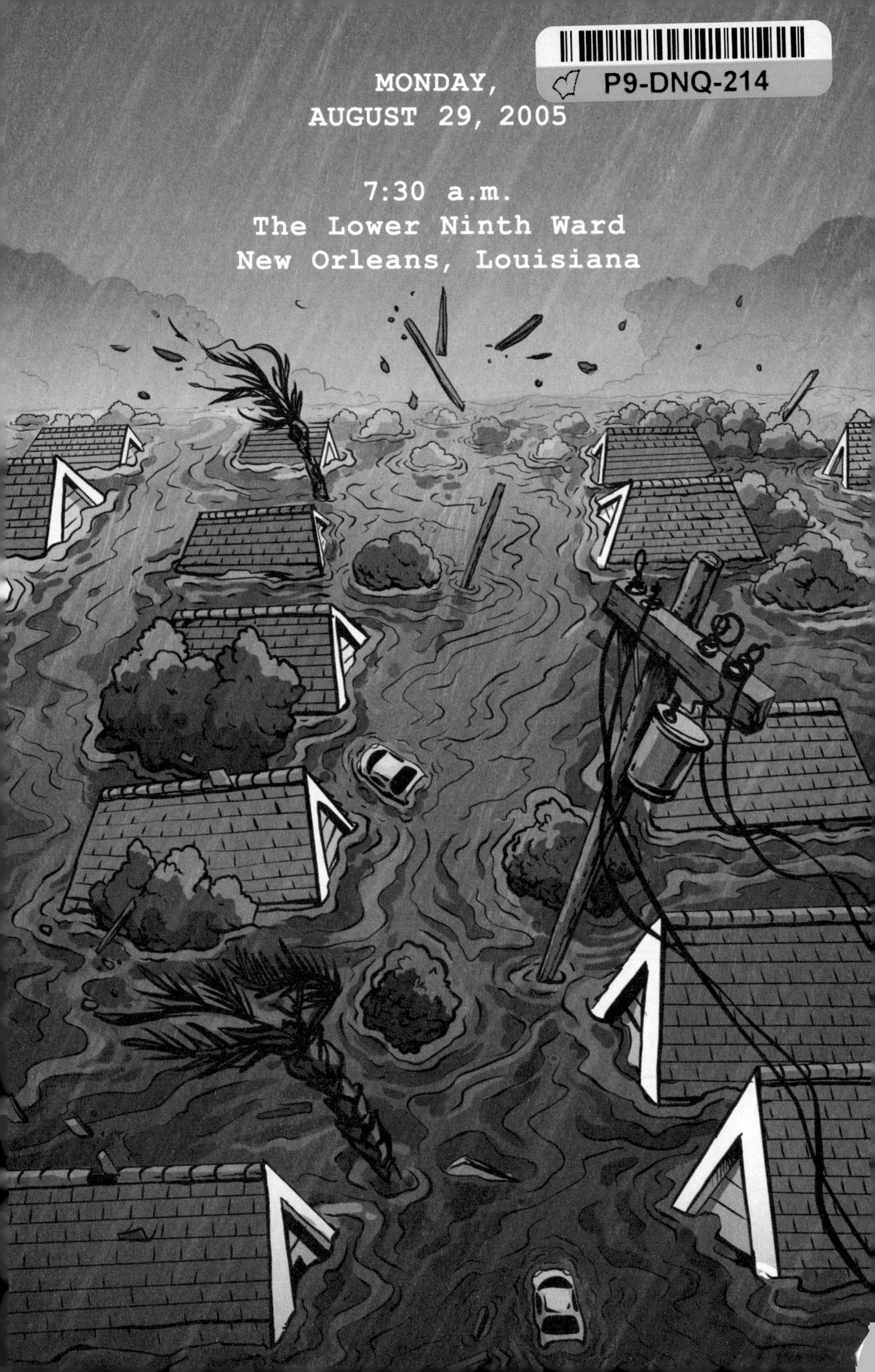
MONDAY,
AUGUST 29, 2005
7:30 a.m.
The Lower Ninth Ward
New Orleans, Louisiana

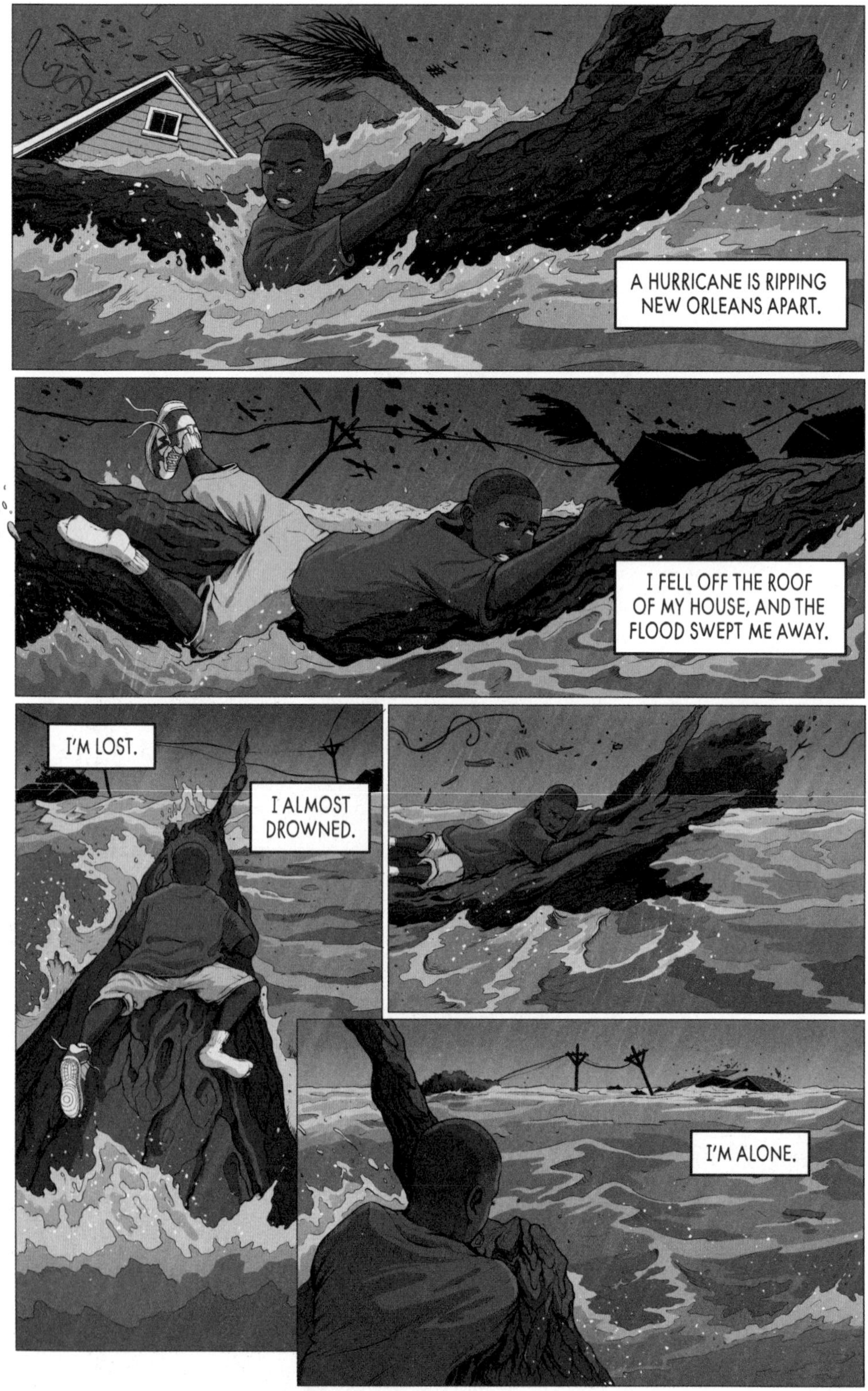
A HURRICANE IS RIPPING NEW ORLEANS APART.
I FELL OFF THE ROOF OF MY HOUSE, AND THE FLOOD SWEPT ME AWAY.
I'M LOST.
I ALMOST DROWNED.
I'M ALONE.

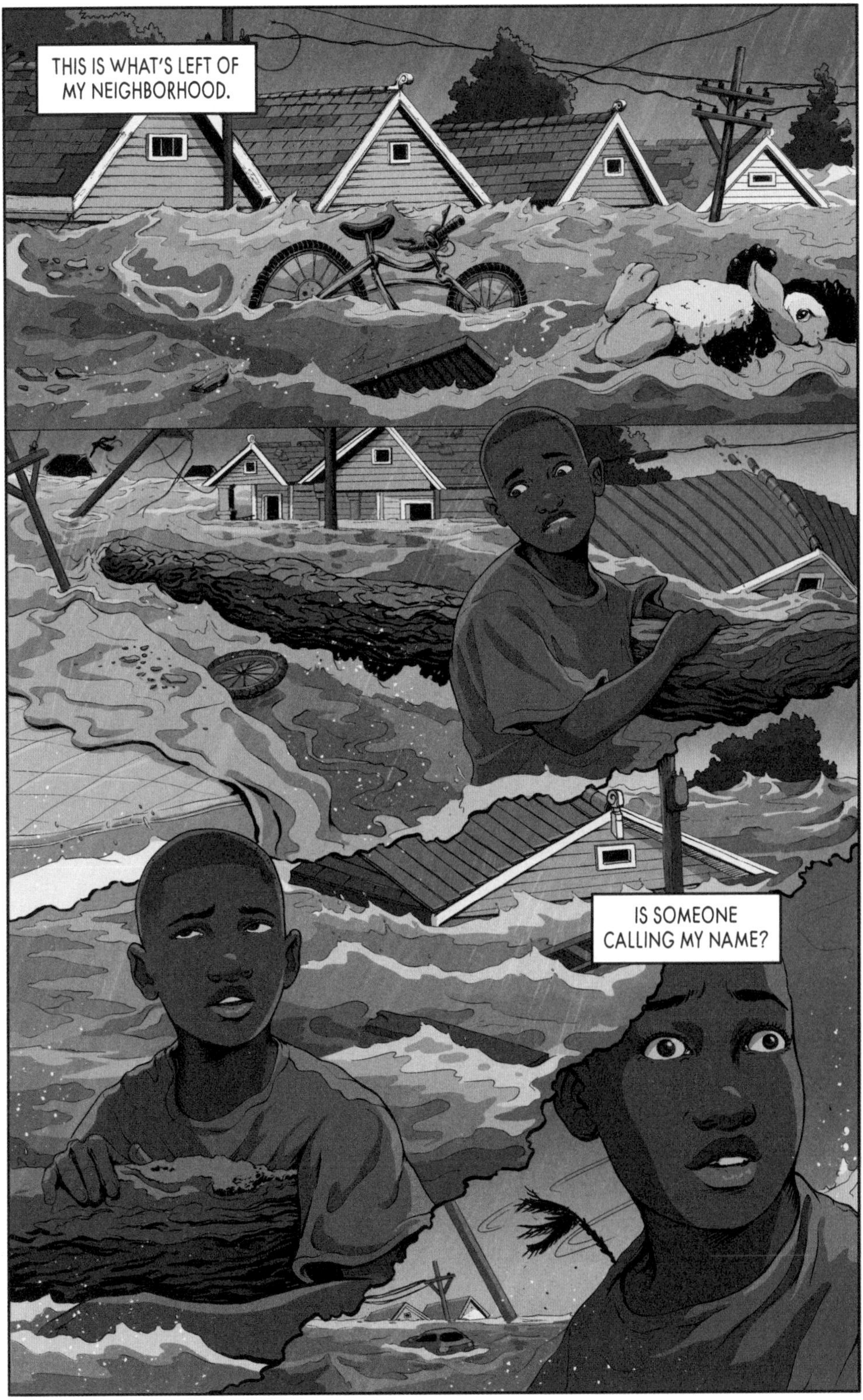
THIS IS WHAT'S LEFT OF MY NEIGHBORHOOD.
IS SOMEONE CALLING MY NAME?

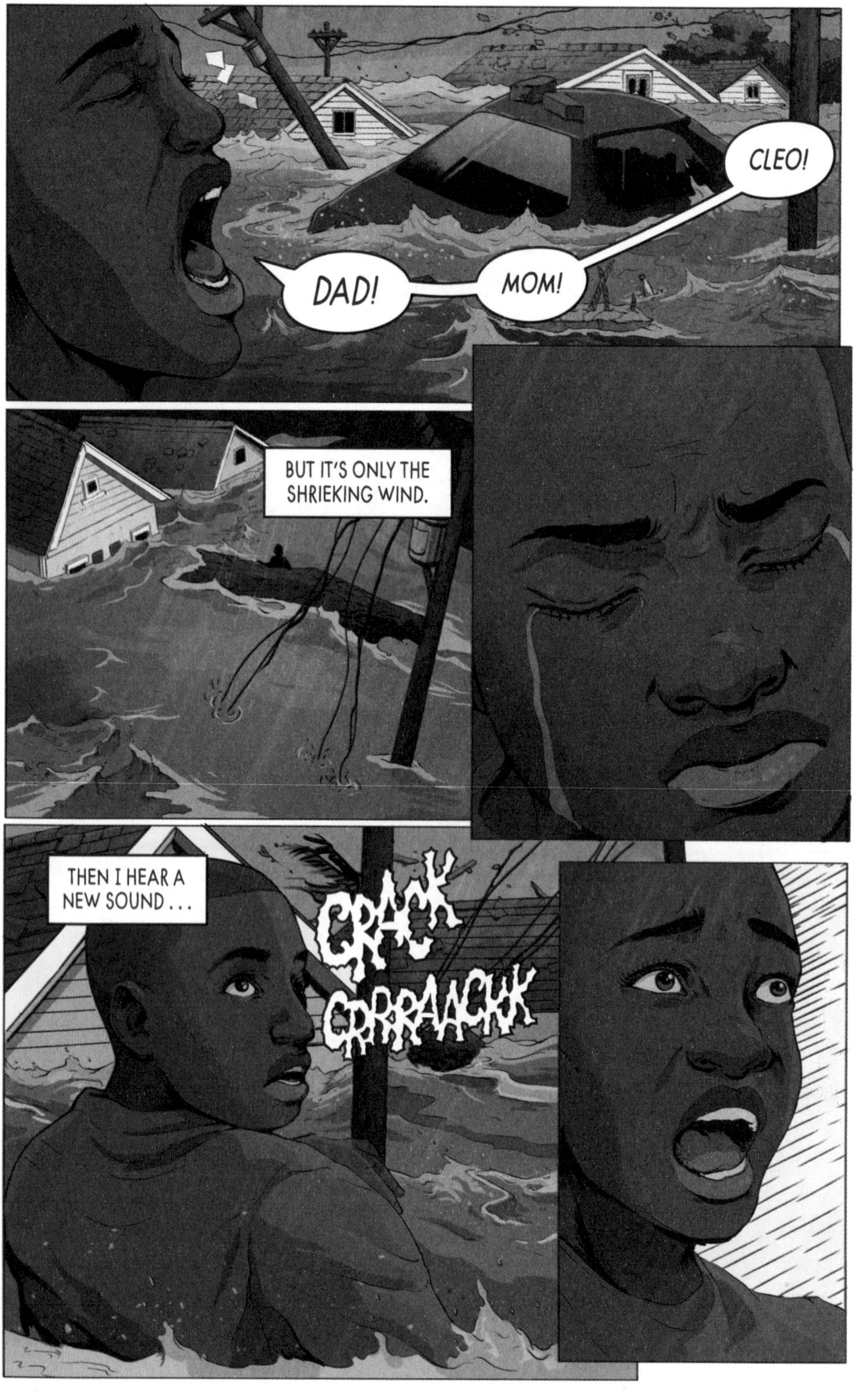
DAD!
MOM!
CLEO!
BUT IT'S ONLY THE SHRIEKING WIND.
THEN I HEAR A NEW SOUND . . .
CRACK
CRRRAAACHK

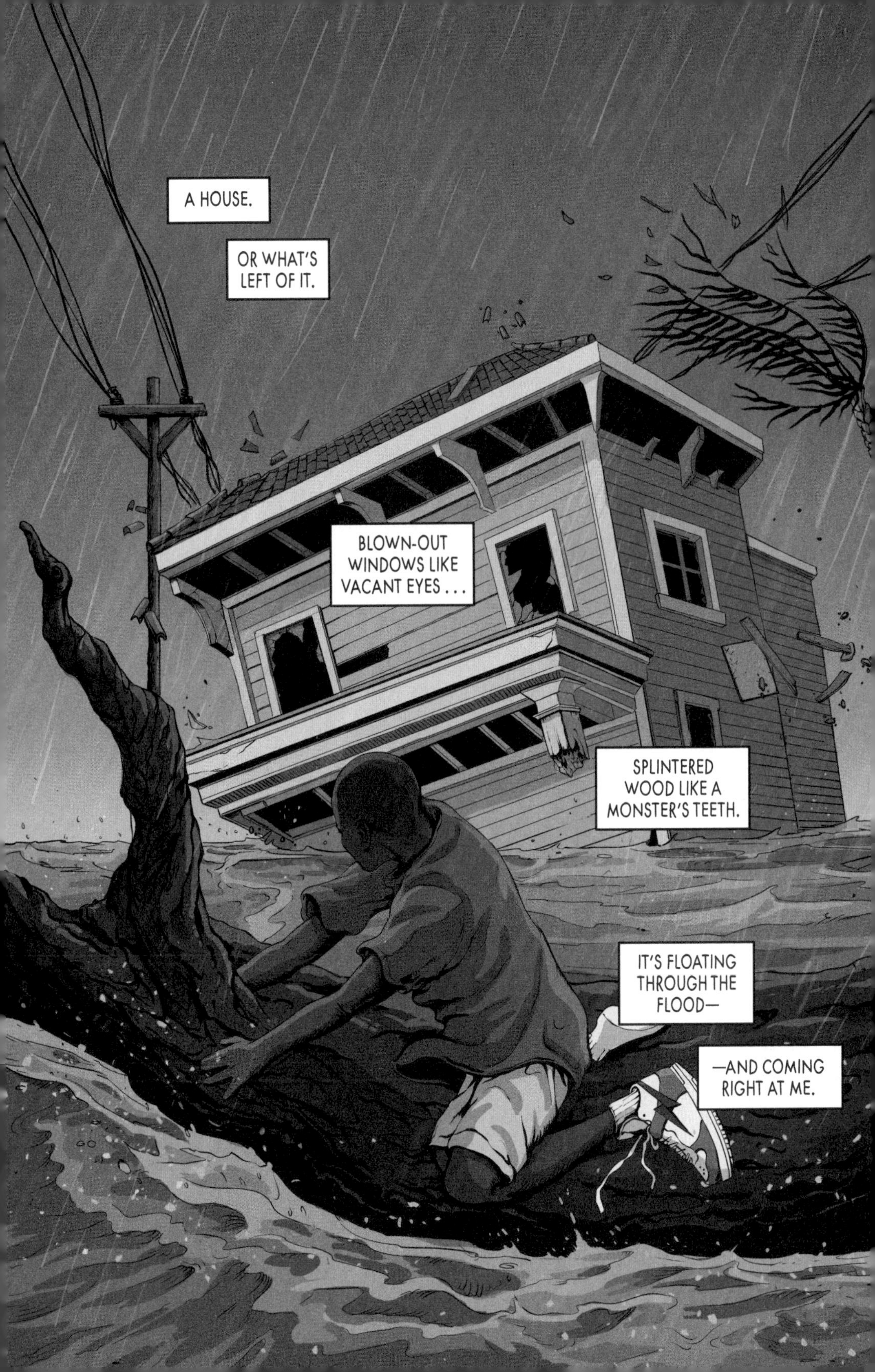
A HOUSE.
OR WHAT'S LEFT OF IT.
BLOWN-OUT WINDOWS LIKE VACANT EYES . . .
SPLINTERED WOOD LIKE A MONSTER'S TEETH.
IT'S FLOATING THROUGH THE FLOOD—
—AND COMING RIGHT AT ME.

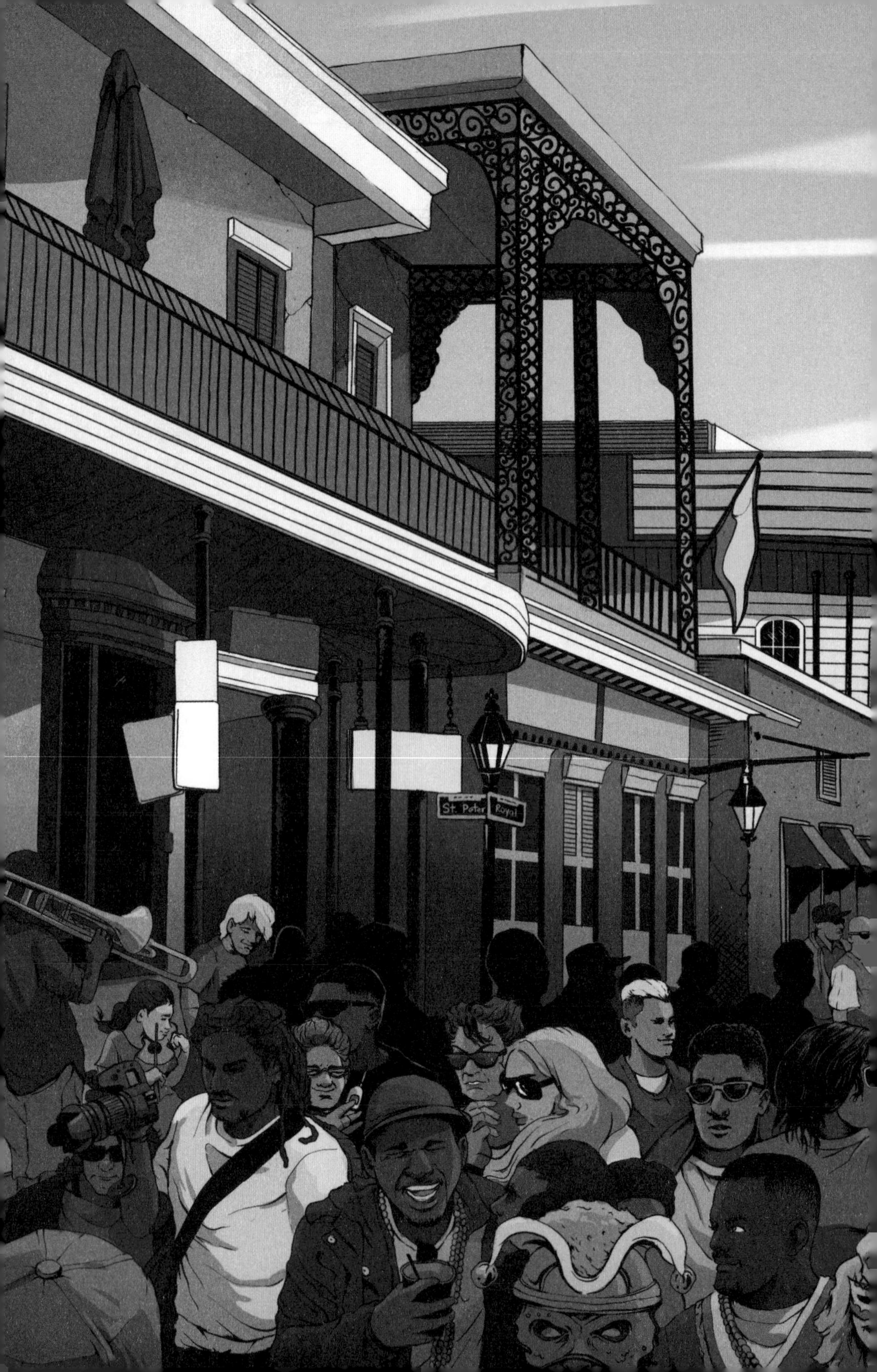
St. Peter
Royal

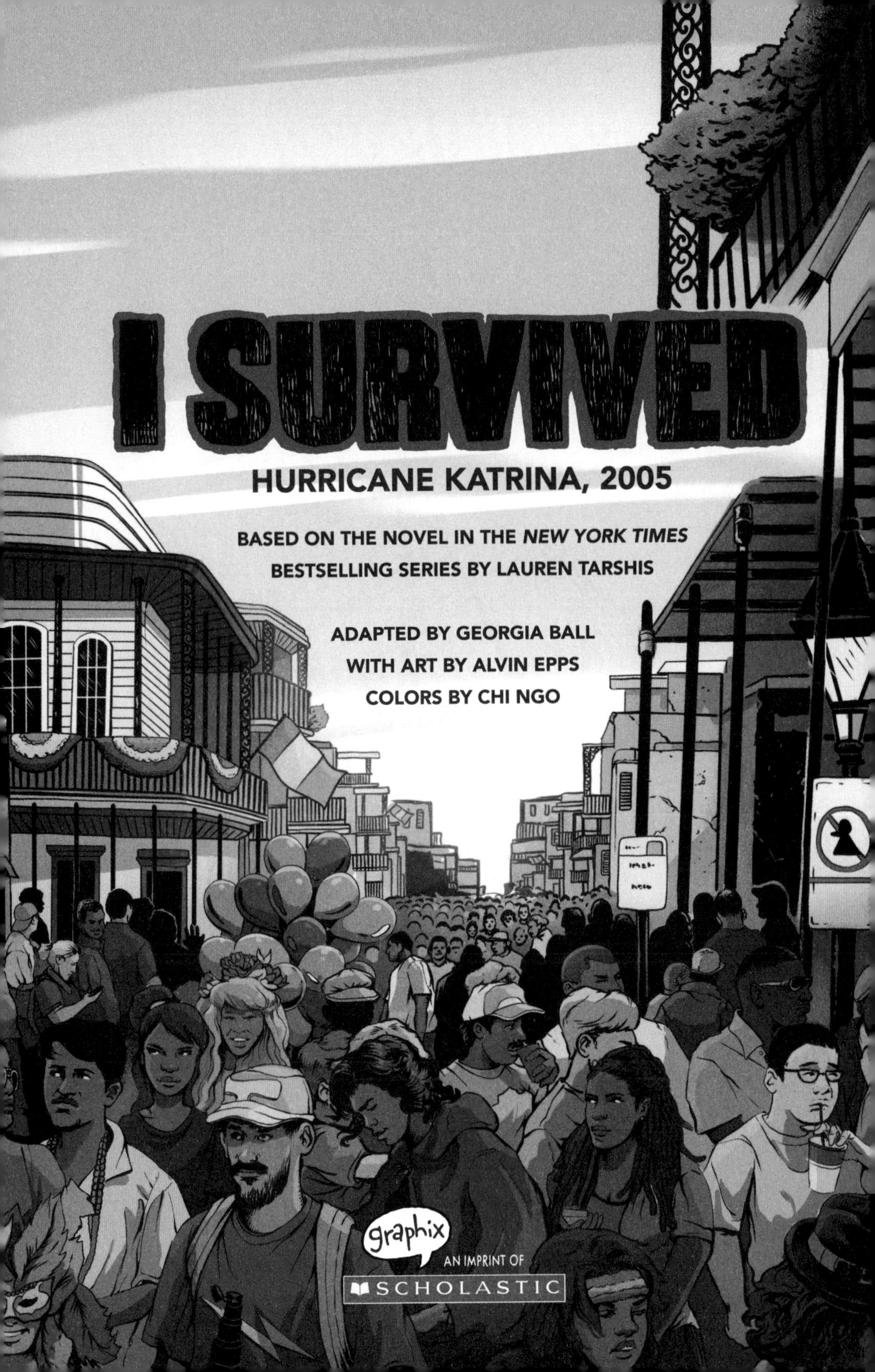

I SURVIVED

HURRICANE KATRINA, 2005

BASED ON THE NOVEL IN THE *NEW YORK TIMES* BESTSELLING SERIES BY LAUREN TARSHIS

ADAPTED BY GEORGIA BALL
WITH ART BY ALVIN EPPS
COLORS BY CHI NGO

graphix
AN IMPRINT OF
SCHOLASTIC

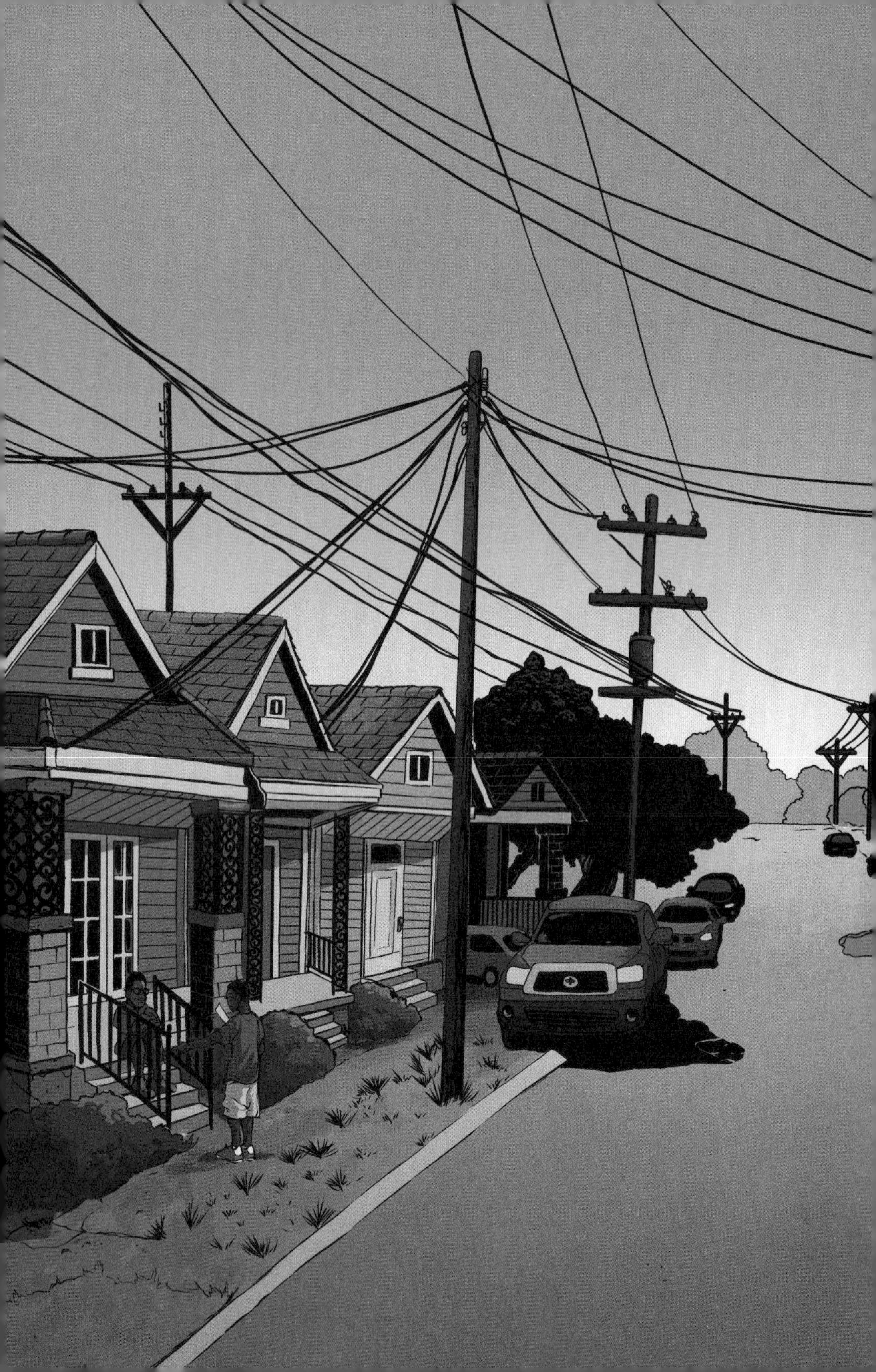

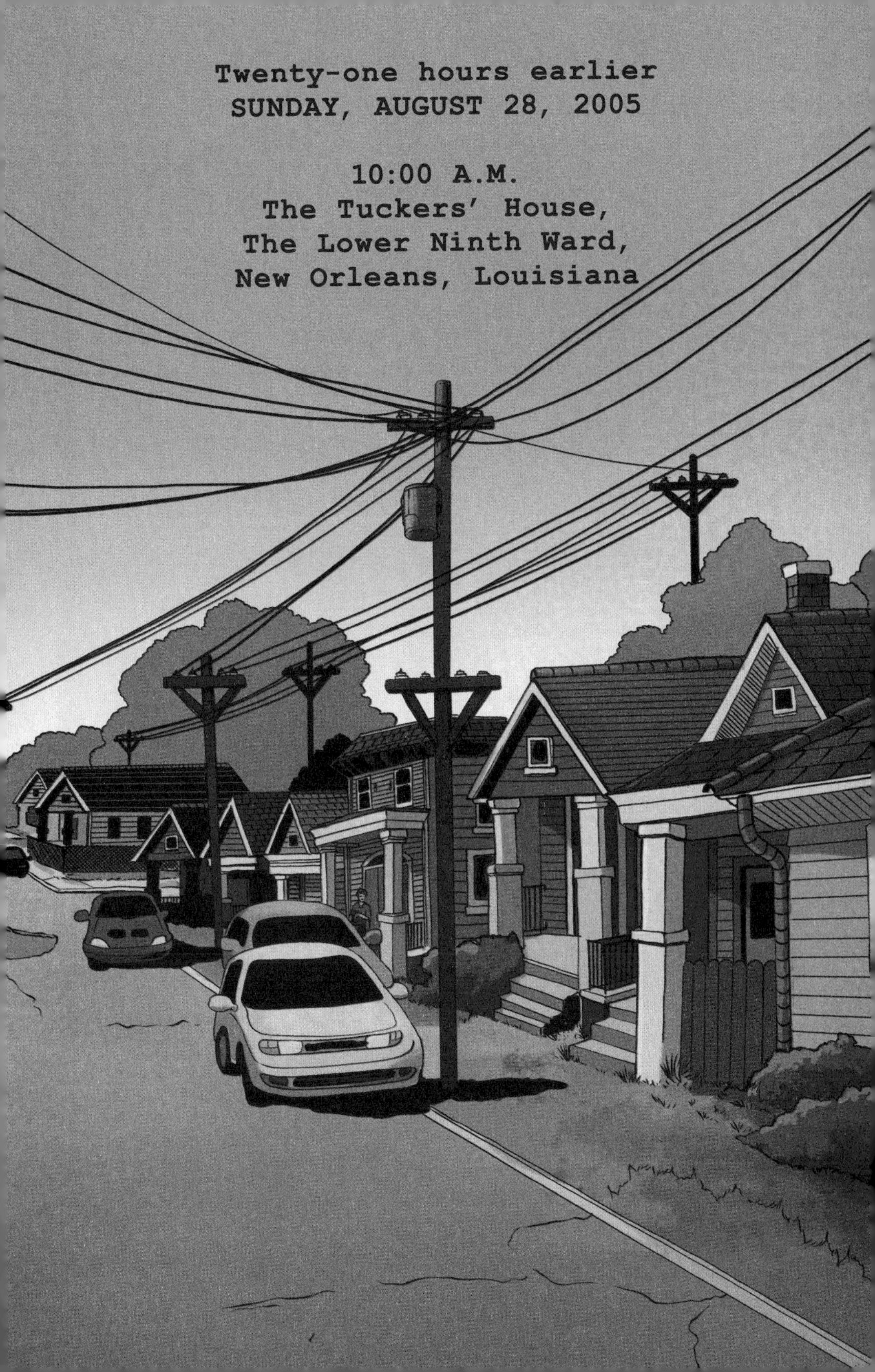
Twenty-one hours earlier
SUNDAY, AUGUST 28, 2005
10:00 A.M.
The Tuckers' House,
The Lower Ninth Ward,
New Orleans, Louisiana

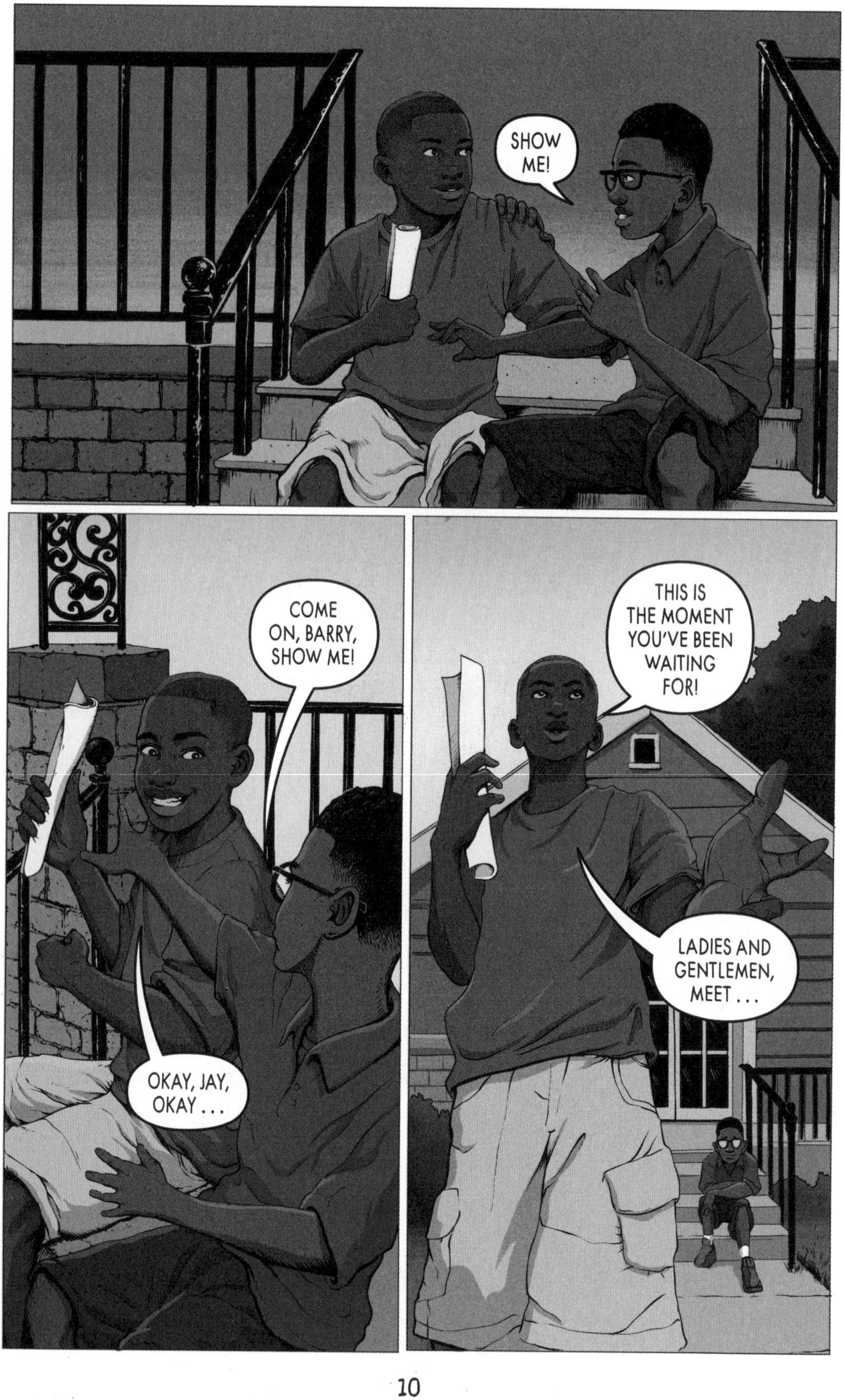
SHOW ME!
COME ON, BARRY, SHOW ME!
OKAY, JAY, OKAY . . .
THIS IS THE MOMENT YOU'VE BEEN WAITING FOR!
LADIES AND GENTLEMEN, MEET . . .

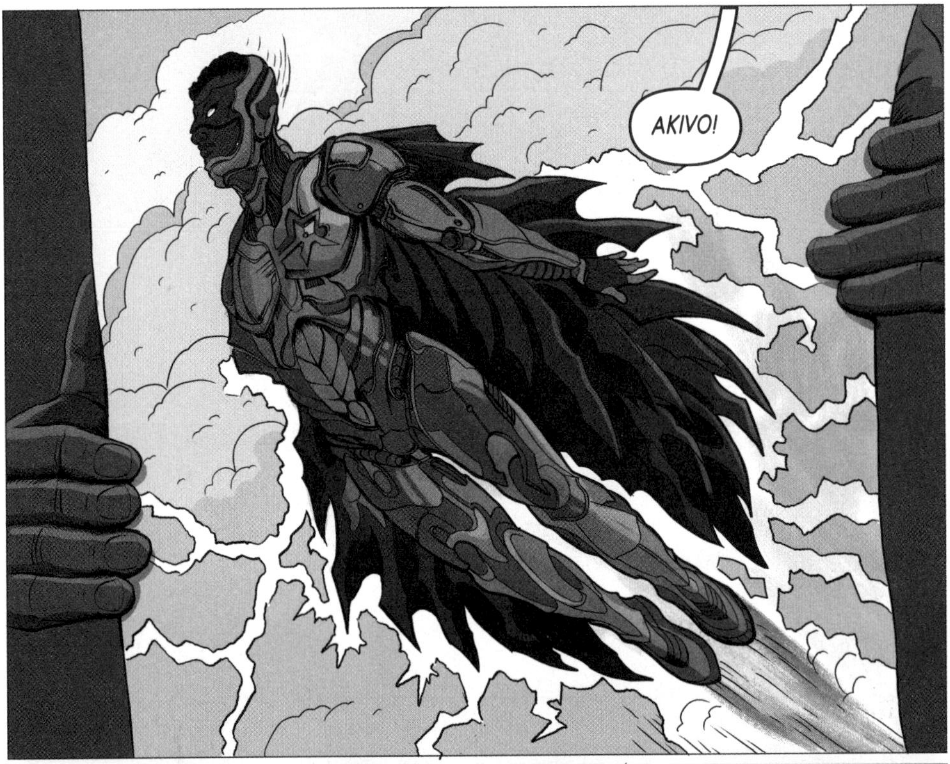
AKIVO!

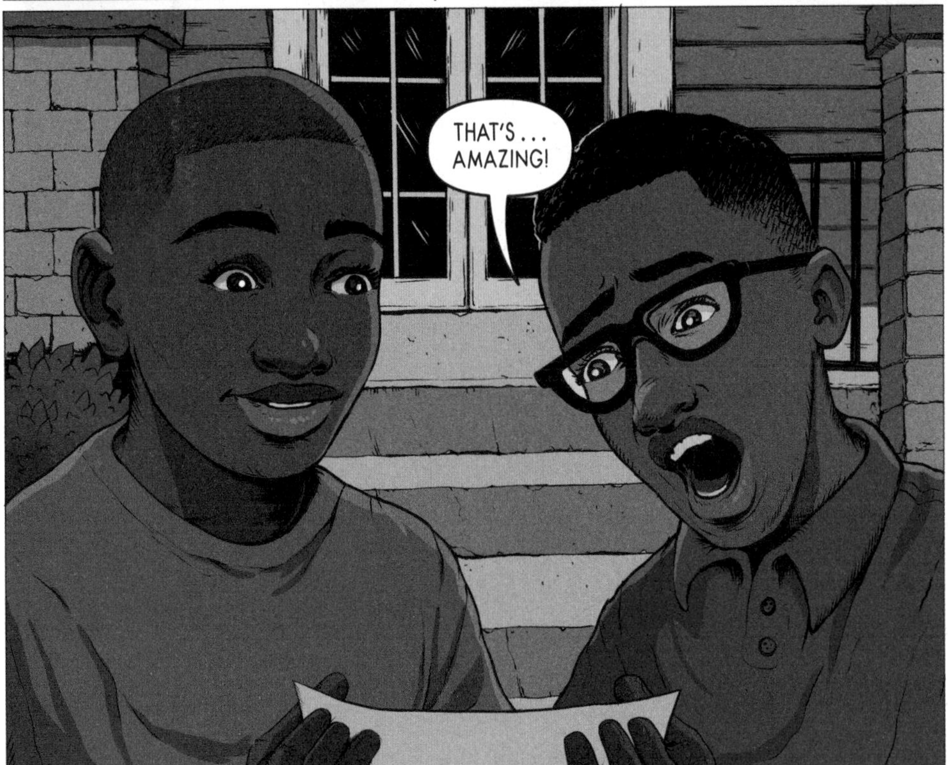
THAT'S . . . AMAZING!

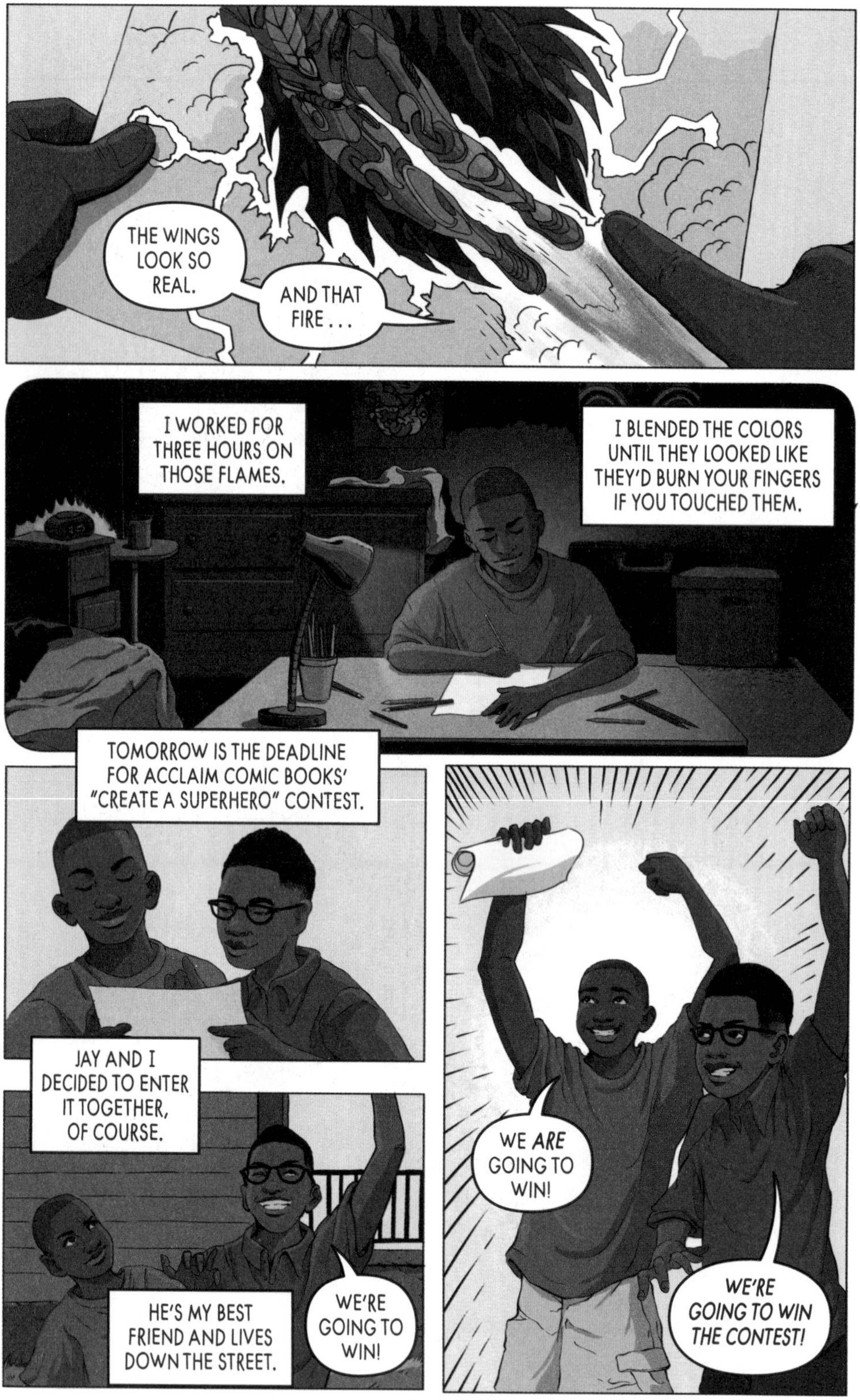
THE WINGS LOOK SO REAL.
AND THAT FIRE . . .
I WORKED FOR THREE HOURS ON THOSE FLAMES.
I BLENDED THE COLORS UNTIL THEY LOOKED LIKE THEY'D BURN YOUR FINGERS IF YOU TOUCHED THEM.
TOMORROW IS THE DEADLINE FOR ACCLAIM COMIC BOOKS' "CREATE A SUPERHERO" CONTEST.
JAY AND I DECIDED TO ENTER IT TOGETHER, OF COURSE.
HE'S MY BEST FRIEND AND LIVES DOWN THE STREET.
WE'RE GOING TO WIN!
WE *ARE* GOING TO WIN!
WE'RE GOING TO WIN THE CONTEST!

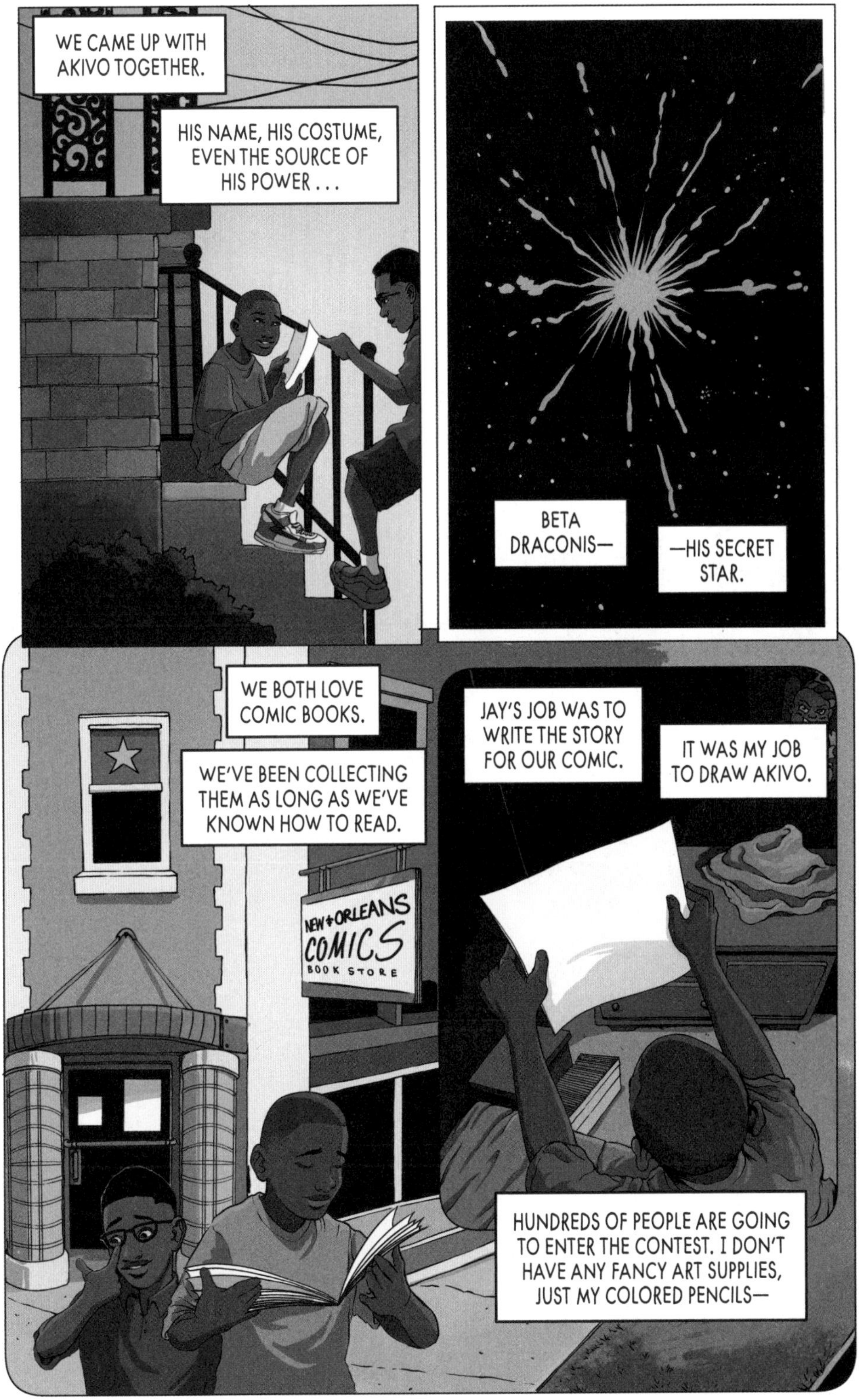
WE CAME UP WITH AKIVO TOGETHER.
HIS NAME, HIS COSTUME, EVEN THE SOURCE OF HIS POWER . . .
BETA DRACONIS—
—HIS SECRET STAR.
WE BOTH LOVE COMIC BOOKS.
WE'VE BEEN COLLECTING THEM AS LONG AS WE'VE KNOWN HOW TO READ.
NEW ORLEANS COMICS BOOK STORE
JAY'S JOB WAS TO WRITE THE STORY FOR OUR COMIC.
IT WAS MY JOB TO DRAW AKIVO.
HUNDREDS OF PEOPLE ARE GOING TO ENTER THE CONTEST. I DON'T HAVE ANY FANCY ART SUPPLIES, JUST MY COLORED PENCILS—

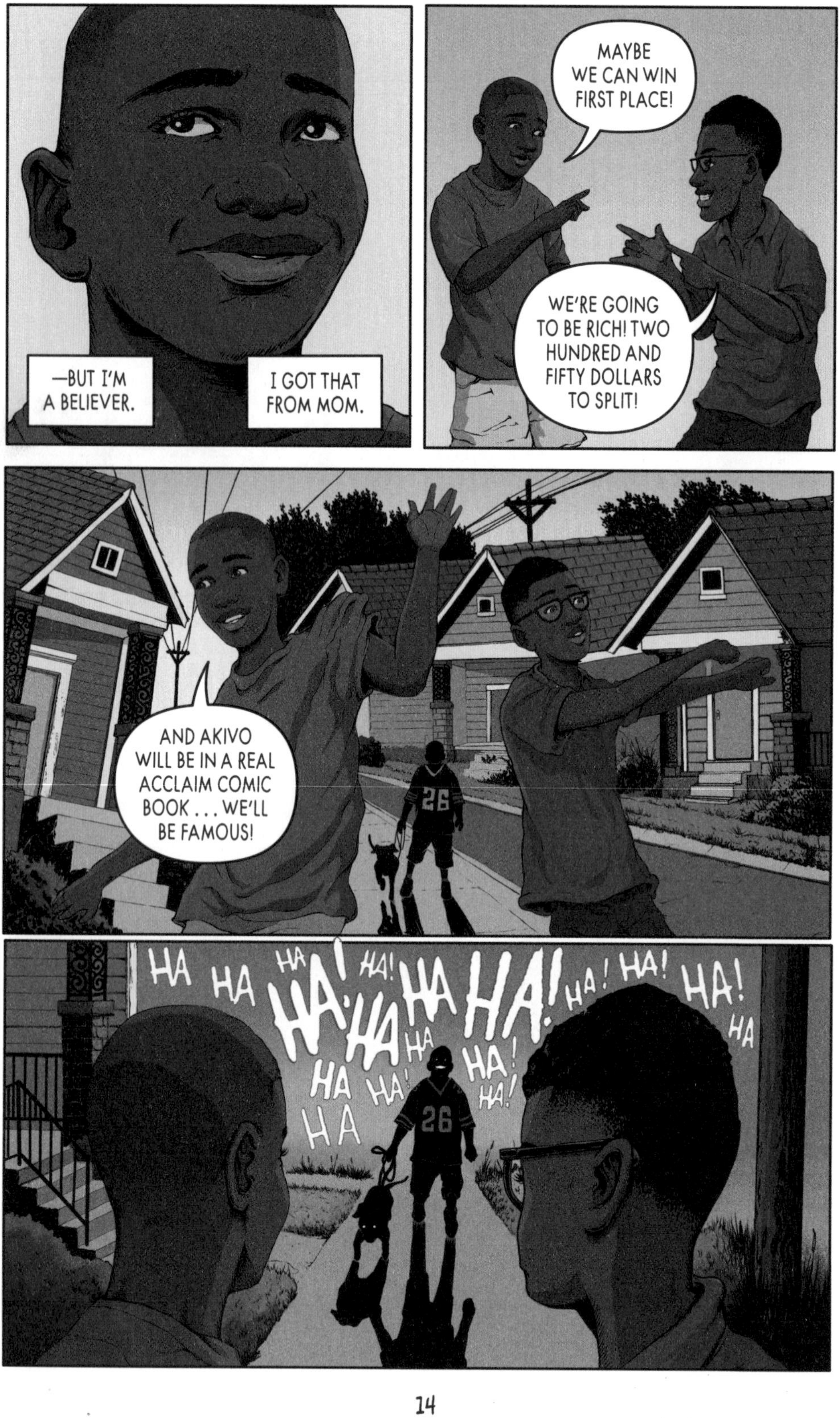
—BUT I'M A BELIEVER.
I GOT THAT FROM MOM.
MAYBE WE CAN WIN FIRST PLACE!
WE'RE GOING TO BE RICH! TWO HUNDRED AND FIFTY DOLLARS TO SPLIT!
AND AKIVO WILL BE IN A REAL ACCLAIM COMIC BOOK . . . WE'LL BE FAMOUS!
26
HA HA HA! HA! HA HA HA HA! HA! HA! HA! HA HA HA HA HA! HA! HA! HA
26

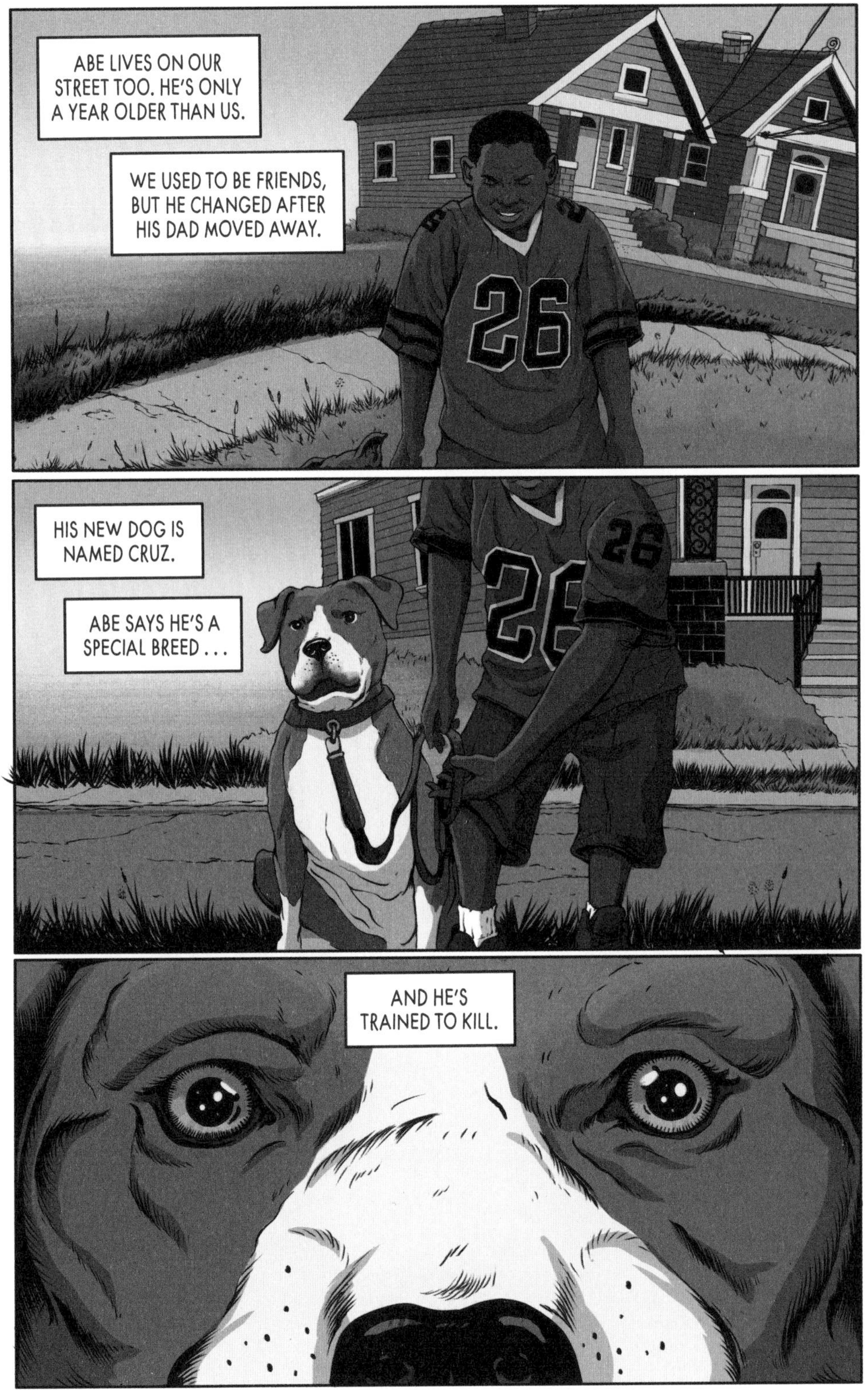
ABE LIVES ON OUR STREET TOO. HE'S ONLY A YEAR OLDER THAN US.
WE USED TO BE FRIENDS, BUT HE CHANGED AFTER HIS DAD MOVED AWAY.
26
HIS NEW DOG IS NAMED CRUZ.
ABE SAYS HE'S A SPECIAL BREED . . .
AND HE'S TRAINED TO KILL.

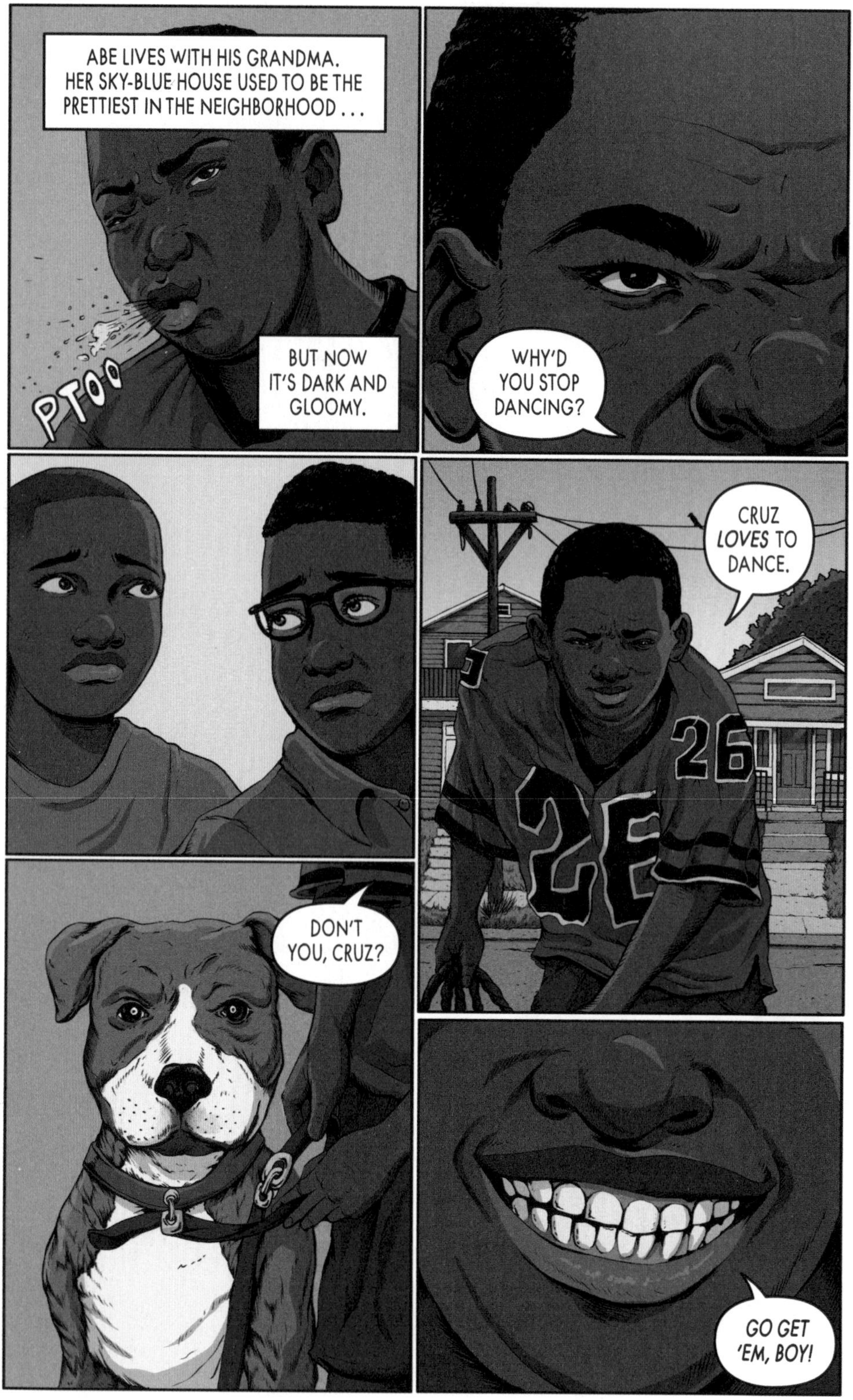
ABE LIVES WITH HIS GRANDMA. HER SKY-BLUE HOUSE USED TO BE THE PRETTIEST IN THE NEIGHBORHOOD . . .
PTOO
BUT NOW IT'S DARK AND GLOOMY.
WHY'D YOU STOP DANCING?
CRUZ *LOVES* TO DANCE.
26
DON'T YOU, CRUZ?
GO GET 'EM, BOY!

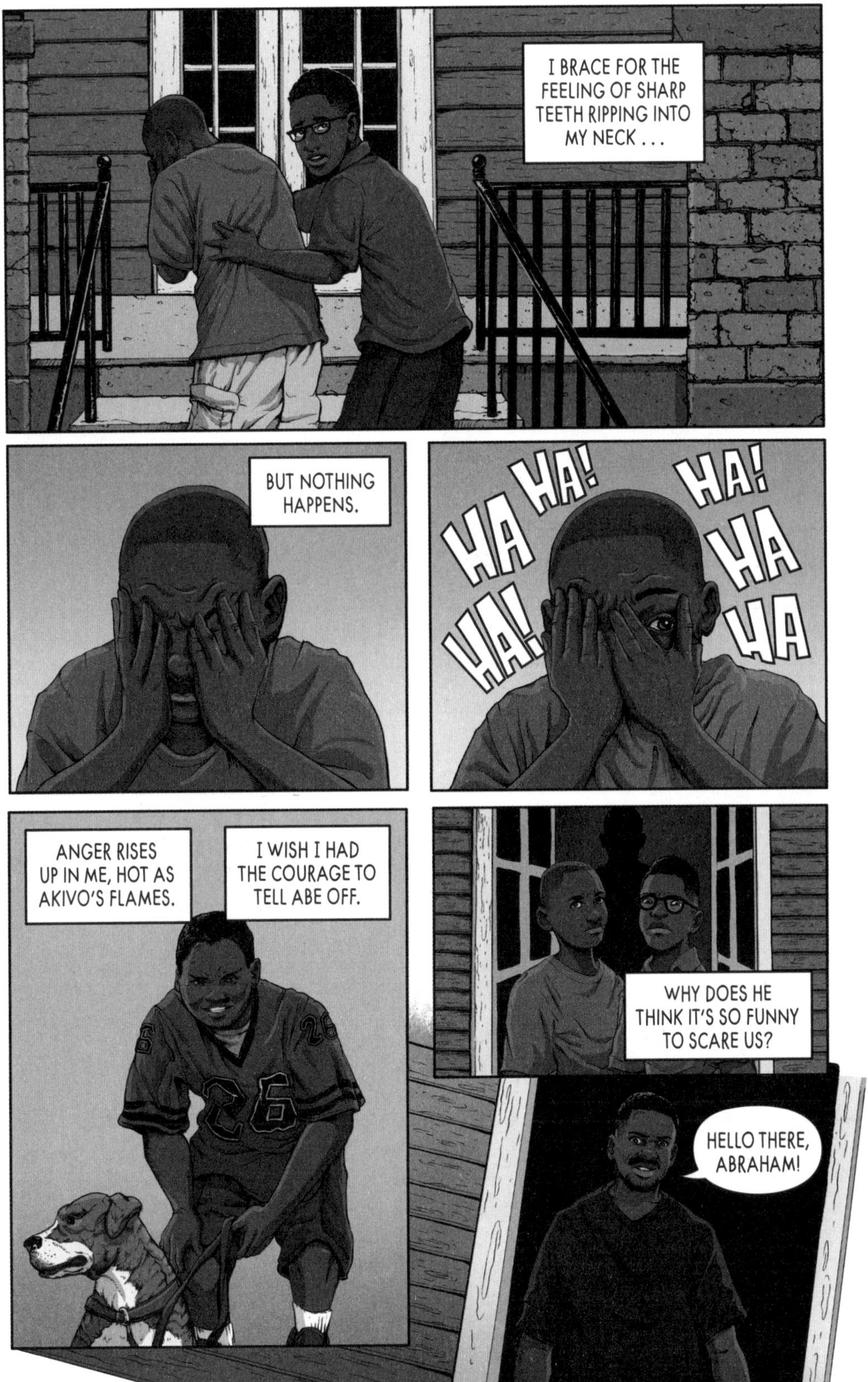
I BRACE FOR THE FEELING OF SHARP TEETH RIPPING INTO MY NECK . . .
BUT NOTHING HAPPENS.
HA HA! HA! HA! HA HA HA
ANGER RISES UP IN ME, HOT AS AKIVO'S FLAMES.
I WISH I HAD THE COURAGE TO TELL ABE OFF.
WHY DOES HE THINK IT'S SO FUNNY TO SCARE US?
HELLO THERE, ABRAHAM!

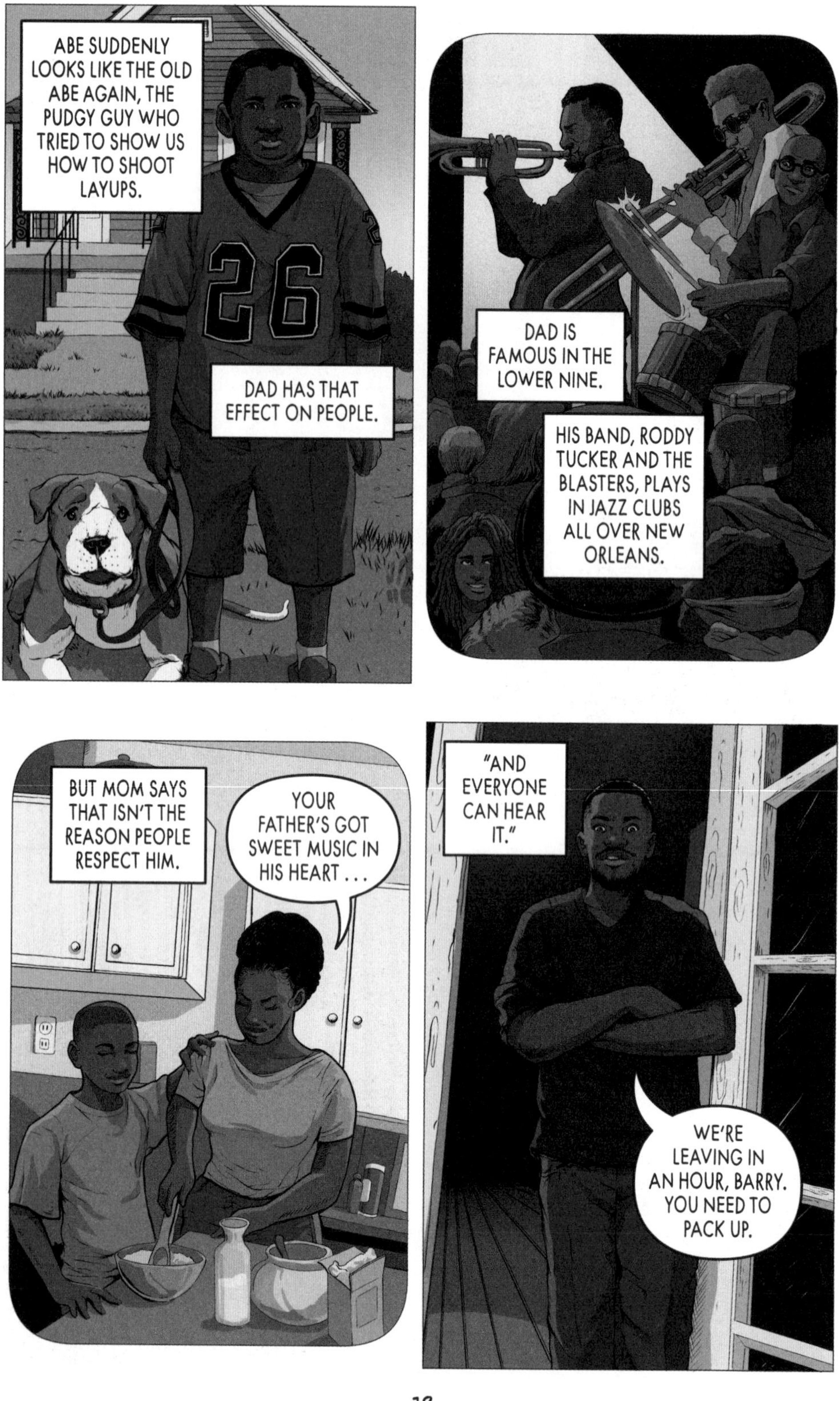
ABE SUDDENLY LOOKS LIKE THE OLD ABE AGAIN, THE PUDGY GUY WHO TRIED TO SHOW US HOW TO SHOOT LAYUPS.
DAD HAS THAT EFFECT ON PEOPLE.
DAD IS FAMOUS IN THE LOWER NINE.
HIS BAND, RODDY TUCKER AND THE BLASTERS, PLAYS IN JAZZ CLUBS ALL OVER NEW ORLEANS.
BUT MOM SAYS THAT ISN'T THE REASON PEOPLE RESPECT HIM.
YOUR FATHER'S GOT SWEET MUSIC IN HIS HEART . . .
"AND EVERYONE CAN HEAR IT."
WE'RE LEAVING IN AN HOUR, BARRY. YOU NEED TO PACK UP.

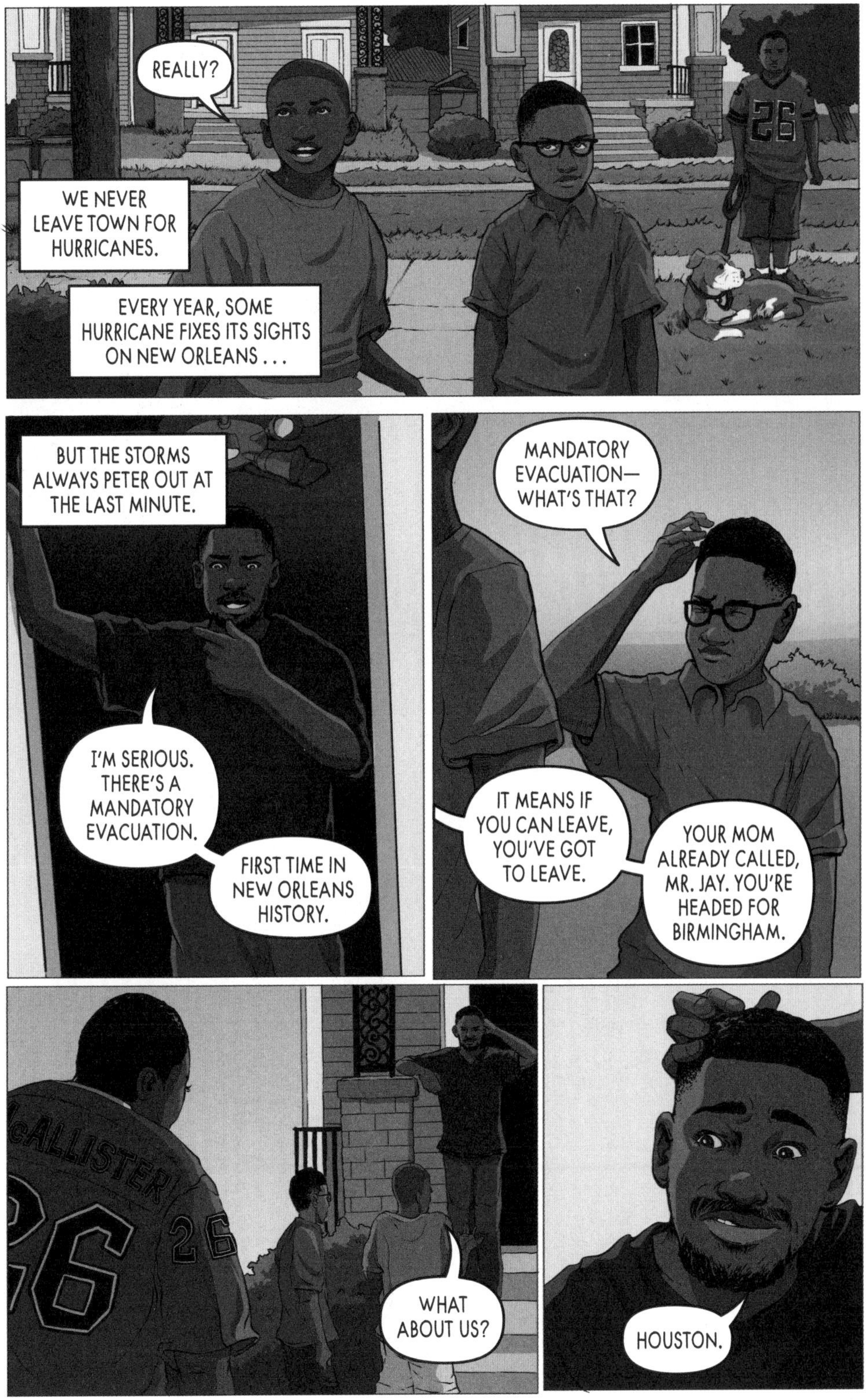
REALLY?
WE NEVER LEAVE TOWN FOR HURRICANES.
EVERY YEAR, SOME HURRICANE FIXES ITS SIGHTS ON NEW ORLEANS . . .
BUT THE STORMS ALWAYS PETER OUT AT THE LAST MINUTE.
I'M SERIOUS. THERE'S A MANDATORY EVACUATION.
FIRST TIME IN NEW ORLEANS HISTORY.
MANDATORY EVACUATION— WHAT'S THAT?
IT MEANS IF YOU CAN LEAVE, YOU'VE GOT TO LEAVE.
YOUR MOM ALREADY CALLED, MR. JAY. YOU'RE HEADED FOR BIRMINGHAM.
WHAT ABOUT US?
HOUSTON.

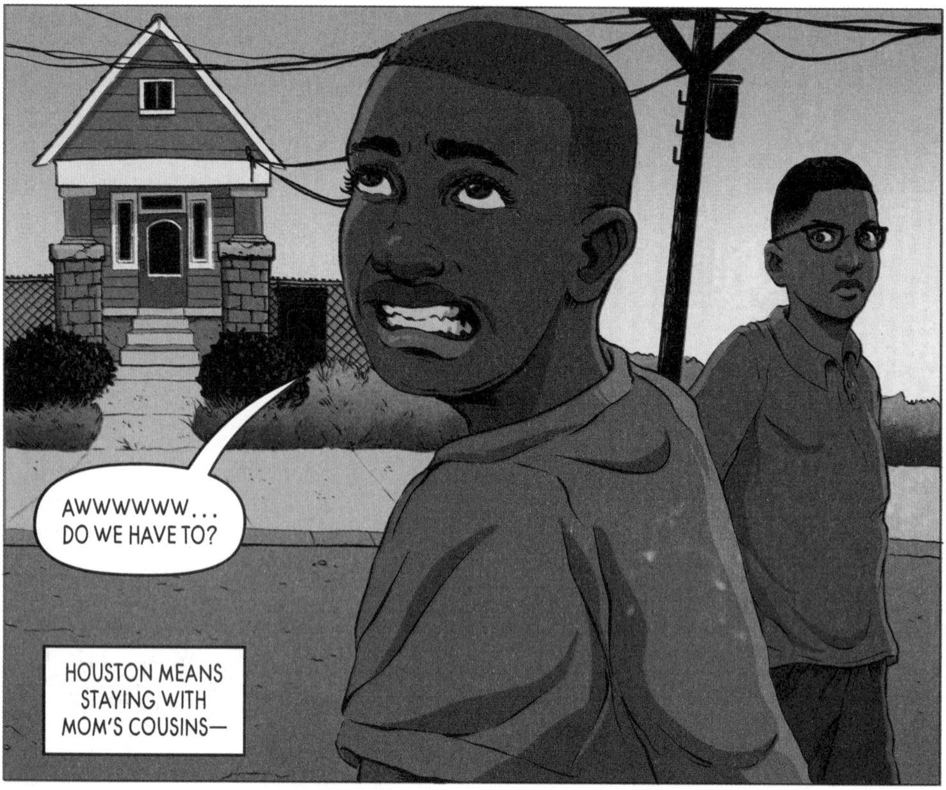
AWWWWWW...
DO WE HAVE TO?
HOUSTON MEANS STAYING WITH MOM'S COUSINS—

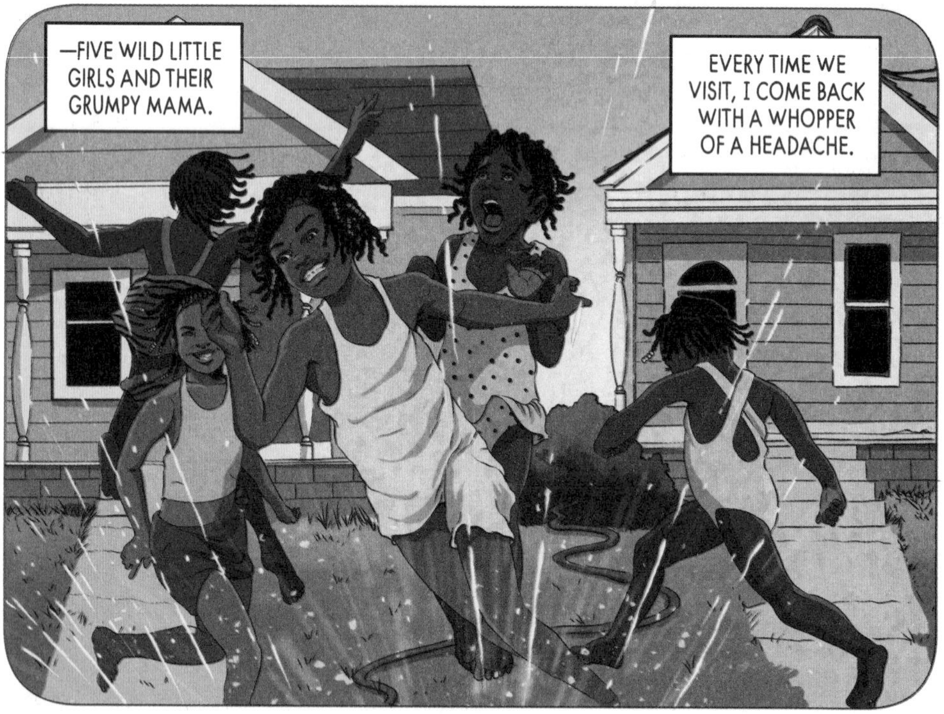
—FIVE WILD LITTLE GIRLS AND THEIR GRUMPY MAMA.
EVERY TIME WE VISIT, I COME BACK WITH A WHOPPER OF A HEADACHE.

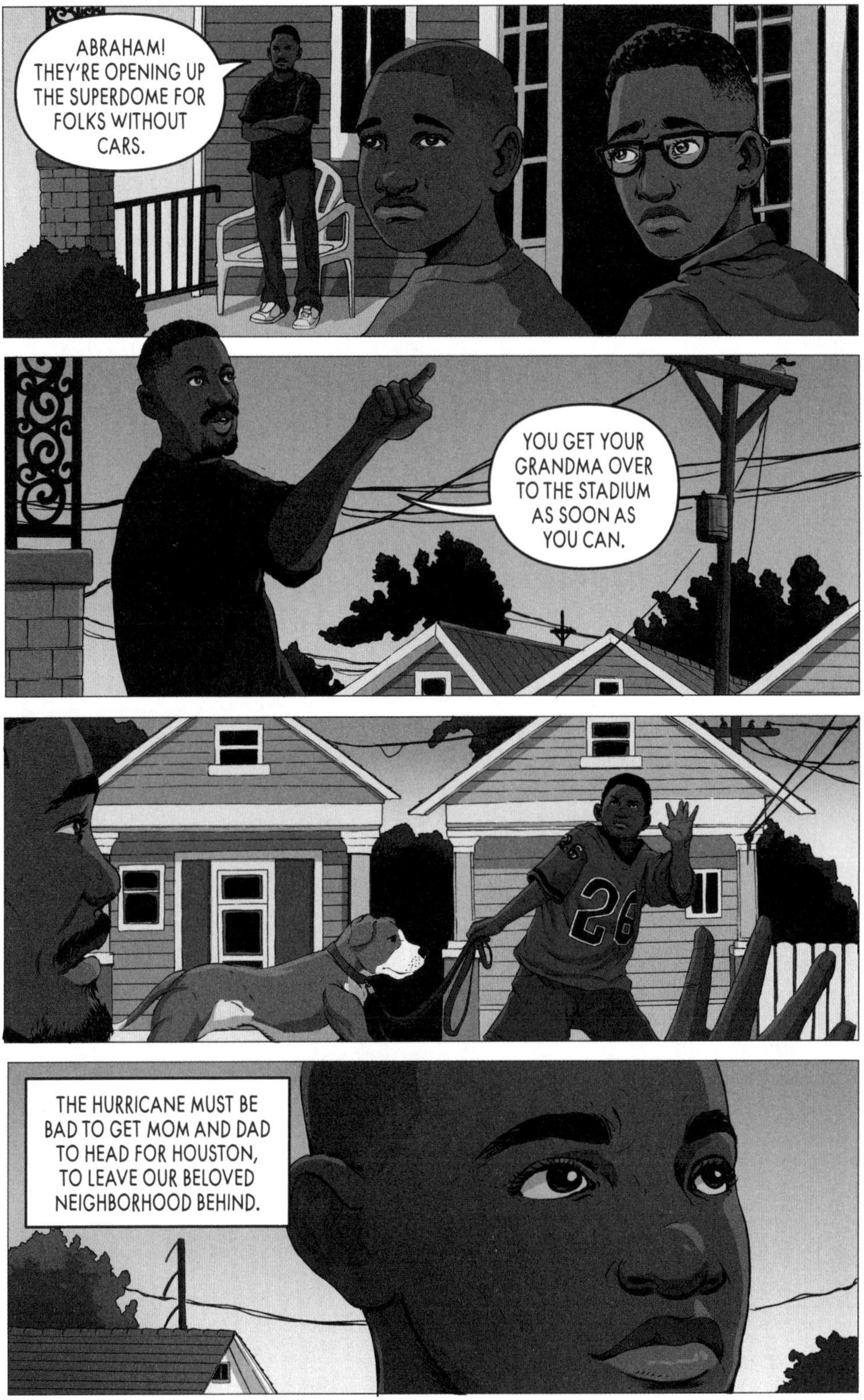
ABRAHAM! THEY'RE OPENING UP THE SUPERDOME FOR FOLKS WITHOUT CARS.
YOU GET YOUR GRANDMA OVER TO THE STADIUM AS SOON AS YOU CAN.
THE HURRICANE MUST BE BAD TO GET MOM AND DAD TO HEAD FOR HOUSTON, TO LEAVE OUR BELOVED NEIGHBORHOOD BEHIND.

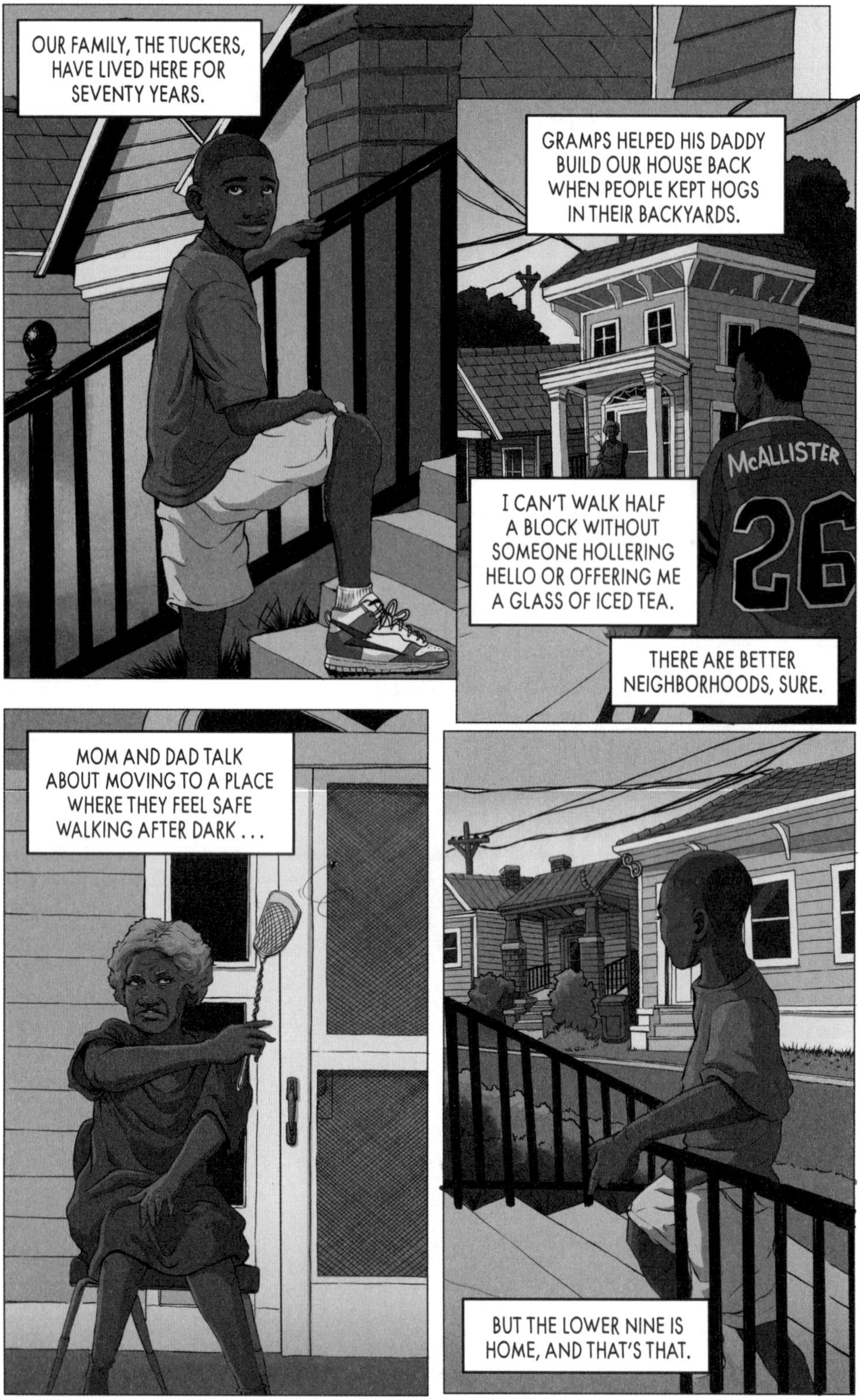
OUR FAMILY, THE TUCKERS, HAVE LIVED HERE FOR SEVENTY YEARS.
GRAMPS HELPED HIS DADDY BUILD OUR HOUSE BACK WHEN PEOPLE KEPT HOGS IN THEIR BACKYARDS.
McALLISTER
26
I CAN'T WALK HALF A BLOCK WITHOUT SOMEONE HOLLERING HELLO OR OFFERING ME A GLASS OF ICED TEA.
THERE ARE BETTER NEIGHBORHOODS, SURE.
MOM AND DAD TALK ABOUT MOVING TO A PLACE WHERE THEY FEEL SAFE WALKING AFTER DARK . . .
BUT THE LOWER NINE IS HOME, AND THAT'S THAT.

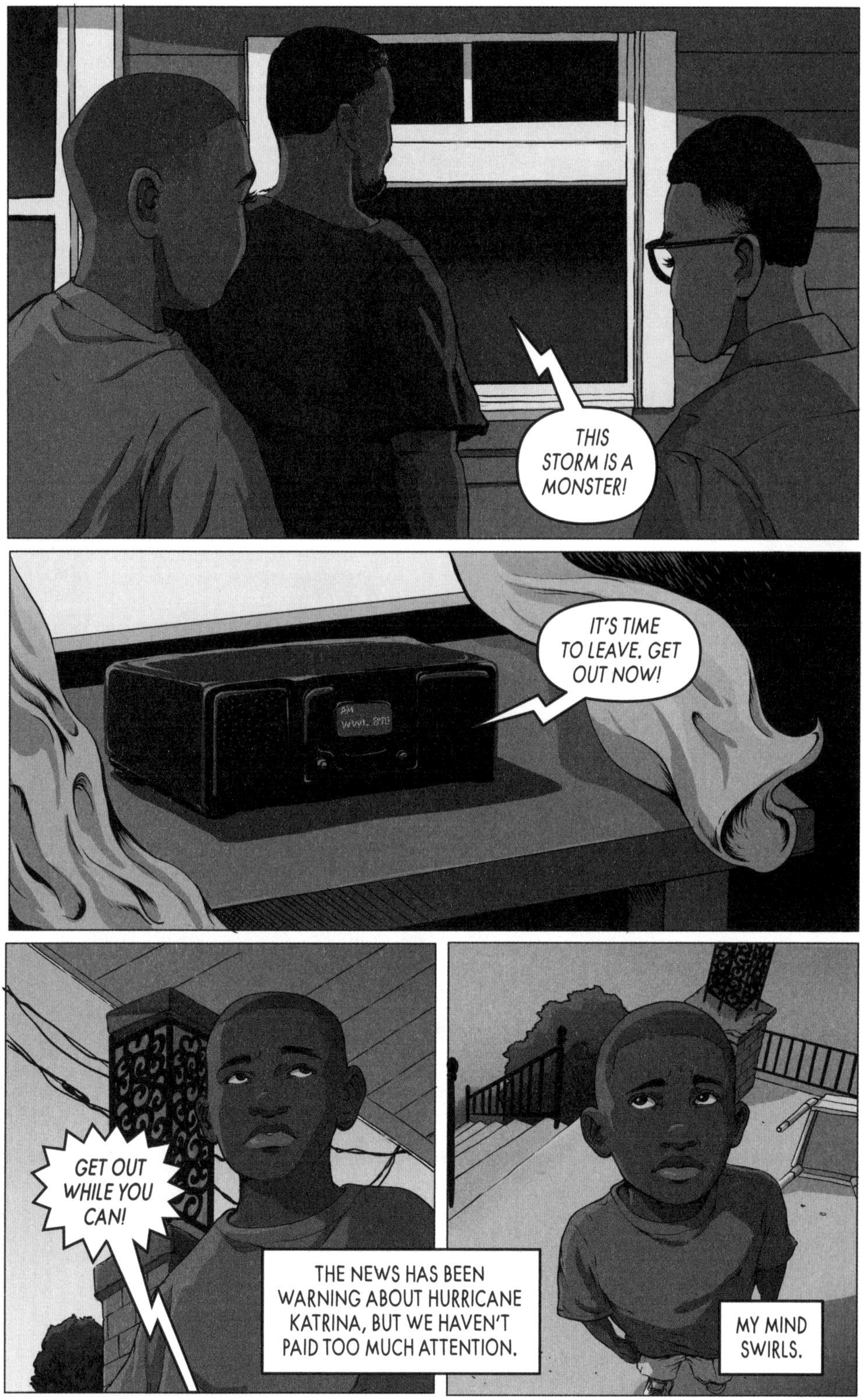
THIS STORM IS A MONSTER!
IT'S TIME TO LEAVE. GET OUT NOW!
GET OUT WHILE YOU CAN!
THE NEWS HAS BEEN WARNING ABOUT HURRICANE KATRINA, BUT WE HAVEN'T PAID TOO MUCH ATTENTION.
MY MIND SWIRLS.

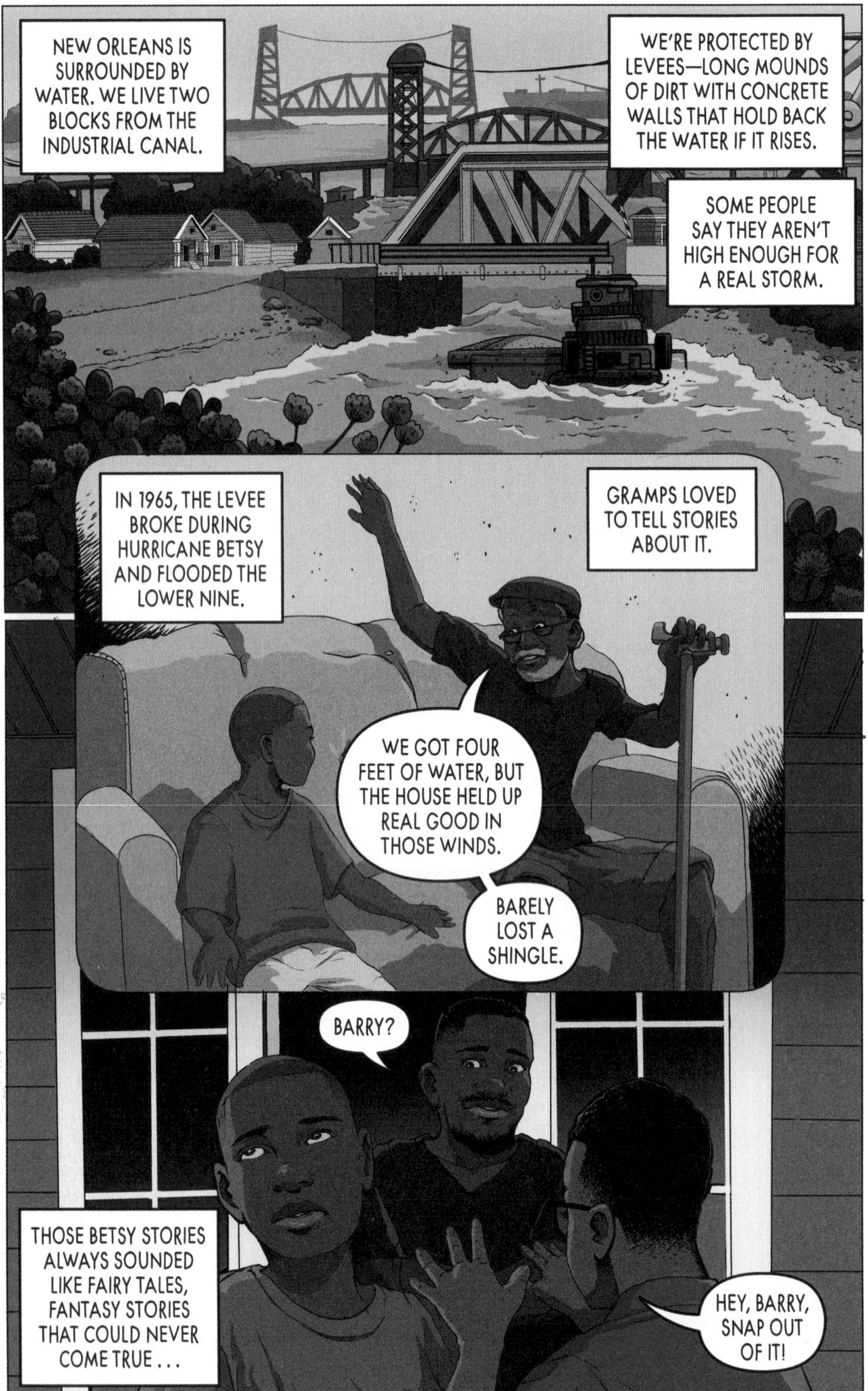

NEW ORLEANS IS SURROUNDED BY WATER. WE LIVE TWO BLOCKS FROM THE INDUSTRIAL CANAL.
WE'RE PROTECTED BY LEVEES—LONG MOUNDS OF DIRT WITH CONCRETE WALLS THAT HOLD BACK THE WATER IF IT RISES.
SOME PEOPLE SAY THEY AREN'T HIGH ENOUGH FOR A REAL STORM.
IN 1965, THE LEVEE BROKE DURING HURRICANE BETSY AND FLOODED THE LOWER NINE.
GRAMPS LOVED TO TELL STORIES ABOUT IT.
WE GOT FOUR FEET OF WATER, BUT THE HOUSE HELD UP REAL GOOD IN THOSE WINDS.
BARELY LOST A SHINGLE.
BARRY?
THOSE BETSY STORIES ALWAYS SOUNDED LIKE FAIRY TALES, FANTASY STORIES THAT COULD NEVER COME TRUE . . .
HEY, BARRY, SNAP OUT OF IT!

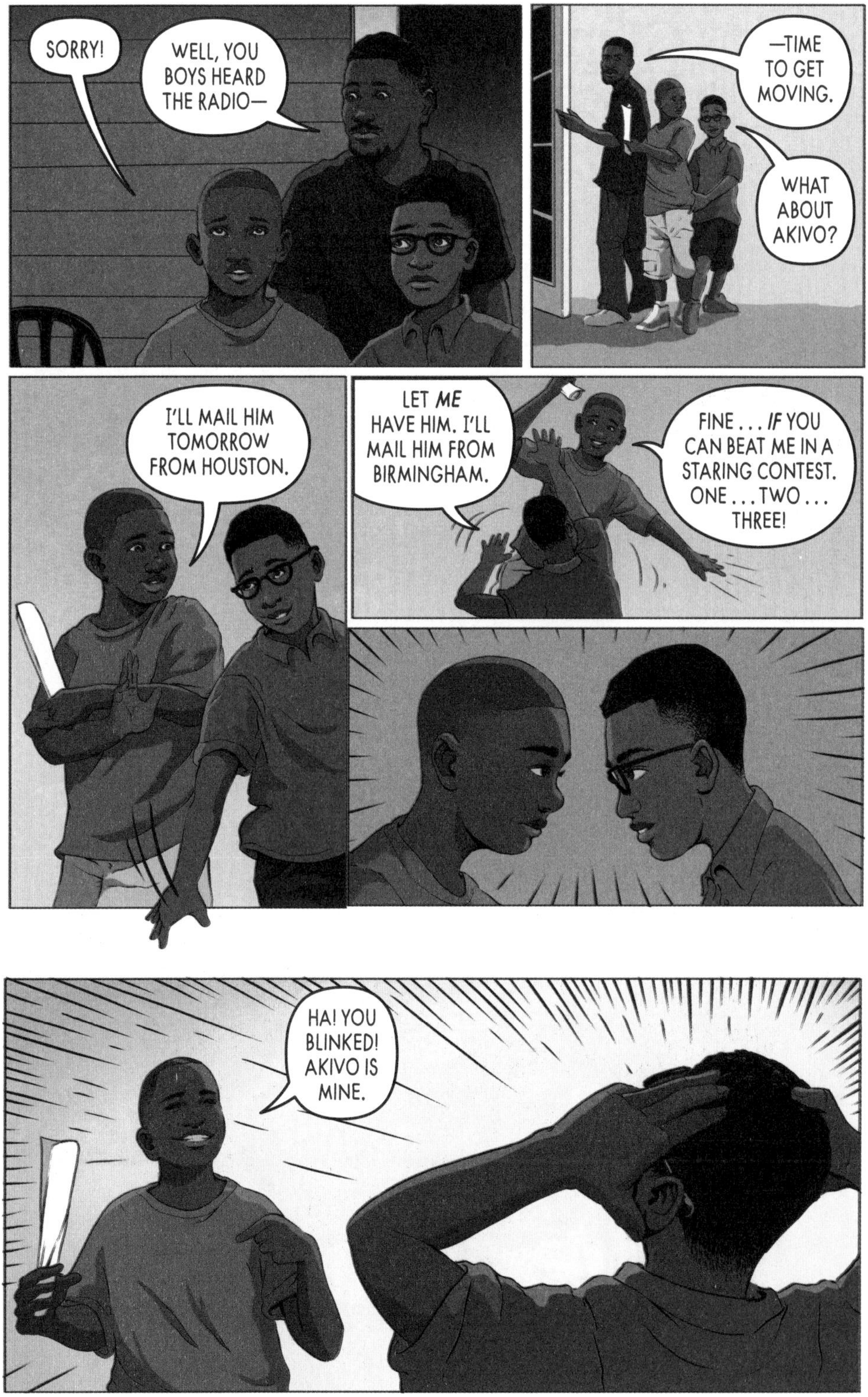

SORRY!
WELL, YOU BOYS HEARD THE RADIO—
—TIME TO GET MOVING.
WHAT ABOUT AKIVO?
I'LL MAIL HIM TOMORROW FROM HOUSTON.
LET *ME* HAVE HIM. I'LL MAIL HIM FROM BIRMINGHAM.
FINE . . . *IF* YOU CAN BEAT ME IN A STARING CONTEST. ONE . . . TWO . . . THREE!
HA! YOU BLINKED! AKIVO IS MINE.

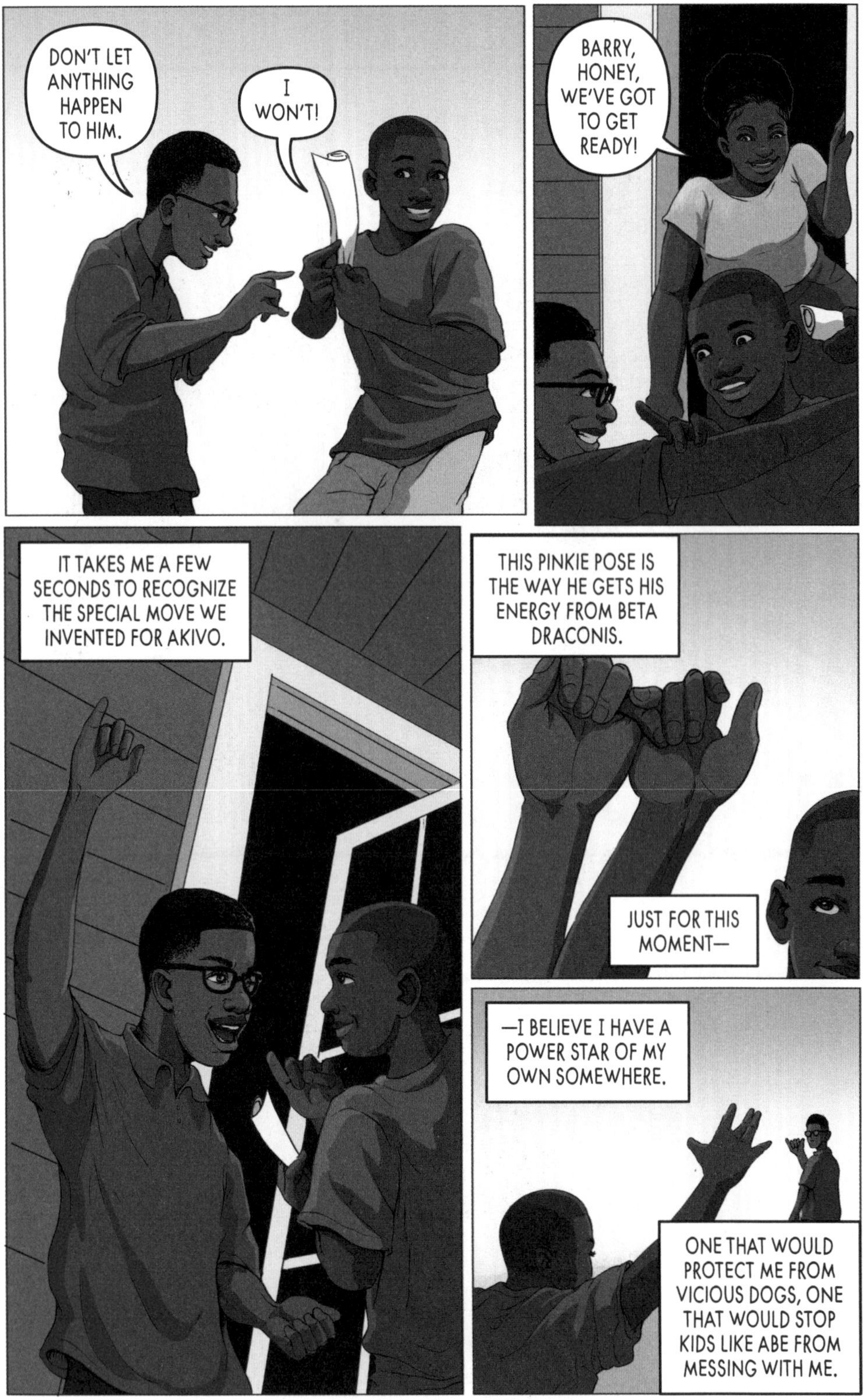
DON'T LET ANYTHING HAPPEN TO HIM.
I WON'T!
BARRY, HONEY, WE'VE GOT TO GET READY!
IT TAKES ME A FEW SECONDS TO RECOGNIZE THE SPECIAL MOVE WE INVENTED FOR AKIVO.
THIS PINKIE POSE IS THE WAY HE GETS HIS ENERGY FROM BETA DRACONIS.
JUST FOR THIS MOMENT—
—I BELIEVE I HAVE A POWER STAR OF MY OWN SOMEWHERE.
ONE THAT WOULD PROTECT ME FROM VICIOUS DOGS, ONE THAT WOULD STOP KIDS LIKE ABE FROM MESSING WITH ME.

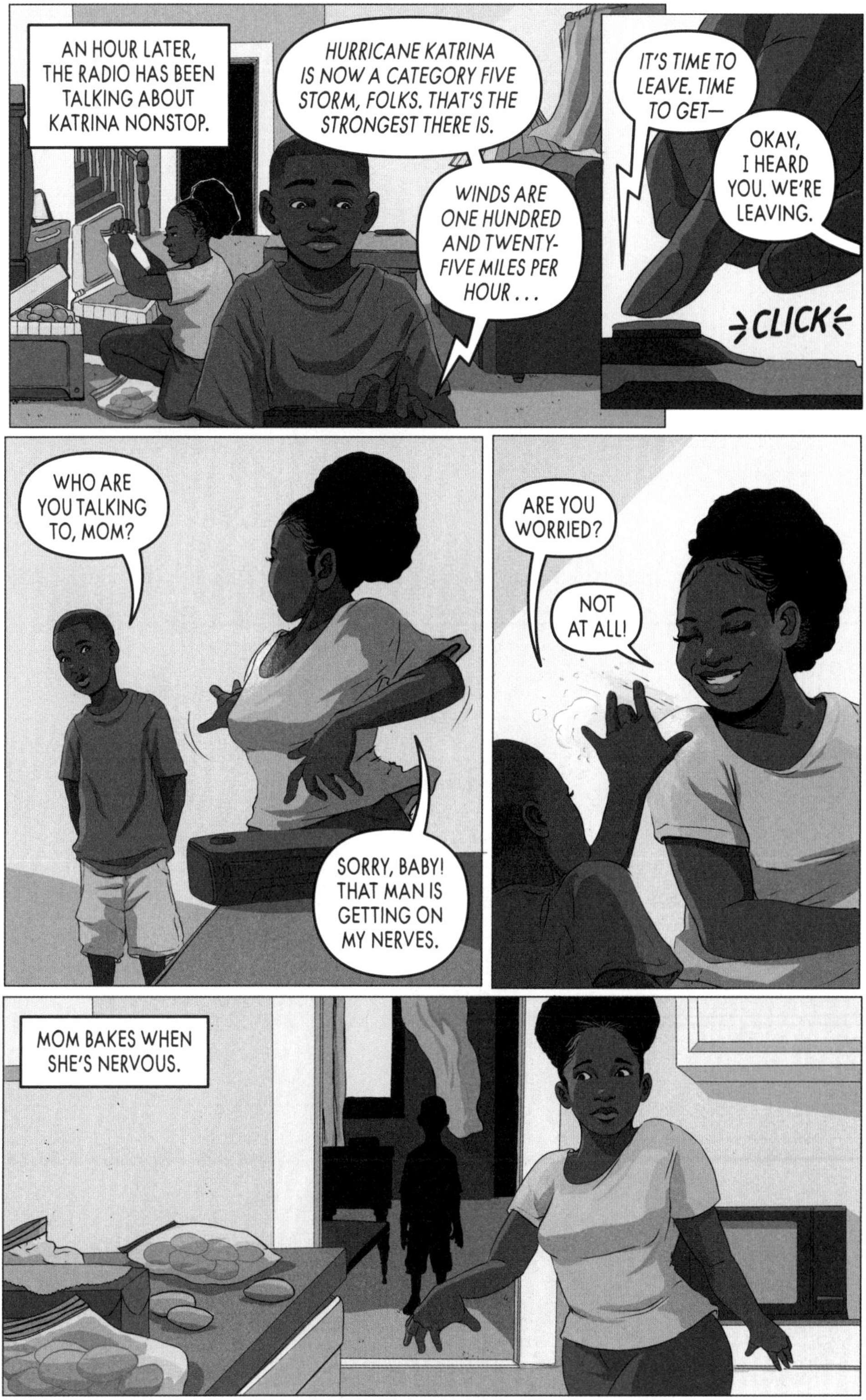
AN HOUR LATER, THE RADIO HAS BEEN TALKING ABOUT KATRINA NONSTOP.
HURRICANE KATRINA IS NOW A CATEGORY FIVE STORM, FOLKS. THAT'S THE STRONGEST THERE IS.
WINDS ARE ONE HUNDRED AND TWENTY-FIVE MILES PER HOUR . . .
IT'S TIME TO LEAVE. TIME TO GET—
OKAY, I HEARD YOU. WE'RE LEAVING.
CLICK
WHO ARE YOU TALKING TO, MOM?
SORRY, BABY! THAT MAN IS GETTING ON MY NERVES.
ARE YOU WORRIED?
NOT AT ALL!
MOM BAKES WHEN SHE'S NERVOUS.

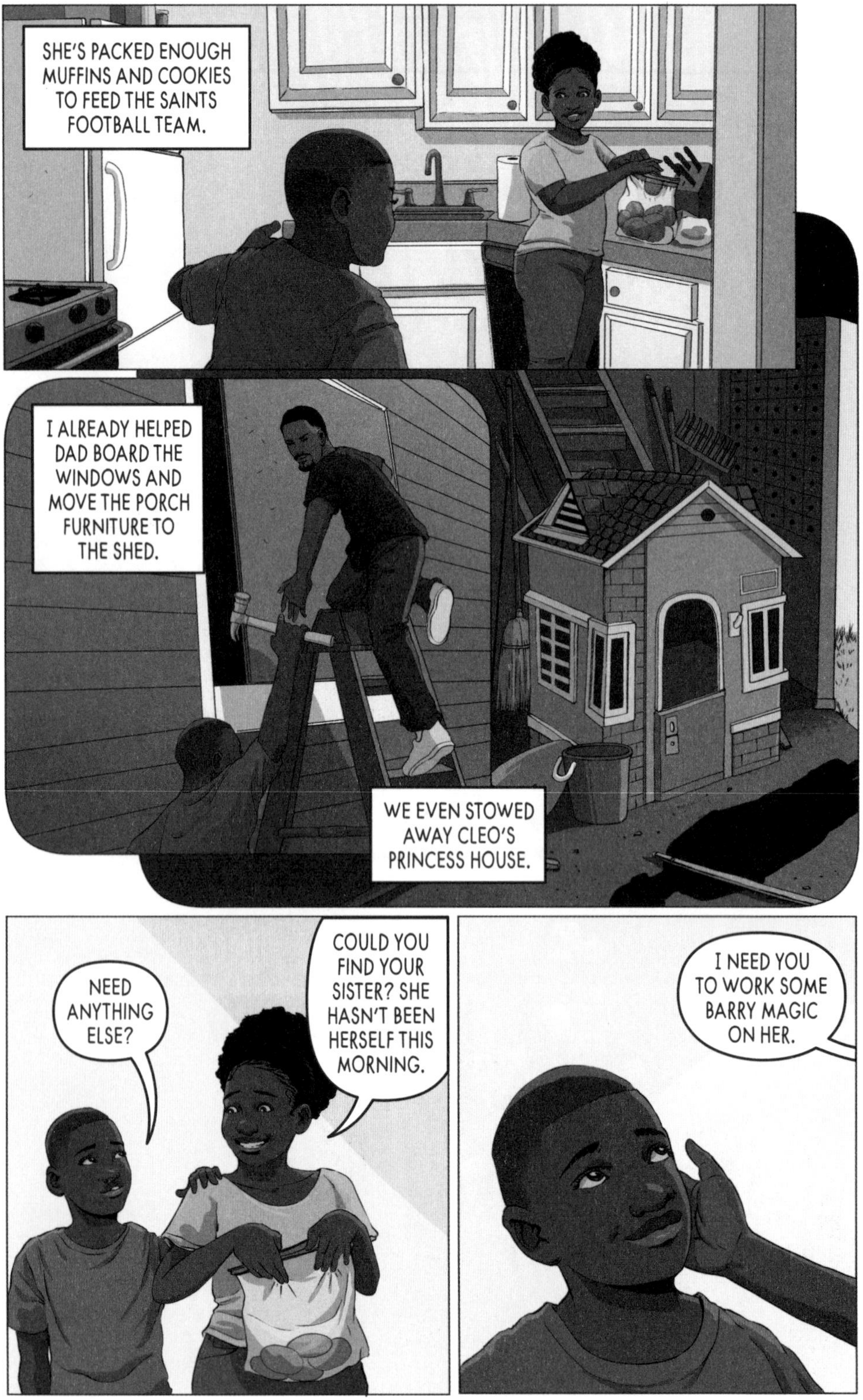

SHE'S PACKED ENOUGH MUFFINS AND COOKIES TO FEED THE SAINTS FOOTBALL TEAM.
I ALREADY HELPED DAD BOARD THE WINDOWS AND MOVE THE PORCH FURNITURE TO THE SHED.
WE EVEN STOWED AWAY CLEO'S PRINCESS HOUSE.
NEED ANYTHING ELSE?
COULD YOU FIND YOUR SISTER? SHE HASN'T BEEN HERSELF THIS MORNING.
I NEED YOU TO WORK SOME BARRY MAGIC ON HER.

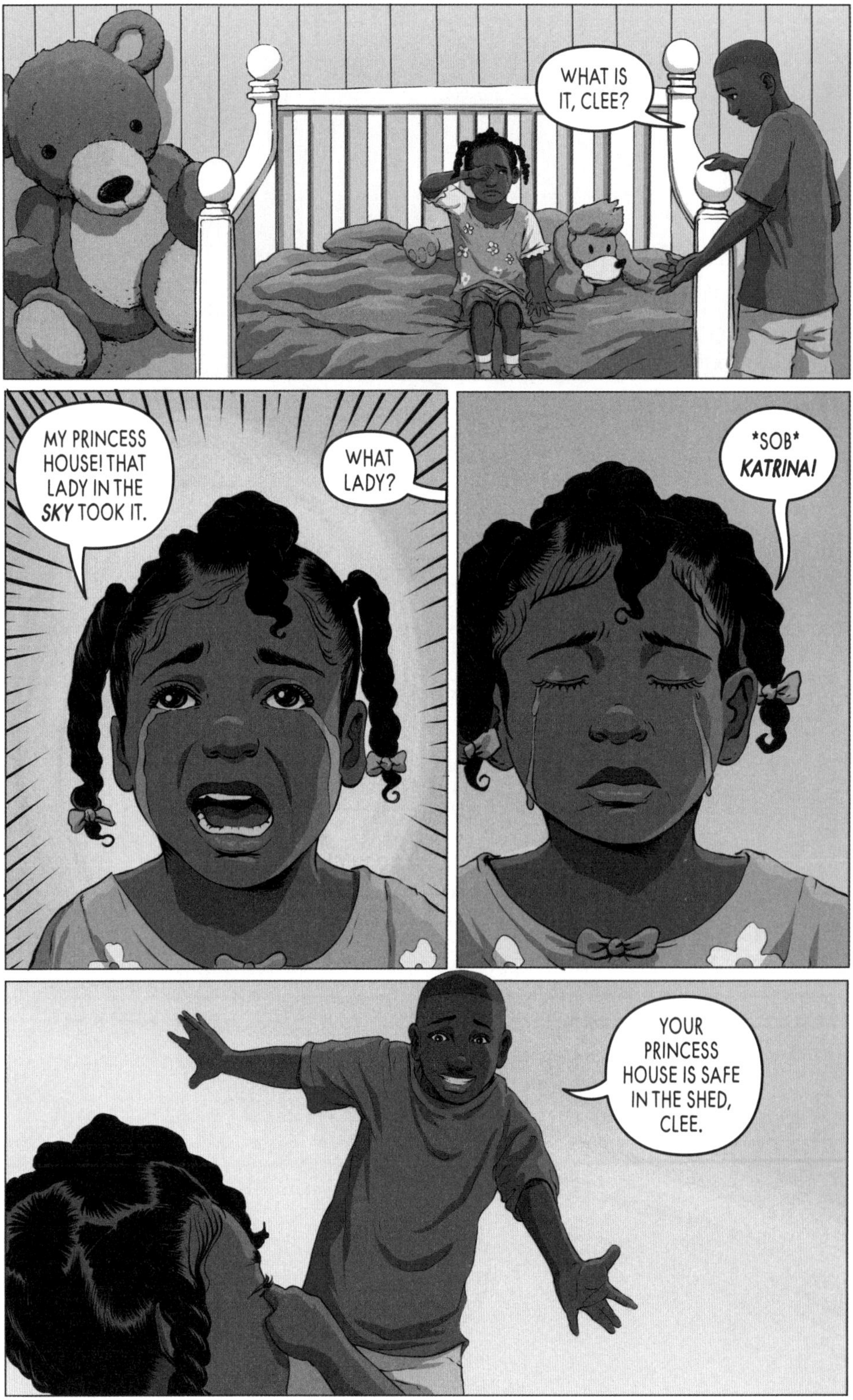
WHAT IS IT, CLEE?
MY PRINCESS HOUSE! THAT LADY IN THE *SKY* TOOK IT.
WHAT LADY?
SOB *KATRINA!*
YOUR PRINCESS HOUSE IS SAFE IN THE SHED, CLEE.

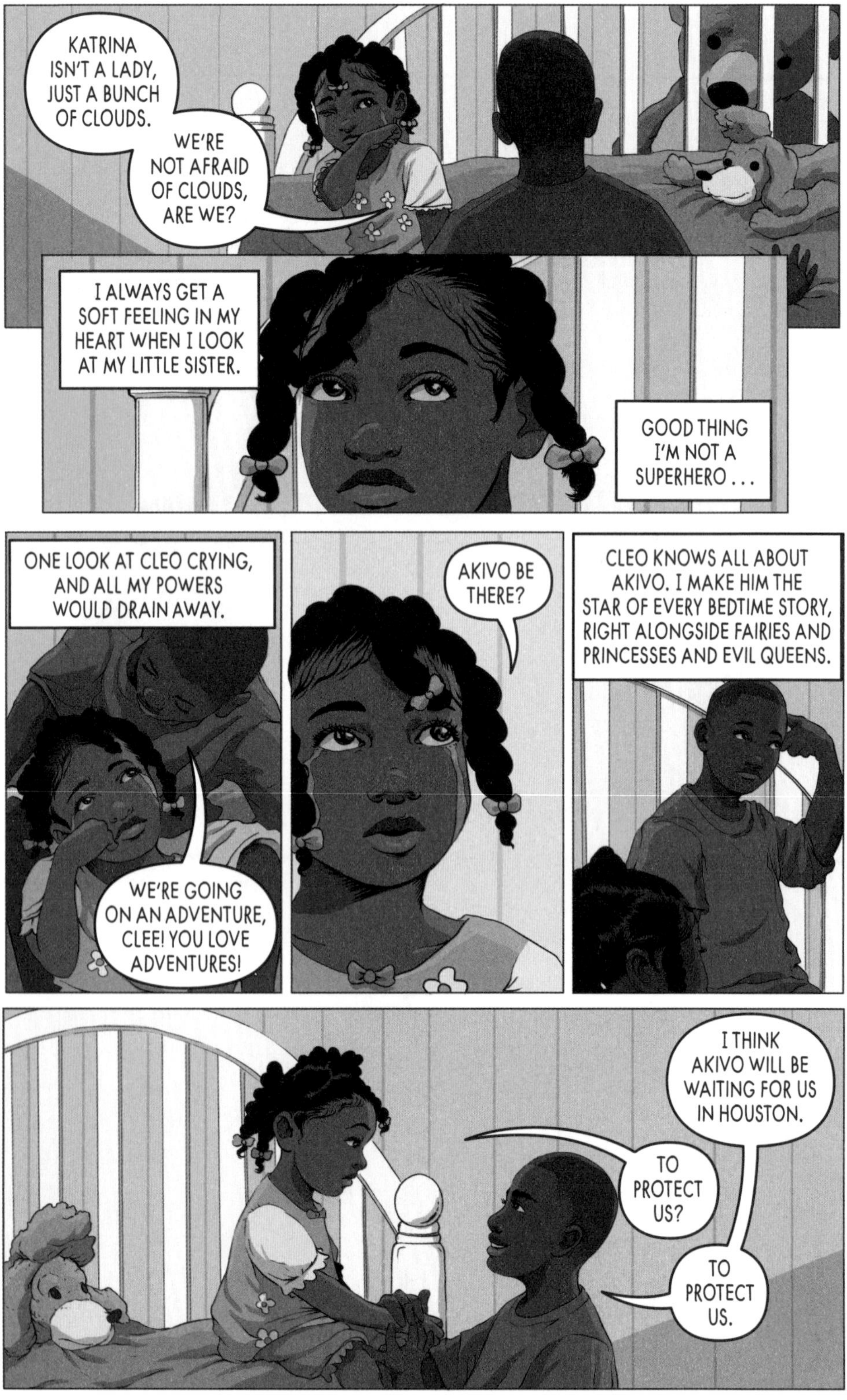
KATRINA ISN'T A LADY, JUST A BUNCH OF CLOUDS.
WE'RE NOT AFRAID OF CLOUDS, ARE WE?
I ALWAYS GET A SOFT FEELING IN MY HEART WHEN I LOOK AT MY LITTLE SISTER.
GOOD THING I'M NOT A SUPERHERO . . .
ONE LOOK AT CLEO CRYING, AND ALL MY POWERS WOULD DRAIN AWAY.
WE'RE GOING ON AN ADVENTURE, CLEE! YOU LOVE ADVENTURES!
AKIVO BE THERE?
CLEO KNOWS ALL ABOUT AKIVO. I MAKE HIM THE STAR OF EVERY BEDTIME STORY, RIGHT ALONGSIDE FAIRIES AND PRINCESSES AND EVIL QUEENS.
I THINK AKIVO WILL BE WAITING FOR US IN HOUSTON.
TO PROTECT US?
TO PROTECT US.

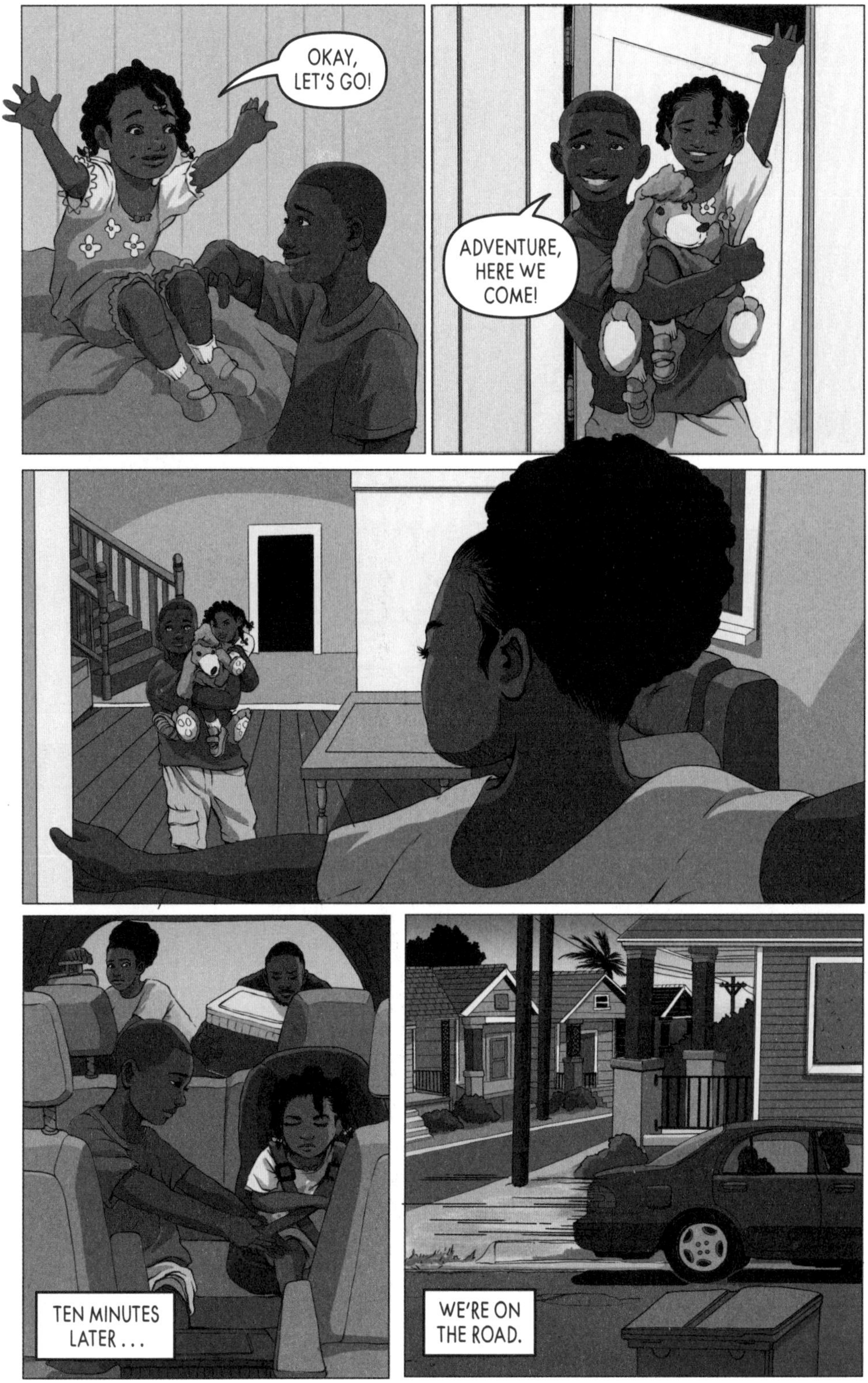
OKAY, LET'S GO!
ADVENTURE, HERE WE COME!
TEN MINUTES LATER . . .
WE'RE ON THE ROAD.

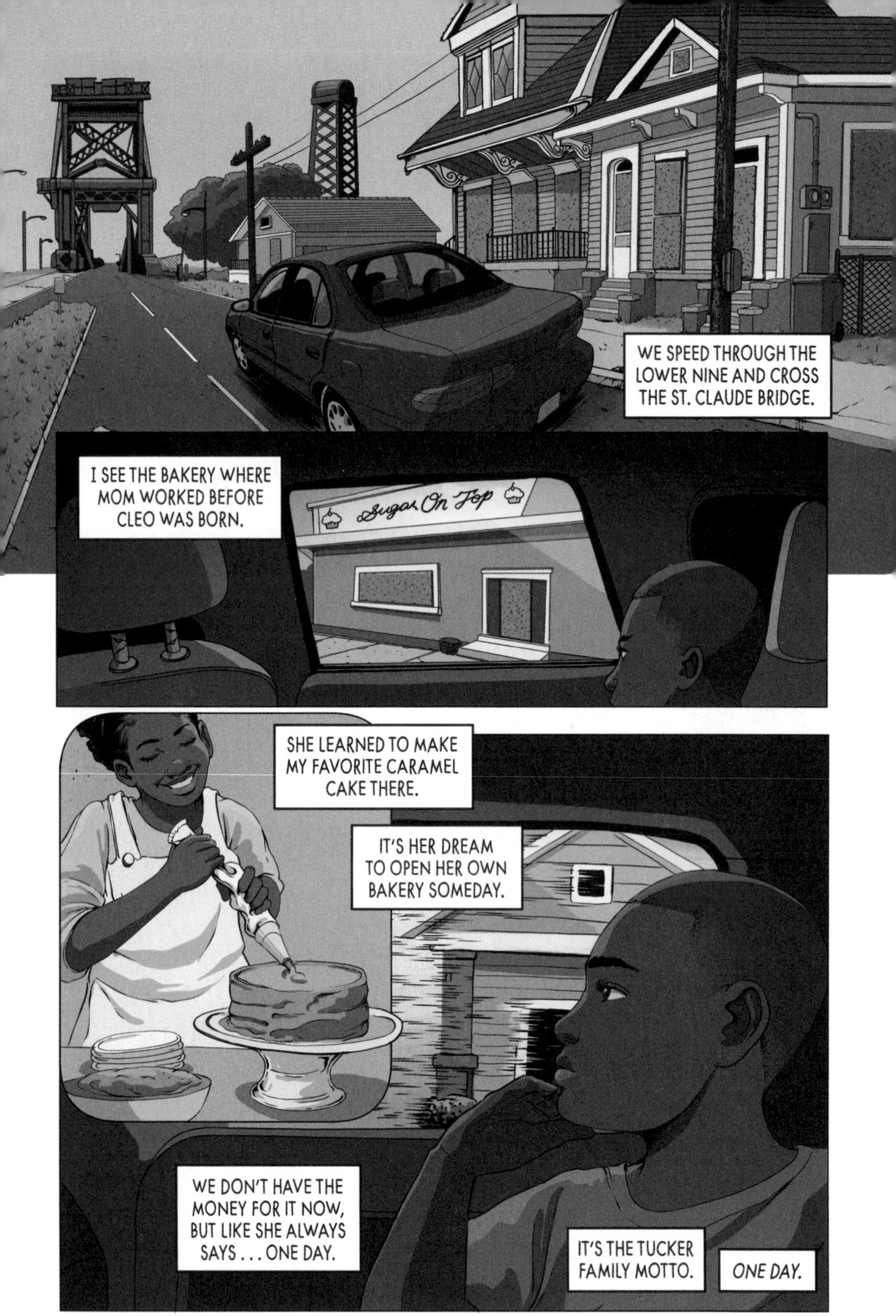
WE SPEED THROUGH THE LOWER NINE AND CROSS THE ST. CLAUDE BRIDGE.
I SEE THE BAKERY WHERE MOM WORKED BEFORE CLEO WAS BORN.
Sugar On Top
SHE LEARNED TO MAKE MY FAVORITE CARAMEL CAKE THERE.
IT'S HER DREAM TO OPEN HER OWN BAKERY SOMEDAY.
WE DON'T HAVE THE MONEY FOR IT NOW, BUT LIKE SHE ALWAYS SAYS . . . ONE DAY.
IT'S THE TUCKER FAMILY MOTTO.
ONE DAY.

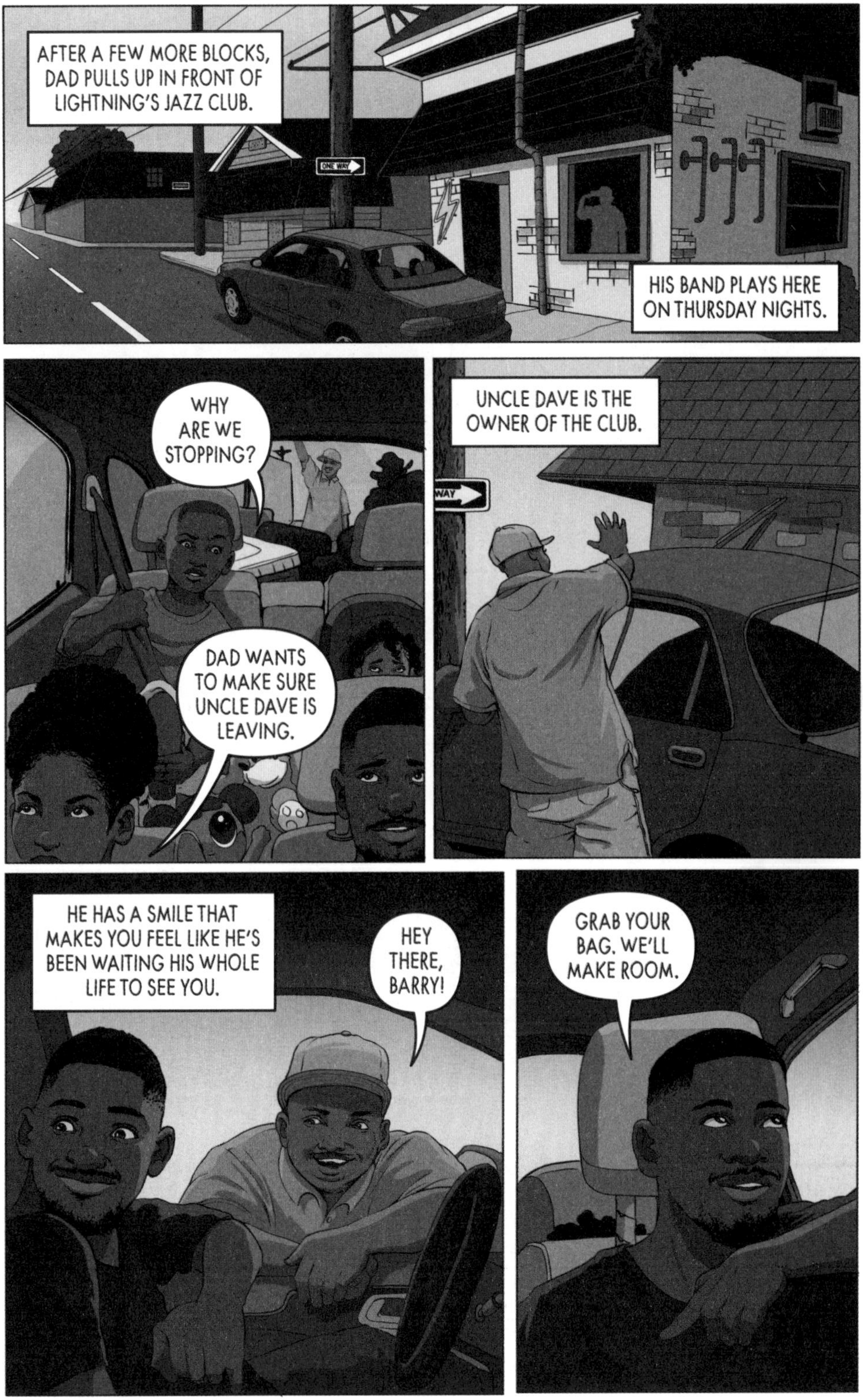
AFTER A FEW MORE BLOCKS, DAD PULLS UP IN FRONT OF LIGHTNING'S JAZZ CLUB.
ONE WAY
HIS BAND PLAYS HERE ON THURSDAY NIGHTS.
WHY ARE WE STOPPING?
DAD WANTS TO MAKE SURE UNCLE DAVE IS LEAVING.
UNCLE DAVE IS THE OWNER OF THE CLUB.
WAY
HE HAS A SMILE THAT MAKES YOU FEEL LIKE HE'S BEEN WAITING HIS WHOLE LIFE TO SEE YOU.
HEY THERE, BARRY!
GRAB YOUR BAG. WE'LL MAKE ROOM.

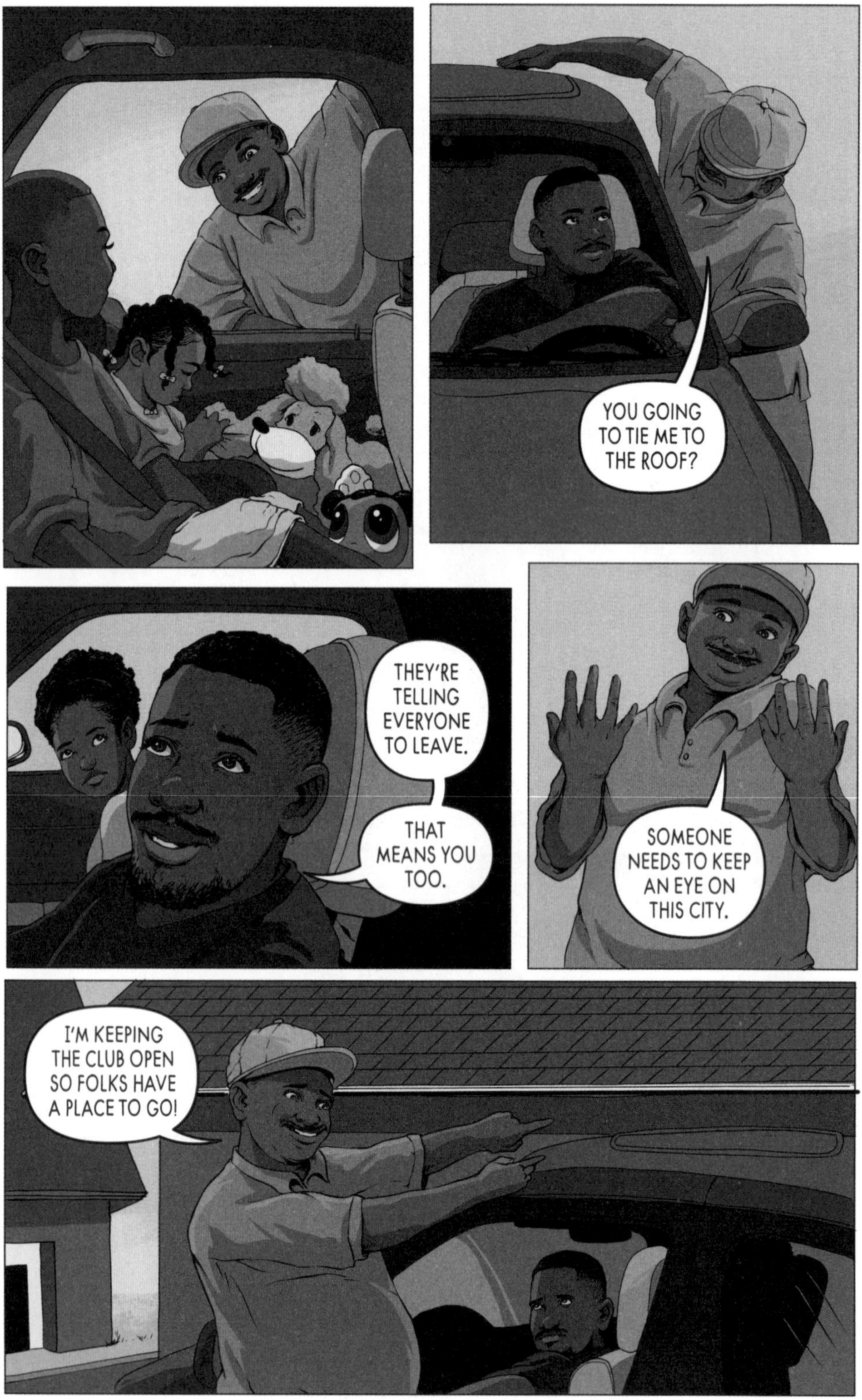
YOU GOING TO TIE ME TO THE ROOF?
THEY'RE TELLING EVERYONE TO LEAVE.
THAT MEANS YOU TOO.
SOMEONE NEEDS TO KEEP AN EYE ON THIS CITY.
I'M KEEPING THE CLUB OPEN SO FOLKS HAVE A PLACE TO GO!

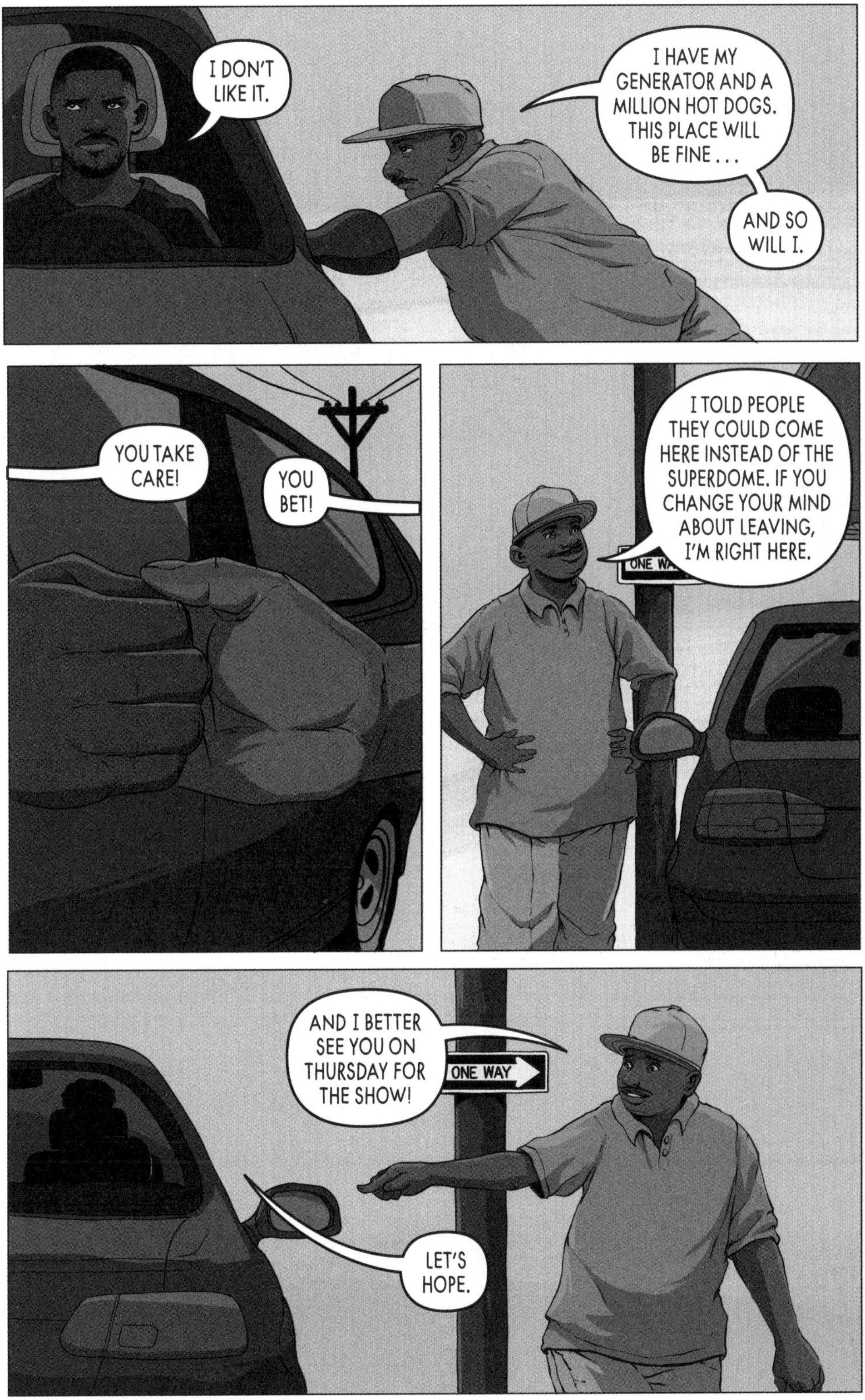
I DON'T LIKE IT.
I HAVE MY GENERATOR AND A MILLION HOT DOGS. THIS PLACE WILL BE FINE . . .
AND SO WILL I.
YOU TAKE CARE!
YOU BET!
I TOLD PEOPLE THEY COULD COME HERE INSTEAD OF THE SUPERDOME. IF YOU CHANGE YOUR MIND ABOUT LEAVING, I'M RIGHT HERE.
AND I BETTER SEE YOU ON THURSDAY FOR THE SHOW!
ONE WAY
LET'S HOPE.

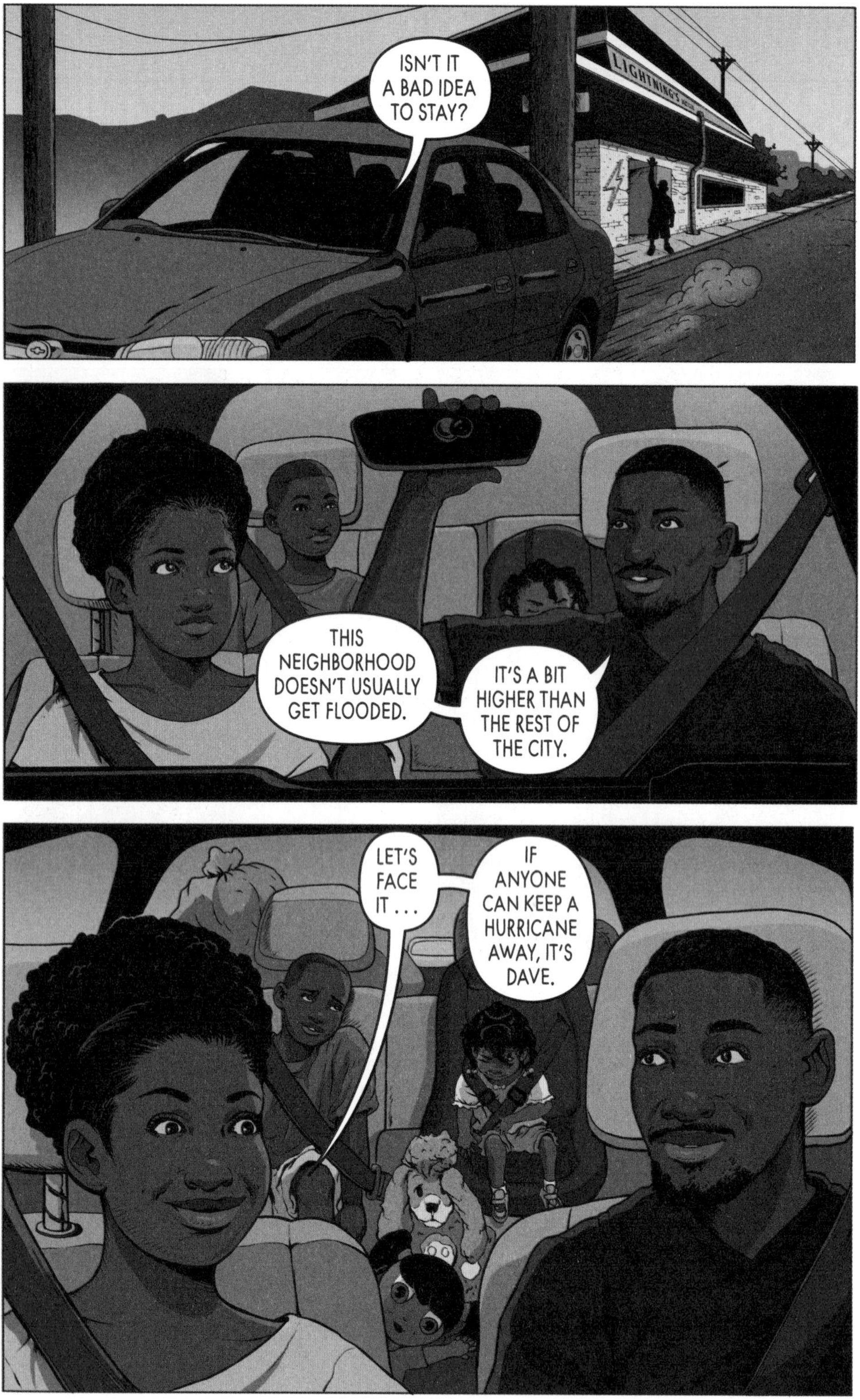
ISN'T IT A BAD IDEA TO STAY?
LIGHTNING'S
THIS NEIGHBORHOOD DOESN'T USUALLY GET FLOODED.
IT'S A BIT HIGHER THAN THE REST OF THE CITY.
LET'S FACE IT . . .
IF ANYONE CAN KEEP A HURRICANE AWAY, IT'S DAVE.

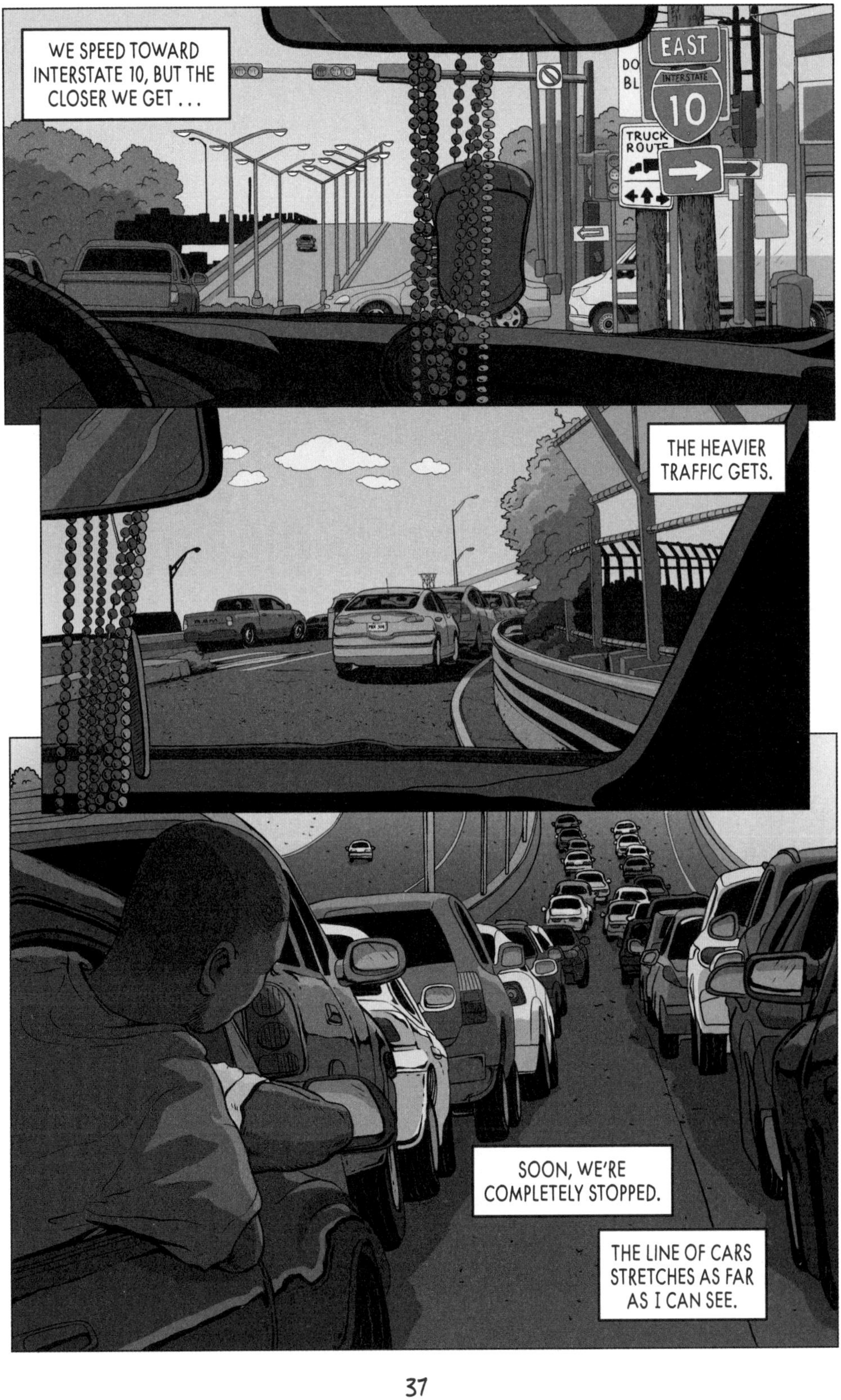
WE SPEED TOWARD INTERSTATE 10, BUT THE CLOSER WE GET . . .
EAST
INTERSTATE
10
TRUCK ROUTE
THE HEAVIER TRAFFIC GETS.
SOON, WE'RE COMPLETELY STOPPED.
THE LINE OF CARS STRETCHES AS FAR AS I CAN SEE.

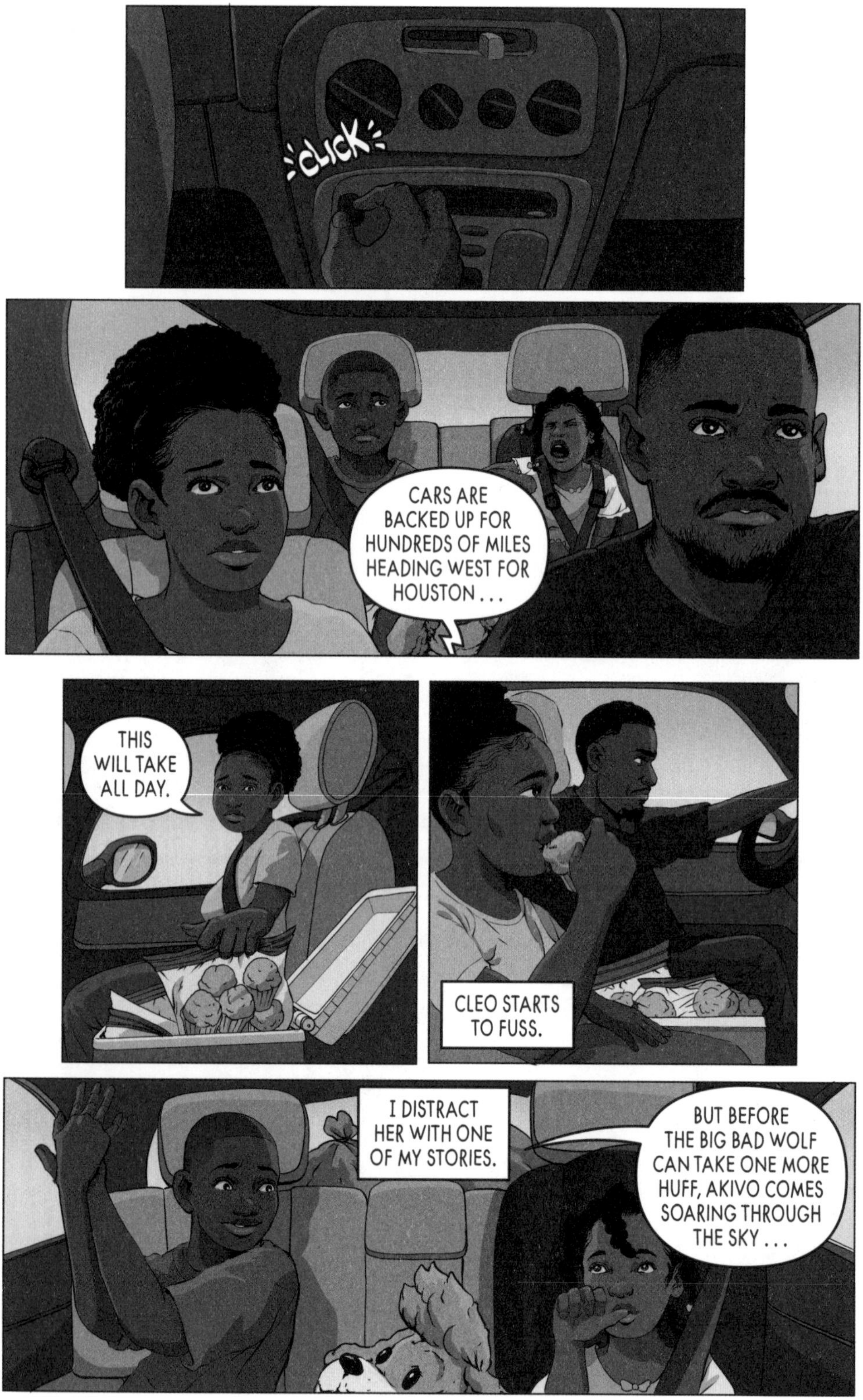
CLICK
CARS ARE BACKED UP FOR HUNDREDS OF MILES HEADING WEST FOR HOUSTON . . .
THIS WILL TAKE ALL DAY.
CLEO STARTS TO FUSS.
I DISTRACT HER WITH ONE OF MY STORIES.
BUT BEFORE THE BIG BAD WOLF CAN TAKE ONE MORE HUFF, AKIVO COMES SOARING THROUGH THE SKY . . .

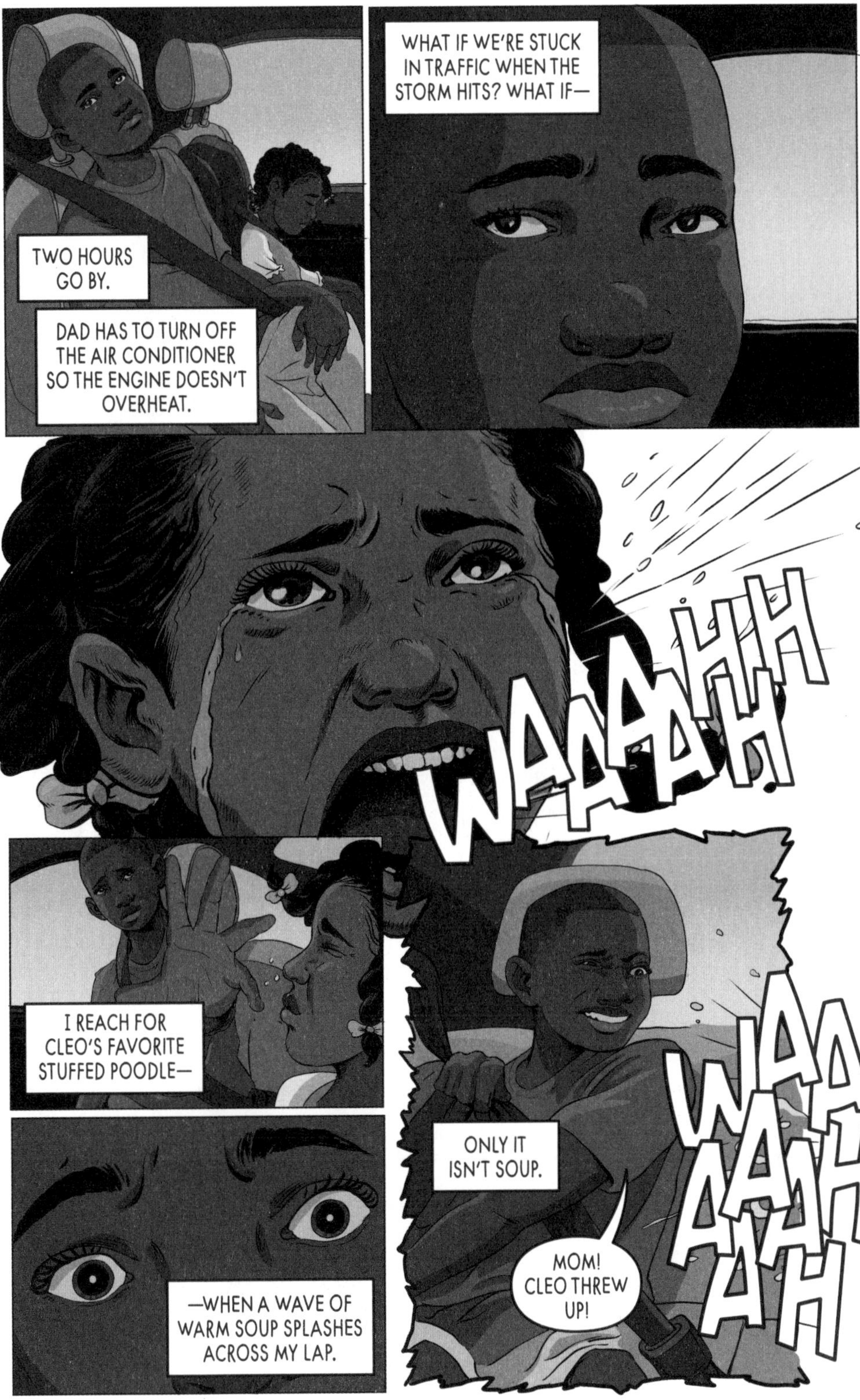
TWO HOURS GO BY.
DAD HAS TO TURN OFF THE AIR CONDITIONER SO THE ENGINE DOESN'T OVERHEAT.
WHAT IF WE'RE STUCK IN TRAFFIC WHEN THE STORM HITS? WHAT IF—
WAAAAHHH!
I REACH FOR CLEO'S FAVORITE STUFFED POODLE—
—WHEN A WAVE OF WARM SOUP SPLASHES ACROSS MY LAP.
ONLY IT ISN'T SOUP.
MOM! CLEO THREW UP!
WAAAAAAHH

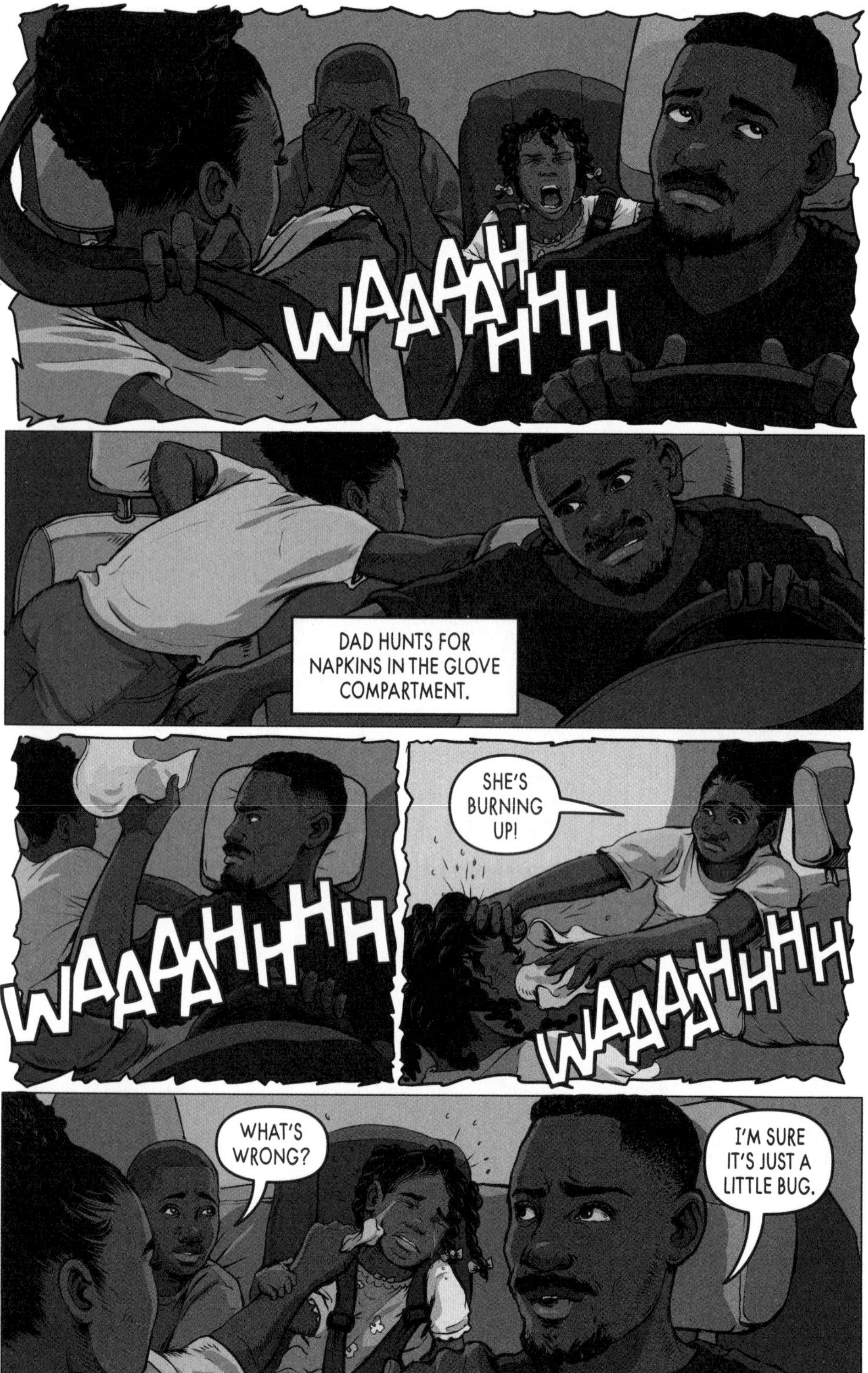
WAAAAHHHH
DAD HUNTS FOR NAPKINS IN THE GLOVE COMPARTMENT.
WAAAAHHHH
SHE'S BURNING UP!
WAAAAHHHH
WHAT'S WRONG?
I'M SURE IT'S JUST A LITTLE BUG.

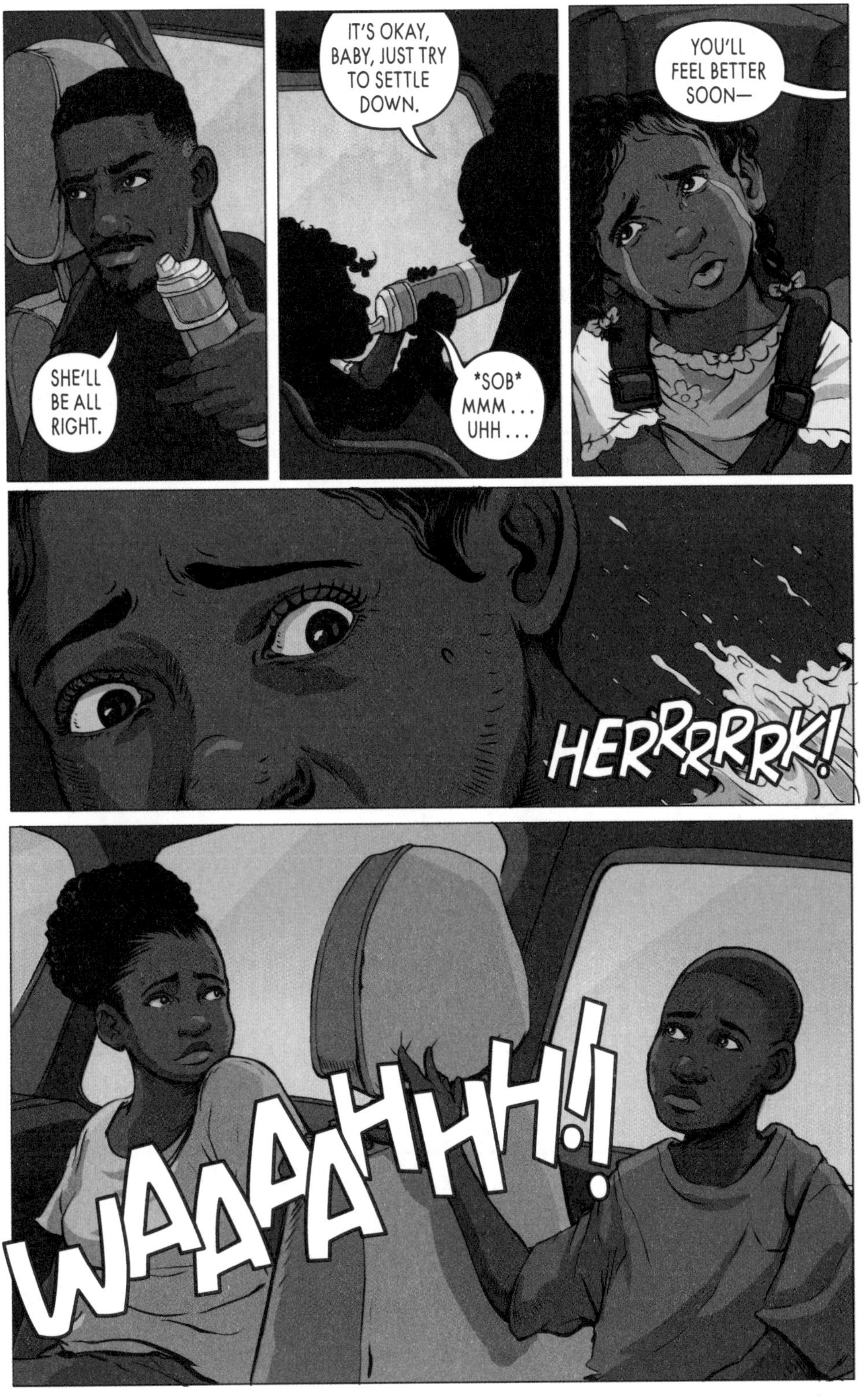

SHE'LL BE ALL RIGHT.
IT'S OKAY, BABY, JUST TRY TO SETTLE DOWN.
SOB MMM . . . UHH . . .
YOU'LL FEEL BETTER SOON—
HERRRRRK!
WAAAAHHH!!

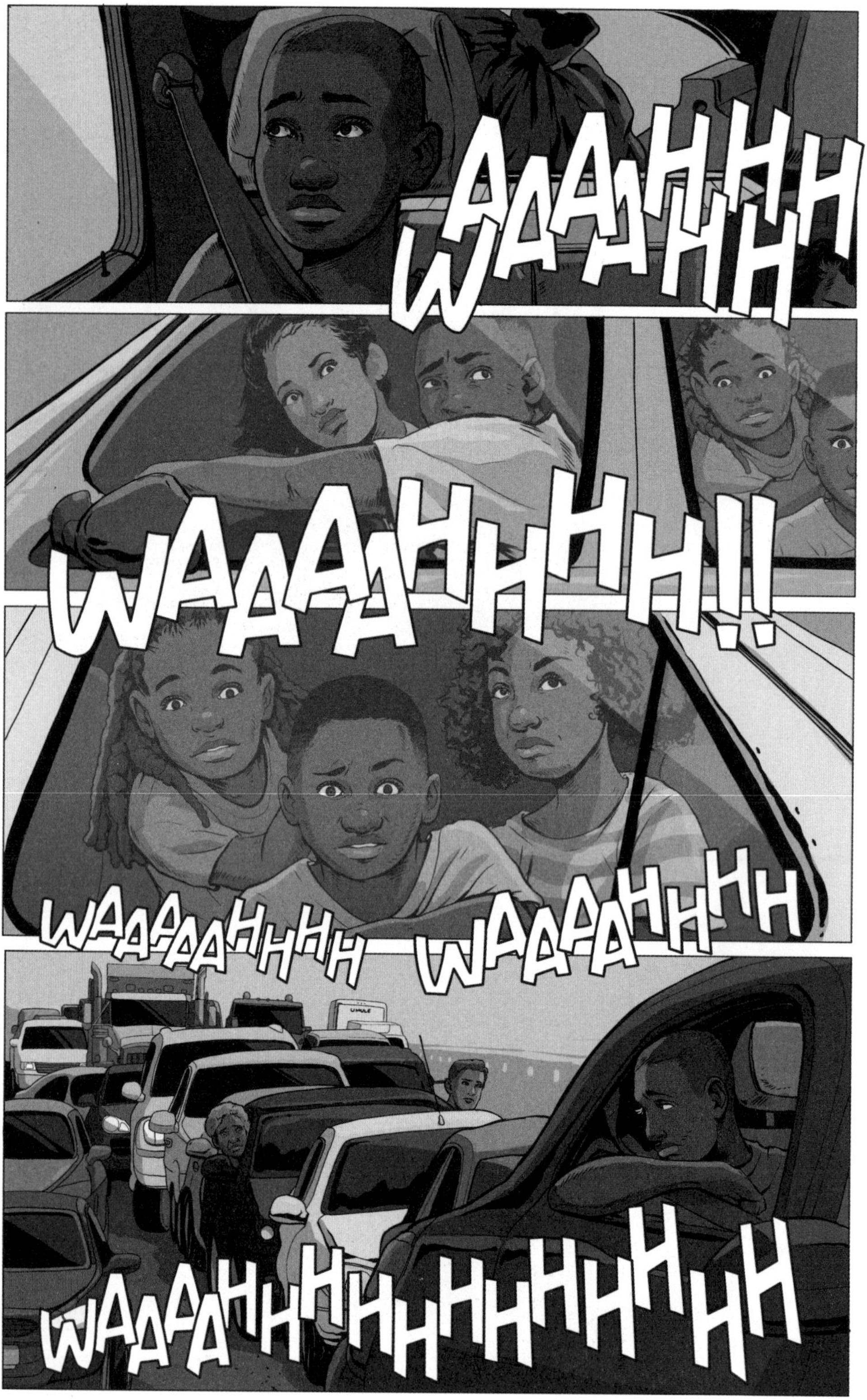
WAAAAHHHHH
WAAAAHHHH!!
WAAAAHHHHH
WAAAAHHHHH
WAAAHHHHHHHHHHHH

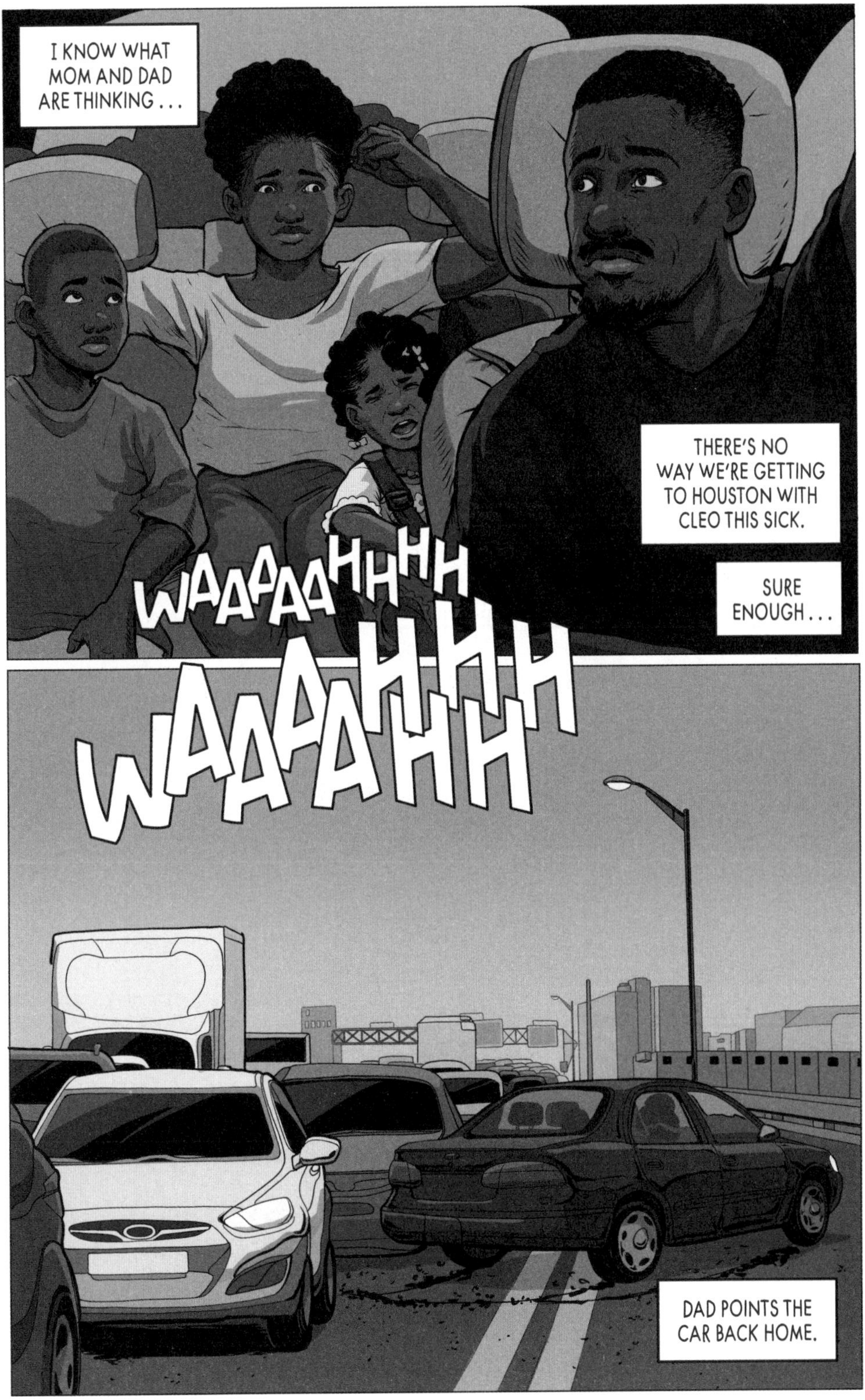
I KNOW WHAT MOM AND DAD ARE THINKING . . .
THERE'S NO WAY WE'RE GETTING TO HOUSTON WITH CLEO THIS SICK.
SURE ENOUGH . . .
WAAAAAHHHH
WAAAAAHHHHHHH
DAD POINTS THE CAR BACK HOME.

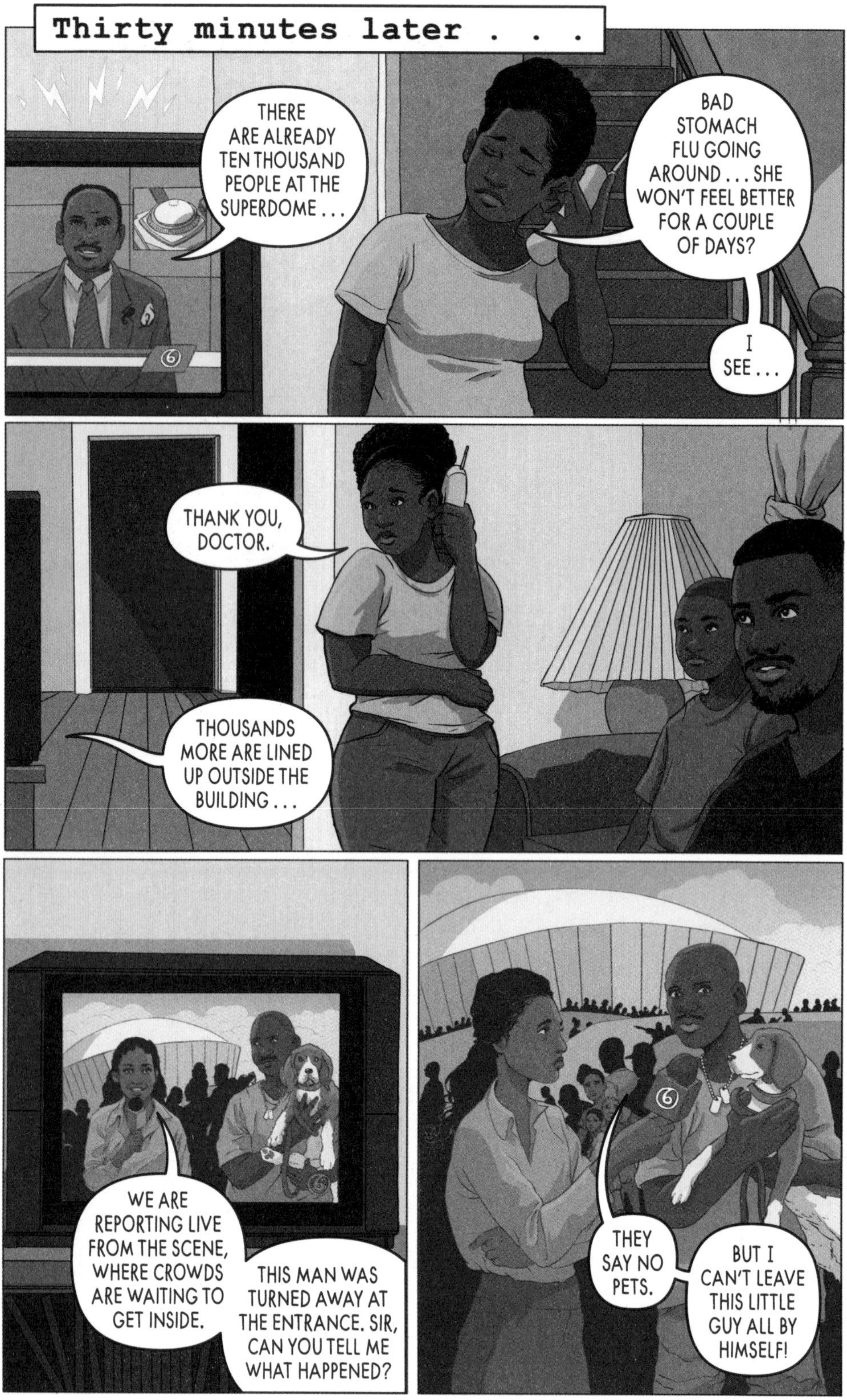
Thirty minutes later . . .
THERE ARE ALREADY TEN THOUSAND PEOPLE AT THE SUPERDOME . . .
BAD STOMACH FLU GOING AROUND . . . SHE WON'T FEEL BETTER FOR A COUPLE OF DAYS?
I SEE . . .
THANK YOU, DOCTOR.
THOUSANDS MORE ARE LINED UP OUTSIDE THE BUILDING . . .
WE ARE REPORTING LIVE FROM THE SCENE, WHERE CROWDS ARE WAITING TO GET INSIDE.
THIS MAN WAS TURNED AWAY AT THE ENTRANCE. SIR, CAN YOU TELL ME WHAT HAPPENED?
THEY SAY NO PETS.
BUT I CAN'T LEAVE THIS LITTLE GUY ALL BY HIMSELF!

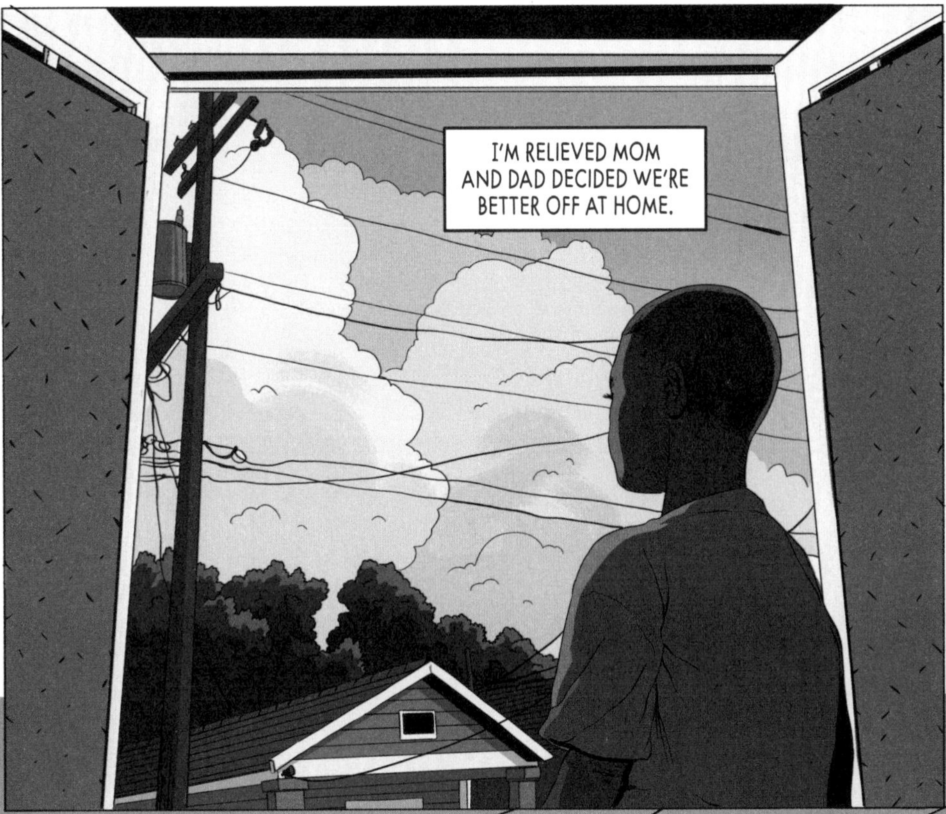
I'M RELIEVED MOM AND DAD DECIDED WE'RE BETTER OFF AT HOME.
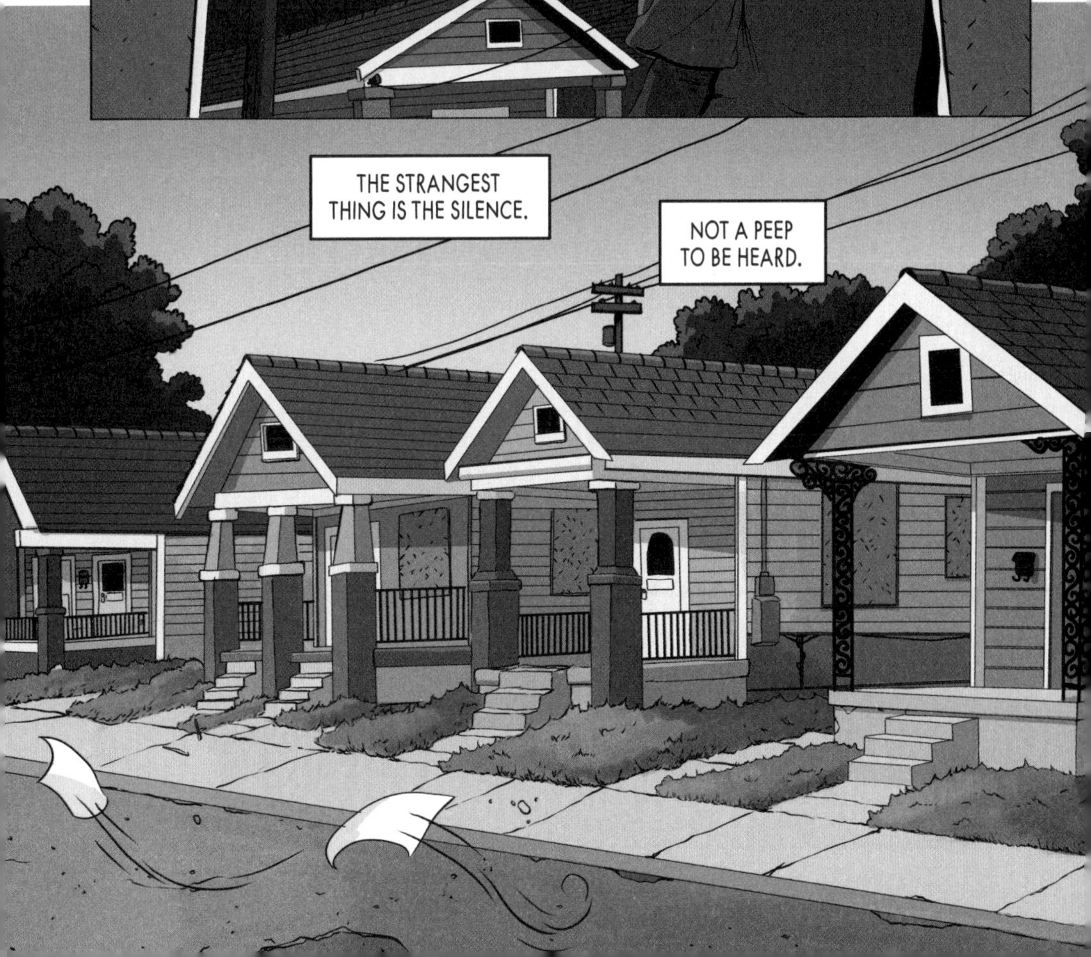
THE STRANGEST THING IS THE SILENCE.
NOT A PEEP TO BE HEARD.

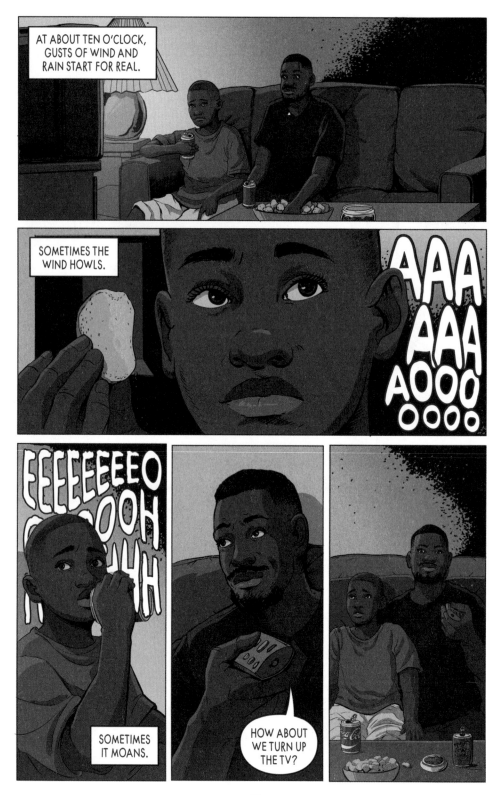

AT ABOUT TEN O'CLOCK, GUSTS OF WIND AND RAIN START FOR REAL.

SOMETIMES THE WIND HOWLS.

AAAAAA AOOO OOOO

EEEEEEEEO OOOH AAH

SOMETIMES IT MOANS.

HOW ABOUT WE TURN UP THE TV?

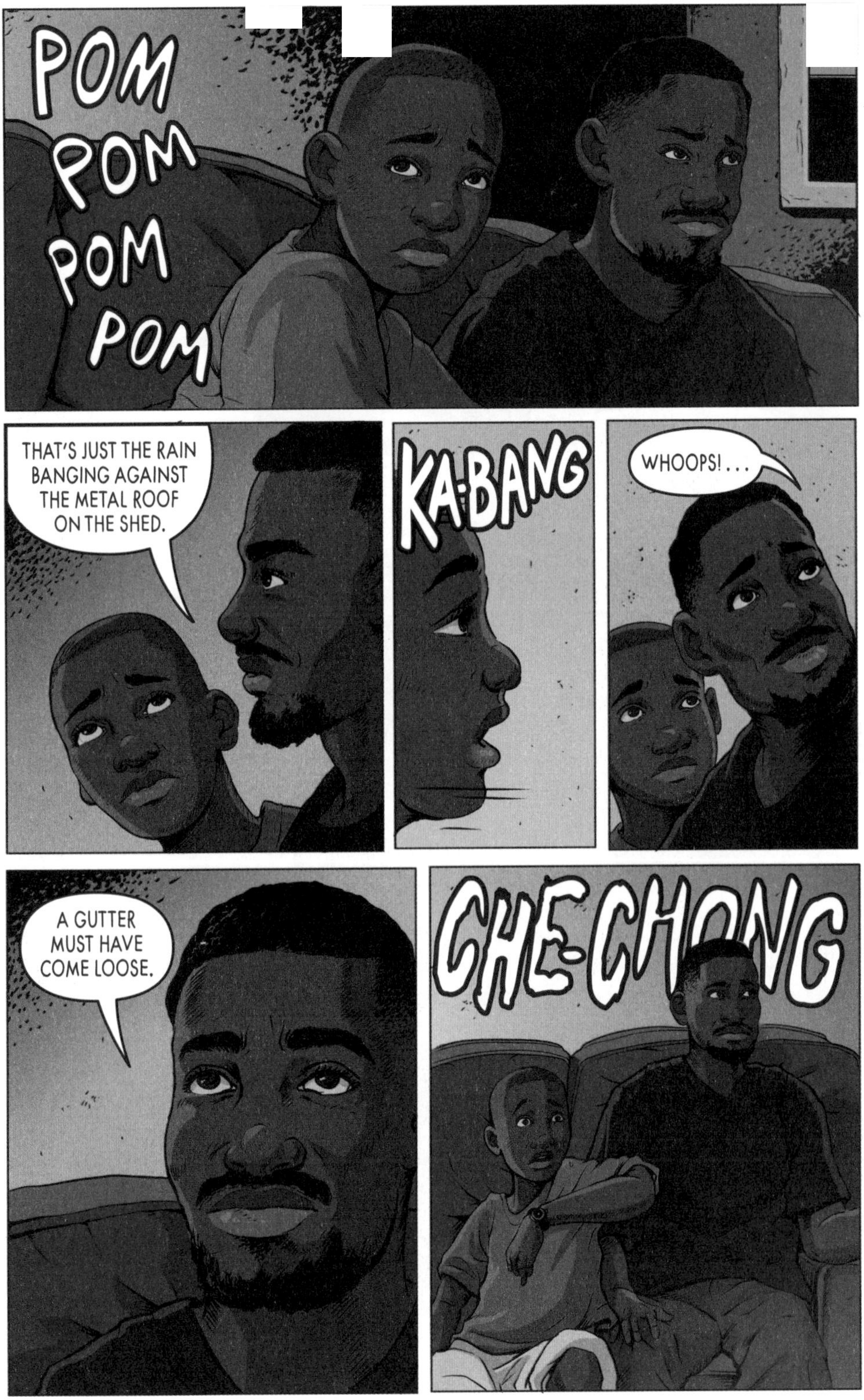
POM
POM
POM
POM
THAT'S JUST THE RAIN BANGING AGAINST THE METAL ROOF ON THE SHED.
KA-BANG
WHOOPS! . . .
A GUTTER MUST HAVE COME LOOSE.
CHE-CHONG

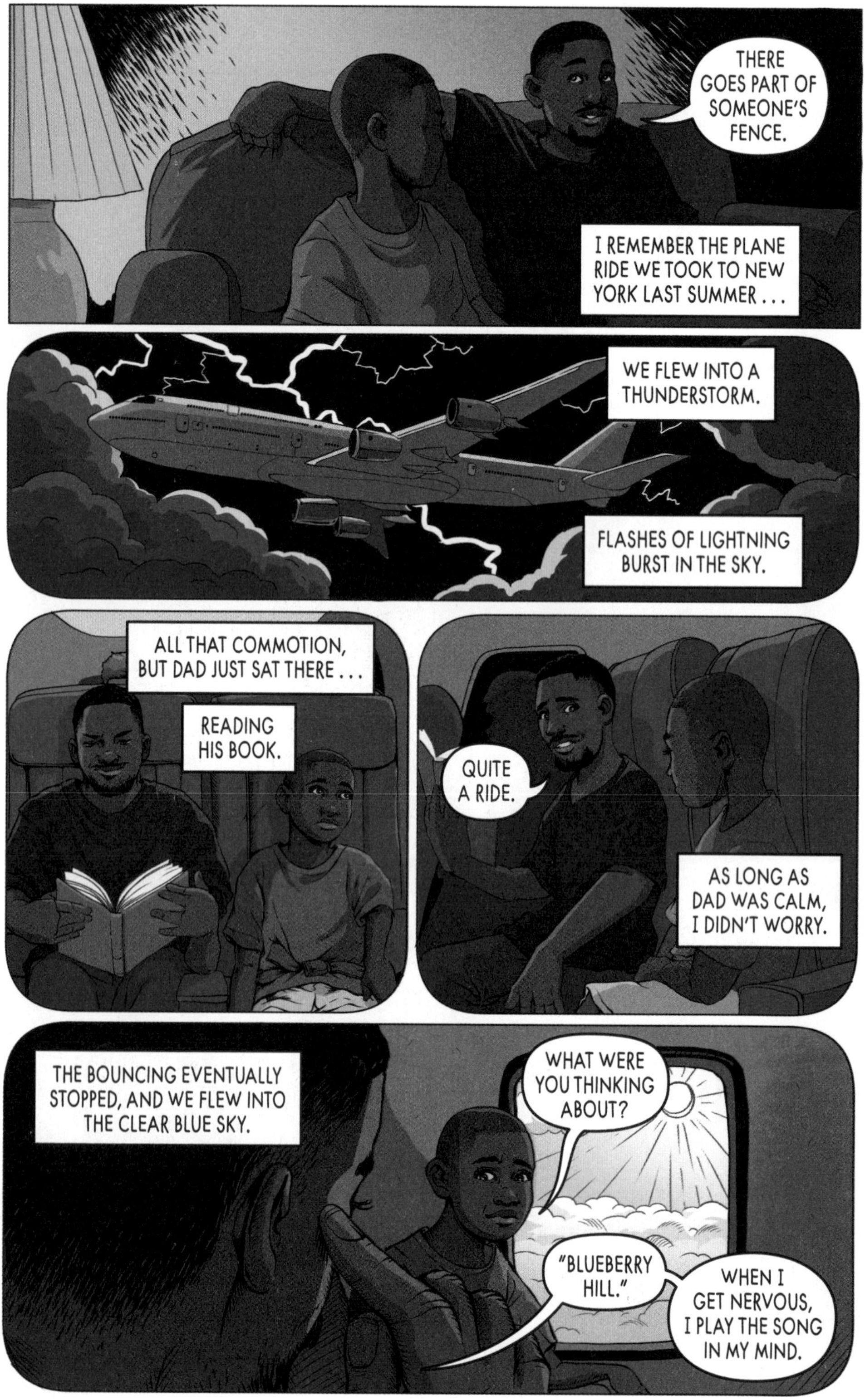
THERE GOES PART OF SOMEONE'S FENCE.
I REMEMBER THE PLANE RIDE WE TOOK TO NEW YORK LAST SUMMER . . .
WE FLEW INTO A THUNDERSTORM.
FLASHES OF LIGHTNING BURST IN THE SKY.
ALL THAT COMMOTION, BUT DAD JUST SAT THERE . . .
READING HIS BOOK.
QUITE A RIDE.
AS LONG AS DAD WAS CALM, I DIDN'T WORRY.
THE BOUNCING EVENTUALLY STOPPED, AND WE FLEW INTO THE CLEAR BLUE SKY.
WHAT WERE YOU THINKING ABOUT?
"BLUEBERRY HILL."
WHEN I GET NERVOUS, I PLAY THE SONG IN MY MIND.

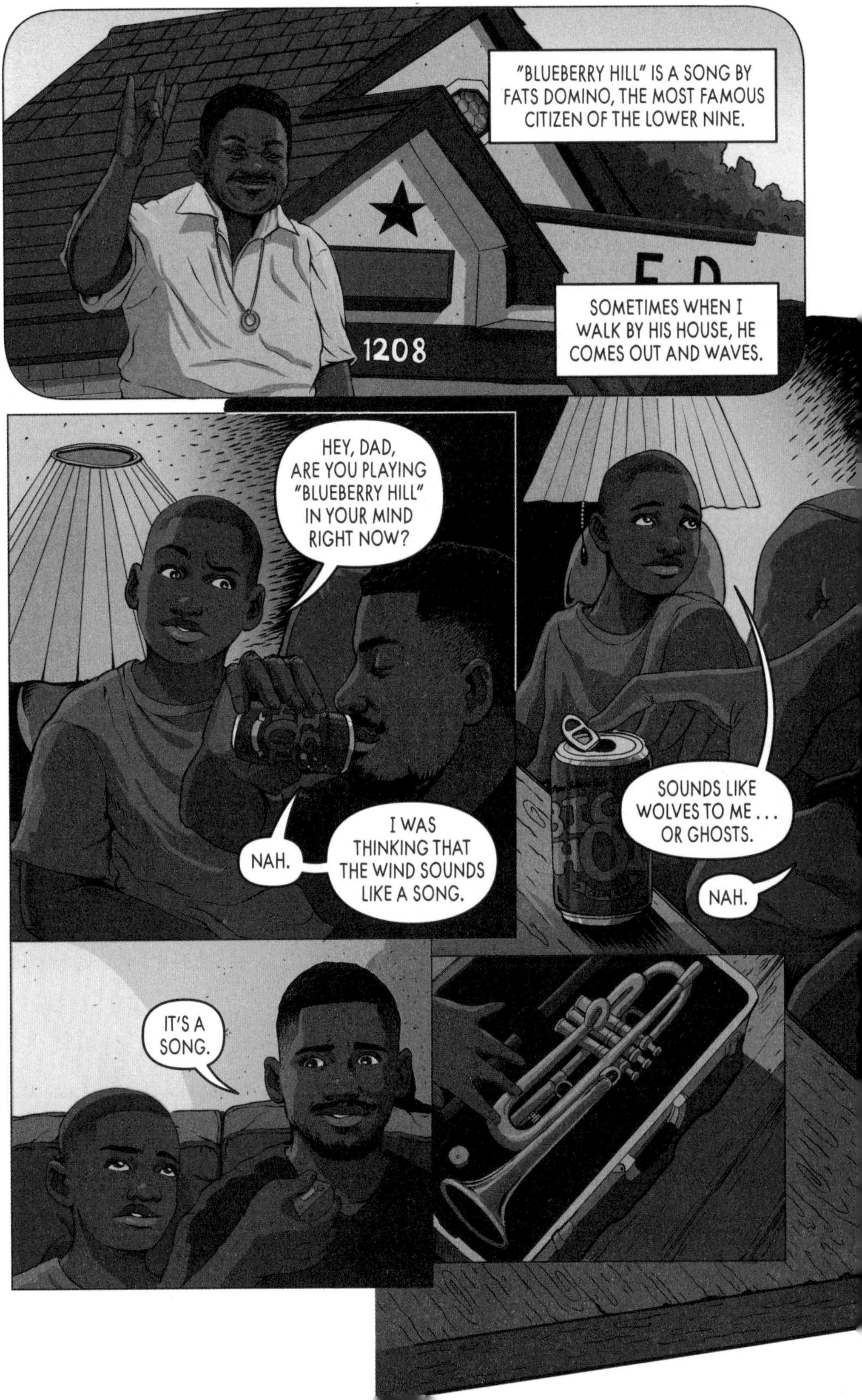
"BLUEBERRY HILL" IS A SONG BY FATS DOMINO, THE MOST FAMOUS CITIZEN OF THE LOWER NINE.
1208
SOMETIMES WHEN I WALK BY HIS HOUSE, HE COMES OUT AND WAVES.
HEY, DAD, ARE YOU PLAYING "BLUEBERRY HILL" IN YOUR MIND RIGHT NOW?
NAH.
I WAS THINKING THAT THE WIND SOUNDS LIKE A SONG.
SOUNDS LIKE WOLVES TO ME . . . OR GHOSTS.
NAH.
IT'S A SONG.

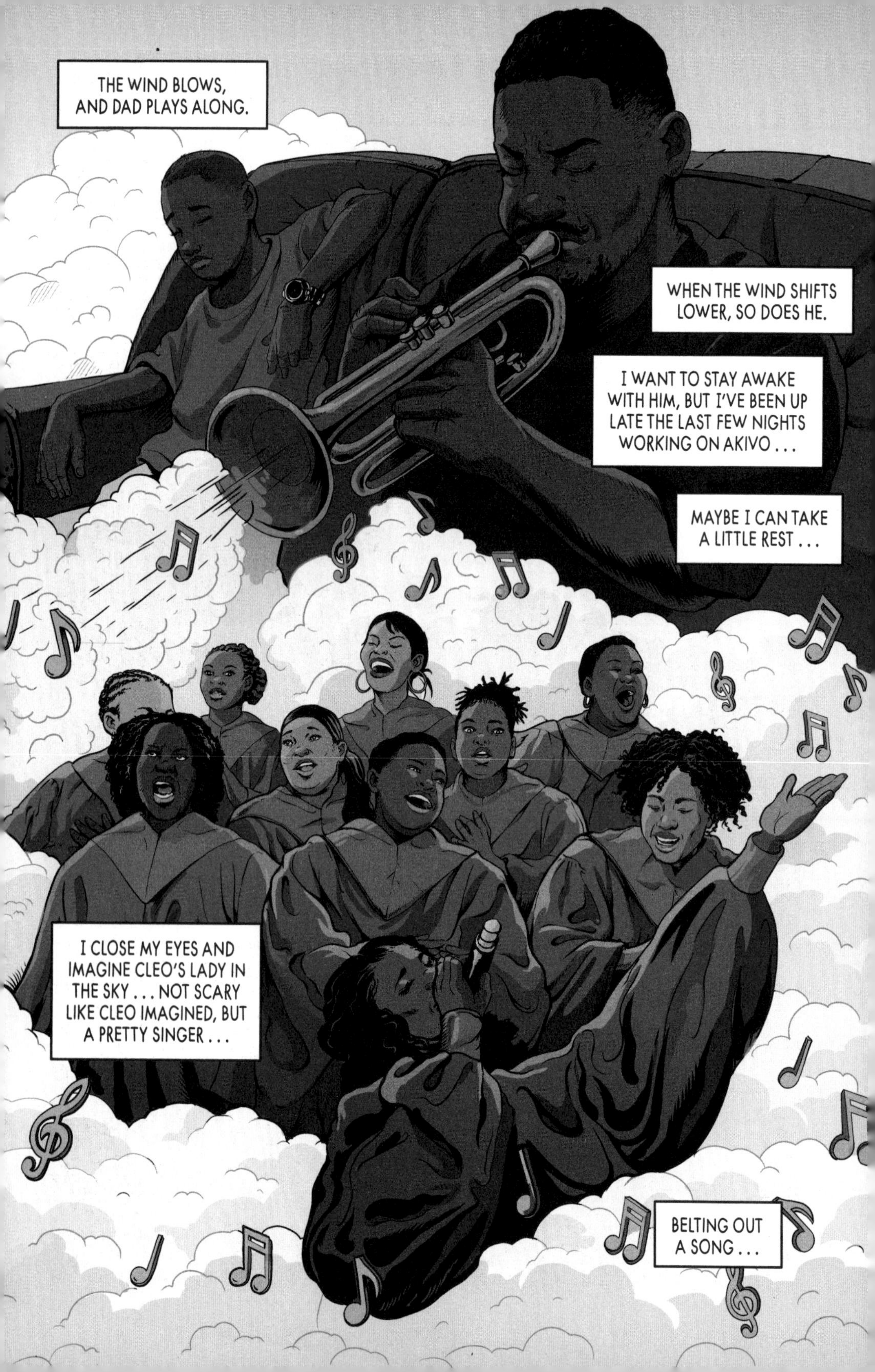
THE WIND BLOWS, AND DAD PLAYS ALONG.
WHEN THE WIND SHIFTS LOWER, SO DOES HE.
I WANT TO STAY AWAKE WITH HIM, BUT I'VE BEEN UP LATE THE LAST FEW NIGHTS WORKING ON AKIVO . . .
MAYBE I CAN TAKE A LITTLE REST . . .
I CLOSE MY EYES AND IMAGINE CLEO'S LADY IN THE SKY . . . NOT SCARY LIKE CLEO IMAGINED, BUT A PRETTY SINGER . . .
BELTING OUT A SONG . . .

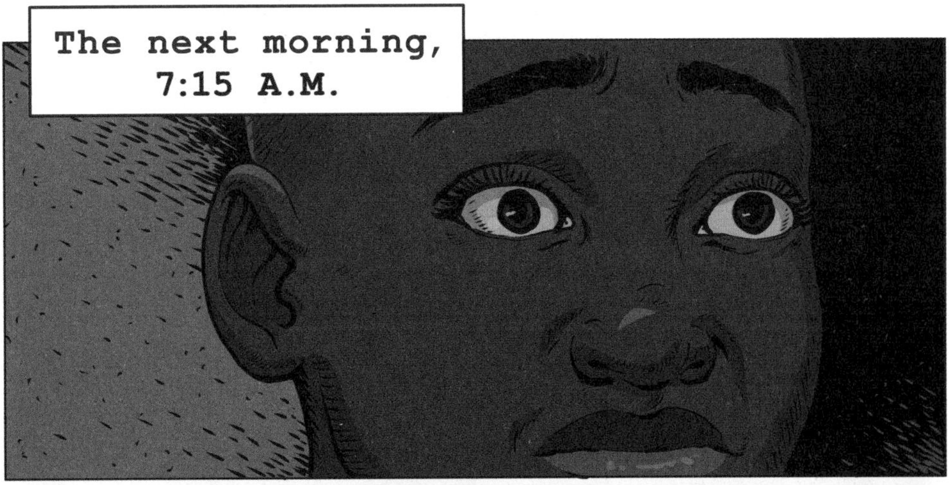
The next morning,
7:15 A.M.

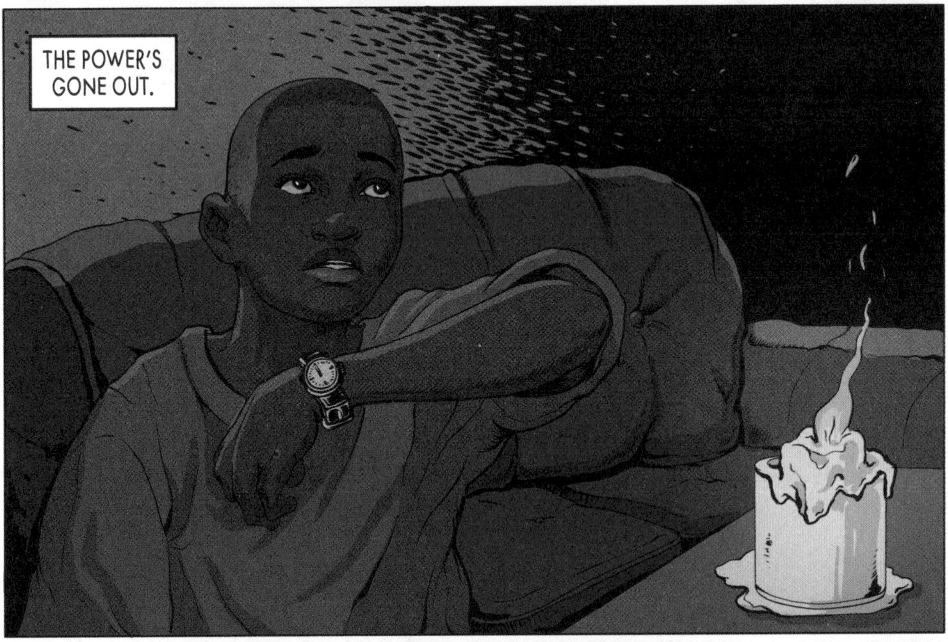
THE POWER'S
GONE OUT.

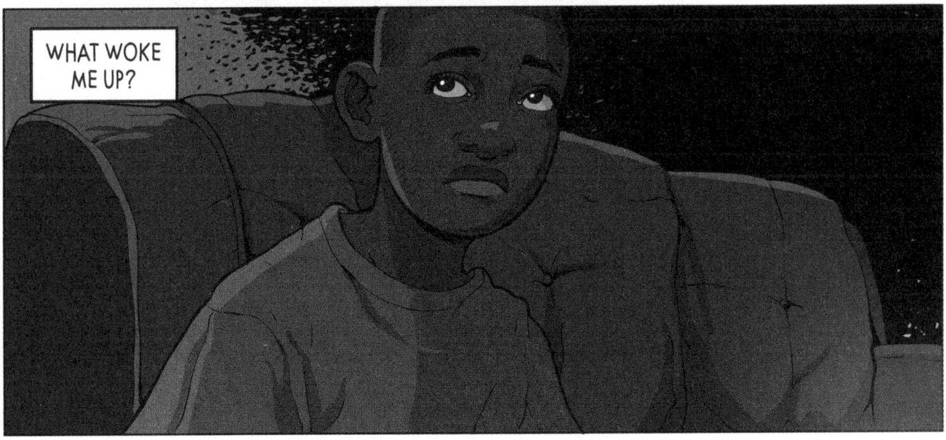
WHAT WOKE
ME UP?

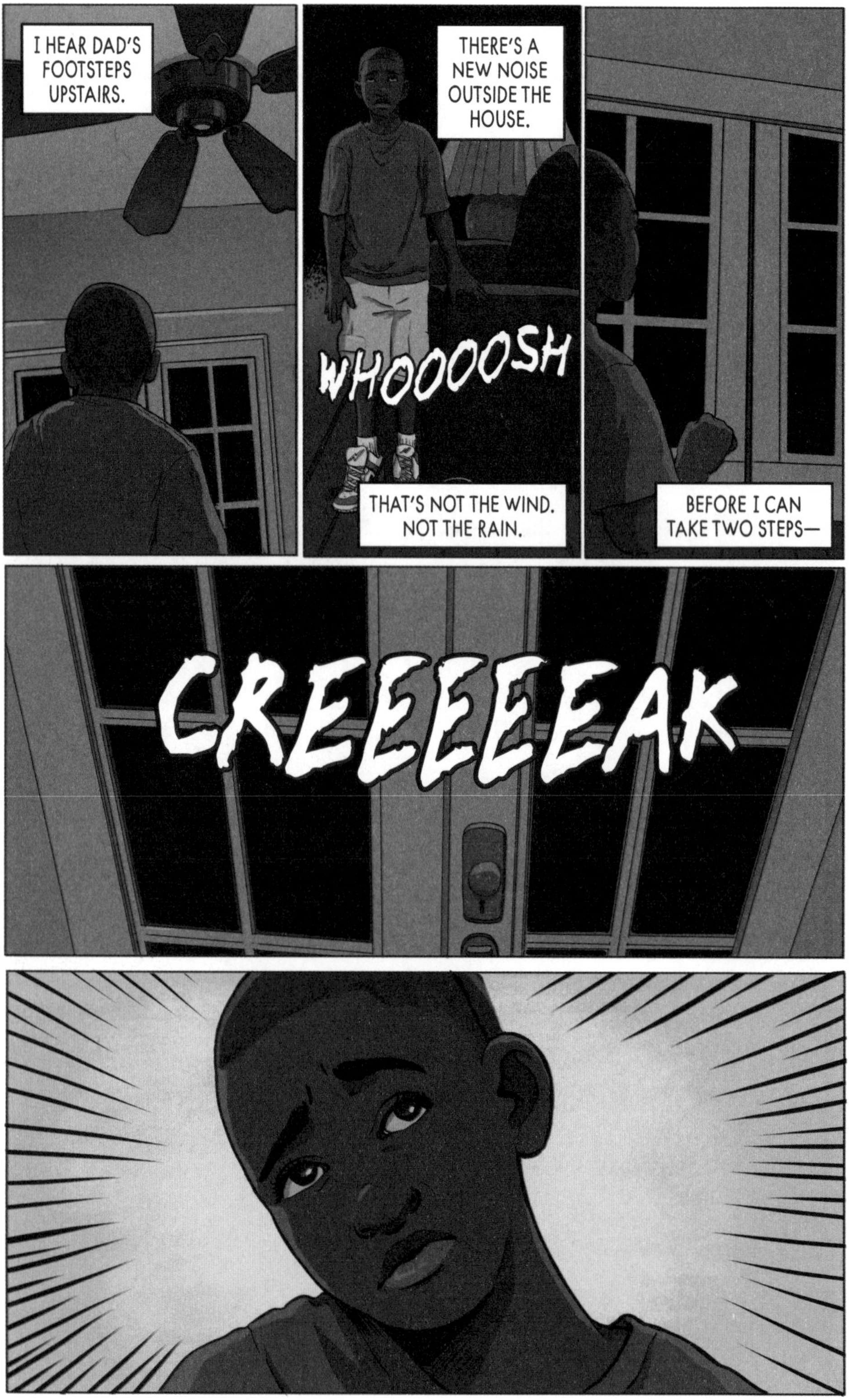
I HEAR DAD'S FOOTSTEPS UPSTAIRS.
THERE'S A NEW NOISE OUTSIDE THE HOUSE.
WHOOOOSH
THAT'S NOT THE WIND. NOT THE RAIN.
BEFORE I CAN TAKE TWO STEPS—
CREEEEEAK

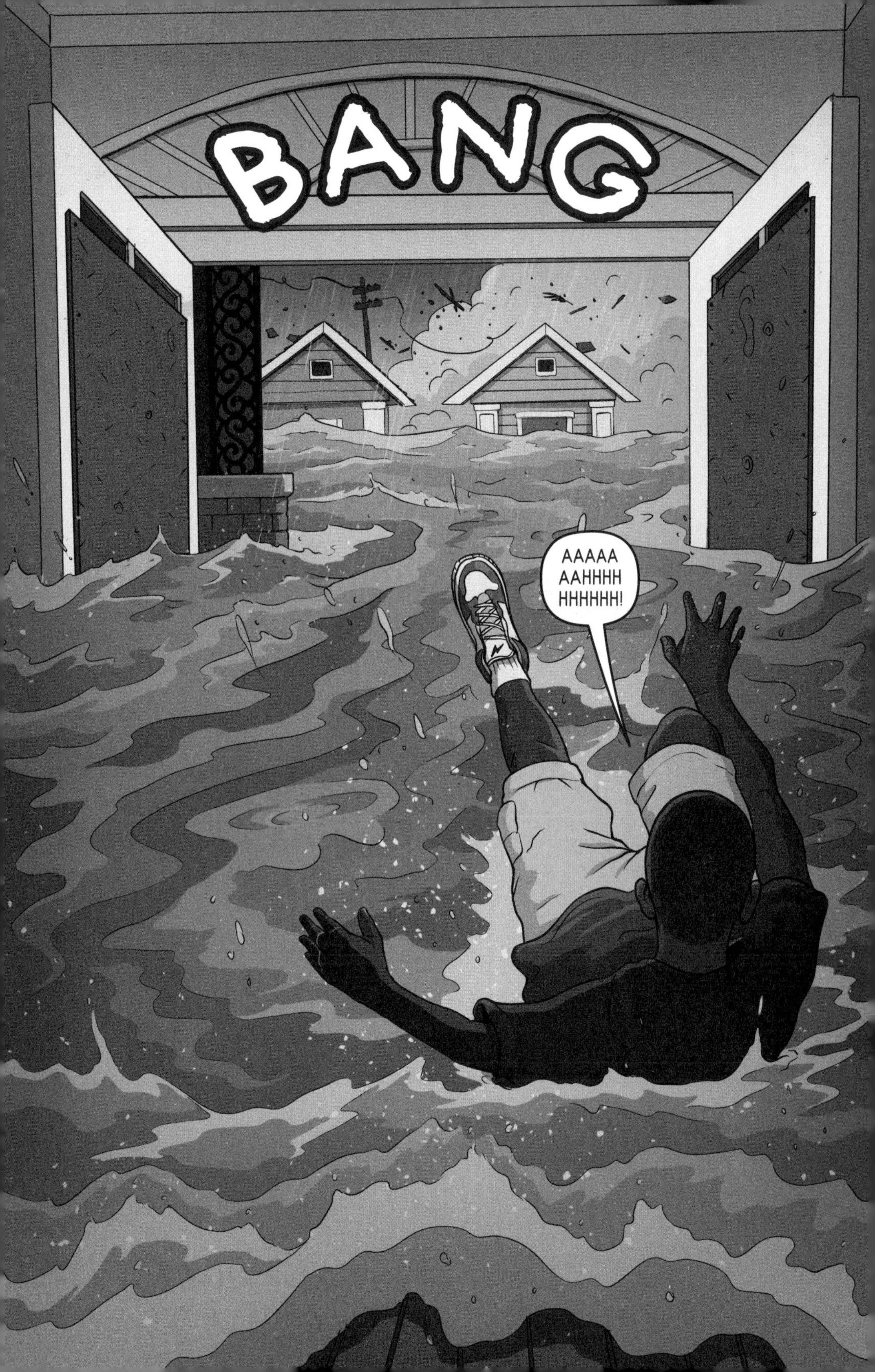
BANG
AAAAA AAHHHH HHHHHH!

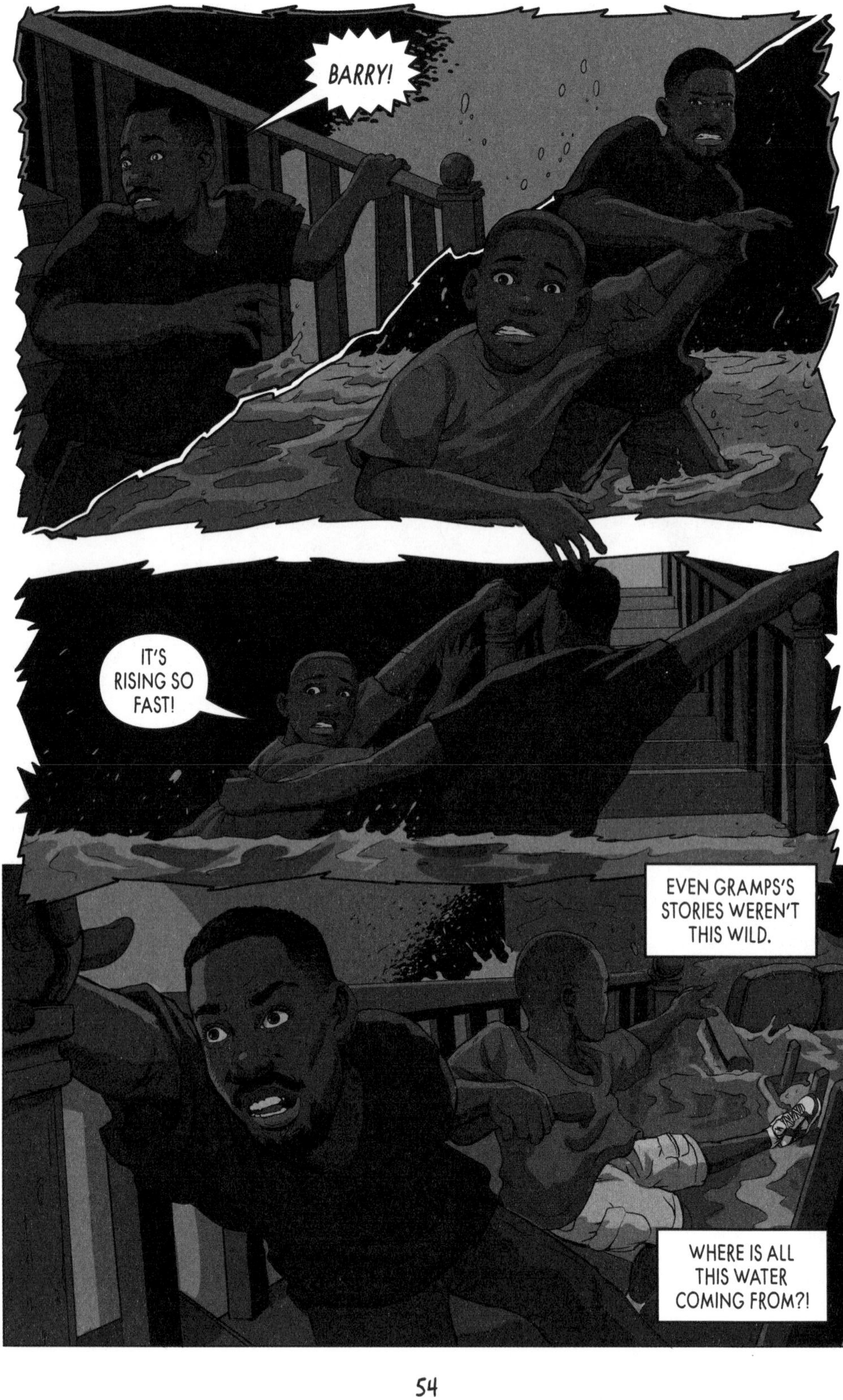
BARRY!
IT'S RISING SO FAST!
EVEN GRAMPS'S STORIES WEREN'T THIS WILD.
WHERE IS ALL THIS WATER COMING FROM?!

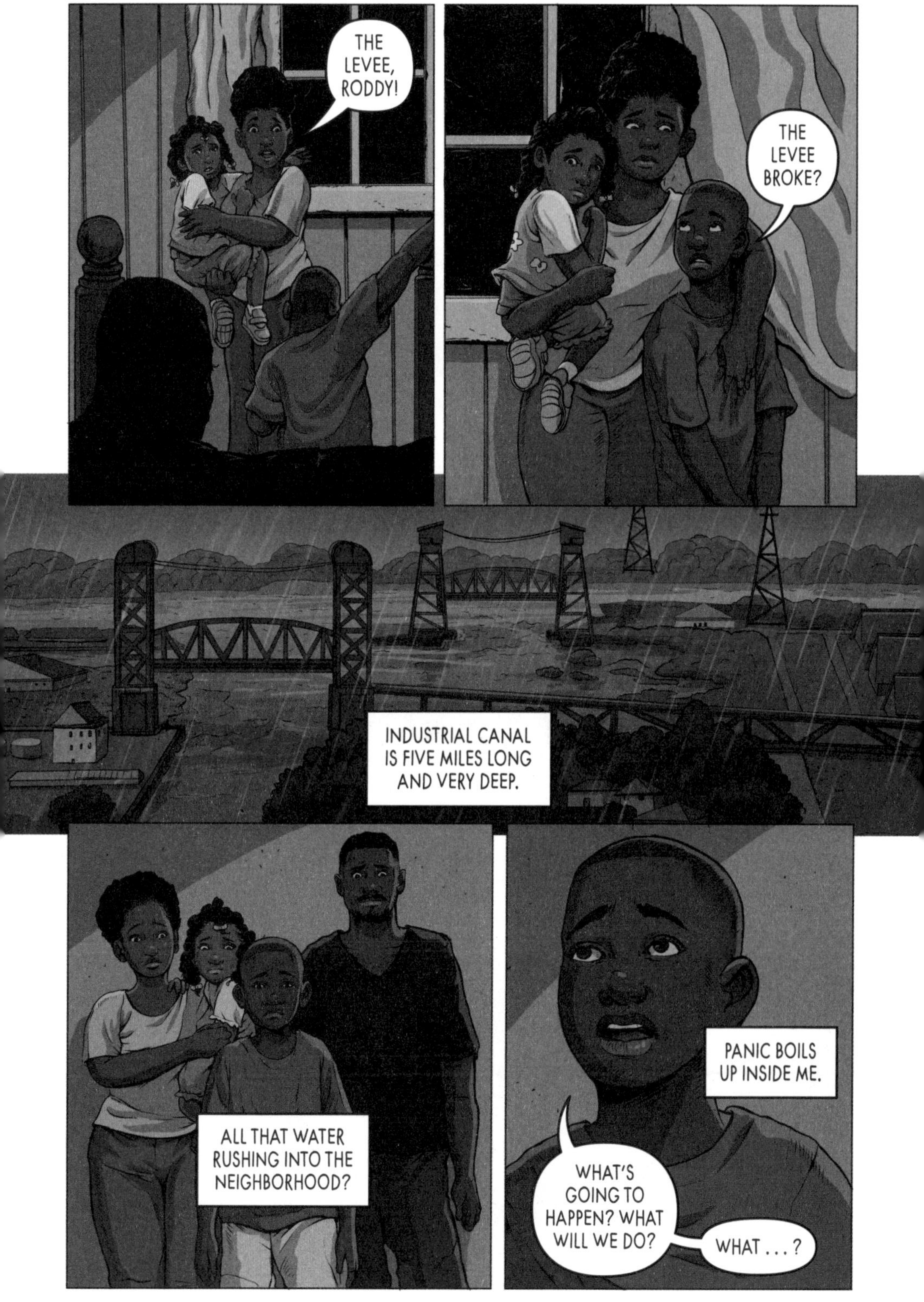
THE LEVEE, RODDY!
THE LEVEE BROKE?
INDUSTRIAL CANAL IS FIVE MILES LONG AND VERY DEEP.
ALL THAT WATER RUSHING INTO THE NEIGHBORHOOD?
PANIC BOILS UP INSIDE ME.
WHAT'S GOING TO HAPPEN? WHAT WILL WE DO?
WHAT . . . ?

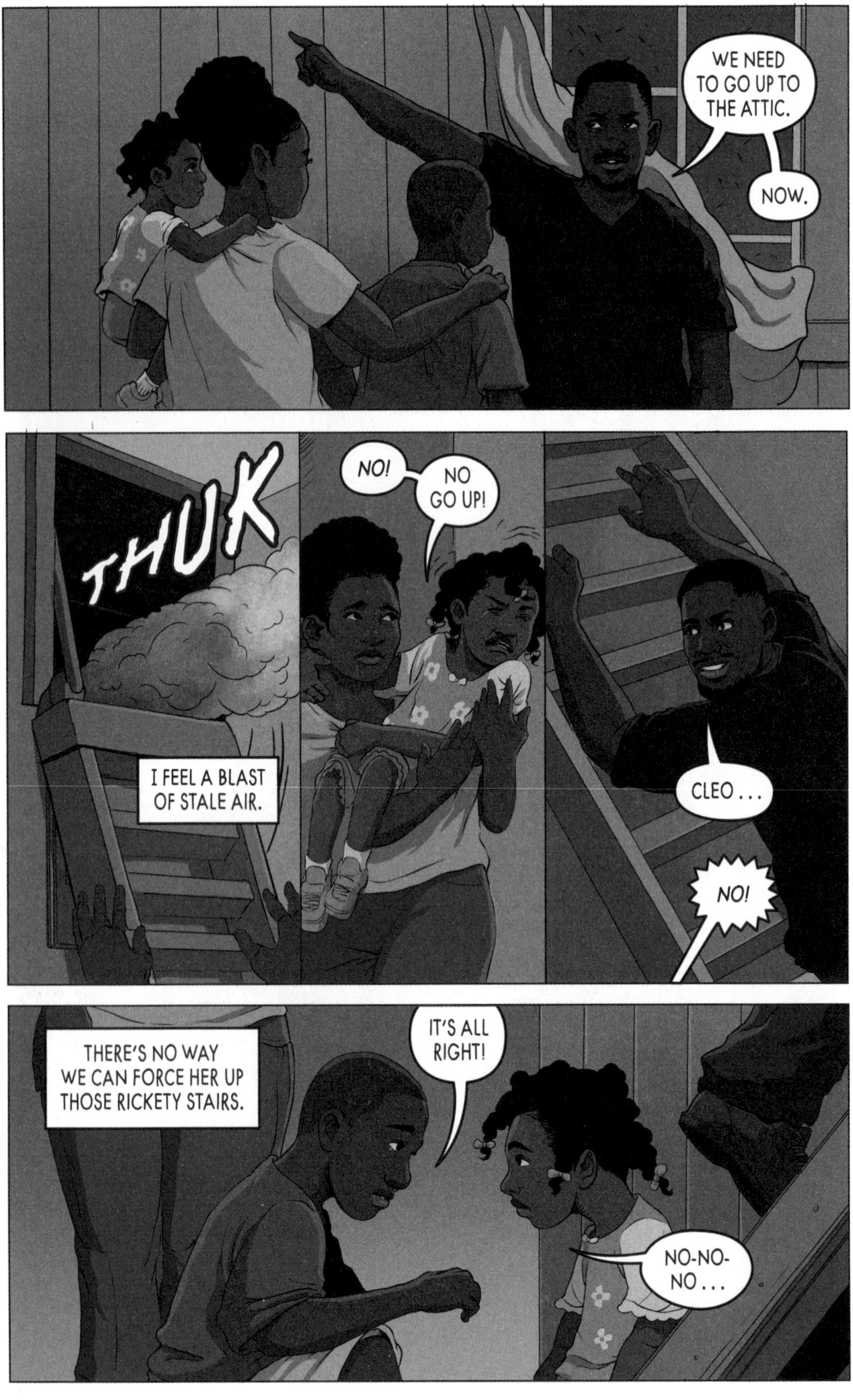
WE NEED TO GO UP TO THE ATTIC.
NOW.
THUK
I FEEL A BLAST OF STALE AIR.
NO!
NO GO UP!
CLEO . . .
NO!
THERE'S NO WAY WE CAN FORCE HER UP THOSE RICKETY STAIRS.
IT'S ALL RIGHT!
NO-NO-NO . . .

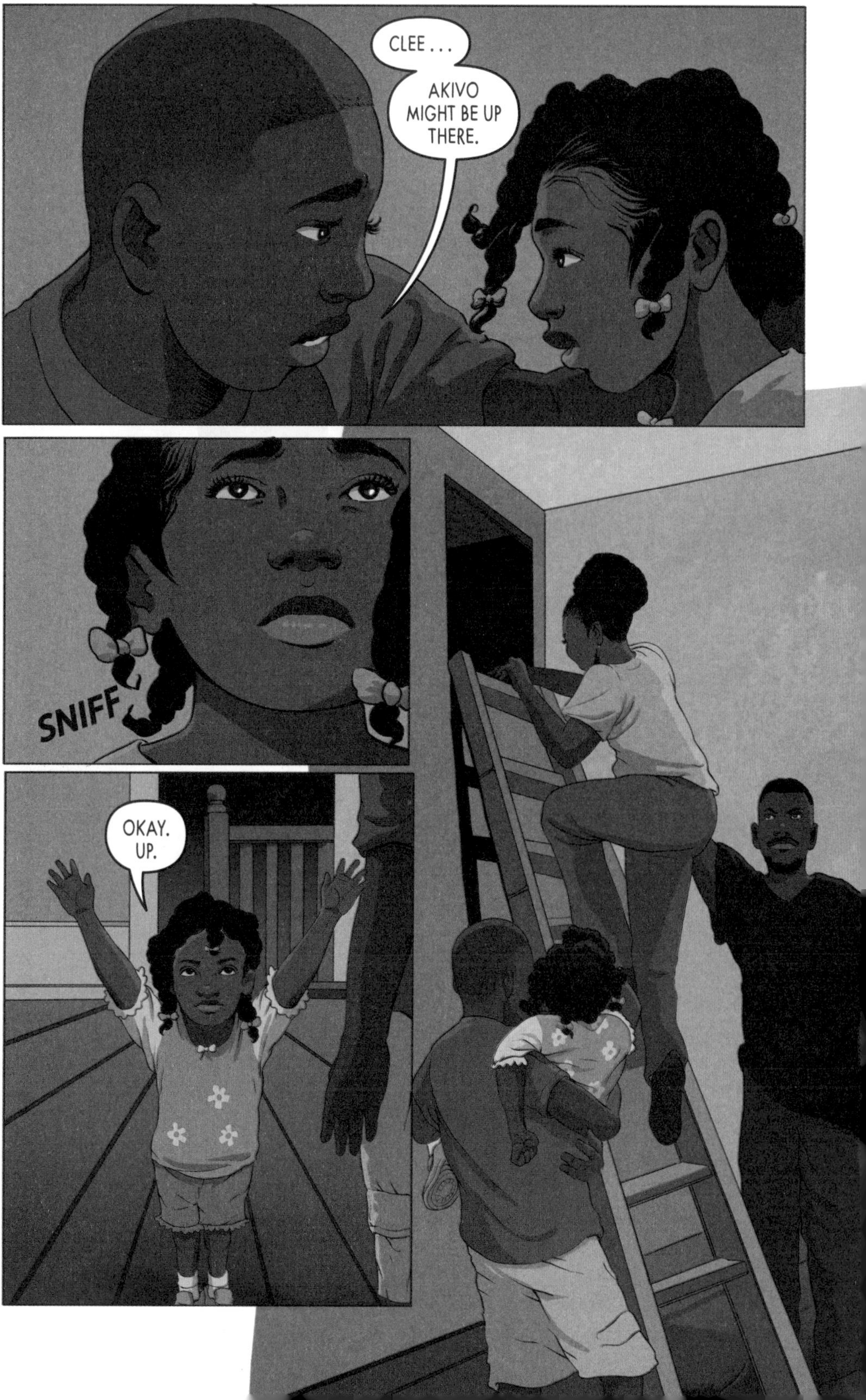
CLEE . . .
AKIVO MIGHT BE UP THERE.
SNIFF
OKAY. UP.

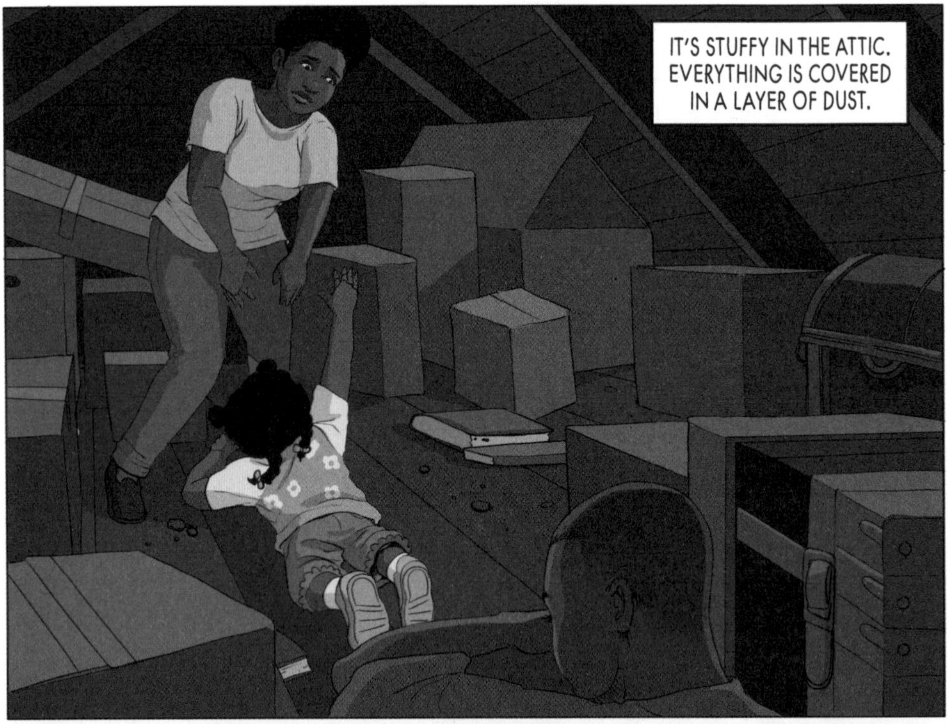
IT'S STUFFY IN THE ATTIC. EVERYTHING IS COVERED IN A LAYER OF DUST.

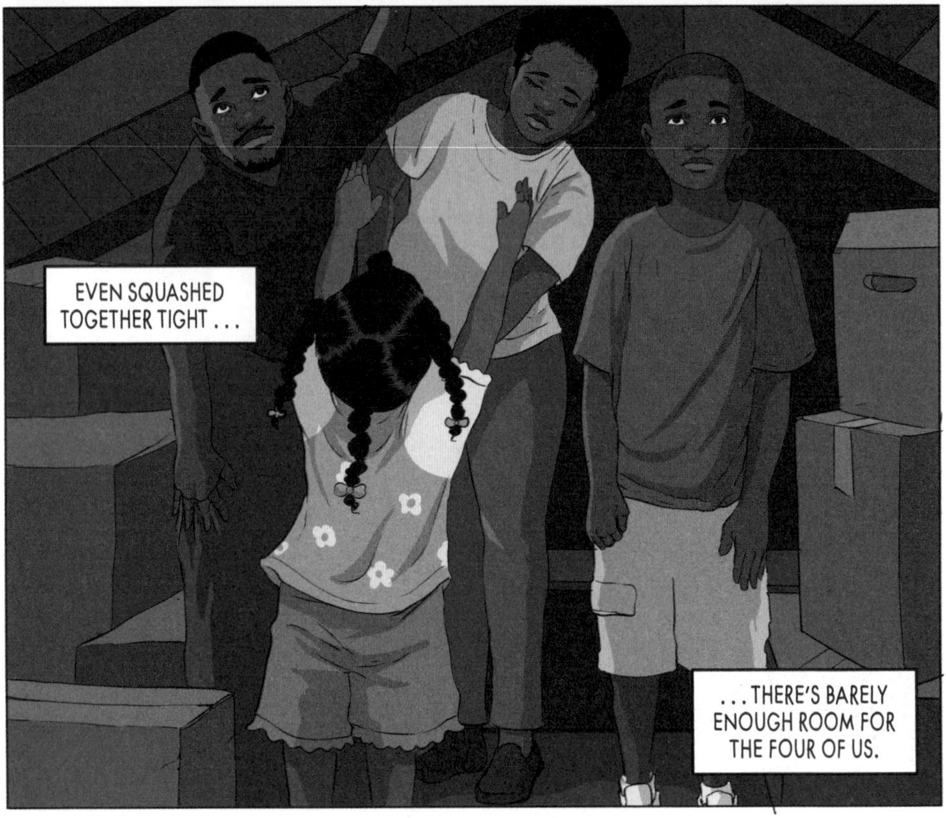
EVEN SQUASHED TOGETHER TIGHT . . .
. . . THERE'S BARELY ENOUGH ROOM FOR THE FOUR OF US.

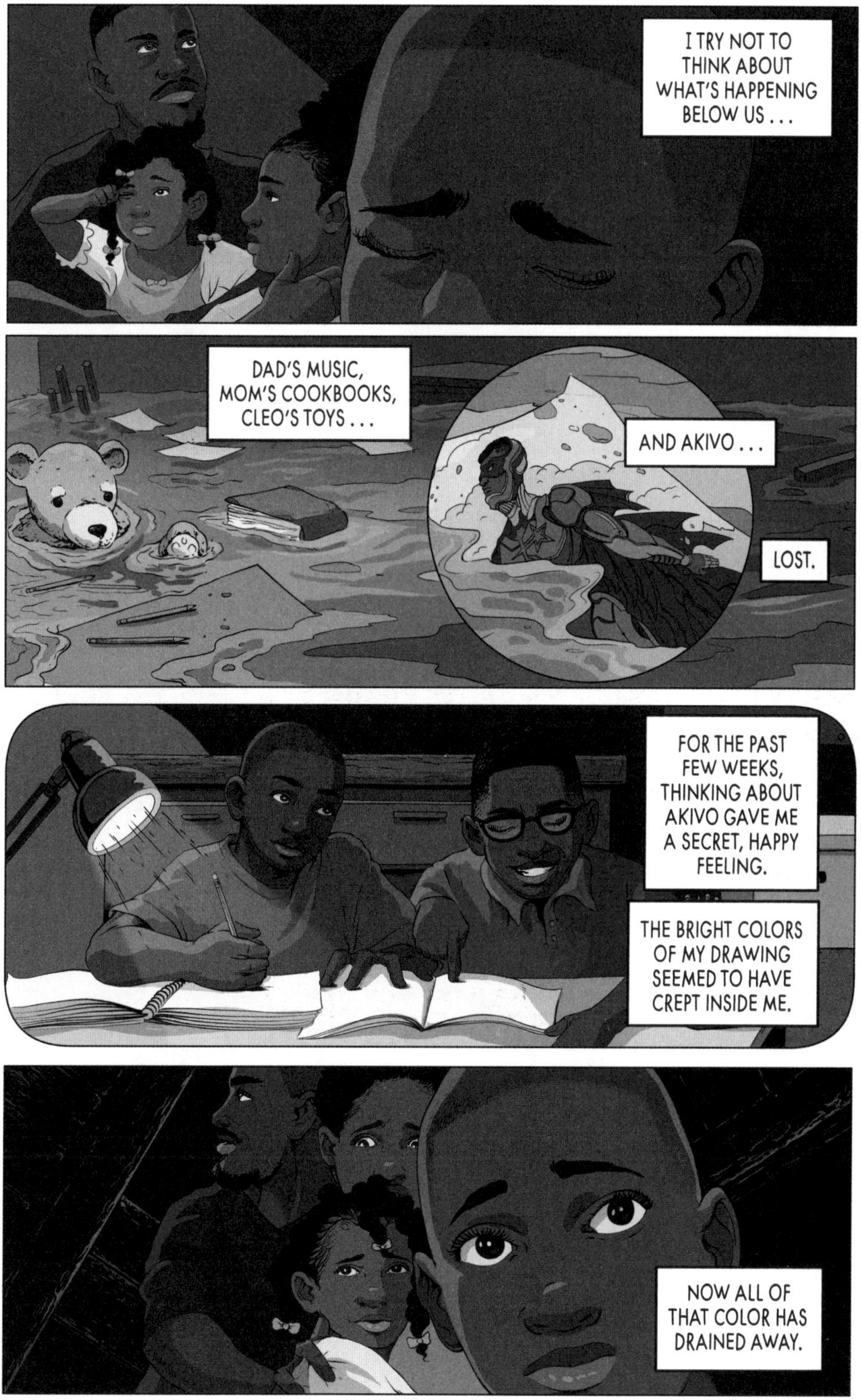
I TRY NOT TO THINK ABOUT WHAT'S HAPPENING BELOW US . . .
DAD'S MUSIC, MOM'S COOKBOOKS, CLEO'S TOYS . . .
AND AKIVO . . .
LOST.
FOR THE PAST FEW WEEKS, THINKING ABOUT AKIVO GAVE ME A SECRET, HAPPY FEELING.
THE BRIGHT COLORS OF MY DRAWING SEEMED TO HAVE CREPT INSIDE ME.
NOW ALL OF THAT COLOR HAS DRAINED AWAY.

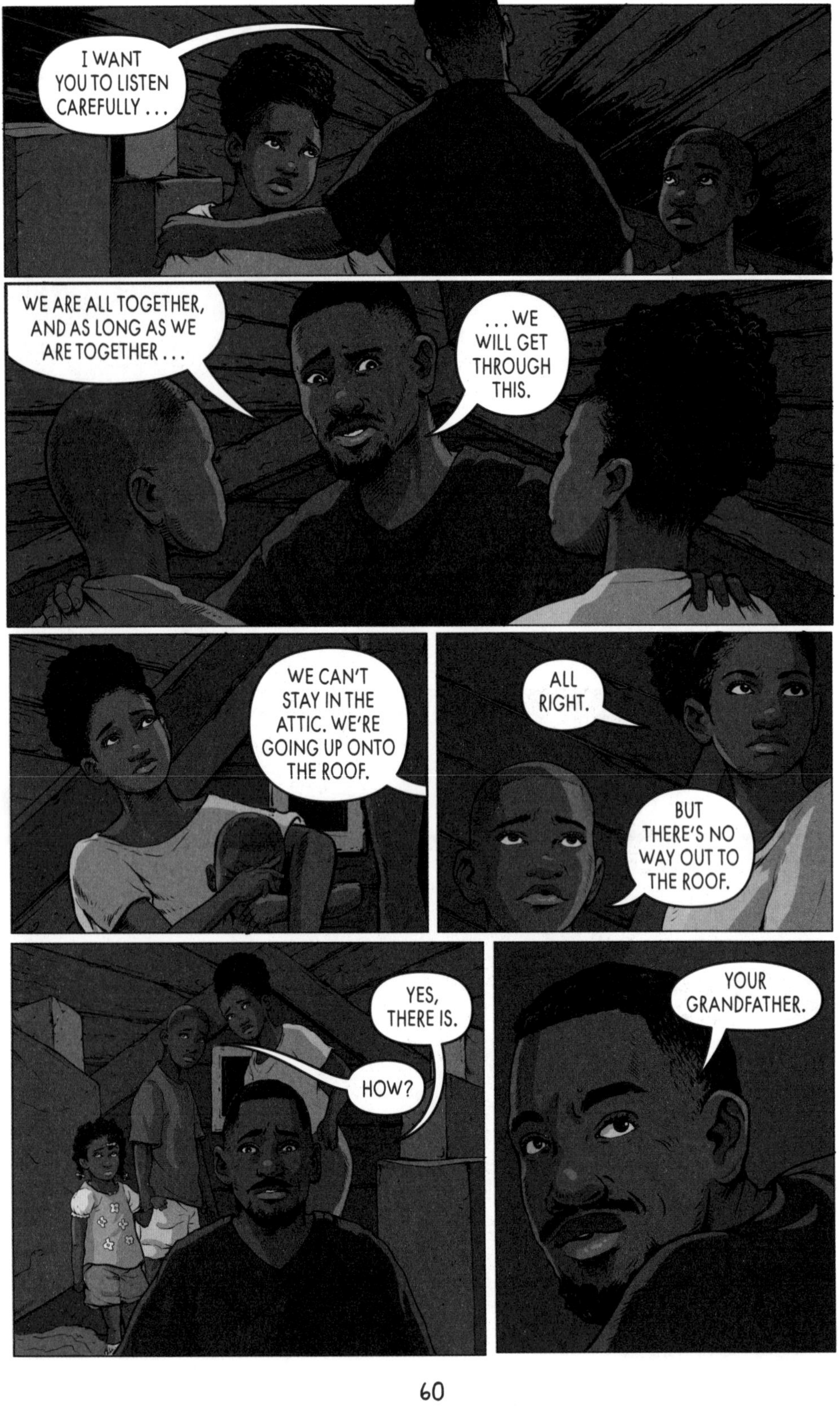
I WANT YOU TO LISTEN CAREFULLY . . .
WE ARE ALL TOGETHER, AND AS LONG AS WE ARE TOGETHER . . .
. . . WE WILL GET THROUGH THIS.
WE CAN'T STAY IN THE ATTIC. WE'RE GOING UP ONTO THE ROOF.
ALL RIGHT.
BUT THERE'S NO WAY OUT TO THE ROOF.
YES, THERE IS.
HOW?
YOUR GRANDFATHER.

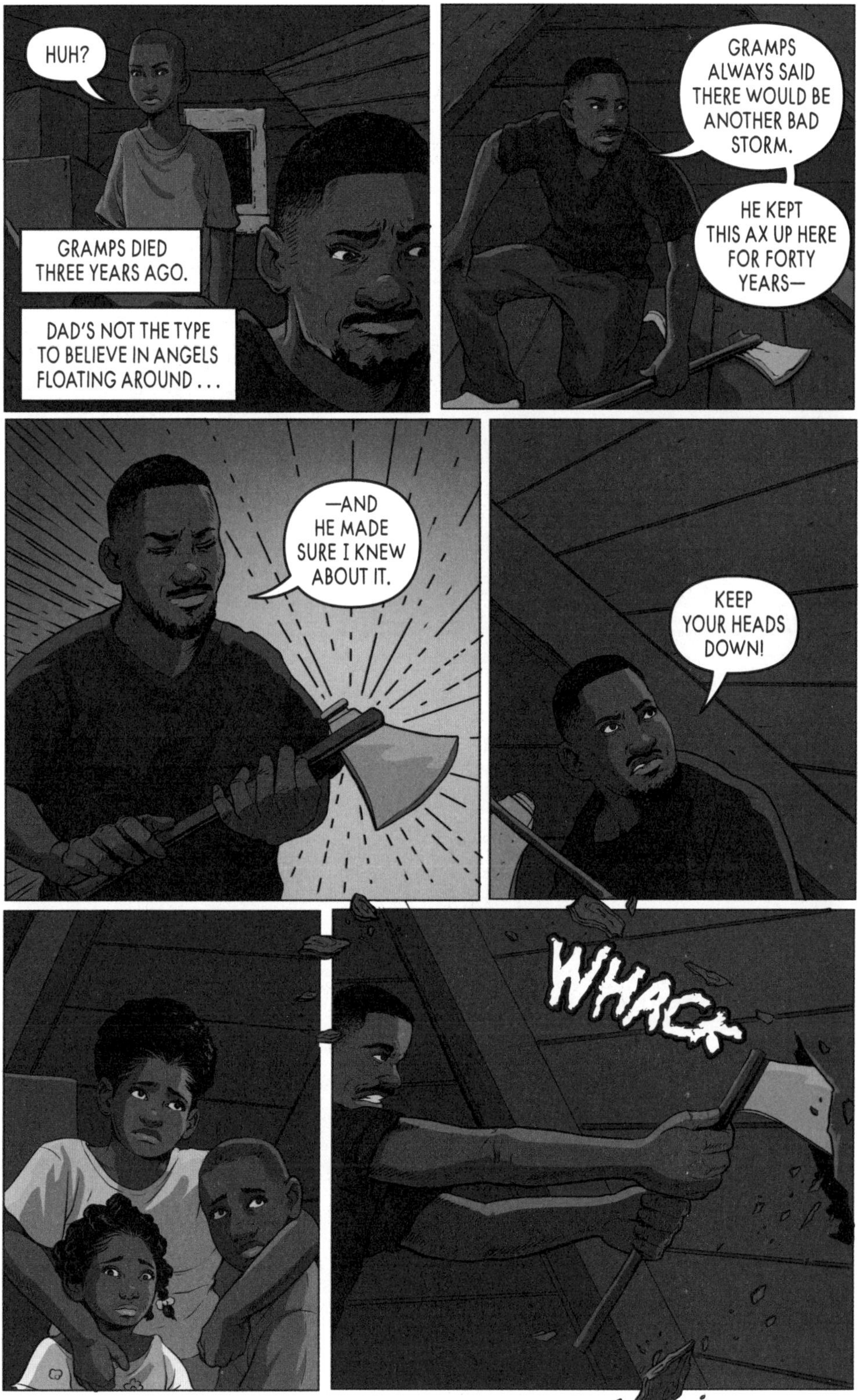
HUH?
GRAMPS DIED THREE YEARS AGO.
DAD'S NOT THE TYPE TO BELIEVE IN ANGELS FLOATING AROUND . . .
GRAMPS ALWAYS SAID THERE WOULD BE ANOTHER BAD STORM.
HE KEPT THIS AX UP HERE FOR FORTY YEARS—
—AND HE MADE SURE I KNEW ABOUT IT.
KEEP YOUR HEADS DOWN!
WHACK

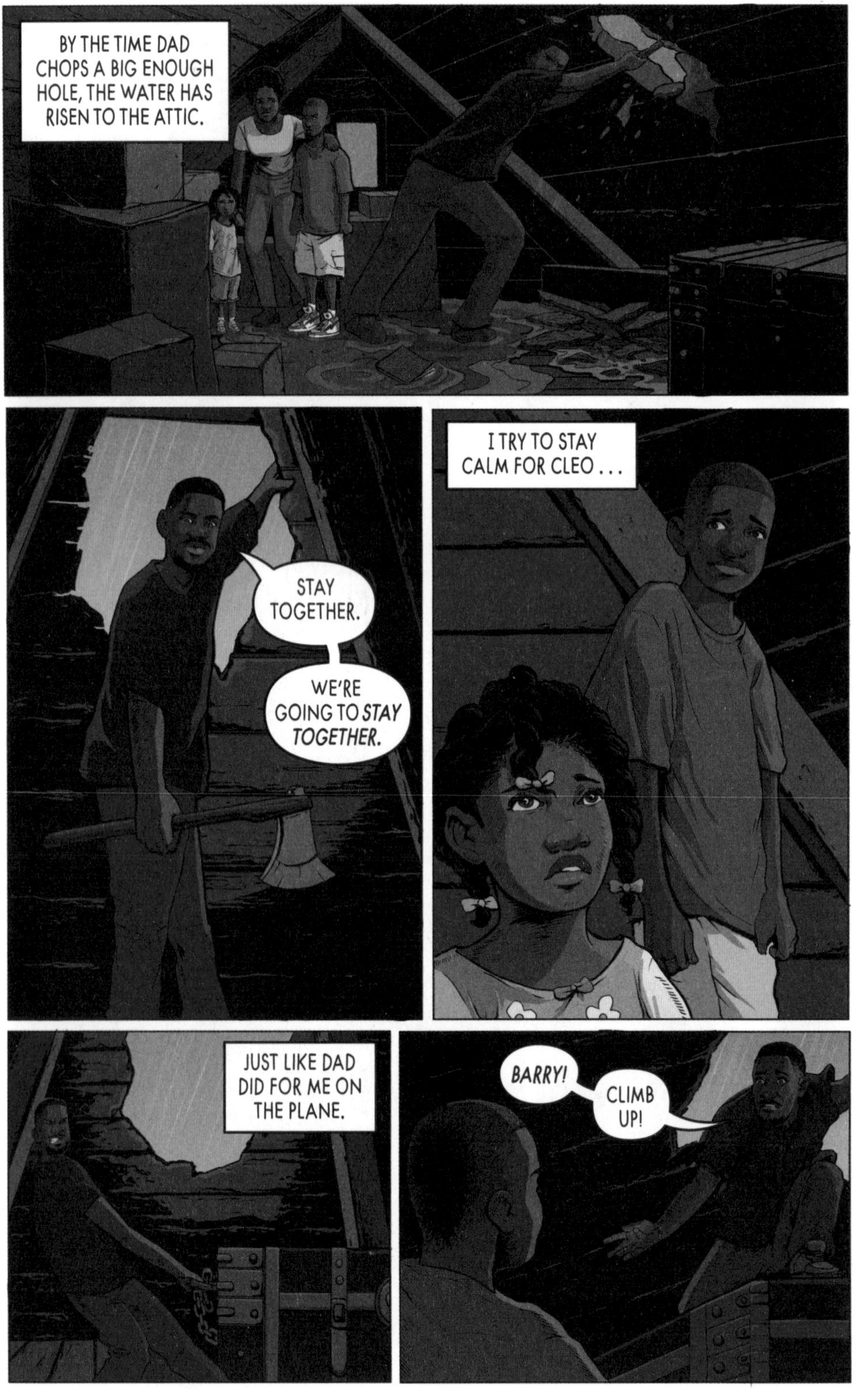

BY THE TIME DAD CHOPS A BIG ENOUGH HOLE, THE WATER HAS RISEN TO THE ATTIC.
STAY TOGETHER.
WE'RE GOING TO *STAY TOGETHER.*
I TRY TO STAY CALM FOR CLEO . . .
JUST LIKE DAD DID FOR ME ON THE PLANE.
BARRY!
CLIMB UP!

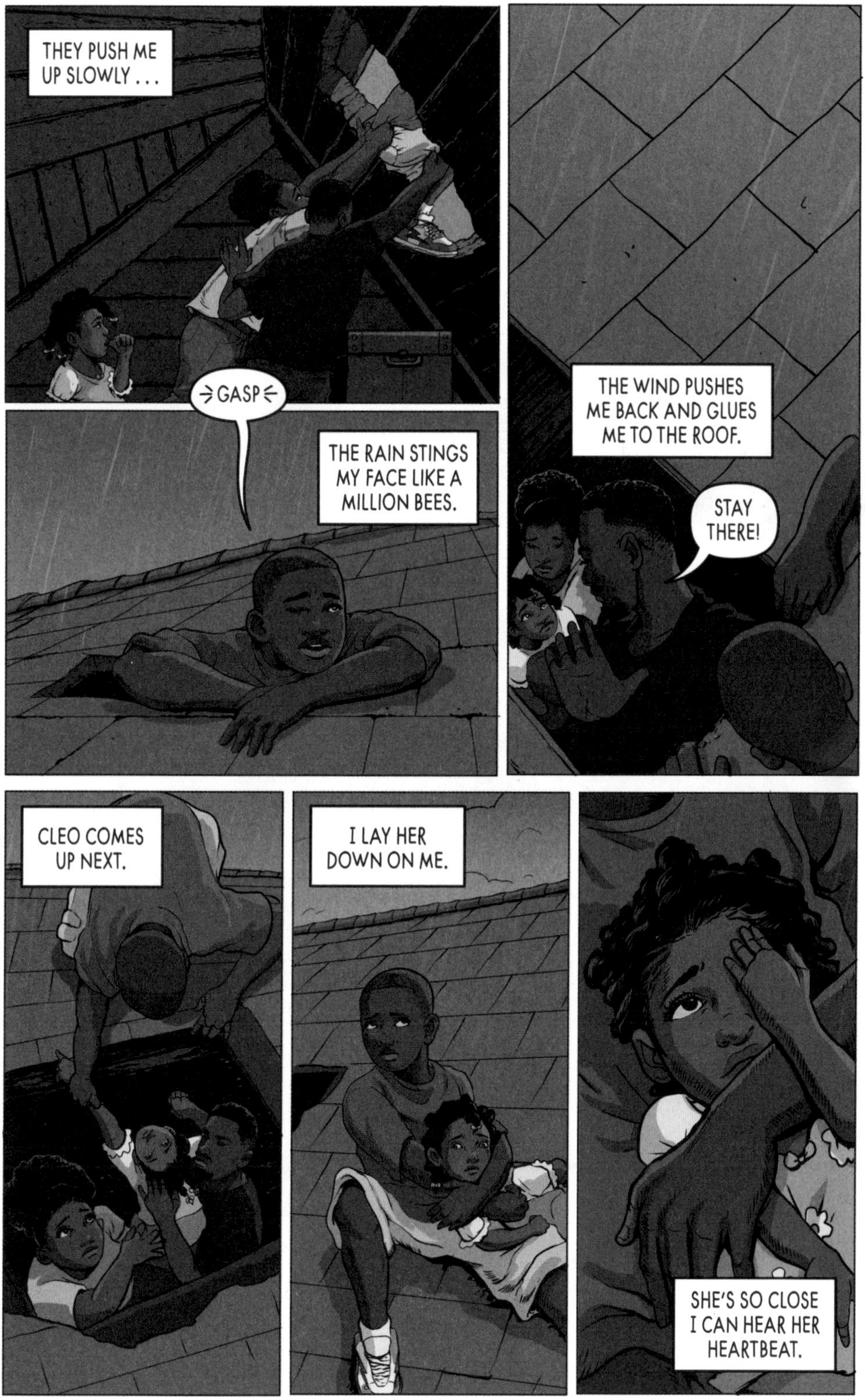
THEY PUSH ME UP SLOWLY . . .
THE WIND PUSHES ME BACK AND GLUES ME TO THE ROOF.
STAY THERE!
GASP
THE RAIN STINGS MY FACE LIKE A MILLION BEES.
CLEO COMES UP NEXT.
I LAY HER DOWN ON ME.
SHE'S SO CLOSE I CAN HEAR HER HEARTBEAT.

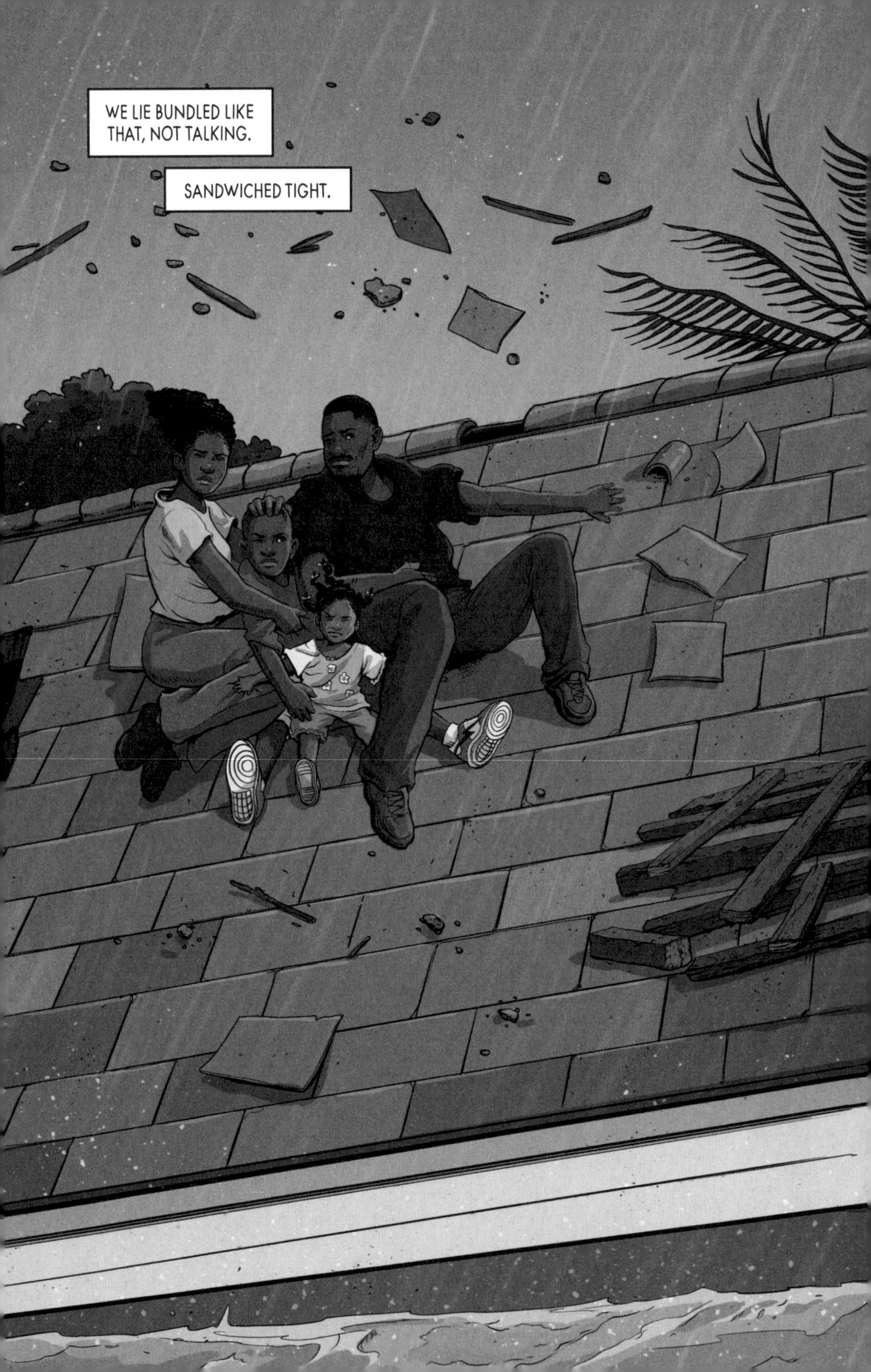
WE LIE BUNDLED LIKE THAT, NOT TALKING.
SANDWICHED TIGHT.

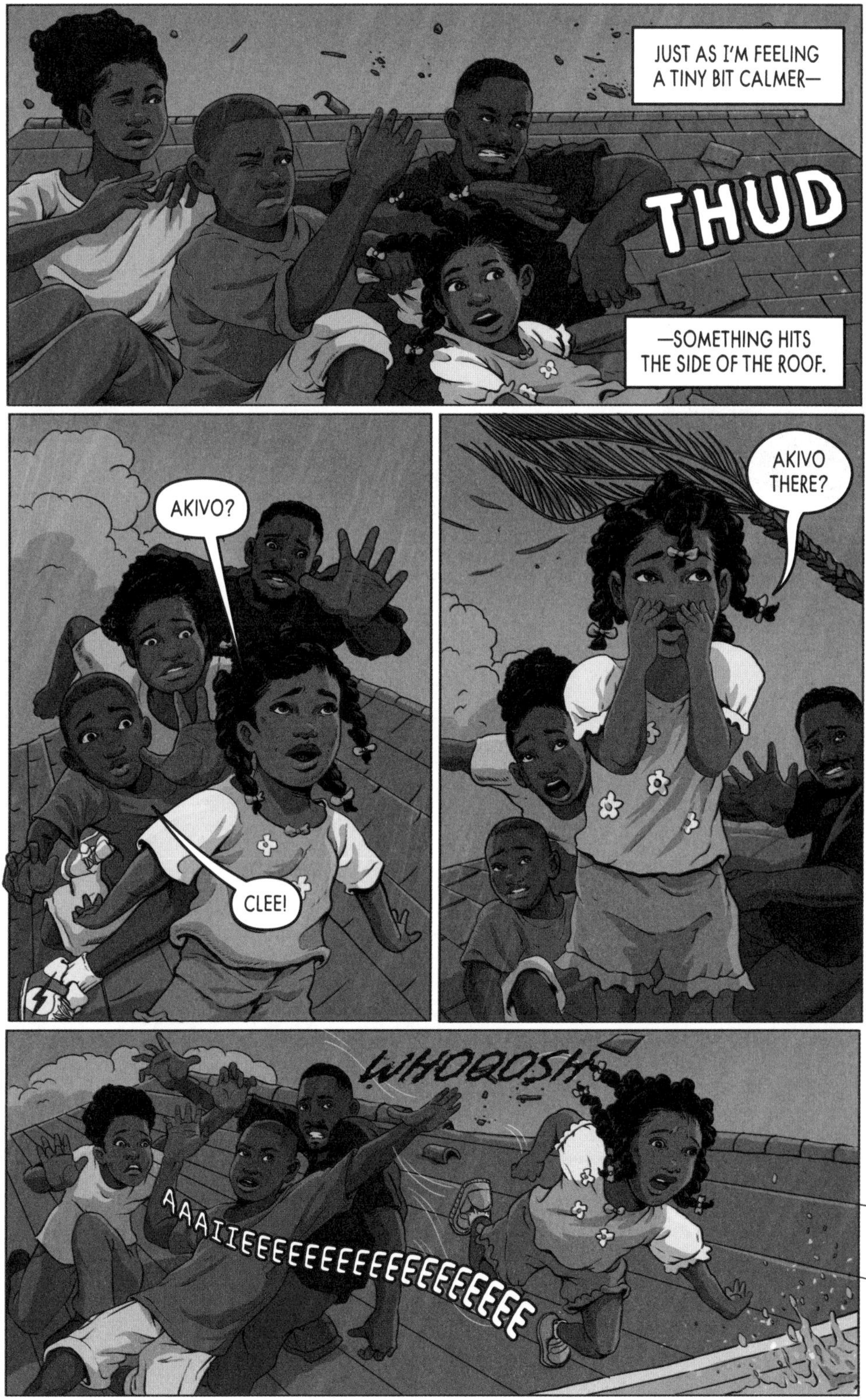
JUST AS I'M FEELING A TINY BIT CALMER—
THUD
—SOMETHING HITS THE SIDE OF THE ROOF.
AKIVO?
CLEE!
AKIVO THERE?
WHOOOSH
AAAIIEEEEEEEEEEEEEEEEEEEE

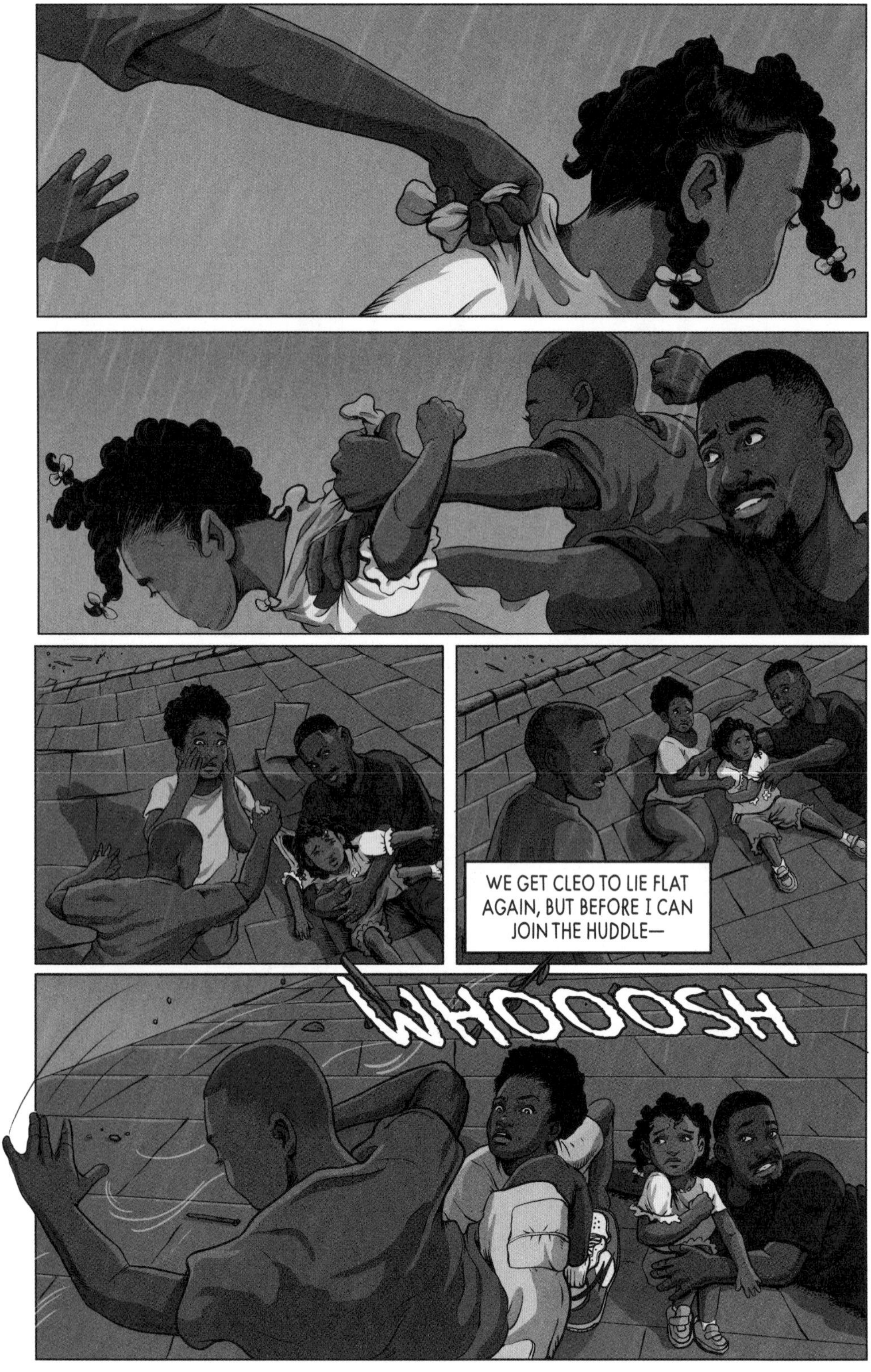
WE GET CLEO TO LIE FLAT AGAIN, BUT BEFORE I CAN JOIN THE HUDDLE—
WHOOOSH

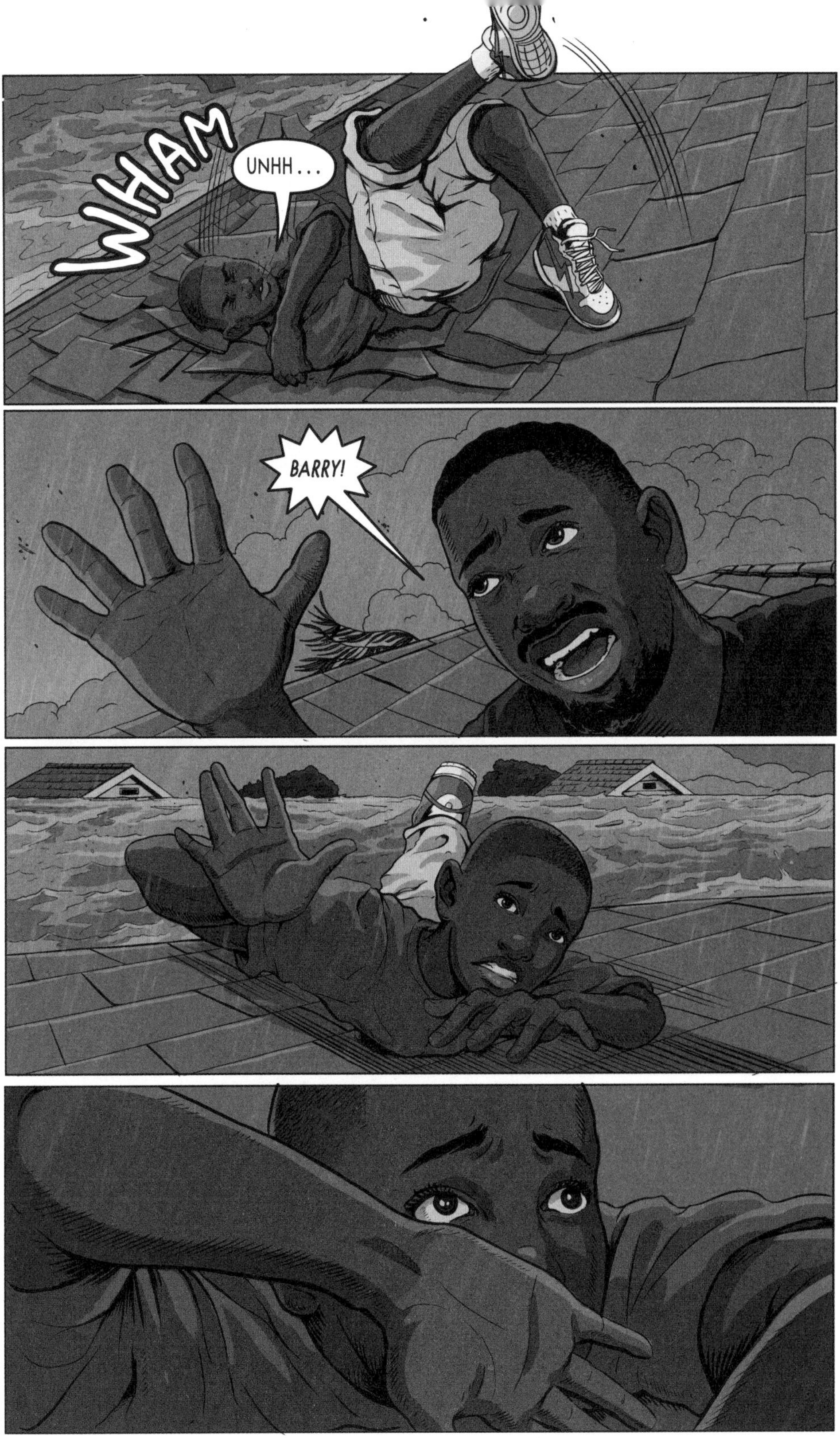
WHAM
UNHH . . .
BARRY!

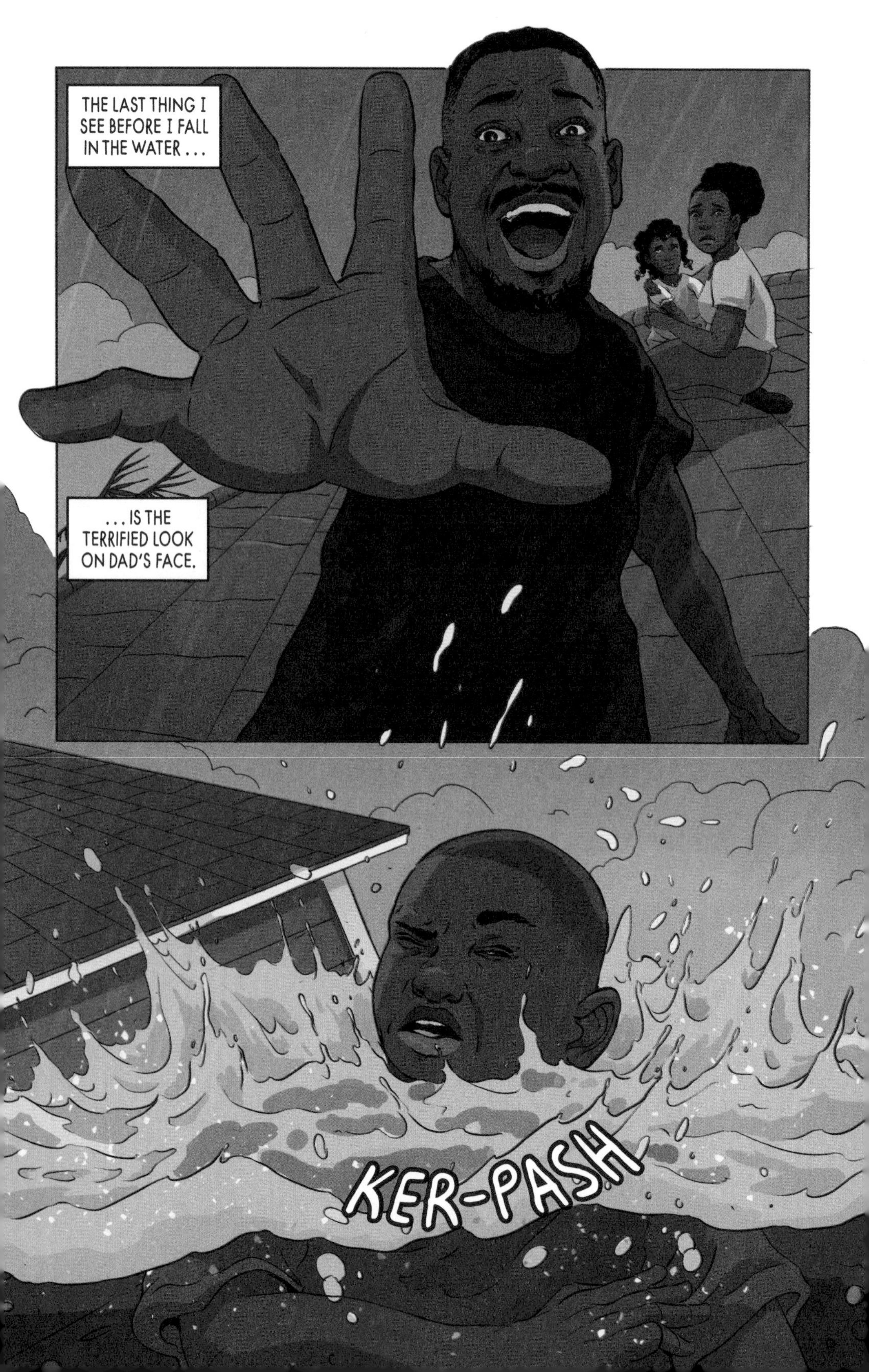
THE LAST THING I SEE BEFORE I FALL IN THE WATER . . .
. . . IS THE TERRIFIED LOOK ON DAD'S FACE.
KER-PASH

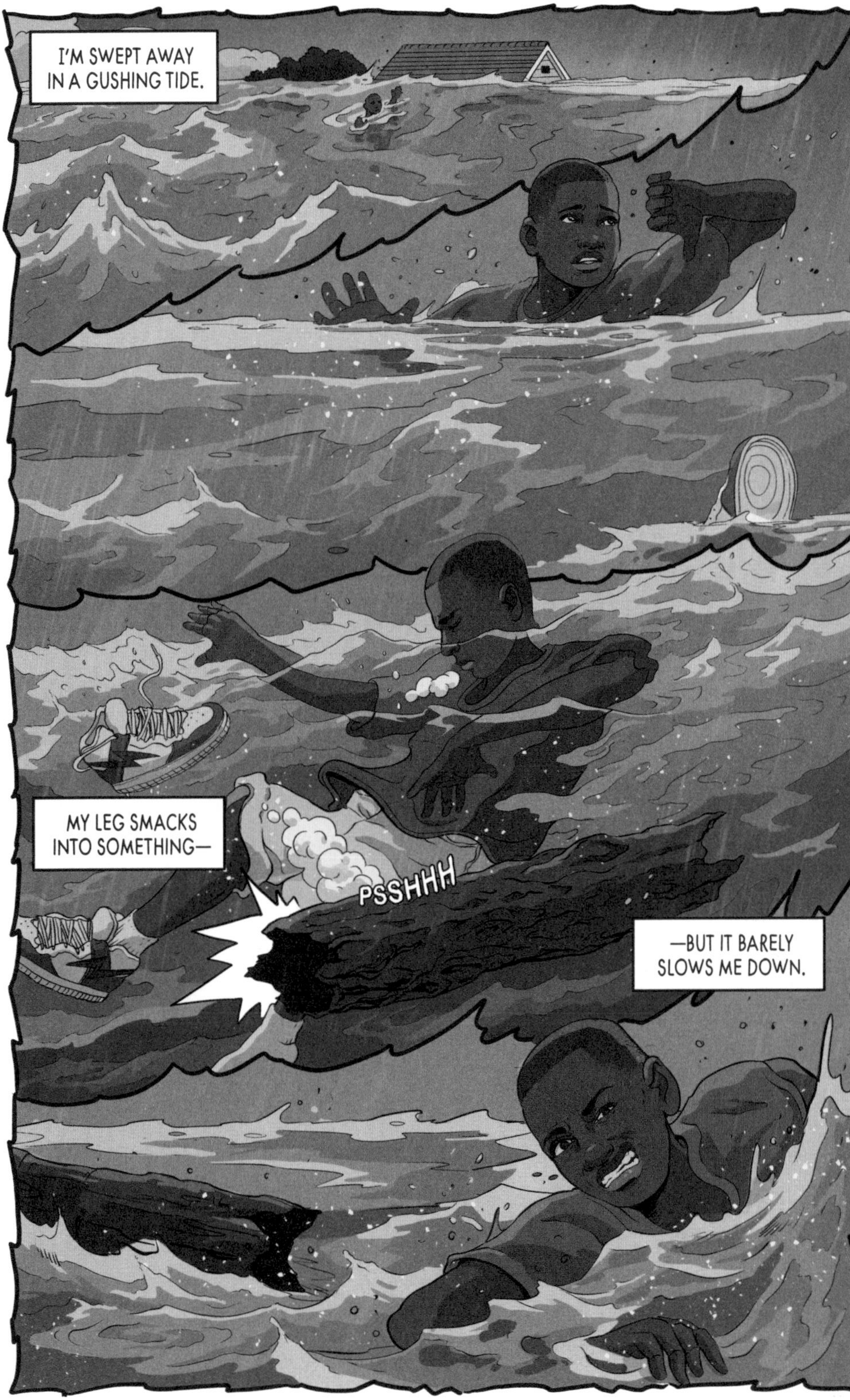
I'M SWEPT AWAY IN A GUSHING TIDE.
MY LEG SMACKS INTO SOMETHING—
PSSHHH
—BUT IT BARELY SLOWS ME DOWN.

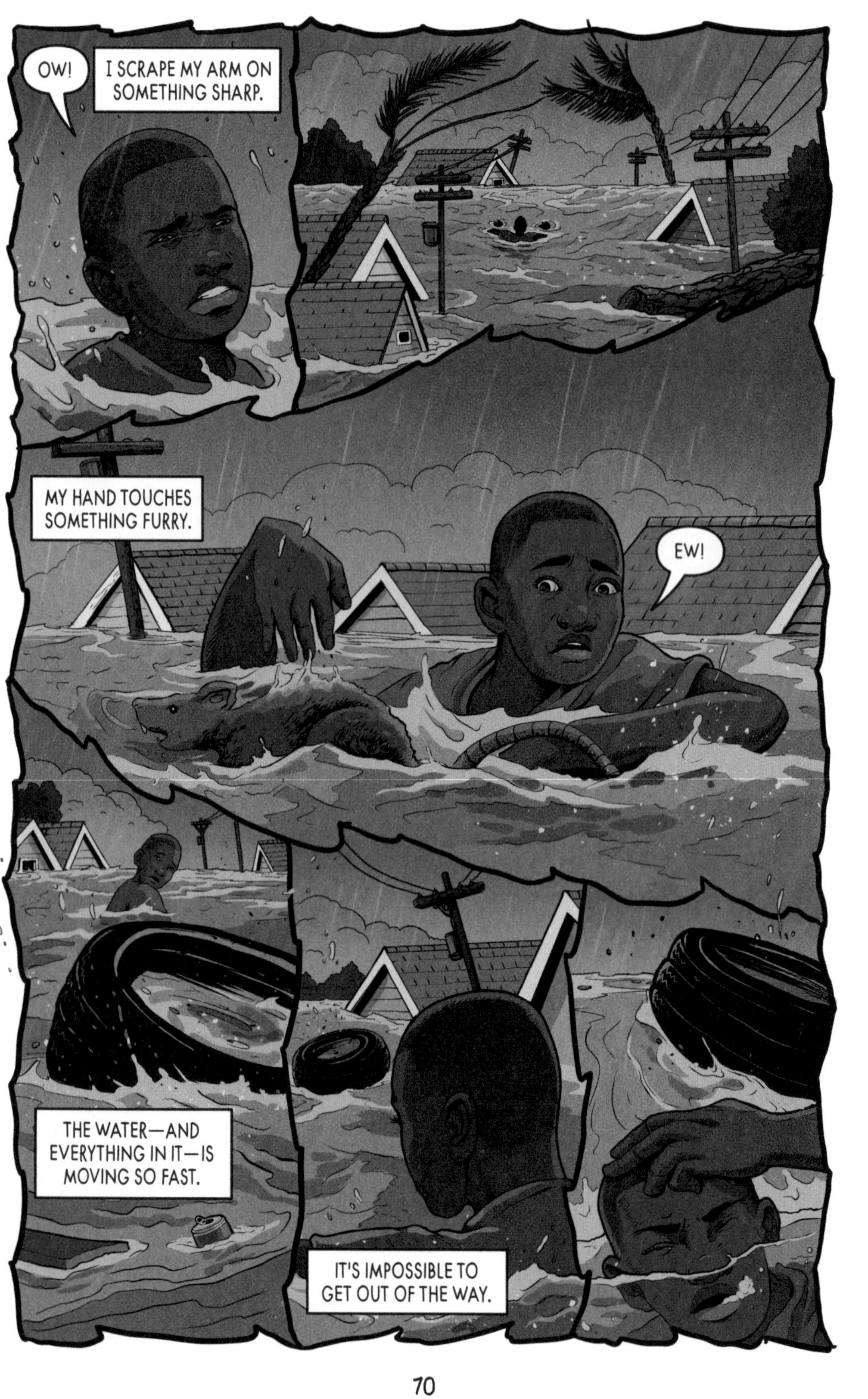
OW!
I SCRAPE MY ARM ON SOMETHING SHARP.
MY HAND TOUCHES SOMETHING FURRY.
EW!
THE WATER—AND EVERYTHING IN IT—IS MOVING SO FAST.
IT'S IMPOSSIBLE TO GET OUT OF THE WAY.

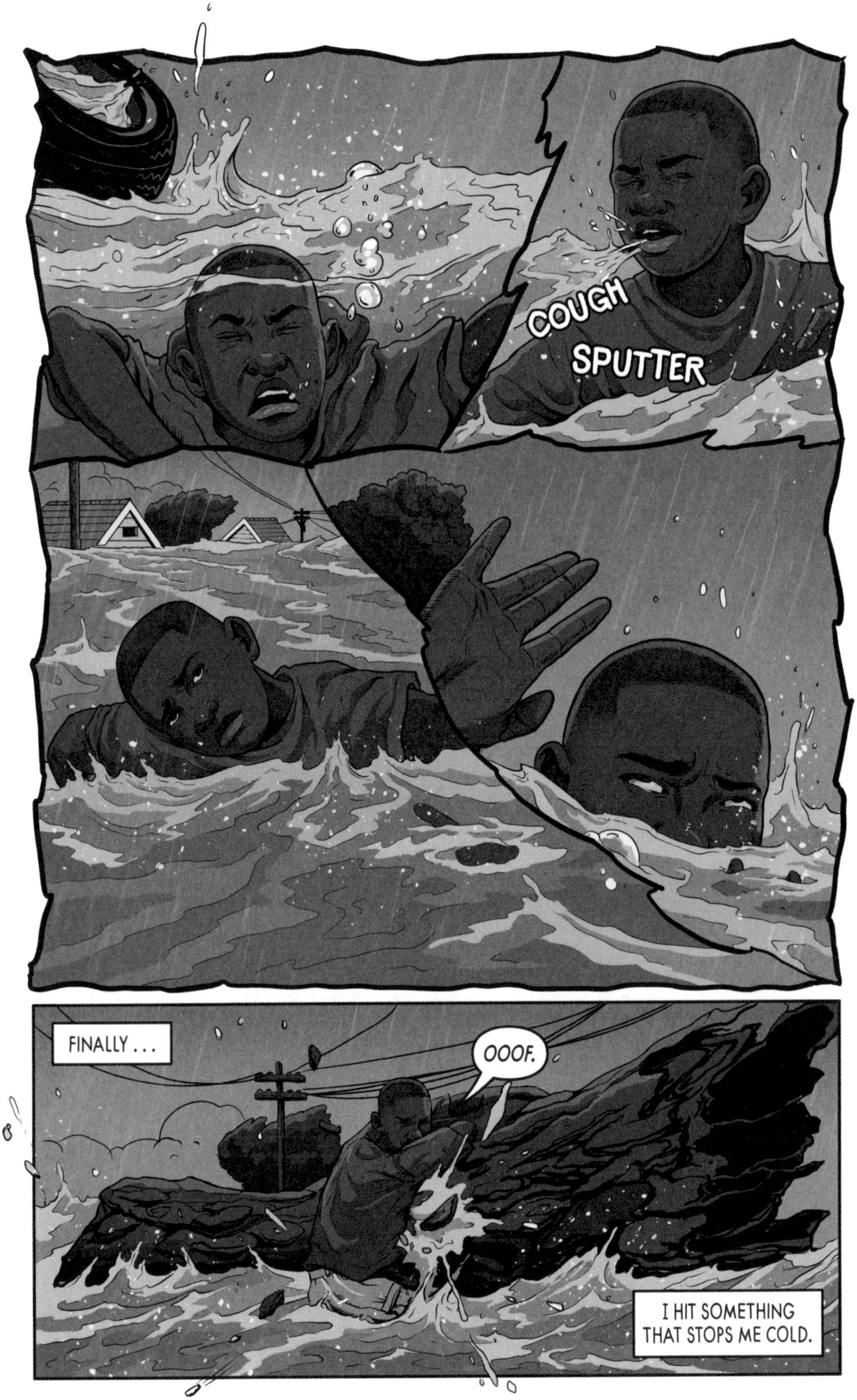
COUGH
SPUTTER
FINALLY . . .
OOOF.
I HIT SOMETHING THAT STOPS ME COLD.

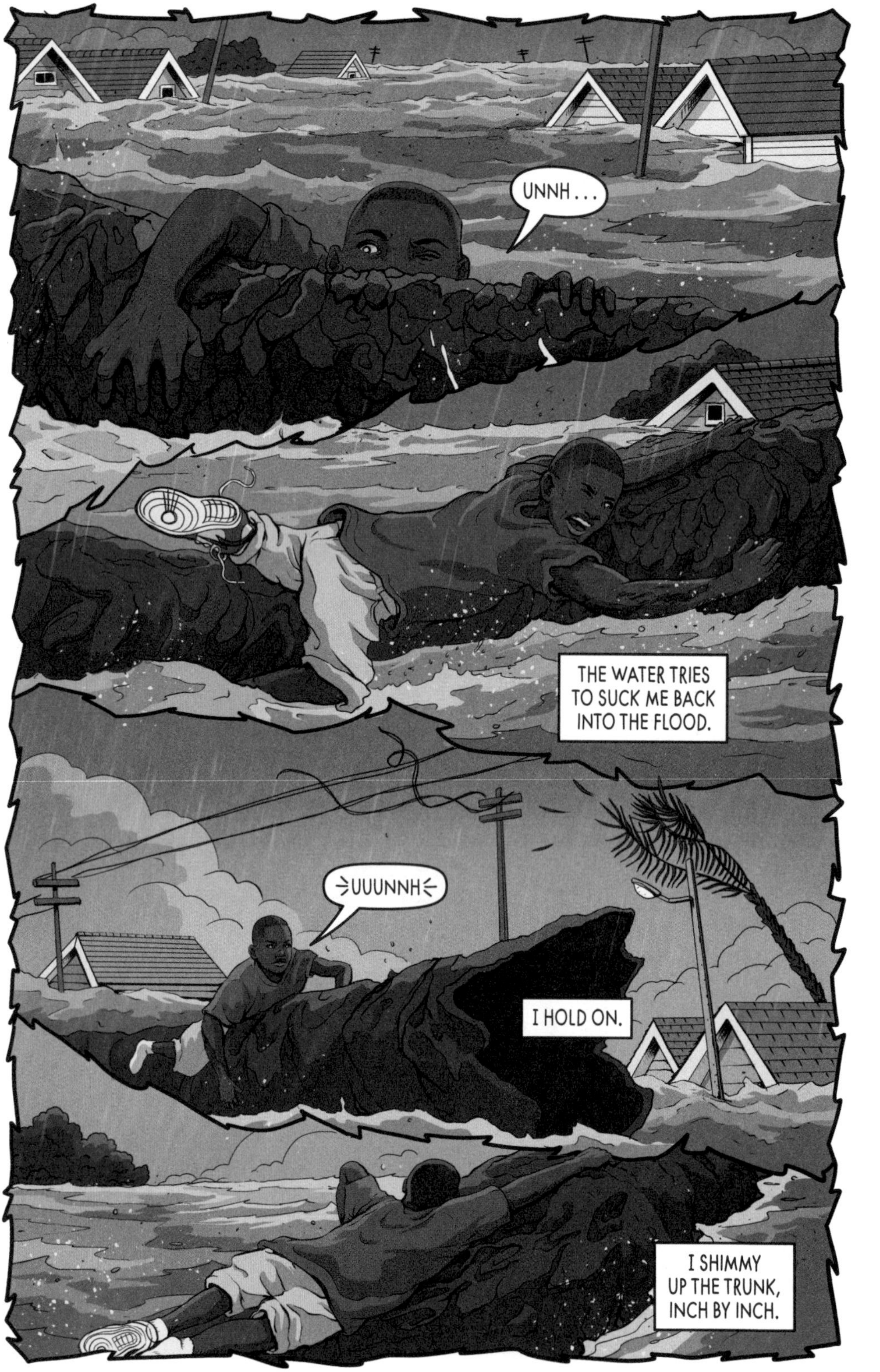
UNNH . . .
THE WATER TRIES TO SUCK ME BACK INTO THE FLOOD.
UUUNNH
I HOLD ON.
I SHIMMY UP THE TRUNK, INCH BY INCH.

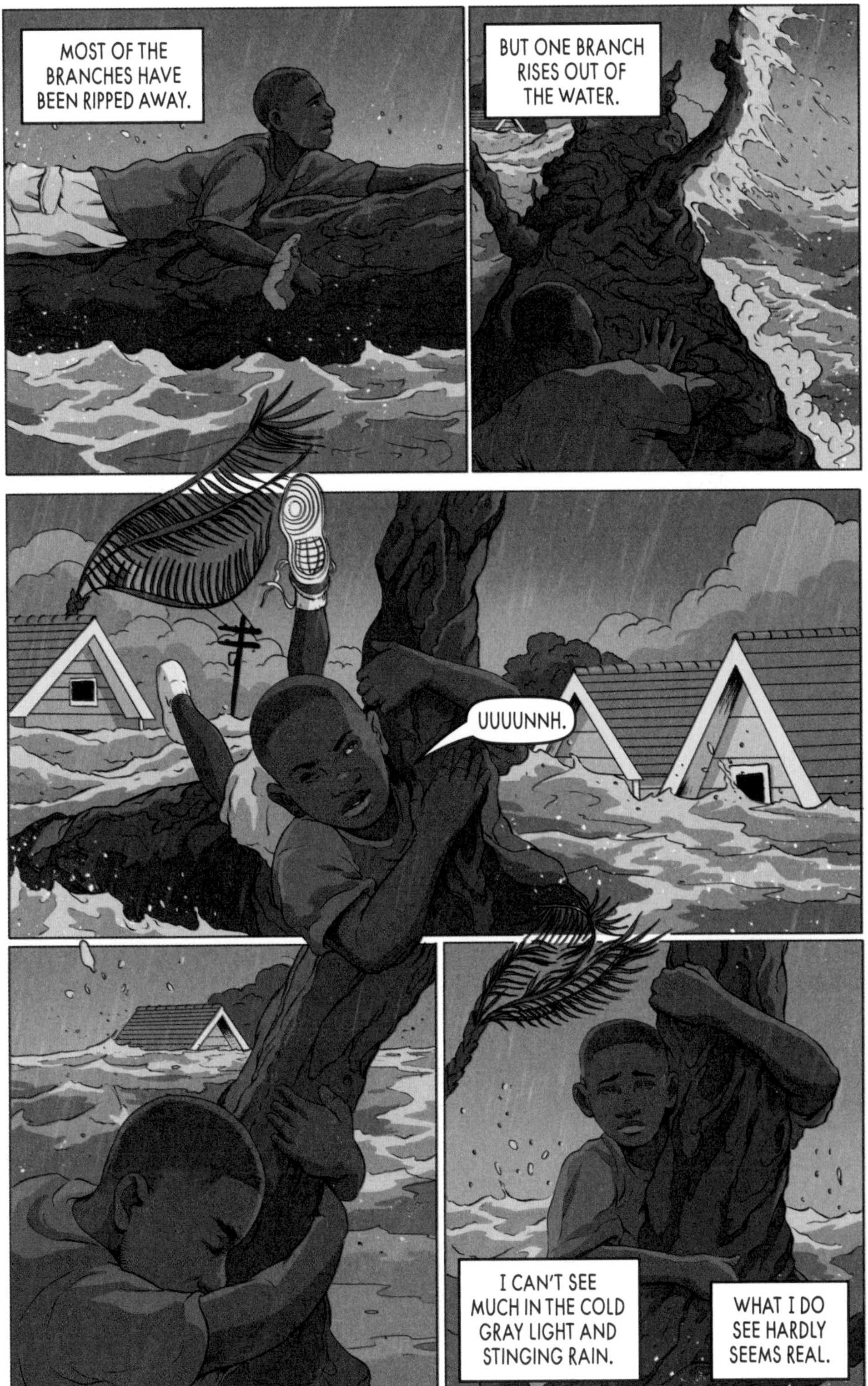

MOST OF THE BRANCHES HAVE BEEN RIPPED AWAY.
BUT ONE BRANCH RISES OUT OF THE WATER.
UUUUNNH.
I CAN'T SEE MUCH IN THE COLD GRAY LIGHT AND STINGING RAIN.
WHAT I DO SEE HARDLY SEEMS REAL.

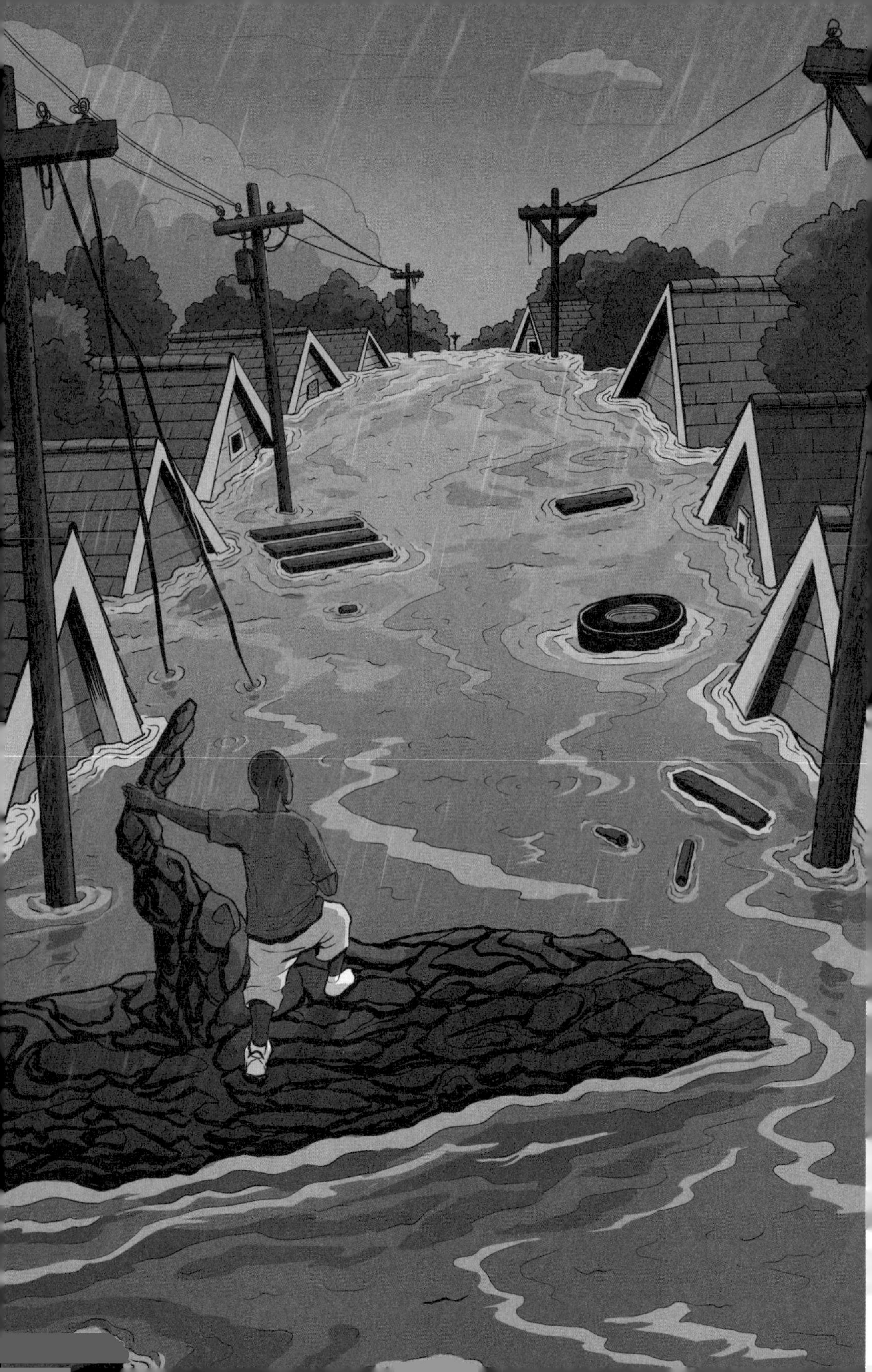

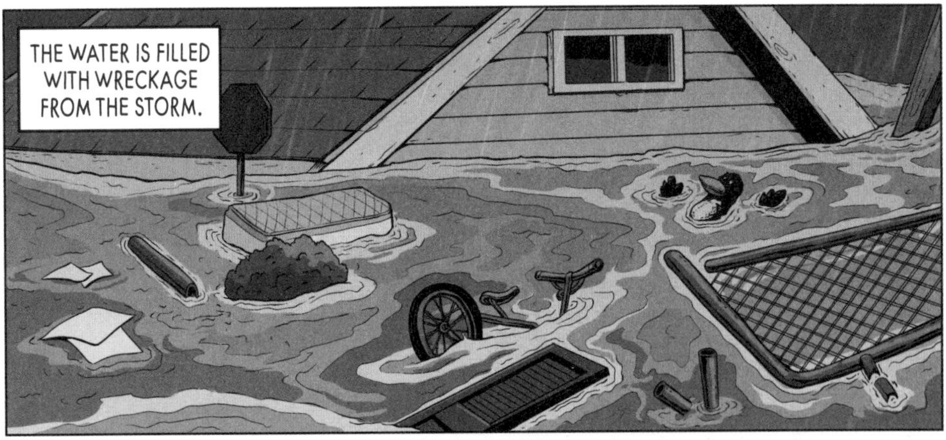
THE WATER IS FILLED WITH WRECKAGE FROM THE STORM.

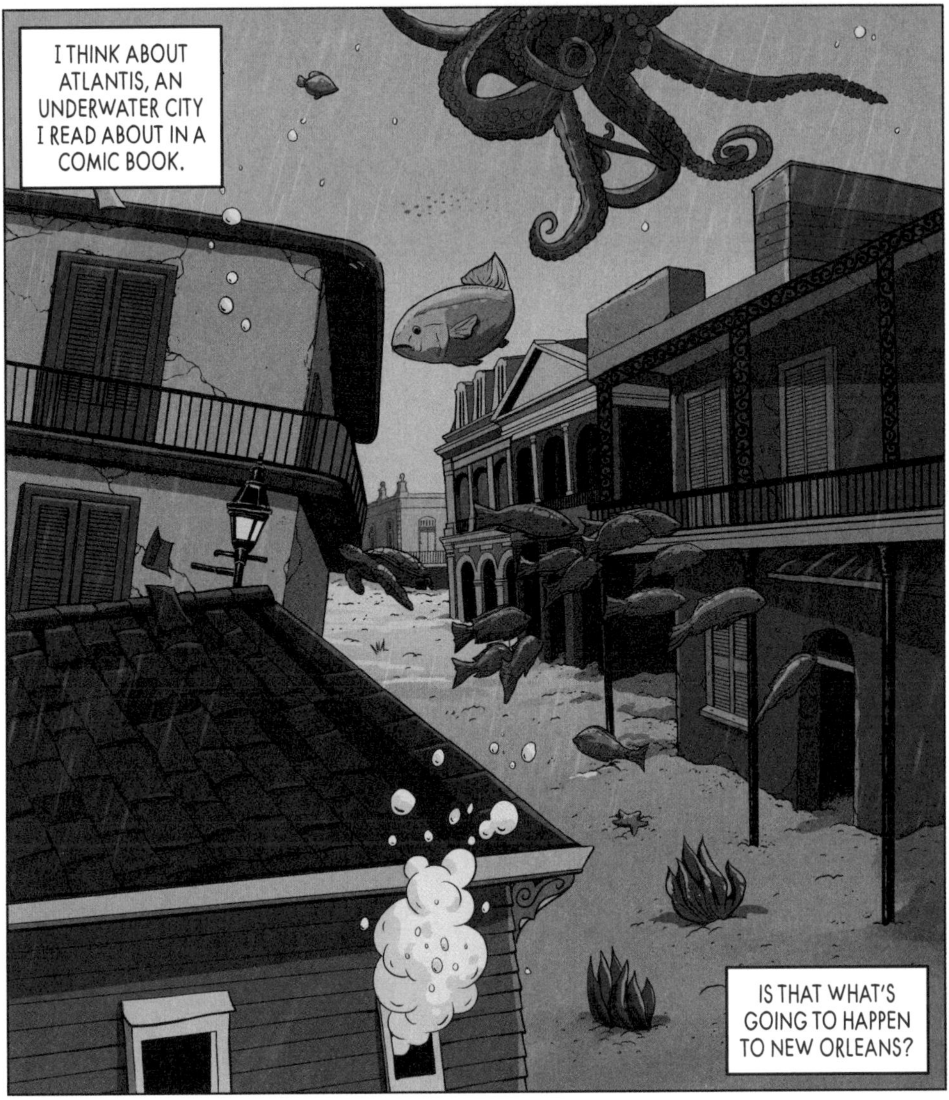
I THINK ABOUT ATLANTIS, AN UNDERWATER CITY I READ ABOUT IN A COMIC BOOK.
IS THAT WHAT'S GOING TO HAPPEN TO NEW ORLEANS?

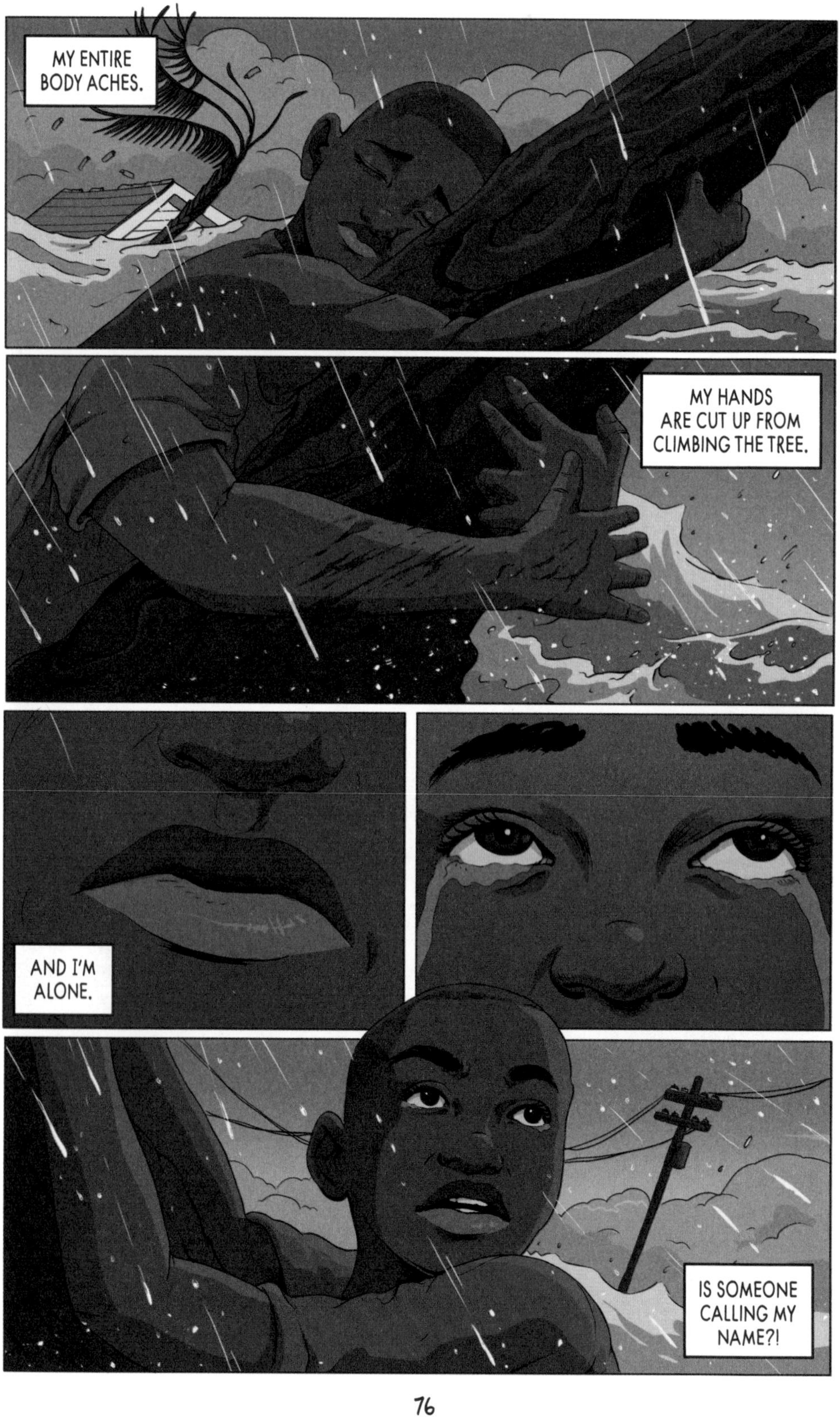
MY ENTIRE BODY ACHES.
MY HANDS ARE CUT UP FROM CLIMBING THE TREE.
AND I'M ALONE.
IS SOMEONE CALLING MY NAME?!

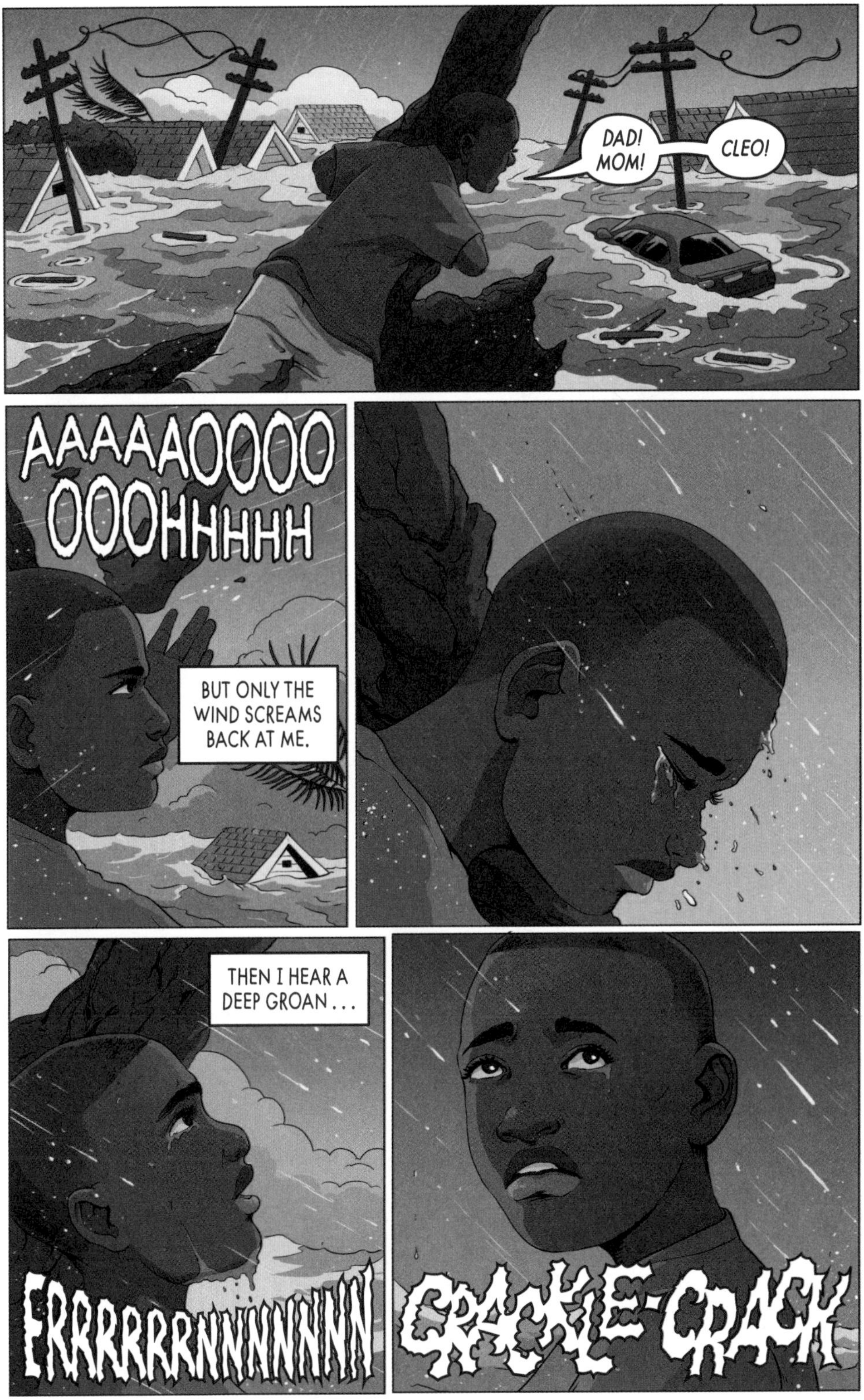
DAD! MOM!
CLEO!
AAAAAOOOO OOOHHHHH
BUT ONLY THE WIND SCREAMS BACK AT ME.
THEN I HEAR A DEEP GROAN . . .
ERRRRRRNNNNNNN
CRACKLE-CRACK

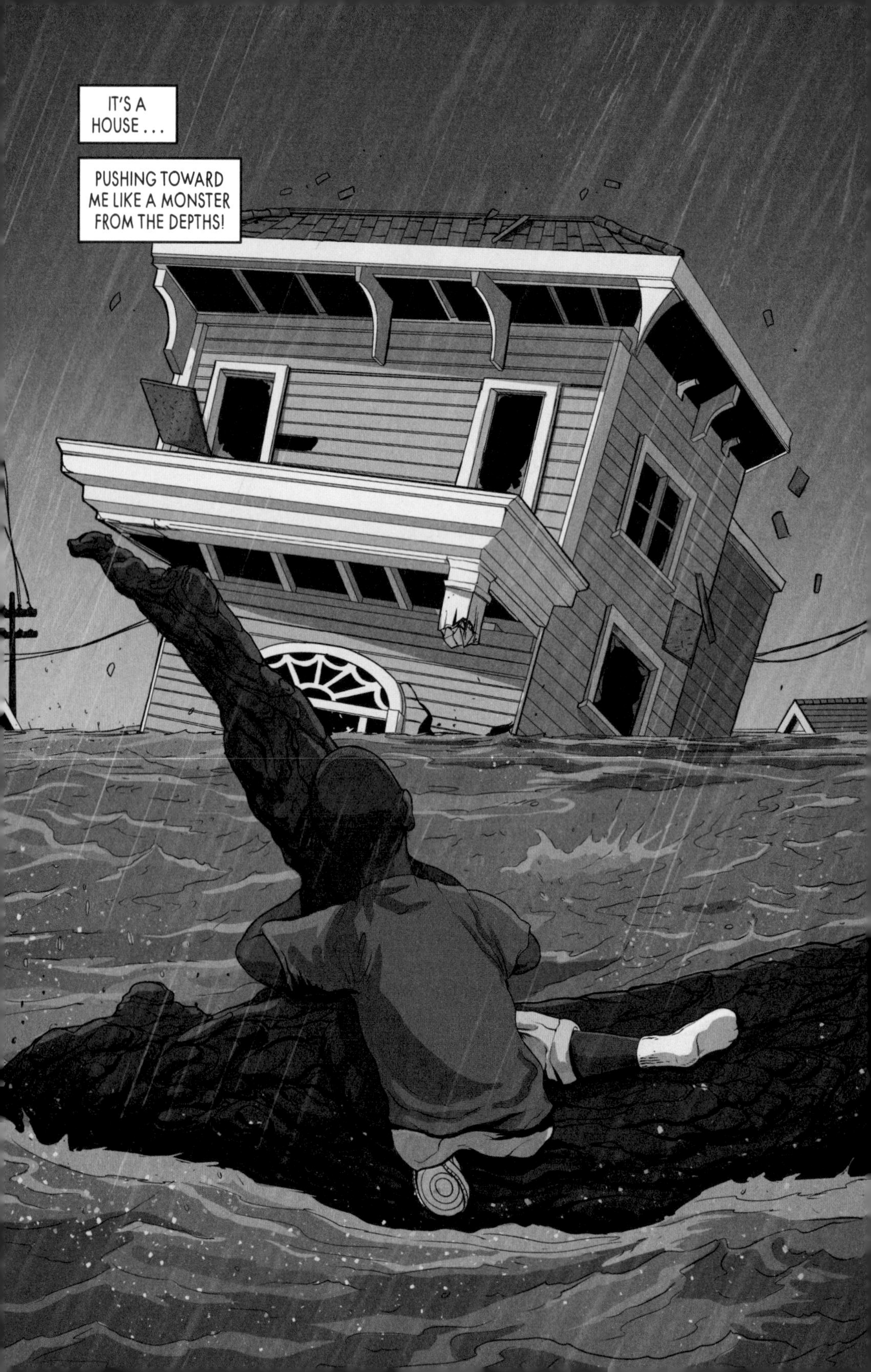
IT'S A HOUSE . . .
PUSHING TOWARD ME LIKE A MONSTER FROM THE DEPTHS!

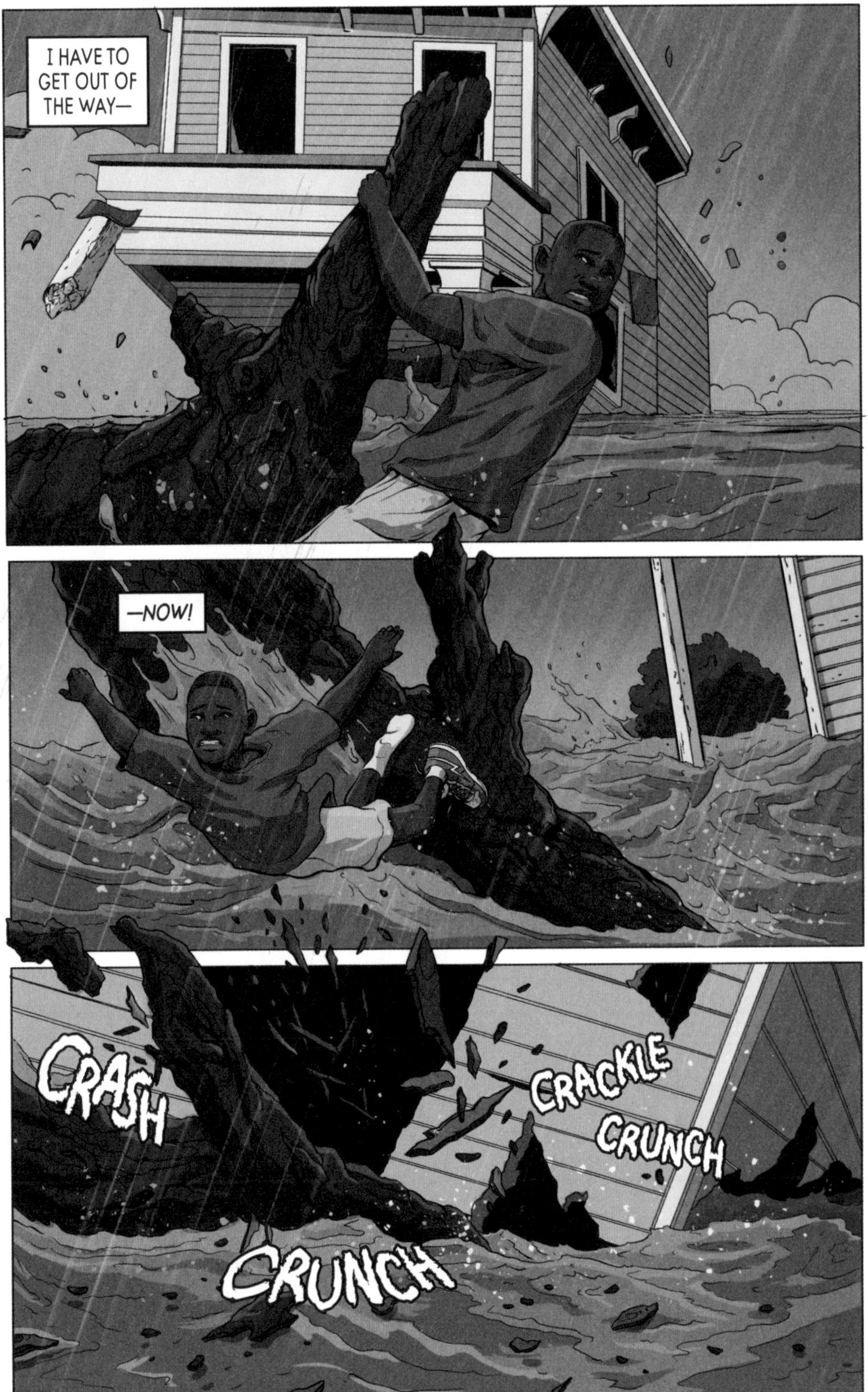
I HAVE TO GET OUT OF THE WAY—
—NOW!
CRASH
CRACKLE
CRUNCH
CRUNCH

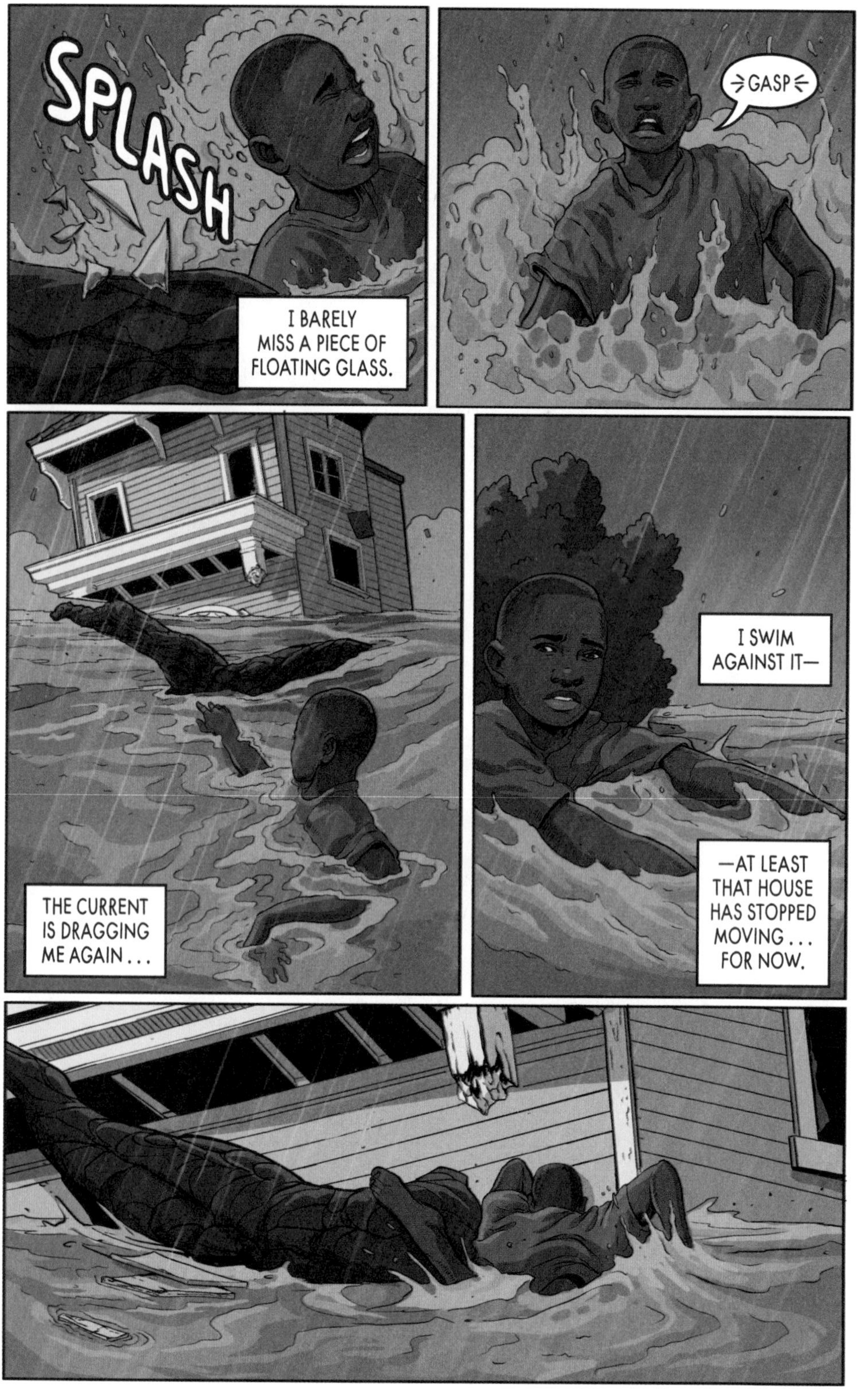
SPLASH
I BARELY MISS A PIECE OF FLOATING GLASS.
GASP
THE CURRENT IS DRAGGING ME AGAIN . . .
I SWIM AGAINST IT—
—AT LEAST THAT HOUSE HAS STOPPED MOVING . . . FOR NOW.

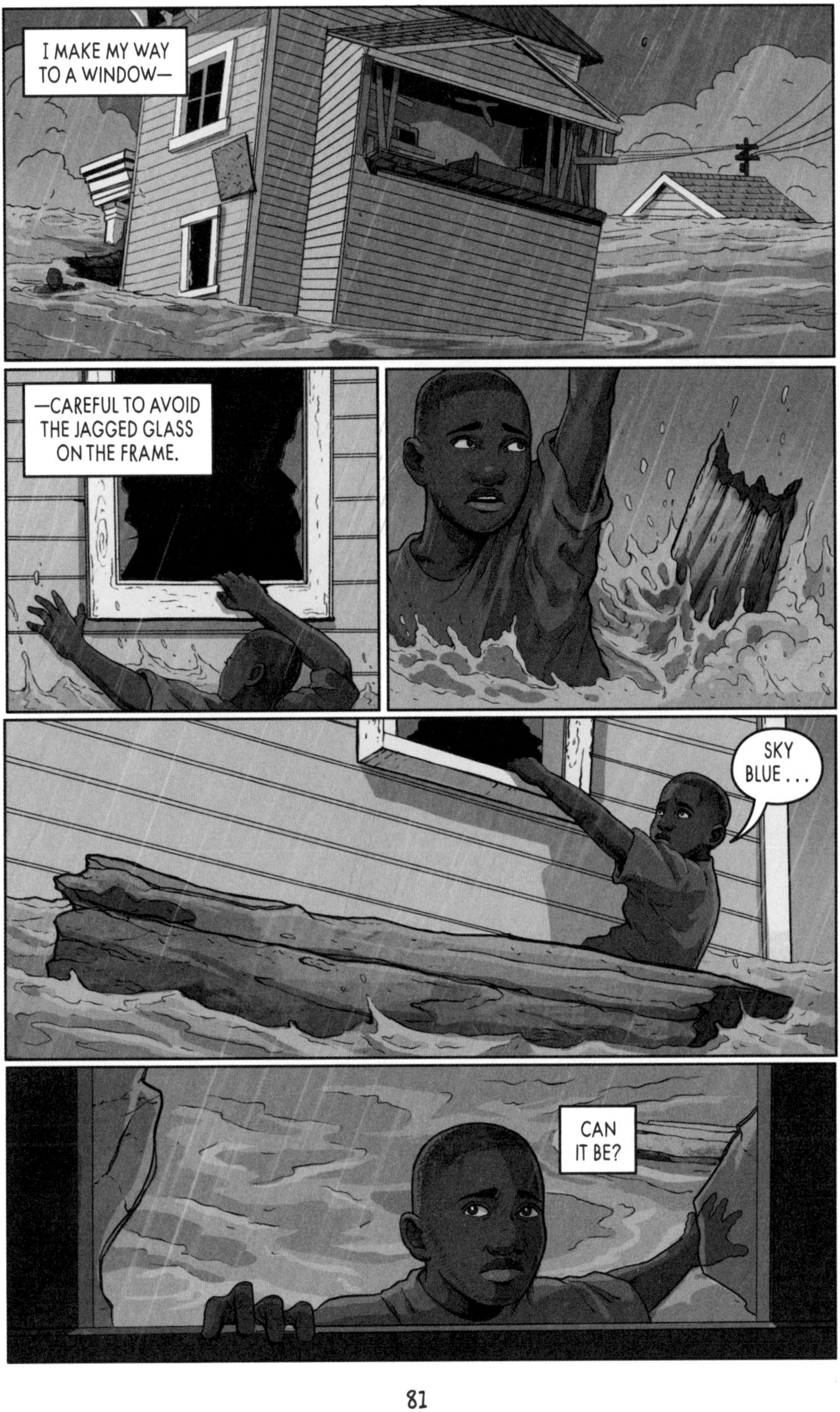
I MAKE MY WAY TO A WINDOW—
—CAREFUL TO AVOID THE JAGGED GLASS ON THE FRAME.
SKY BLUE . . .
CAN IT BE?

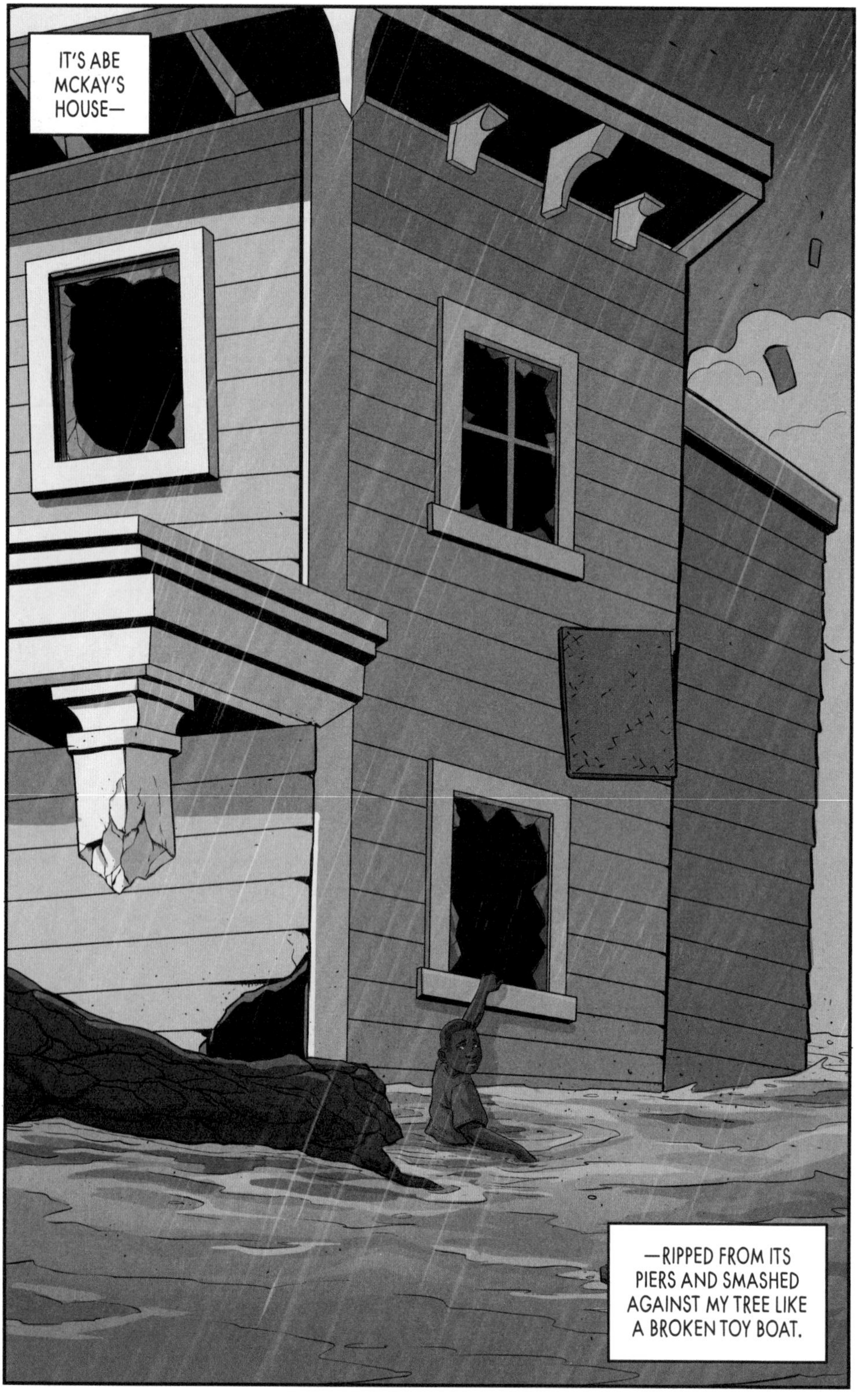
IT'S ABE MCKAY'S HOUSE—
—RIPPED FROM ITS PIERS AND SMASHED AGAINST MY TREE LIKE A BROKEN TOY BOAT.

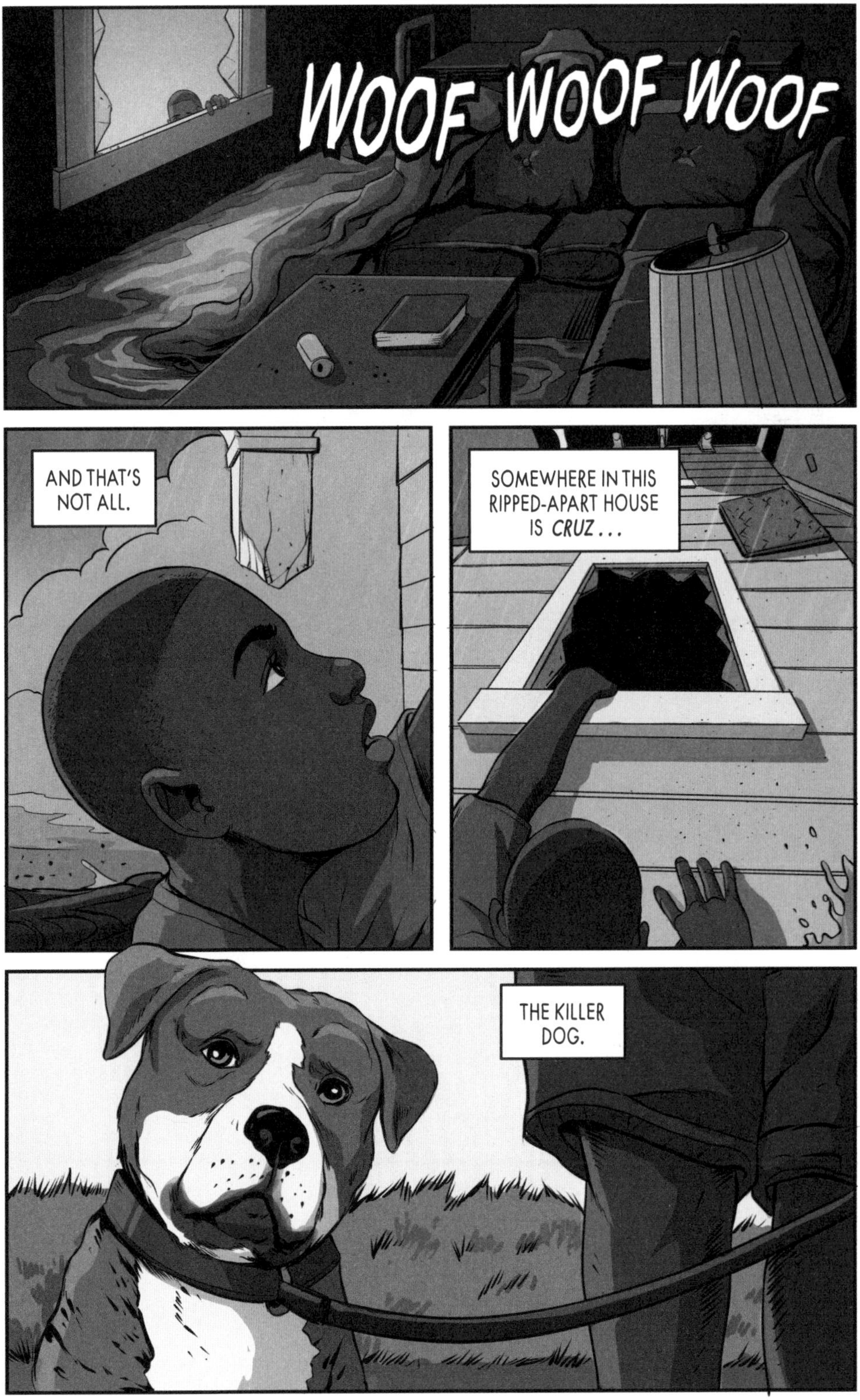
WOOF WOOF WOOF
AND THAT'S NOT ALL.
SOMEWHERE IN THIS RIPPED-APART HOUSE IS *CRUZ*...
THE KILLER DOG.

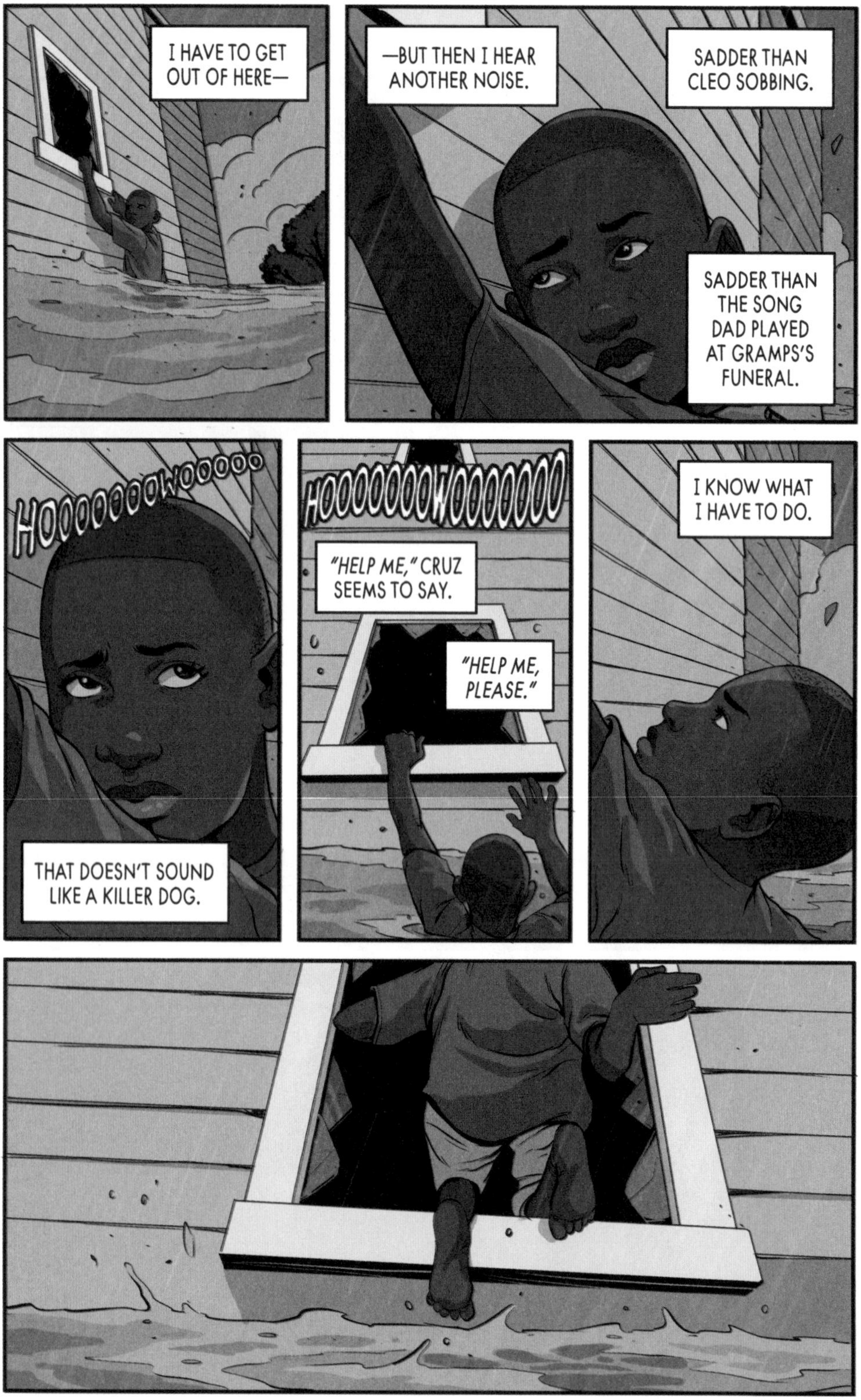
I HAVE TO GET OUT OF HERE—
—BUT THEN I HEAR ANOTHER NOISE.
SADDER THAN CLEO SOBBING.
SADDER THAN THE SONG DAD PLAYED AT GRAMPS'S FUNERAL.
HOOOOOOOWOOOOO
THAT DOESN'T SOUND LIKE A KILLER DOG.
HOOOOOOOWOOOOOOO
"HELP ME," CRUZ SEEMS TO SAY.
"HELP ME, PLEASE."
I KNOW WHAT I HAVE TO DO.

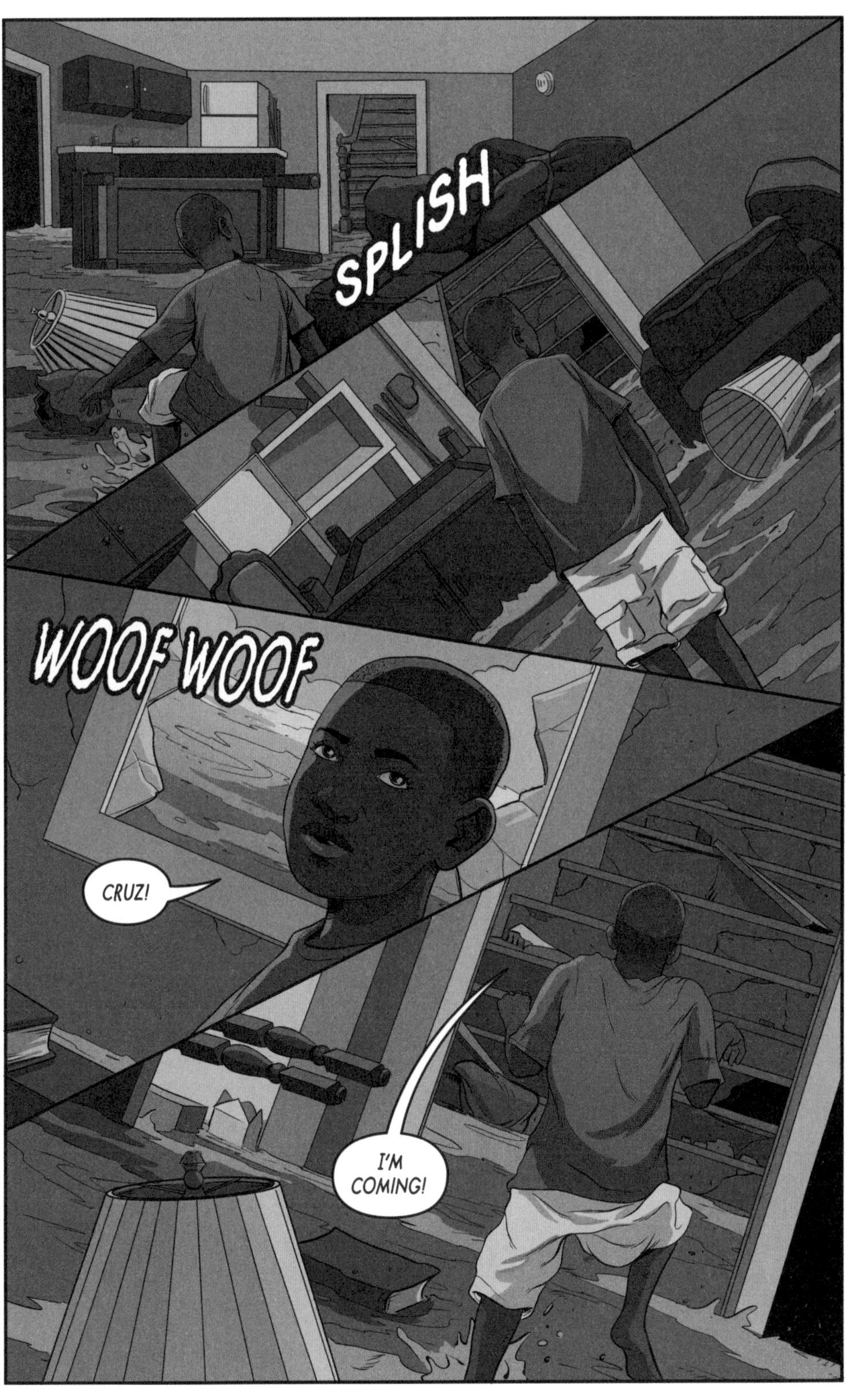
SPLISH
WOOF WOOF
CRUZ!
I'M COMING!

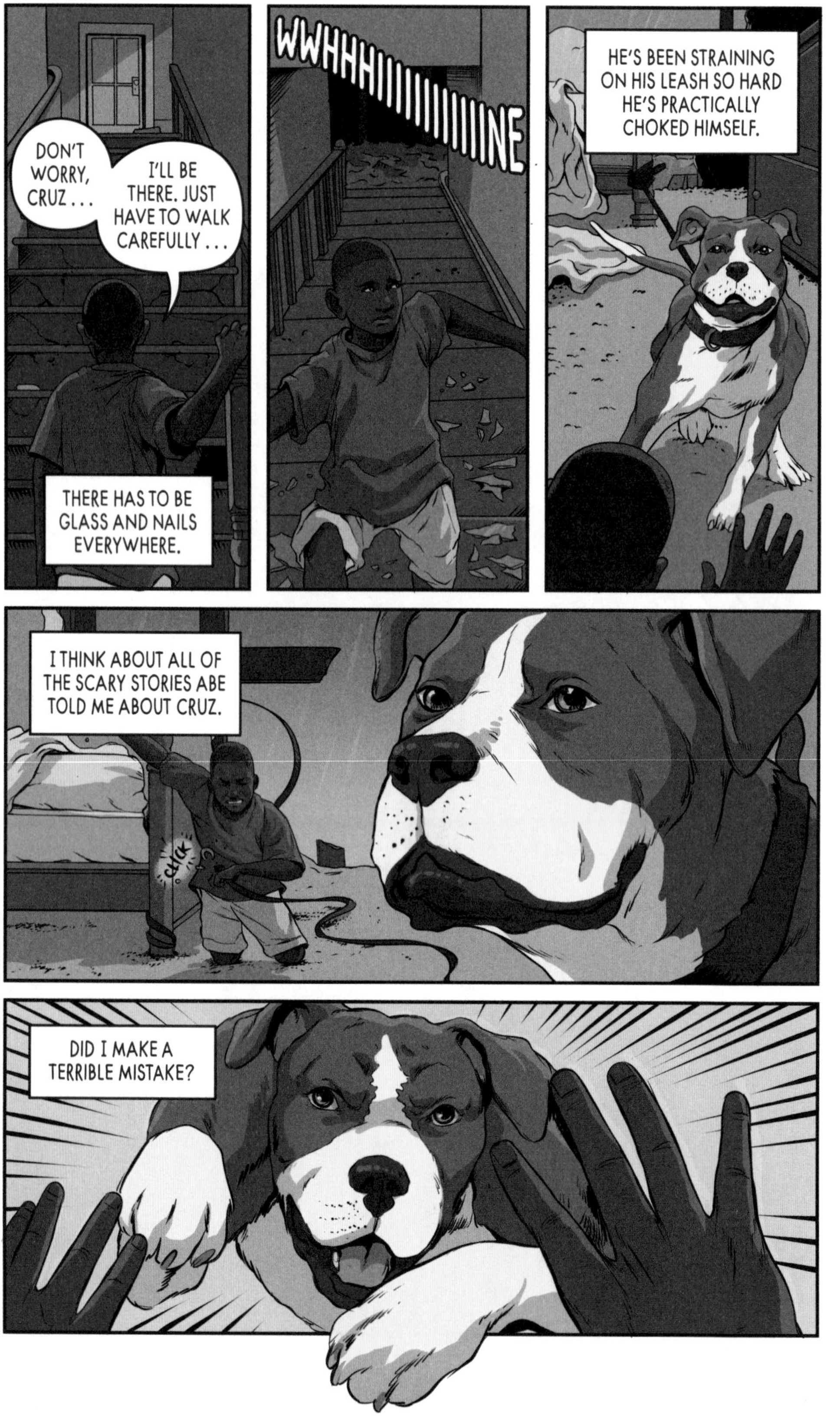
DON'T WORRY, CRUZ . . .
I'LL BE THERE. JUST HAVE TO WALK CAREFULLY . . .
THERE HAS TO BE GLASS AND NAILS EVERYWHERE.
WWHHHIIIIIIIIIIIIINE
HE'S BEEN STRAINING ON HIS LEASH SO HARD HE'S PRACTICALLY CHOKED HIMSELF.
I THINK ABOUT ALL OF THE SCARY STORIES ABE TOLD ME ABOUT CRUZ.
CLICK
DID I MAKE A TERRIBLE MISTAKE?

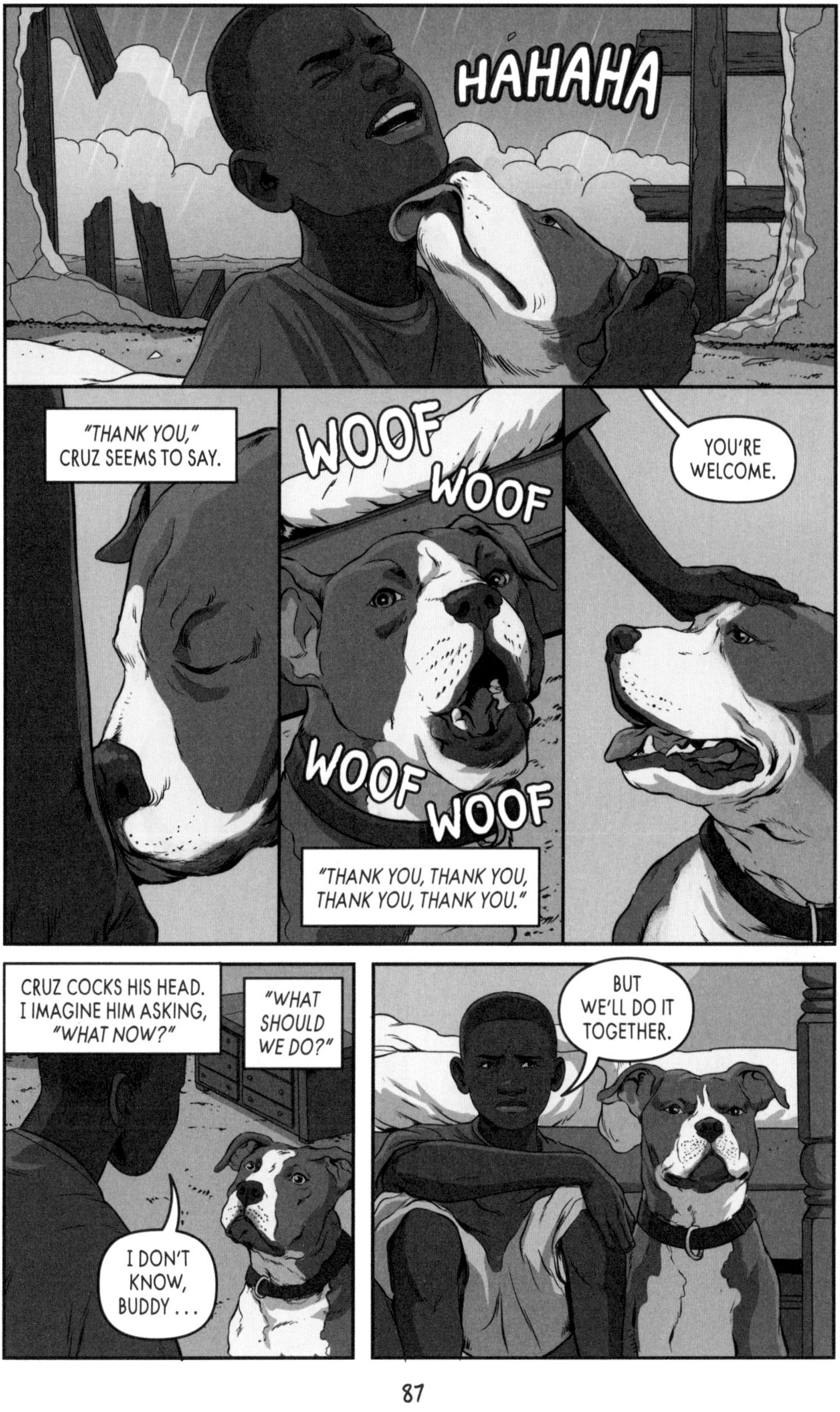
HAHAHA
"THANK YOU," CRUZ SEEMS TO SAY.
WOOF WOOF
WOOF WOOF
"THANK YOU, THANK YOU, THANK YOU, THANK YOU."
YOU'RE WELCOME.
CRUZ COCKS HIS HEAD. I IMAGINE HIM ASKING, "WHAT NOW?"
"WHAT SHOULD WE DO?"
I DON'T KNOW, BUDDY . . .
BUT WE'LL DO IT TOGETHER.

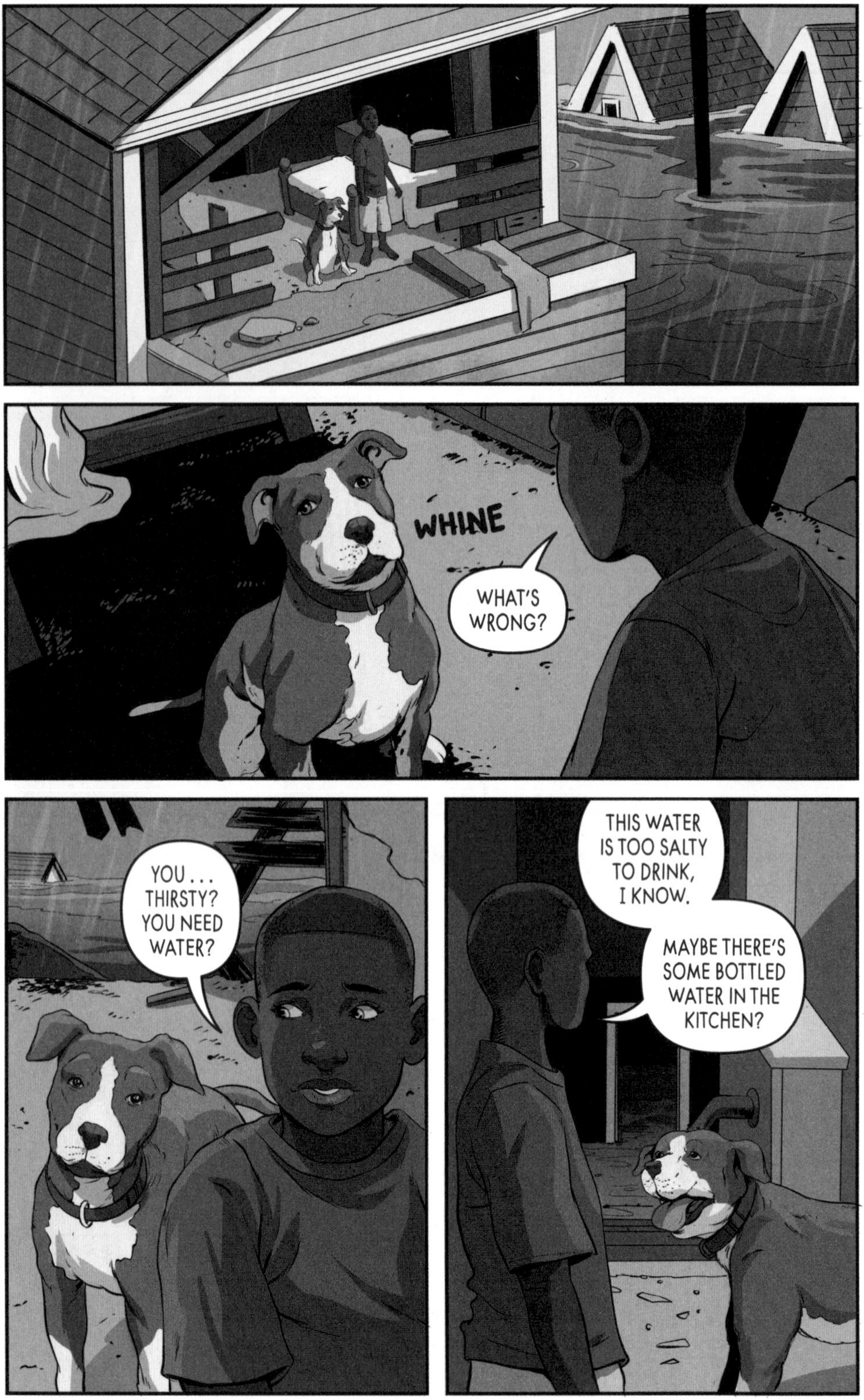
WHINE
WHAT'S WRONG?
YOU . . . THIRSTY? YOU NEED WATER?
THIS WATER IS TOO SALTY TO DRINK, I KNOW.
MAYBE THERE'S SOME BOTTLED WATER IN THE KITCHEN?

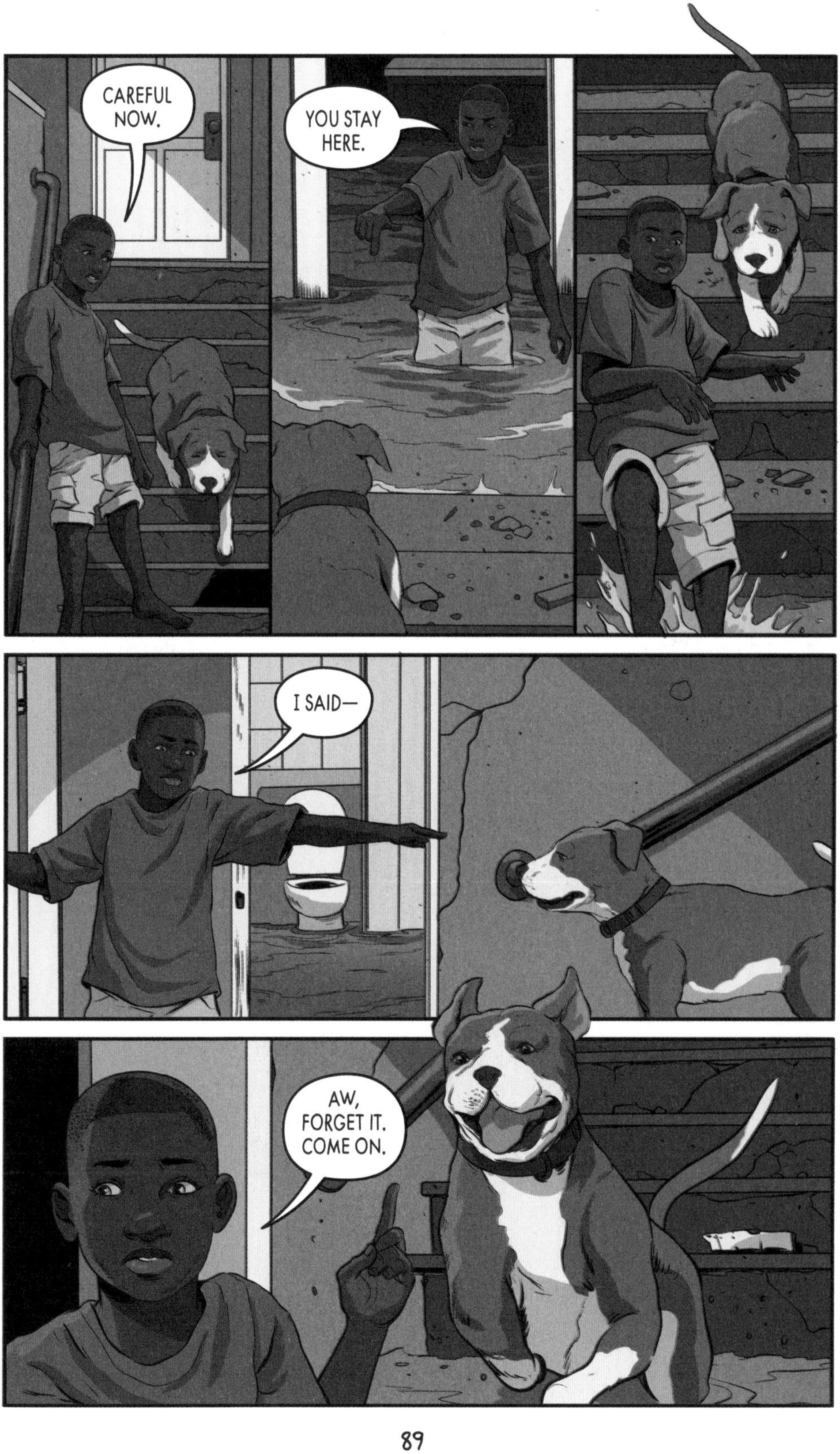
CAREFUL NOW.
YOU STAY HERE.
I SAID—
AW, FORGET IT. COME ON.

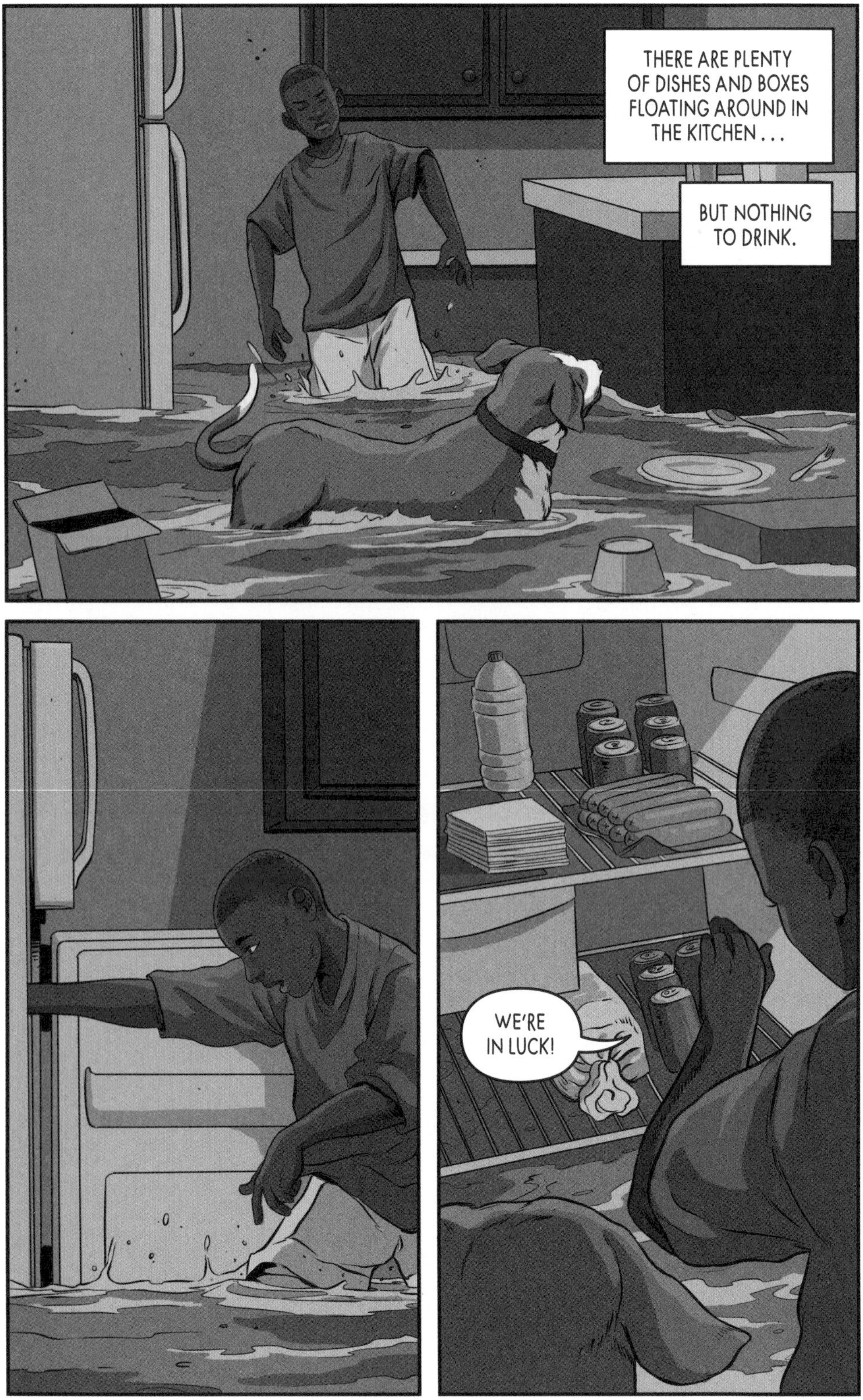
THERE ARE PLENTY OF DISHES AND BOXES FLOATING AROUND IN THE KITCHEN . . .
BUT NOTHING TO DRINK.
WE'RE IN LUCK!

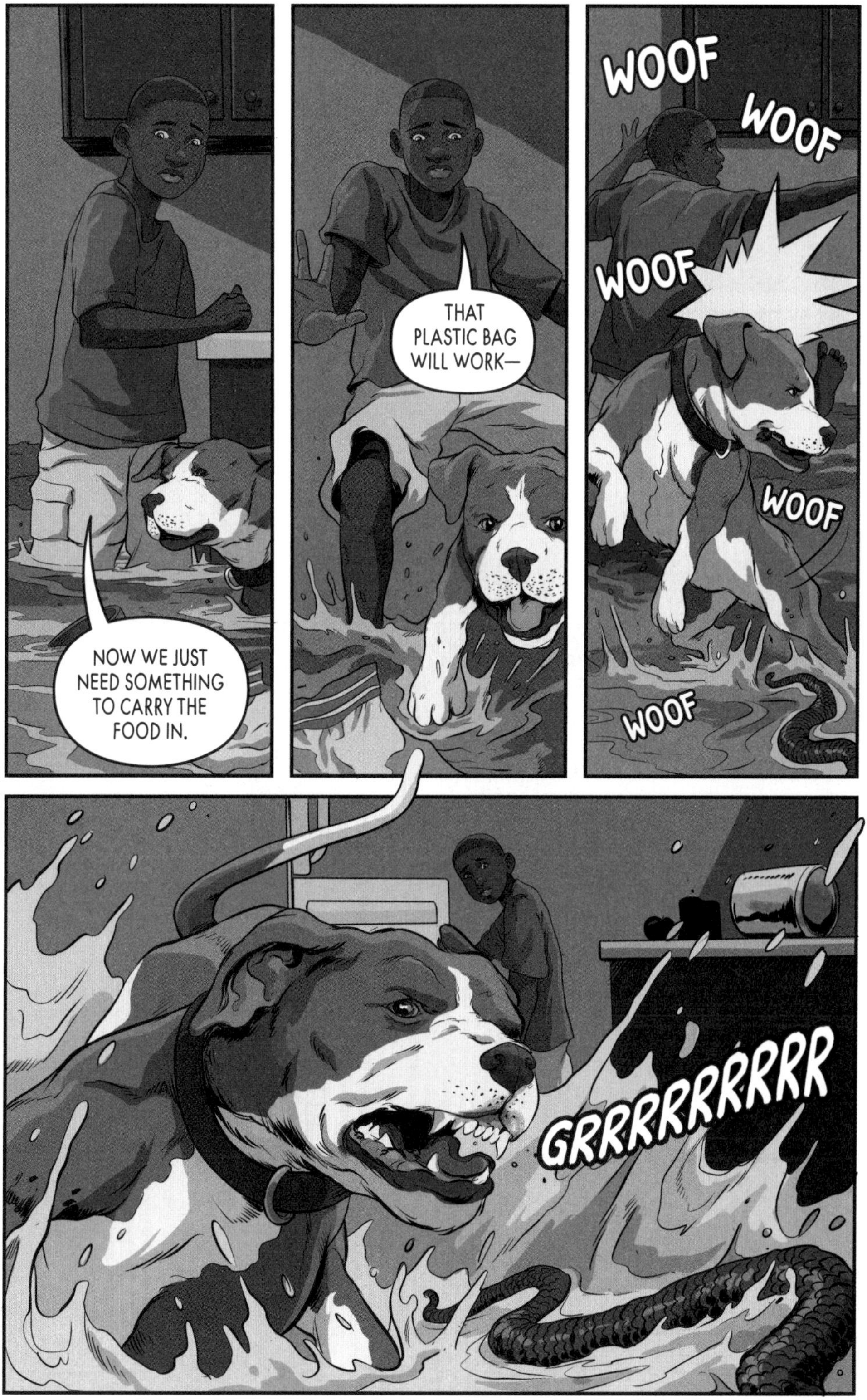
NOW WE JUST NEED SOMETHING TO CARRY THE FOOD IN.
THAT PLASTIC BAG WILL WORK—
WOOF
WOOF
WOOF
WOOF
WOOF
GRRRRRRRR

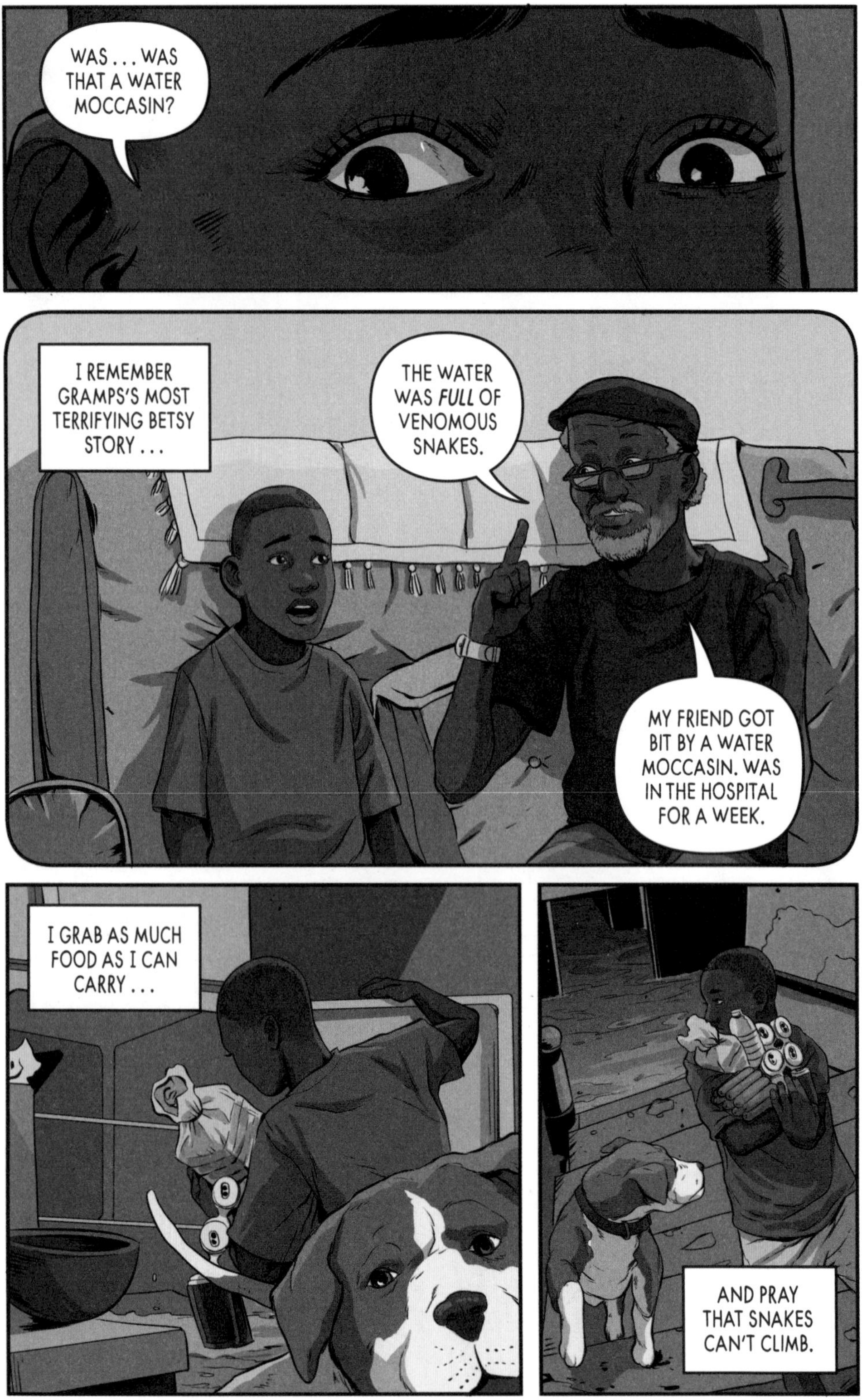
WAS . . . WAS THAT A WATER MOCCASIN?
I REMEMBER GRAMPS'S MOST TERRIFYING BETSY STORY . . .
THE WATER WAS *FULL* OF VENOMOUS SNAKES.
MY FRIEND GOT BIT BY A WATER MOCCASIN. WAS IN THE HOSPITAL FOR A WEEK.
I GRAB AS MUCH FOOD AS I CAN CARRY . . .
AND PRAY THAT SNAKES CAN'T CLIMB.

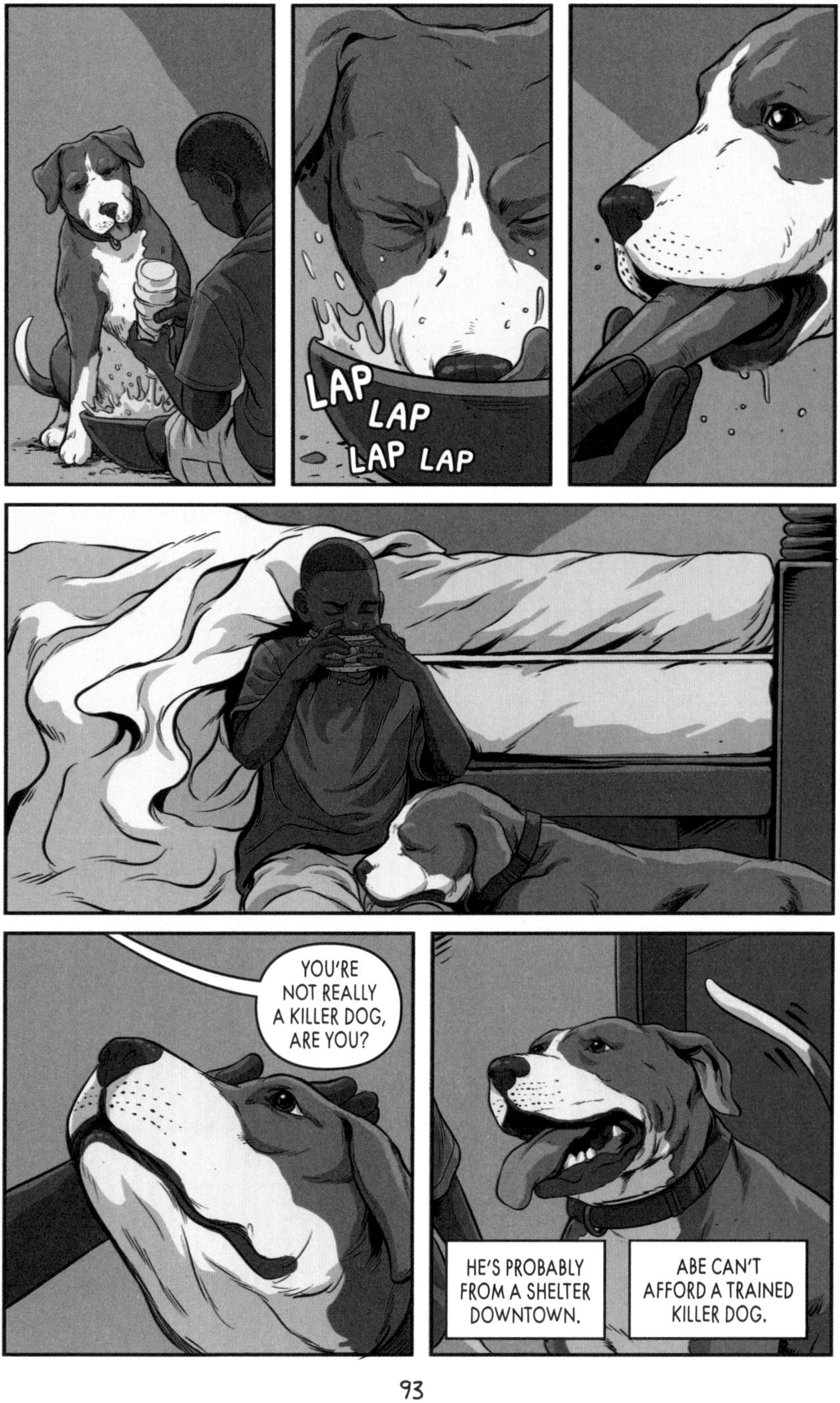
LAP
LAP
LAP LAP
YOU'RE NOT REALLY A KILLER DOG, ARE YOU?
HE'S PROBABLY FROM A SHELTER DOWNTOWN.
ABE CAN'T AFFORD A TRAINED KILLER DOG.

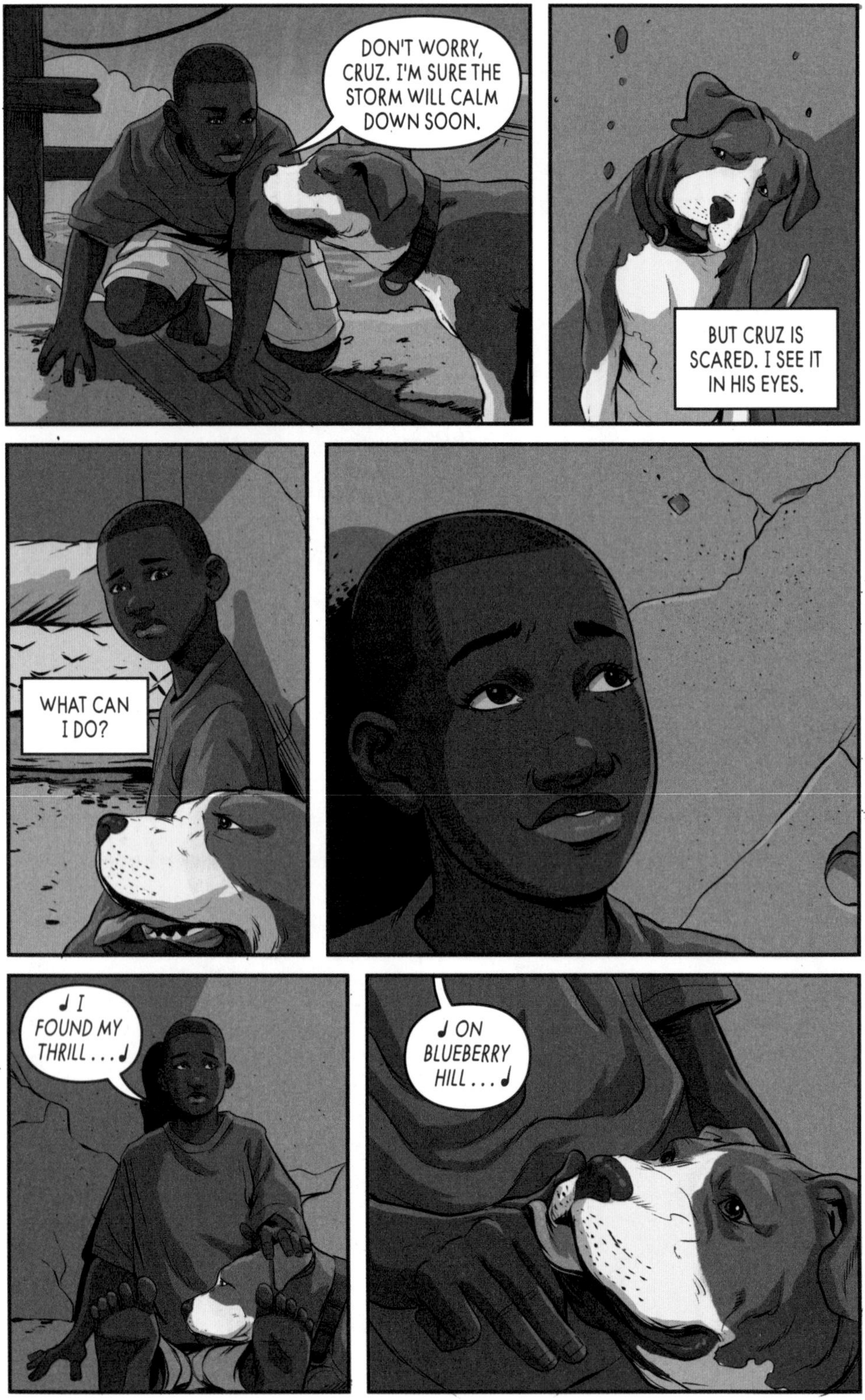
DON'T WORRY, CRUZ. I'M SURE THE STORM WILL CALM DOWN SOON.
BUT CRUZ IS SCARED. I SEE IT IN HIS EYES.
WHAT CAN I DO?
♩ I FOUND MY THRILL . . . ♩
♩ ON BLUEBERRY HILL . . . ♩

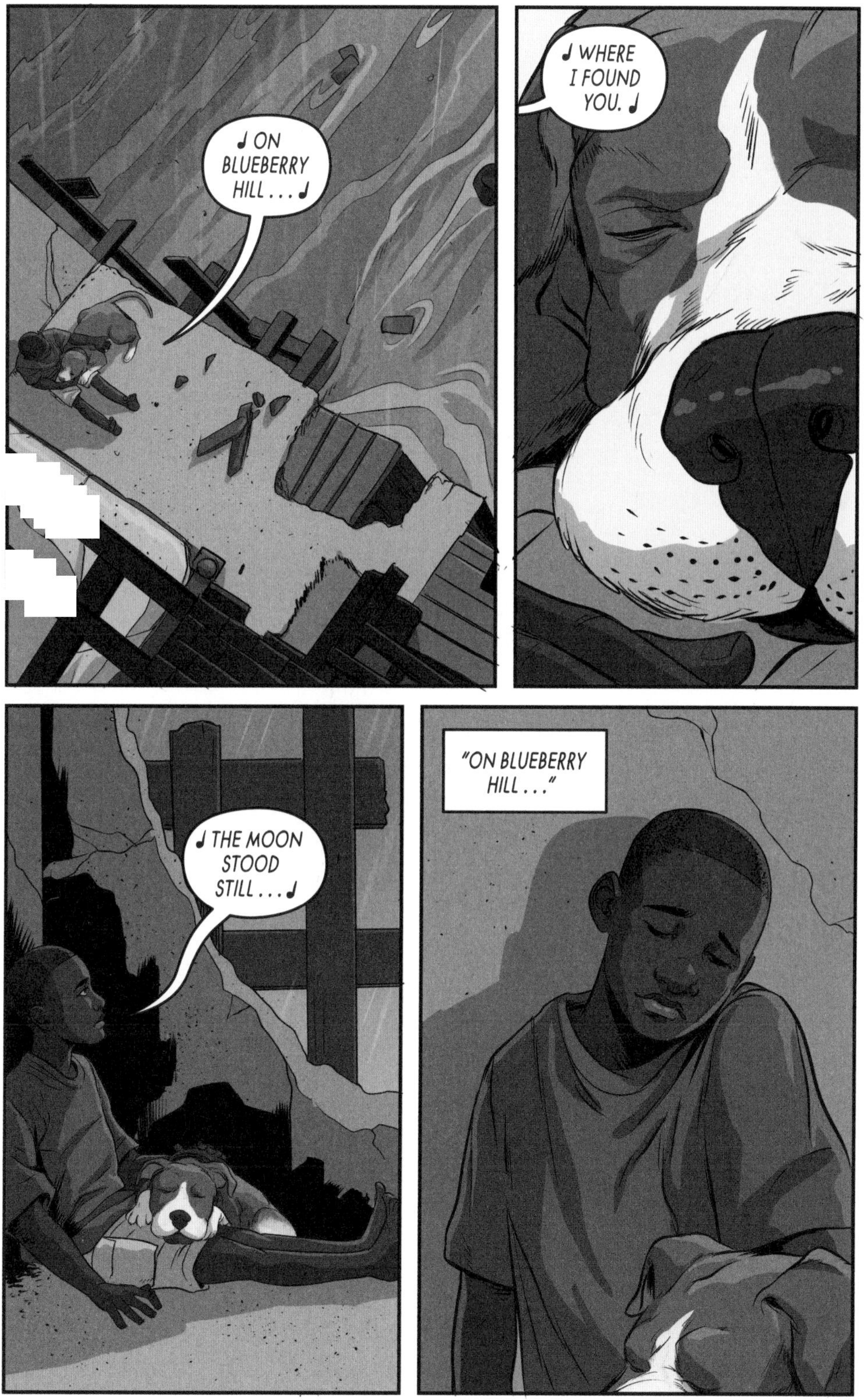
♩ ON BLUEBERRY HILL . . . ♩
♩ WHERE I FOUND YOU. ♩
♩ THE MOON STOOD STILL . . . ♩
"ON BLUEBERRY HILL . . ."

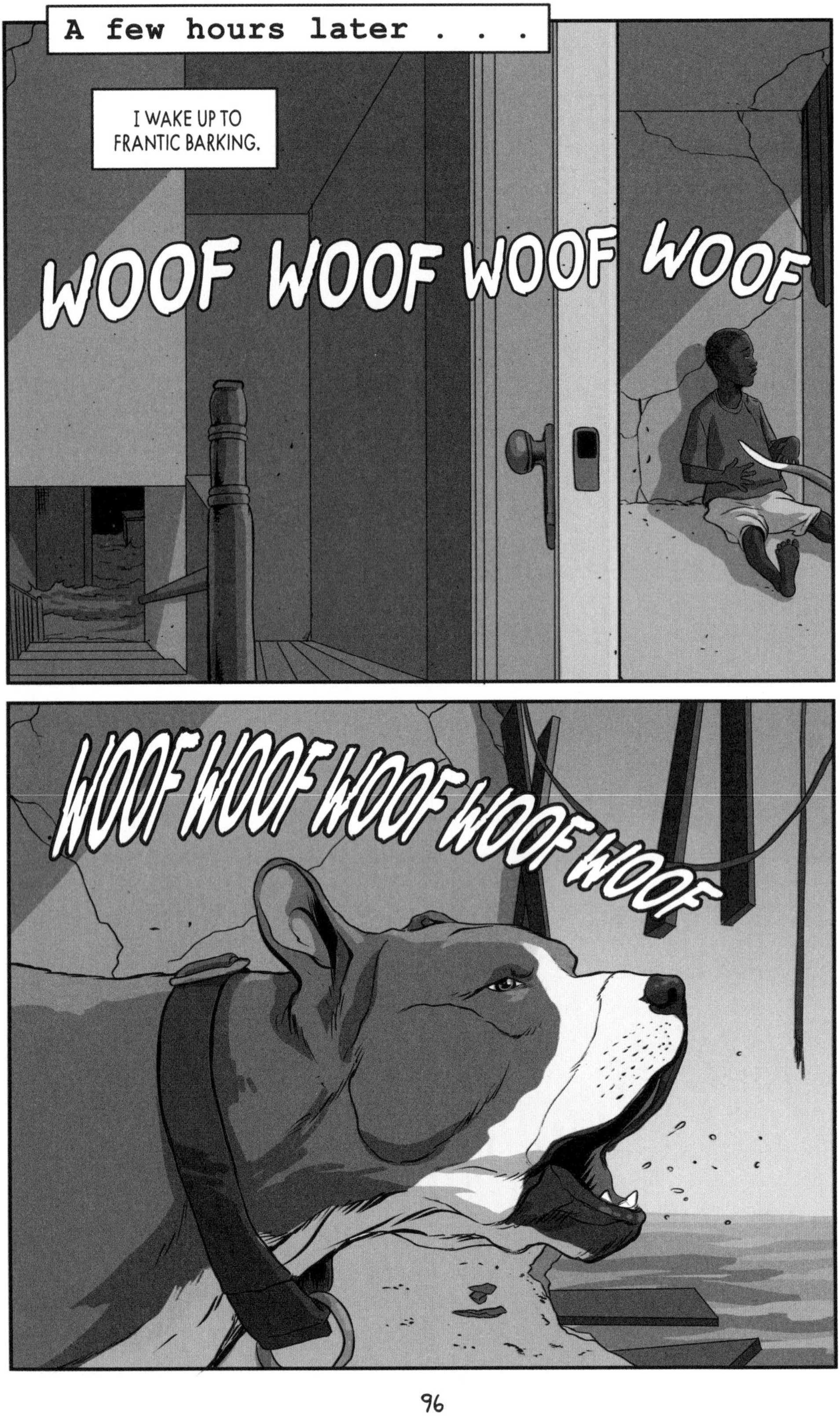
A few hours later . . .
I WAKE UP TO FRANTIC BARKING.
WOOF WOOF WOOF WOOF
WOOF WOOF WOOF WOOF WOOF

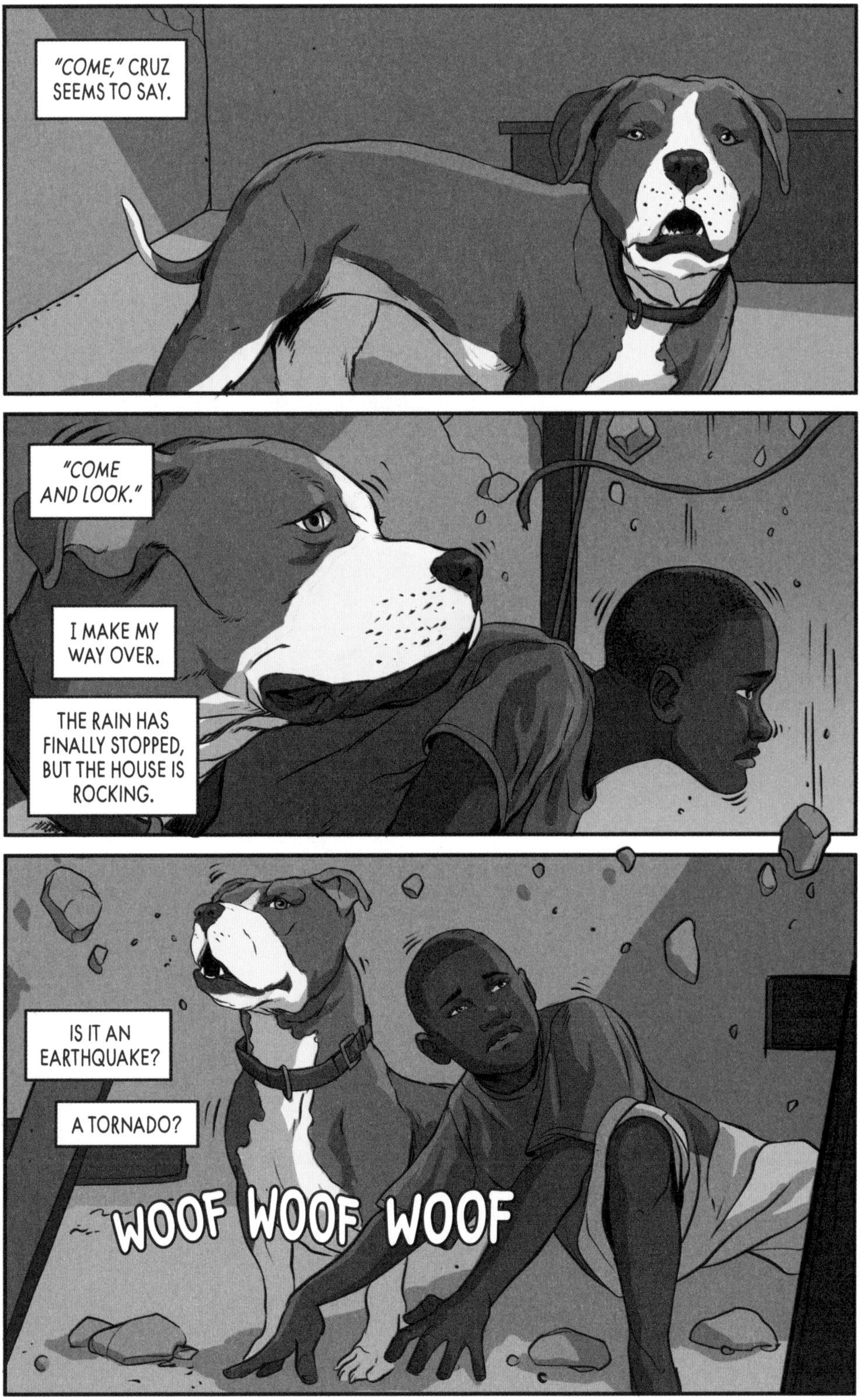
"COME," CRUZ SEEMS TO SAY.
"COME AND LOOK."
I MAKE MY WAY OVER.
THE RAIN HAS FINALLY STOPPED, BUT THE HOUSE IS ROCKING.
IS IT AN EARTHQUAKE?
A TORNADO?
WOOF WOOF WOOF

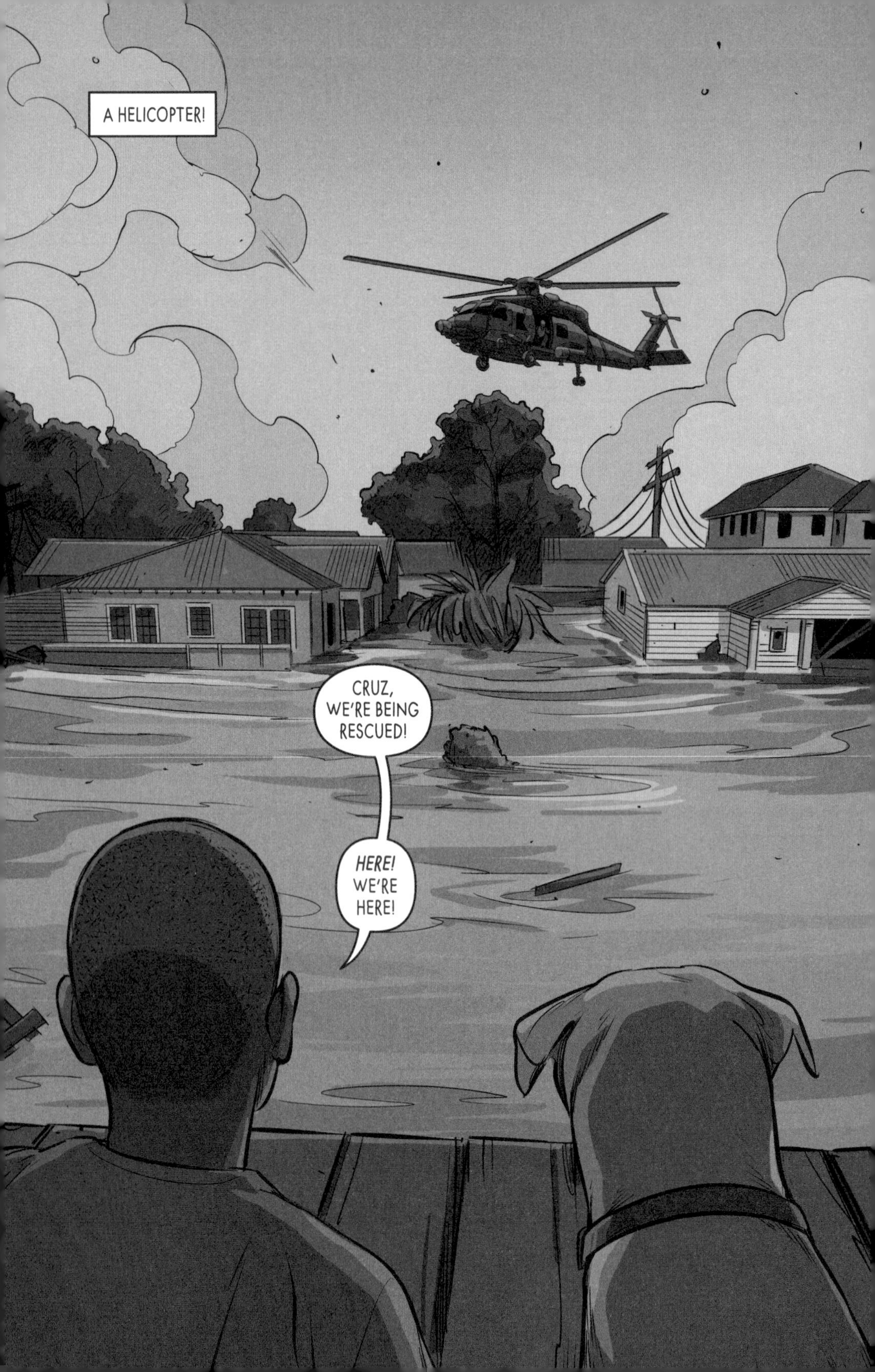
A HELICOPTER!
CRUZ, WE'RE BEING RESCUED!
HERE! WE'RE HERE!

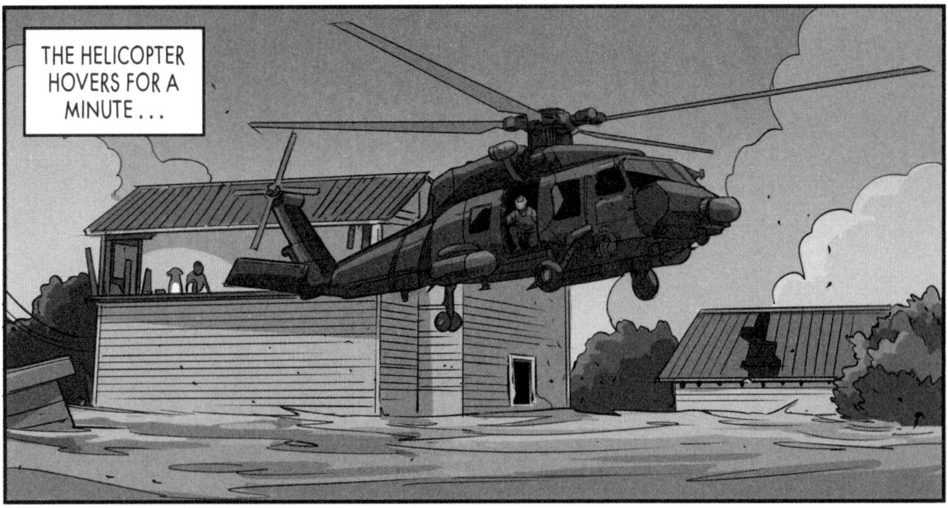
THE HELICOPTER HOVERS FOR A MINUTE . . .

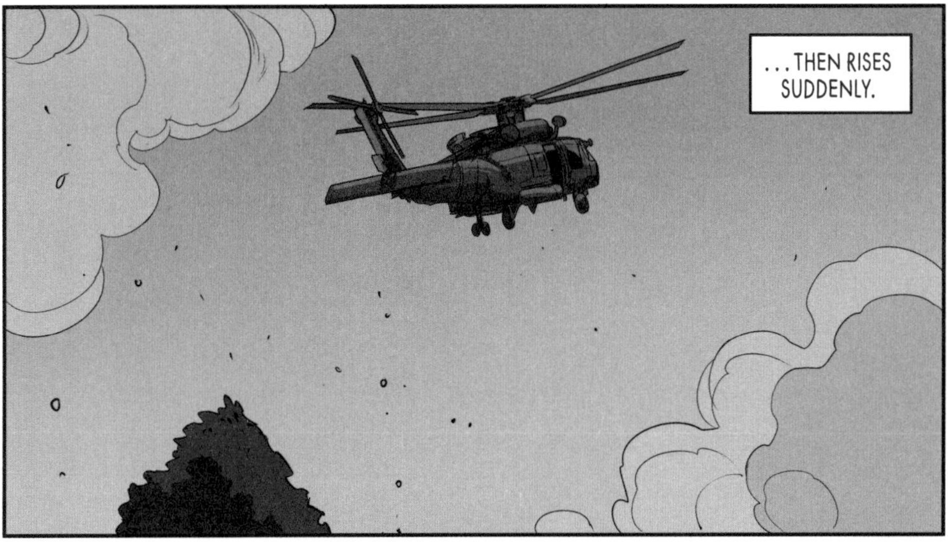
. . . THEN RISES SUDDENLY.

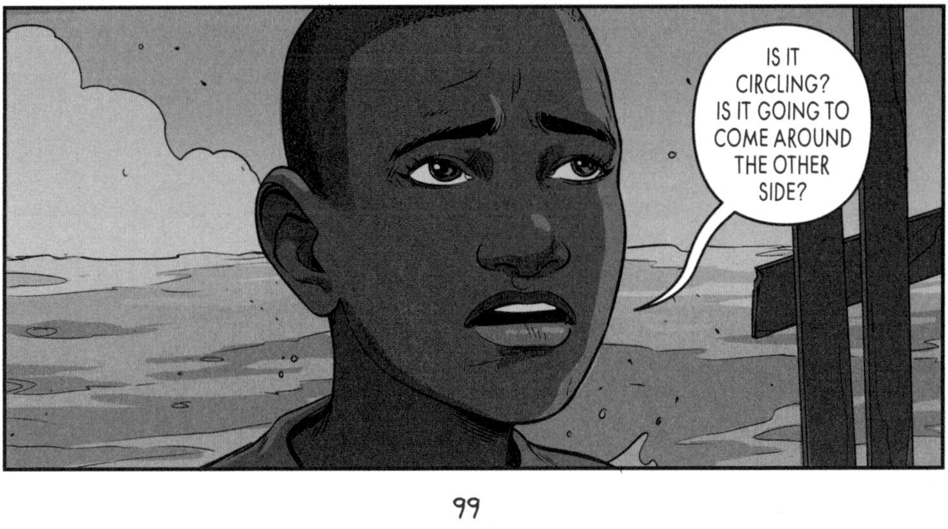
IS IT CIRCLING? IS IT GOING TO COME AROUND THE OTHER SIDE?

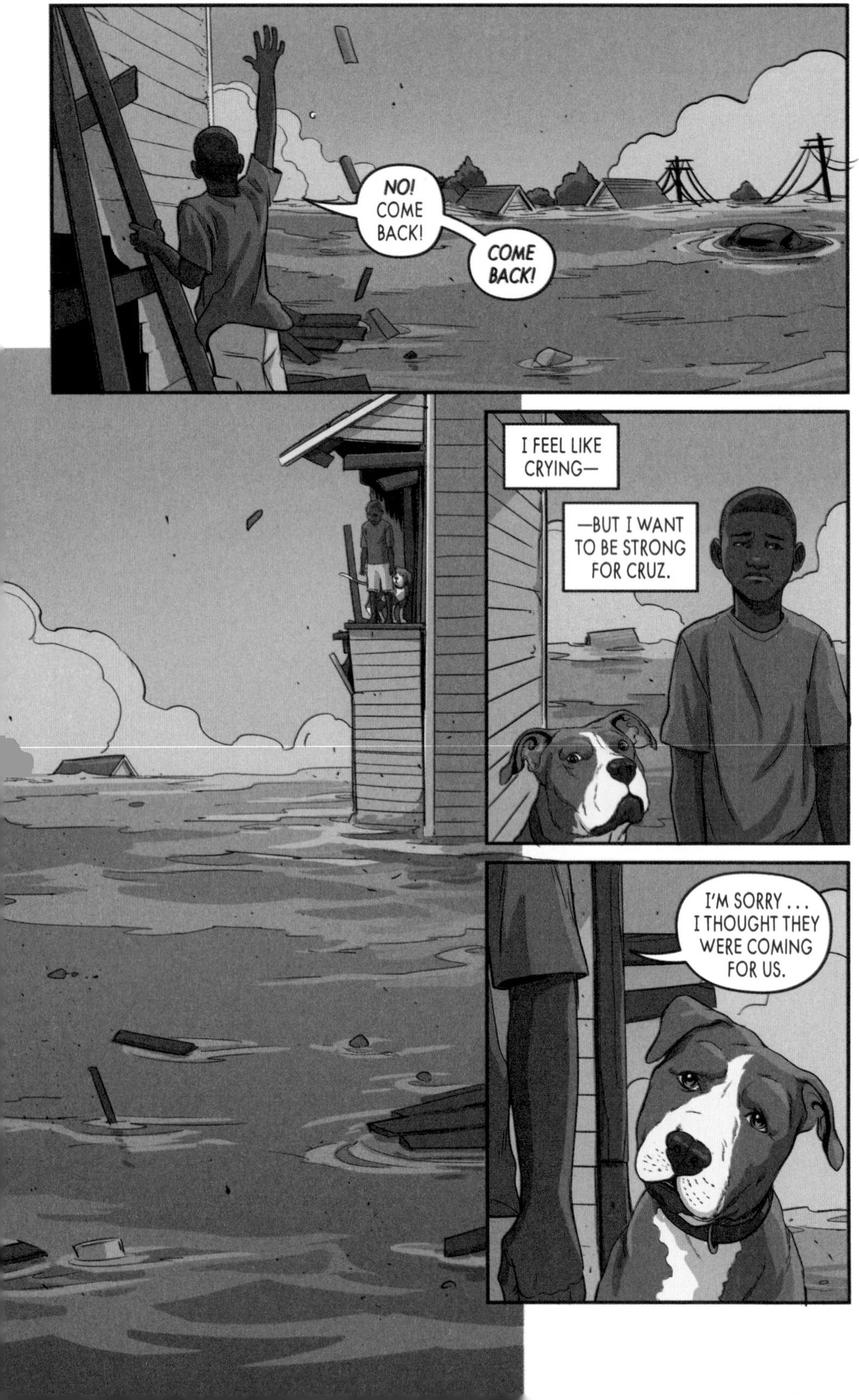
NO! COME BACK!
COME BACK!
I FEEL LIKE CRYING—
—BUT I WANT TO BE STRONG FOR CRUZ.
I'M SORRY . . . I THOUGHT THEY WERE COMING FOR US.

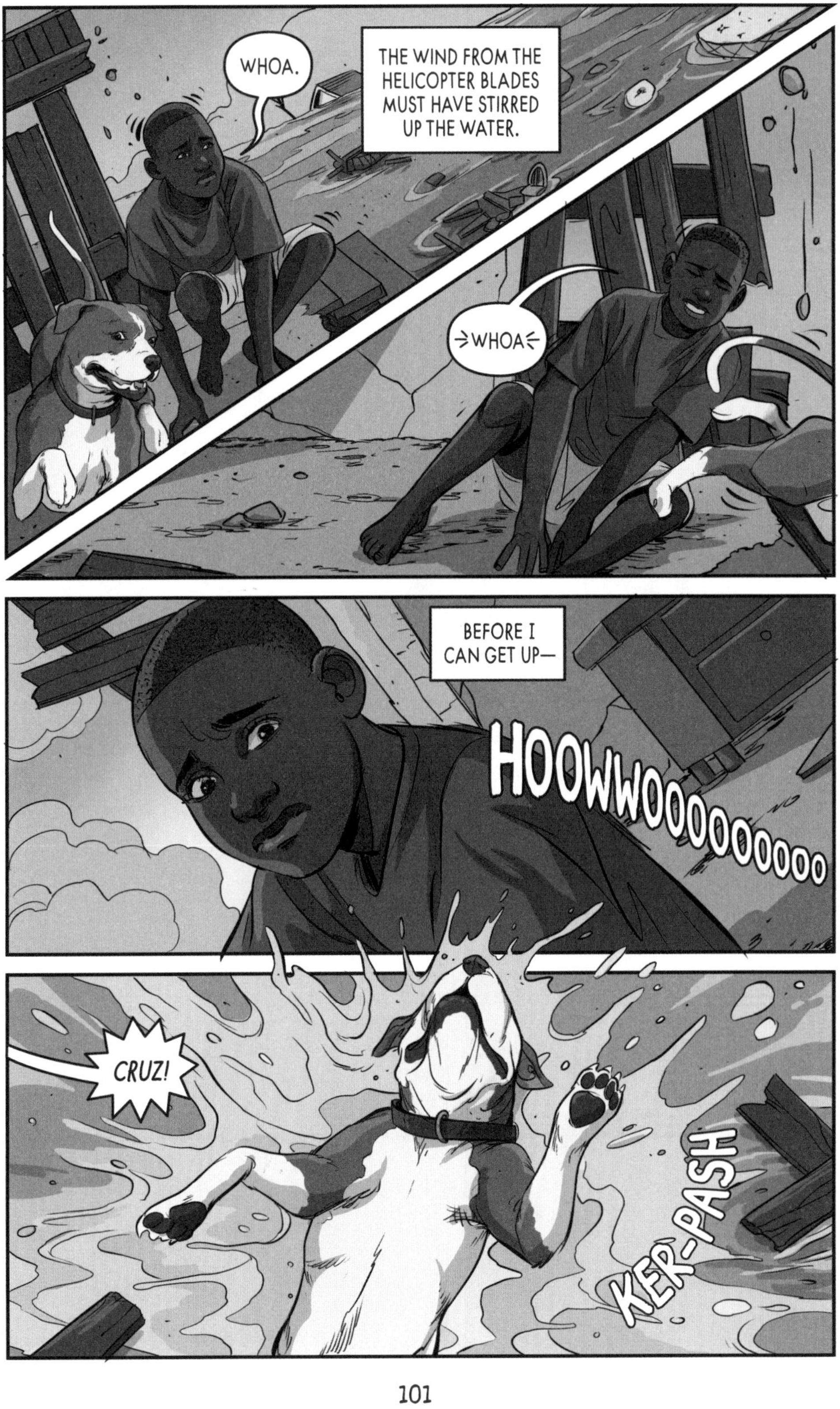
WHOA.
THE WIND FROM THE HELICOPTER BLADES MUST HAVE STIRRED UP THE WATER.
WHOA
BEFORE I CAN GET UP—
HOOWWOOOOOOOOO
CRUZ!
KER-PASH

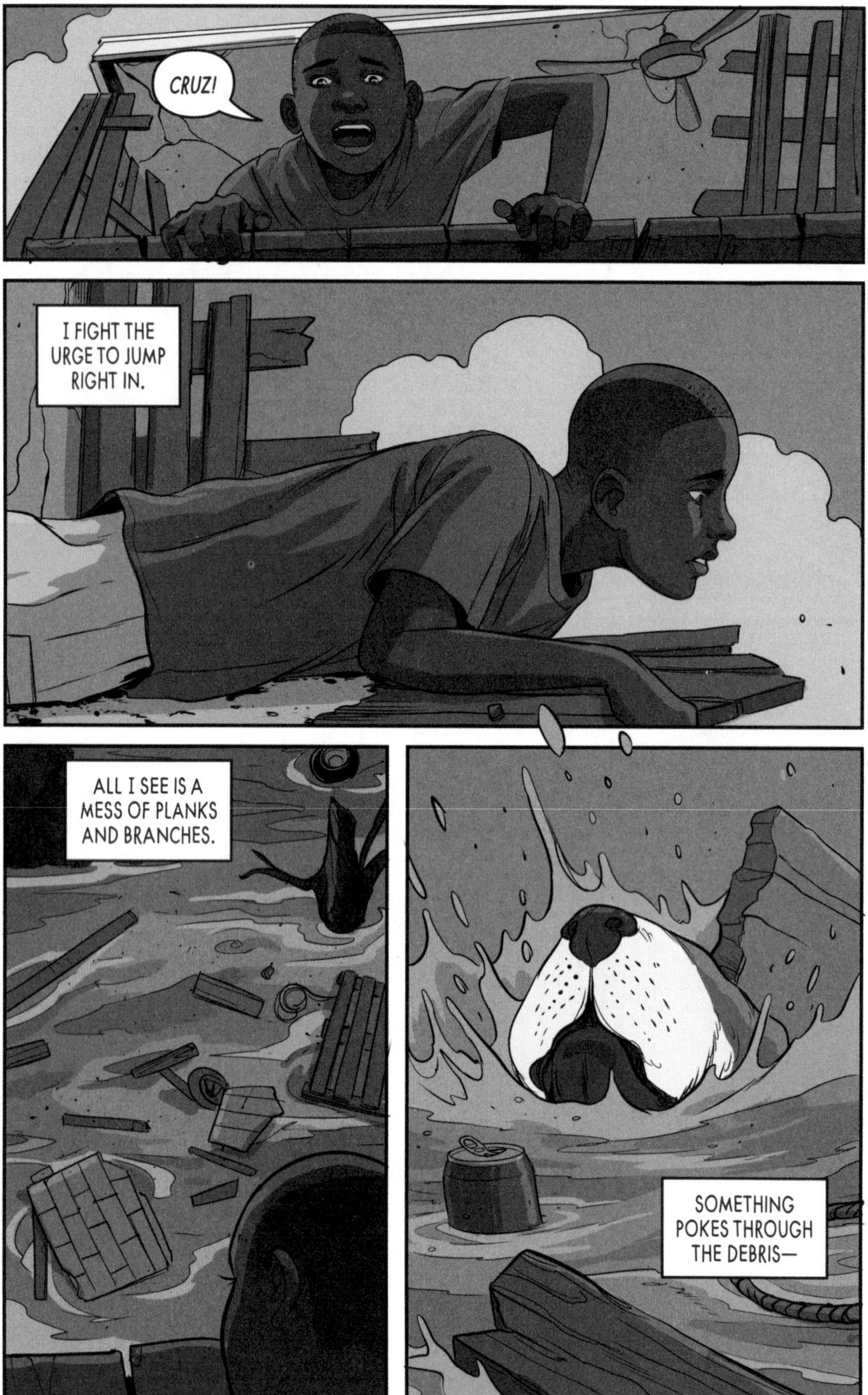
CRUZ!
I FIGHT THE URGE TO JUMP RIGHT IN.
ALL I SEE IS A MESS OF PLANKS AND BRANCHES.
SOMETHING POKES THROUGH THE DEBRIS—

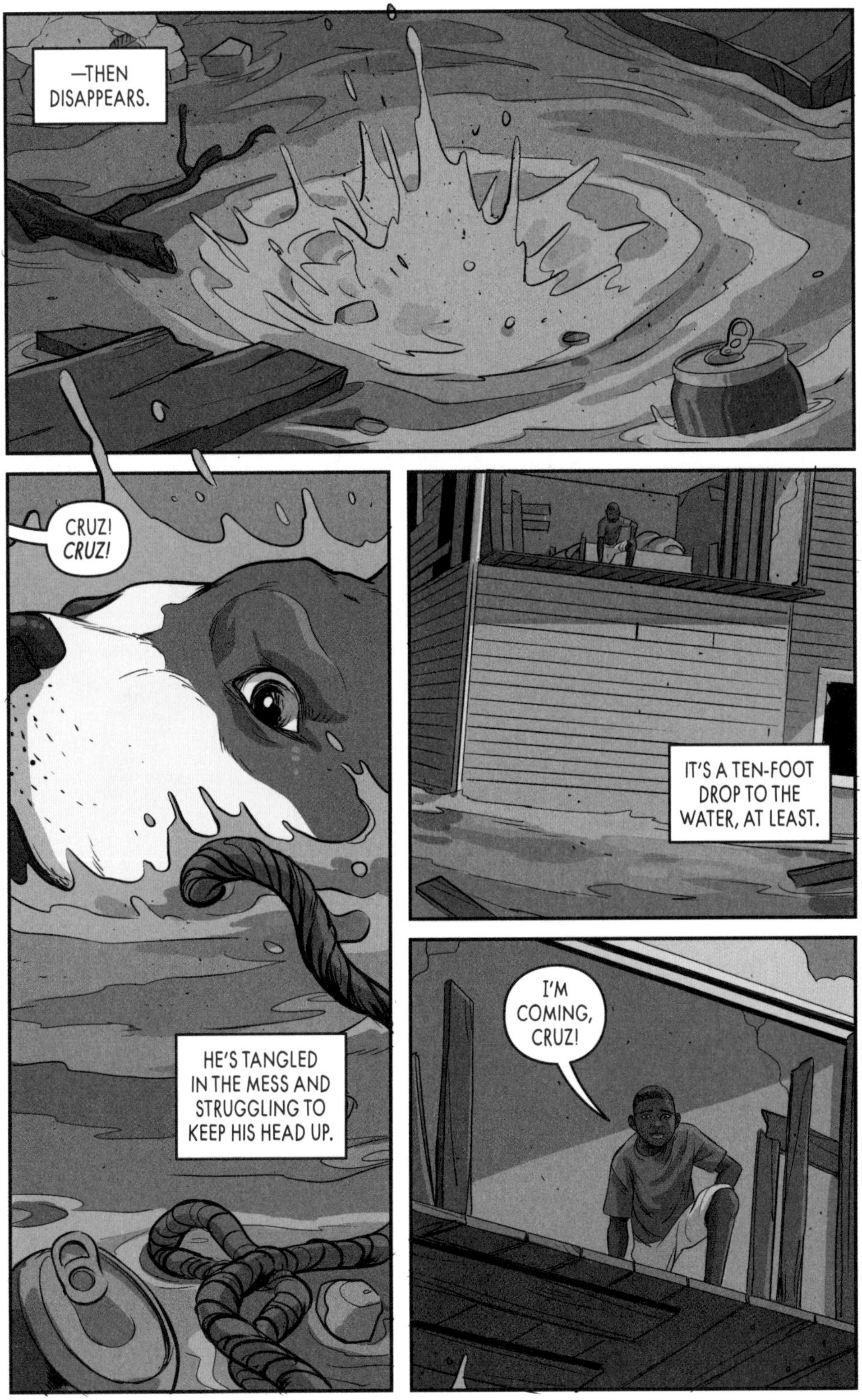
—THEN DISAPPEARS.
CRUZ! *CRUZ!*
HE'S TANGLED IN THE MESS AND STRUGGLING TO KEEP HIS HEAD UP.
IT'S A TEN-FOOT DROP TO THE WATER, AT LEAST.
I'M COMING, CRUZ!

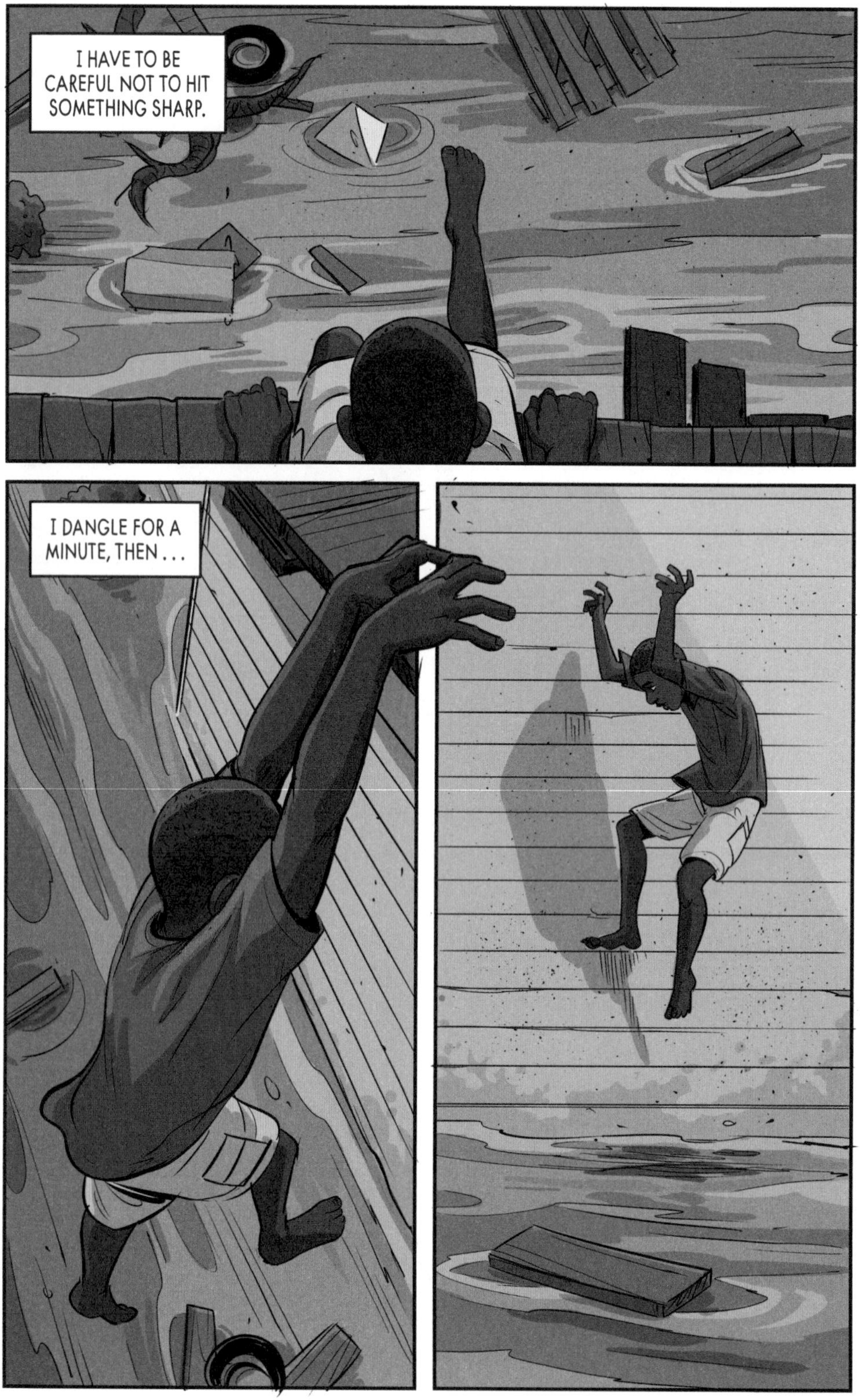
I HAVE TO BE CAREFUL NOT TO HIT SOMETHING SHARP.
I DANGLE FOR A MINUTE, THEN . . .

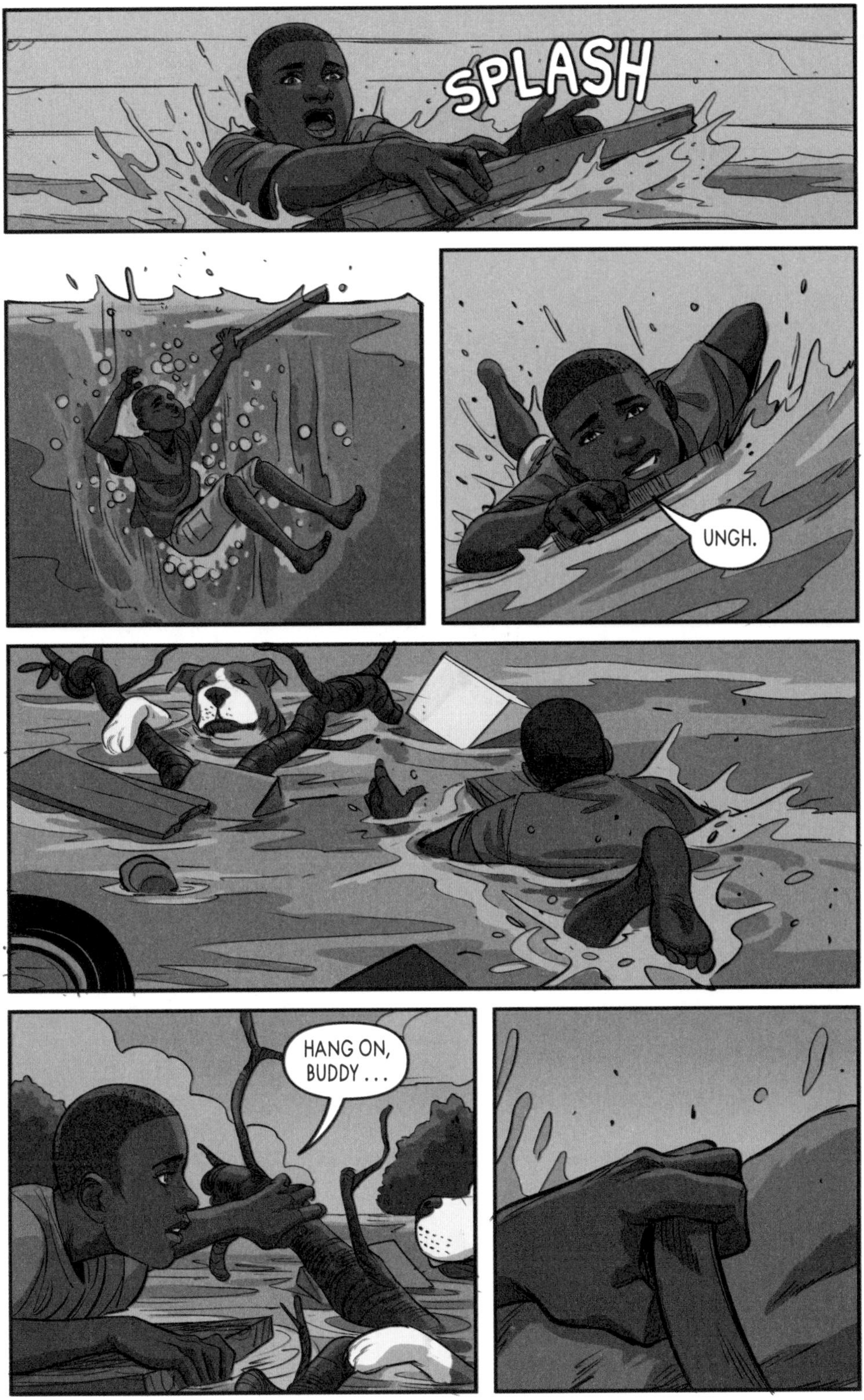
SPLASH
UNGH.
HANG ON, BUDDY . . .

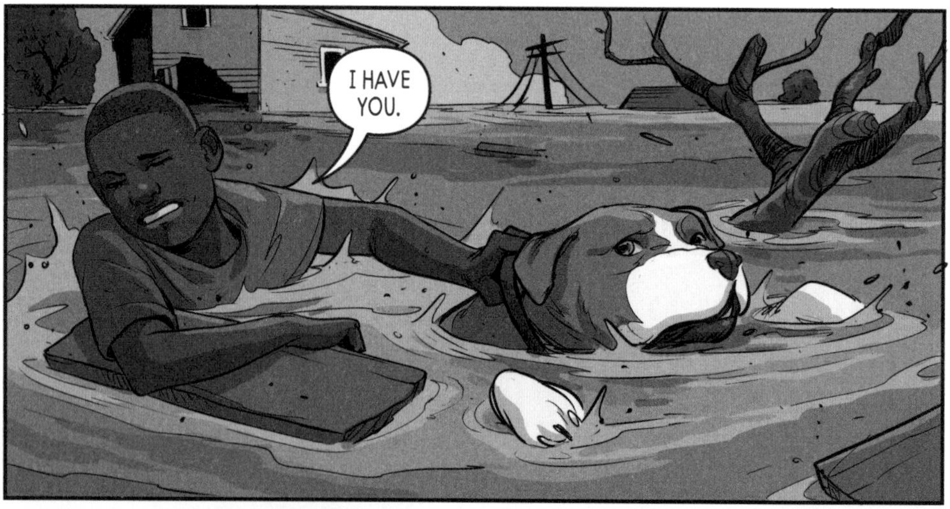
I HAVE YOU.

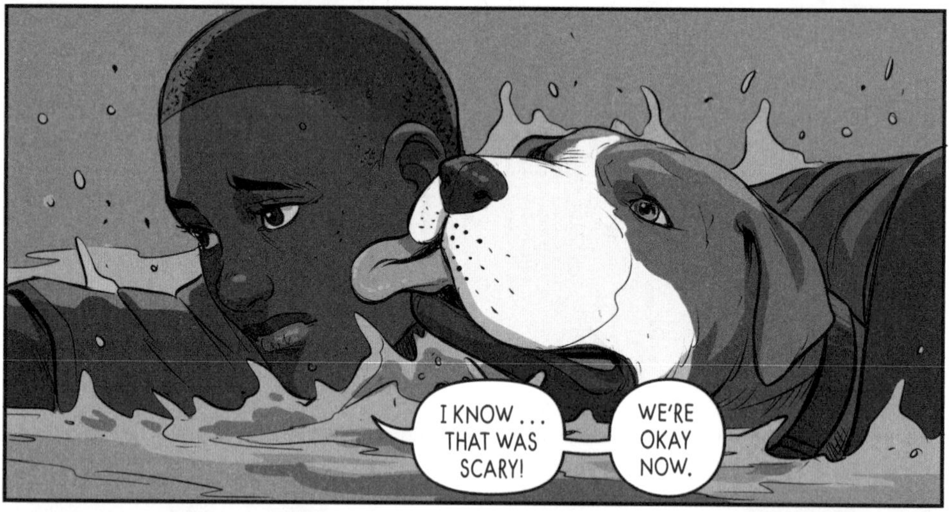
I KNOW . . . THAT WAS SCARY!
WE'RE OKAY NOW.

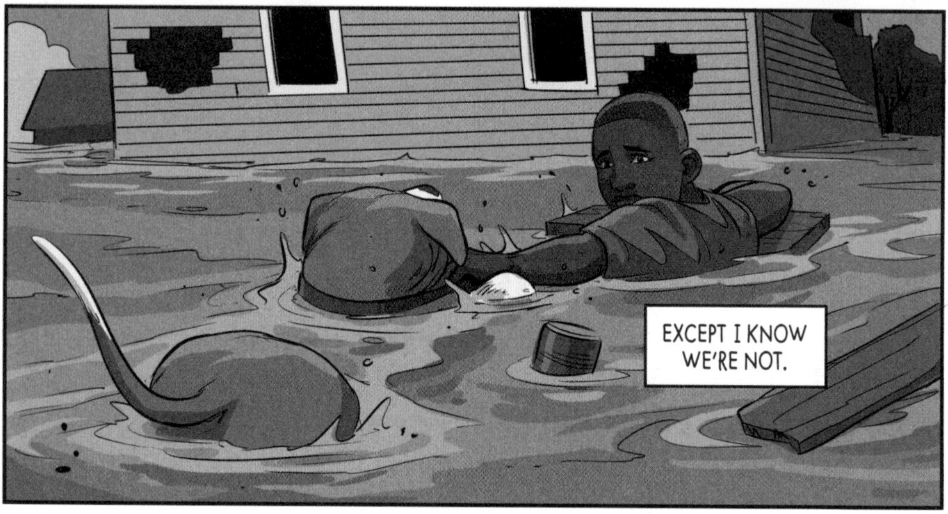
EXCEPT I KNOW WE'RE NOT.

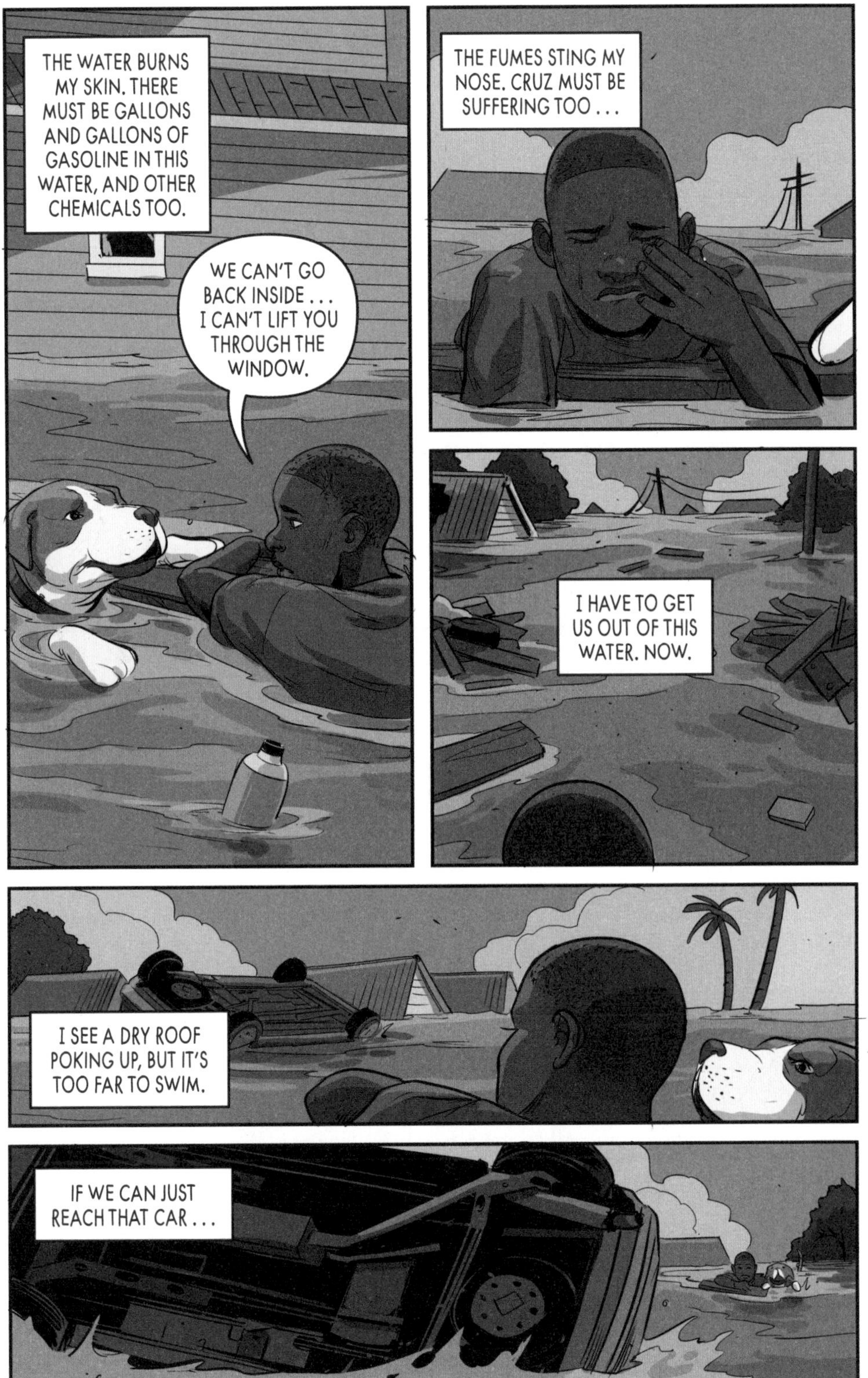
THE WATER BURNS MY SKIN. THERE MUST BE GALLONS AND GALLONS OF GASOLINE IN THIS WATER, AND OTHER CHEMICALS TOO.
WE CAN'T GO BACK INSIDE . . . I CAN'T LIFT YOU THROUGH THE WINDOW.
THE FUMES STING MY NOSE. CRUZ MUST BE SUFFERING TOO . . .
I HAVE TO GET US OUT OF THIS WATER. NOW.
I SEE A DRY ROOF POKING UP, BUT IT'S TOO FAR TO SWIM.
IF WE CAN JUST REACH THAT CAR . . .

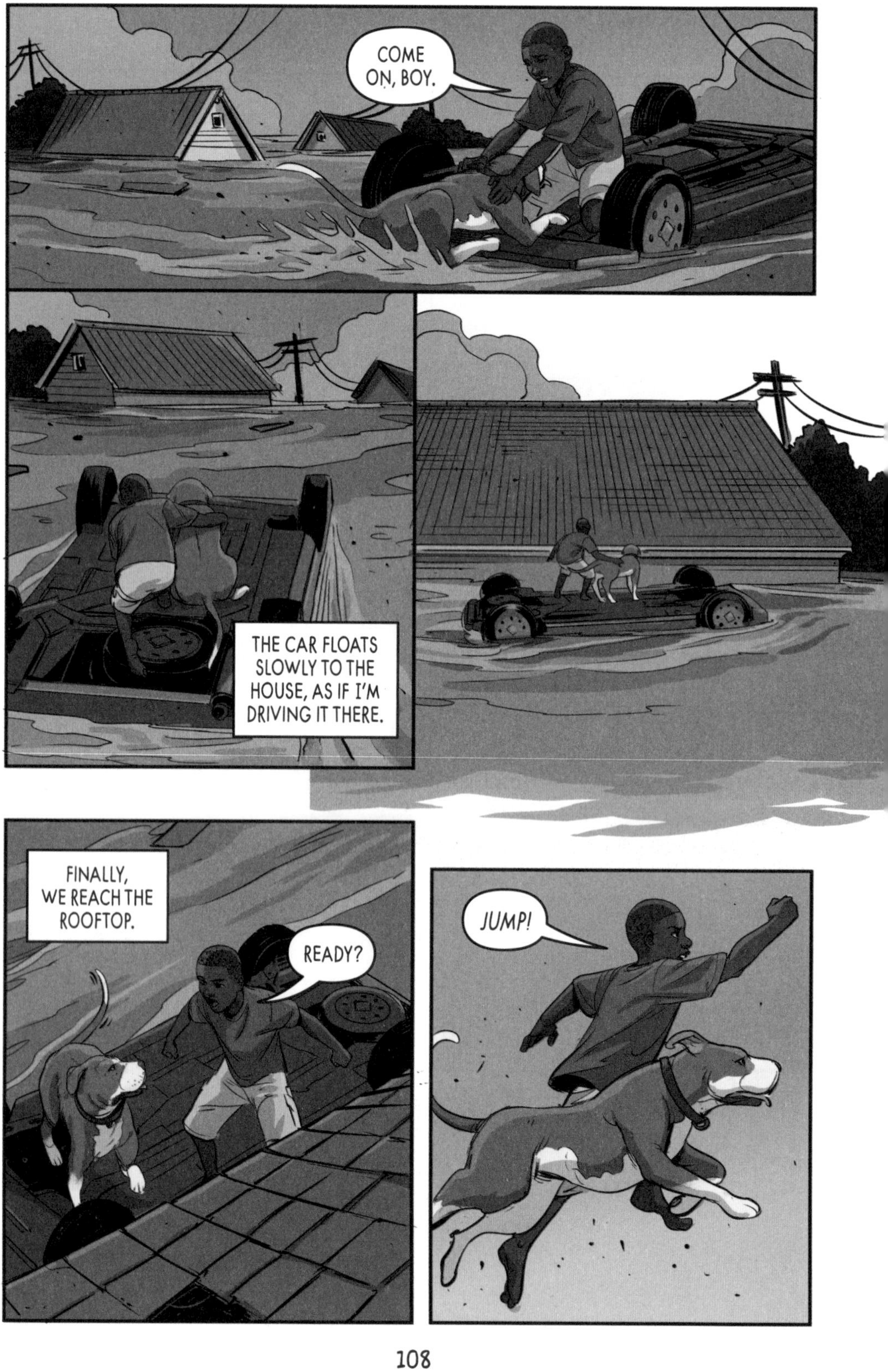
COME ON, BOY.
THE CAR FLOATS SLOWLY TO THE HOUSE, AS IF I'M DRIVING IT THERE.
FINALLY, WE REACH THE ROOFTOP.
READY?
JUMP!

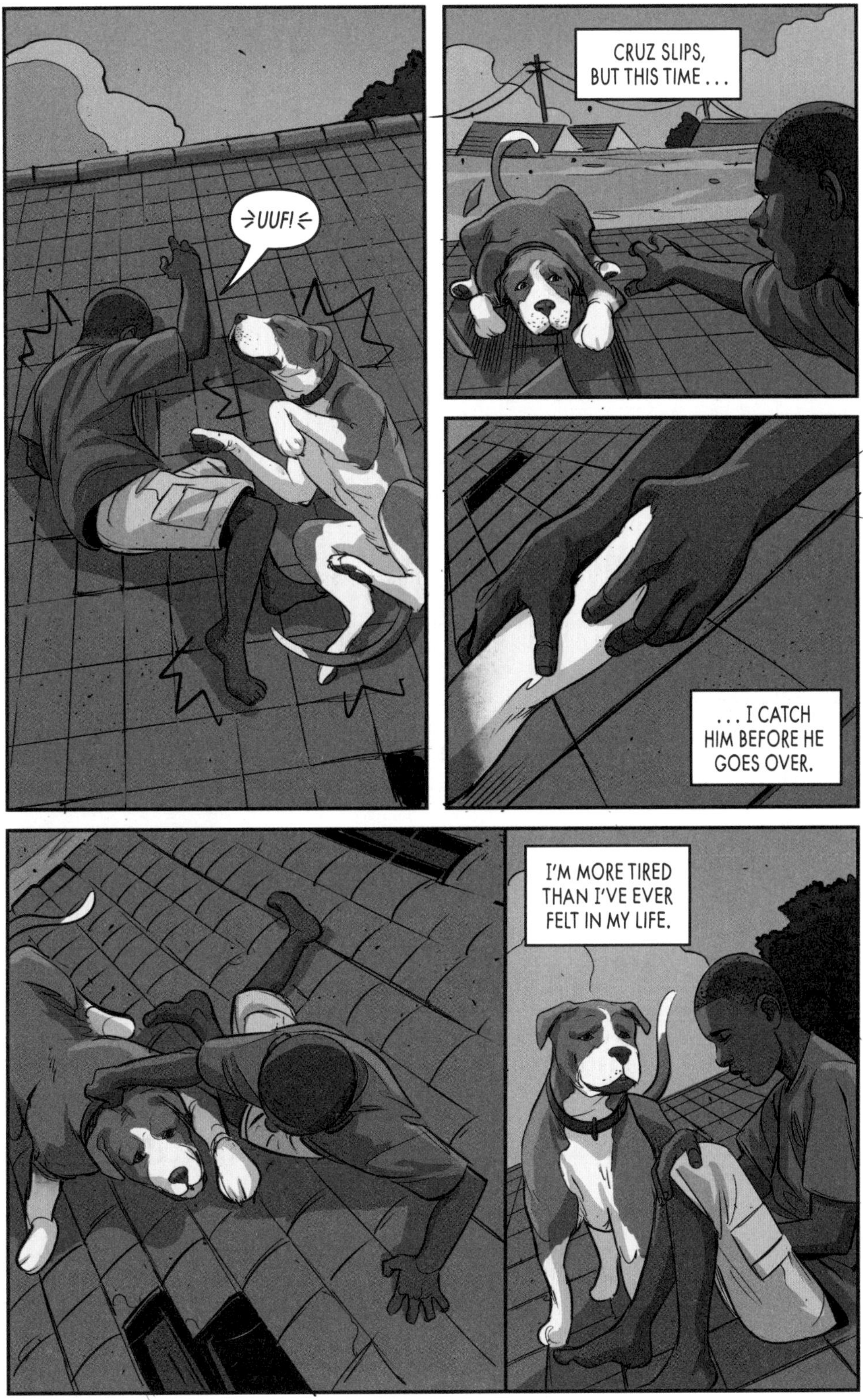
UUF!
CRUZ SLIPS, BUT THIS TIME . . .
. . . I CATCH HIM BEFORE HE GOES OVER.
I'M MORE TIRED THAN I'VE EVER FELT IN MY LIFE.

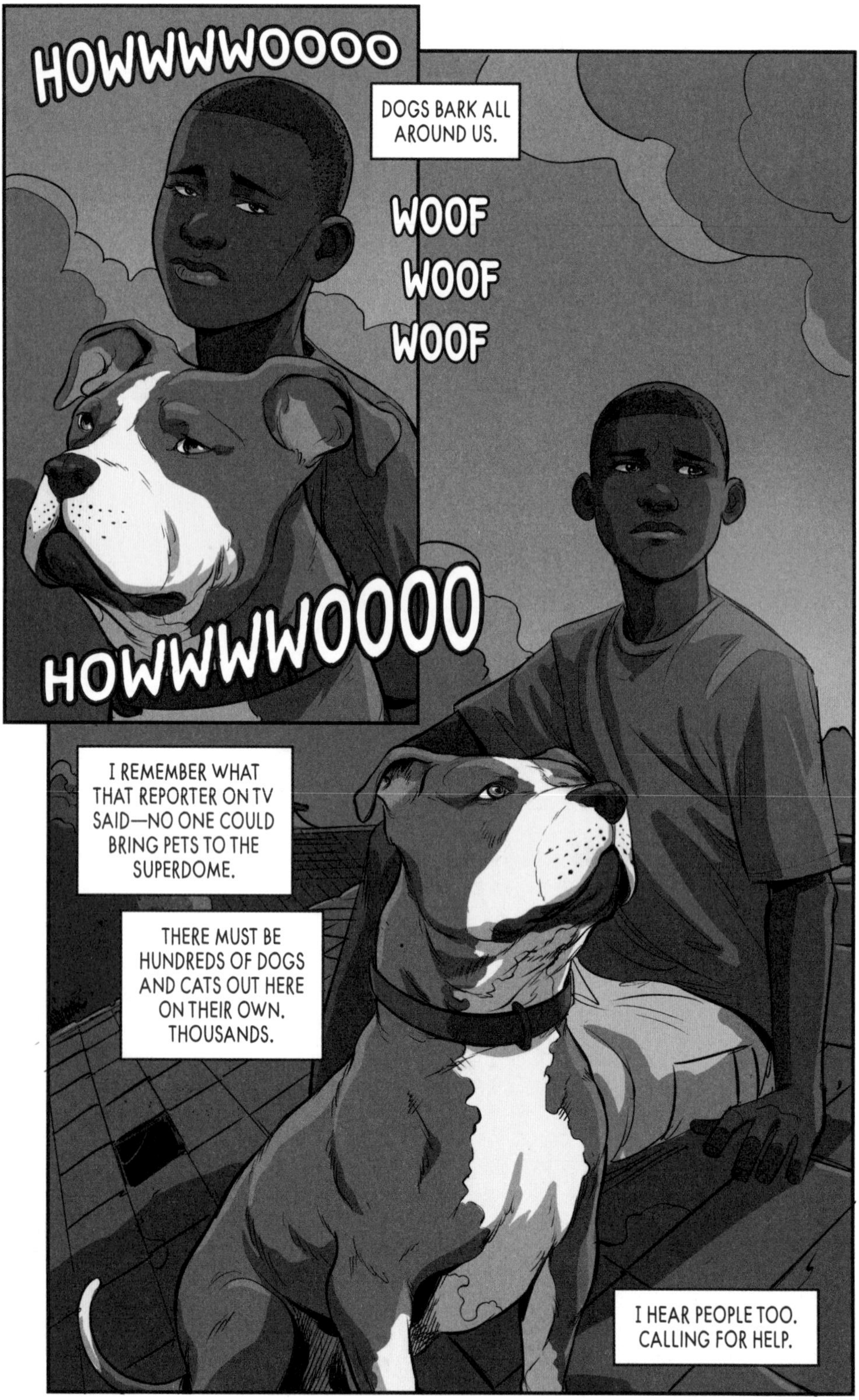
HOWWWWOOOO
DOGS BARK ALL AROUND US.
WOOF
WOOF
WOOF
HOWWWWOOOO
I REMEMBER WHAT THAT REPORTER ON TV SAID—NO ONE COULD BRING PETS TO THE SUPERDOME.
THERE MUST BE HUNDREDS OF DOGS AND CATS OUT HERE ON THEIR OWN. THOUSANDS.
I HEAR PEOPLE TOO. CALLING FOR HELP.

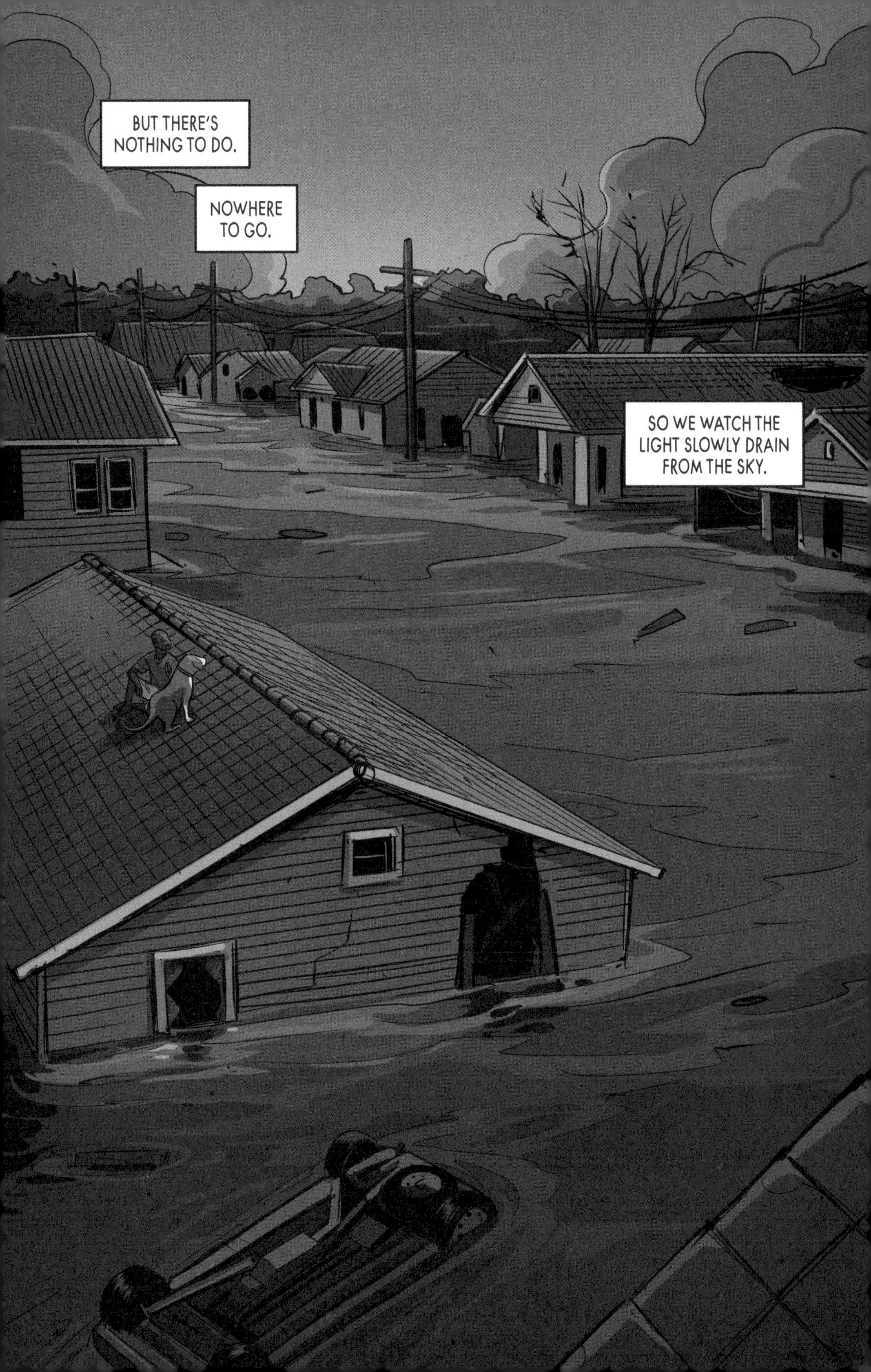
BUT THERE'S NOTHING TO DO.
NOWHERE TO GO.
SO WE WATCH THE LIGHT SLOWLY DRAIN FROM THE SKY.

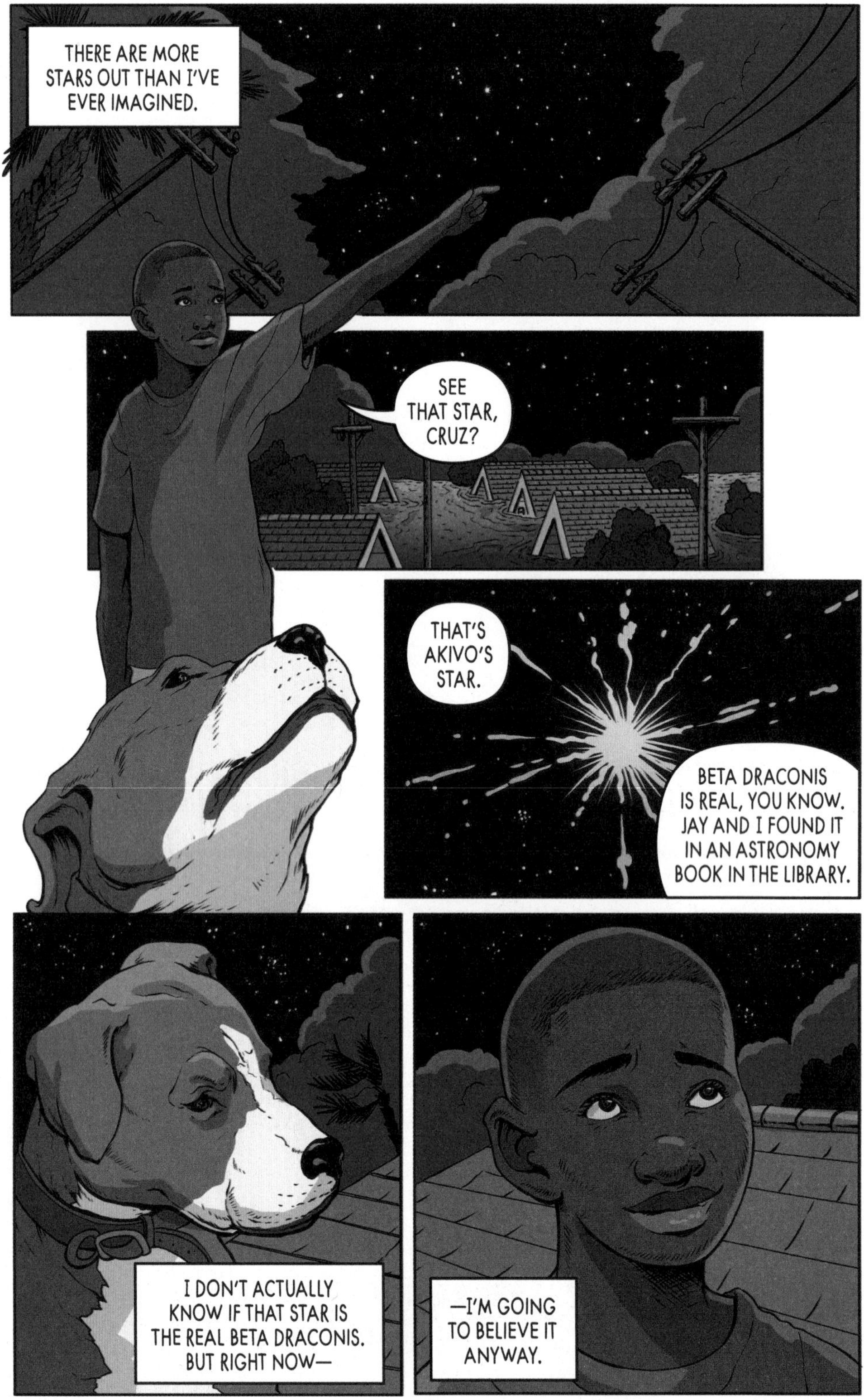
THERE ARE MORE STARS OUT THAN I'VE EVER IMAGINED.
SEE THAT STAR, CRUZ?
THAT'S AKIVO'S STAR.
BETA DRACONIS IS REAL, YOU KNOW. JAY AND I FOUND IT IN AN ASTRONOMY BOOK IN THE LIBRARY.
I DON'T ACTUALLY KNOW IF THAT STAR IS THE REAL BETA DRACONIS. BUT RIGHT NOW—
—I'M GOING TO BELIEVE IT ANYWAY.

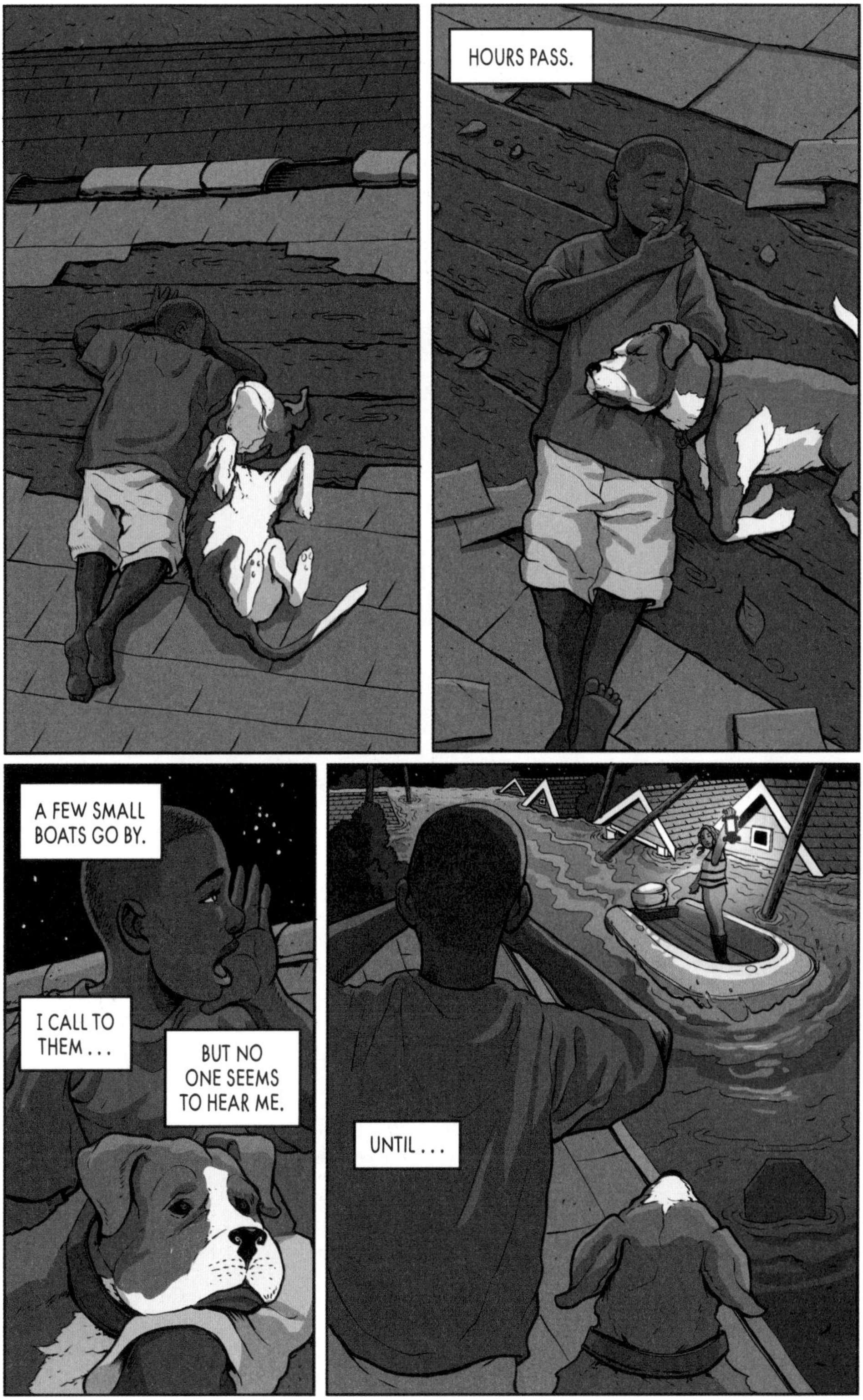
HOURS PASS.
A FEW SMALL BOATS GO BY.
I CALL TO THEM . . .
BUT NO ONE SEEMS TO HEAR ME.
UNTIL . . .

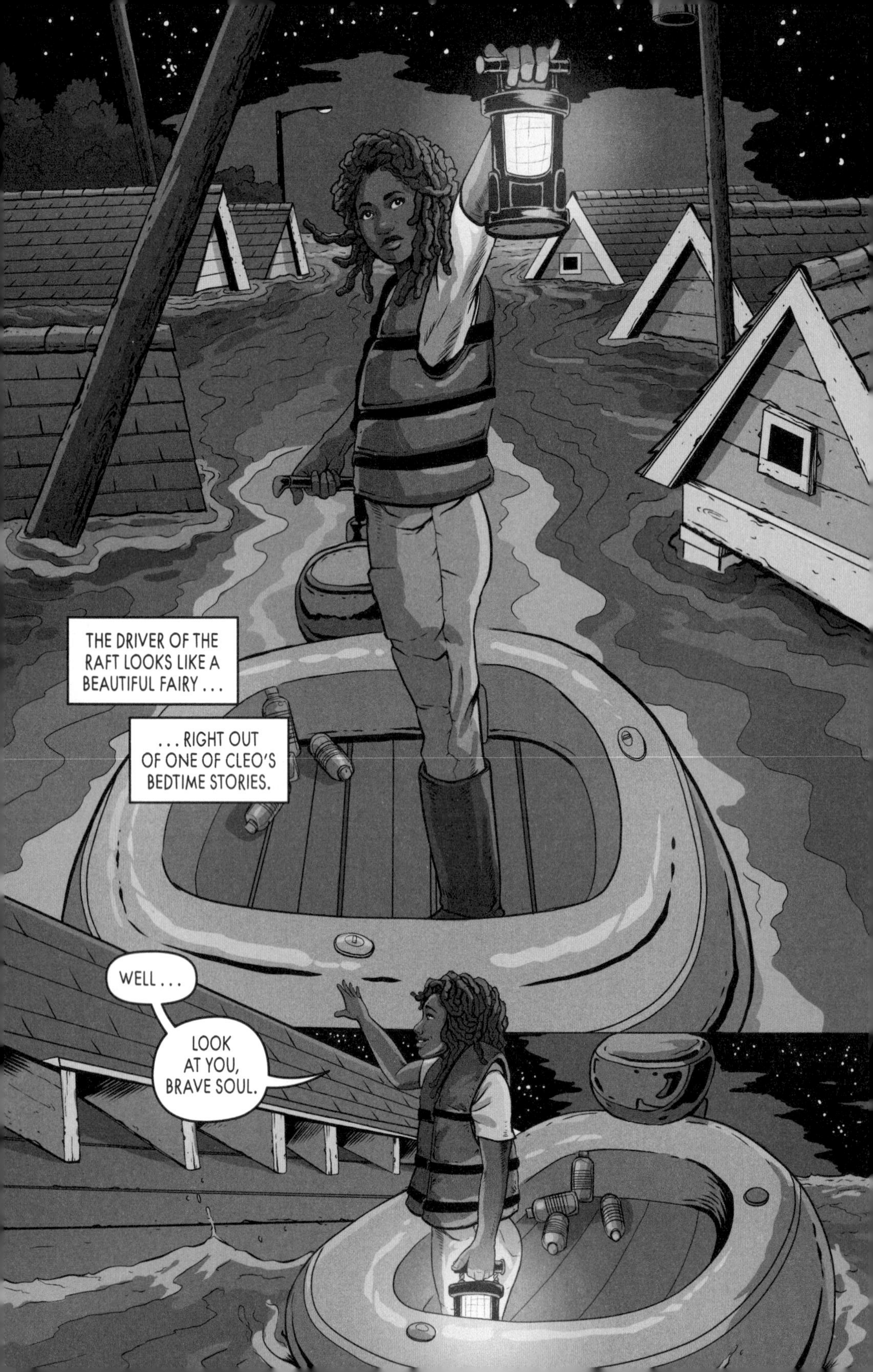
THE DRIVER OF THE RAFT LOOKS LIKE A BEAUTIFUL FAIRY . . .
. . . RIGHT OUT OF ONE OF CLEO'S BEDTIME STORIES.
WELL . . .
LOOK AT YOU, BRAVE SOUL.

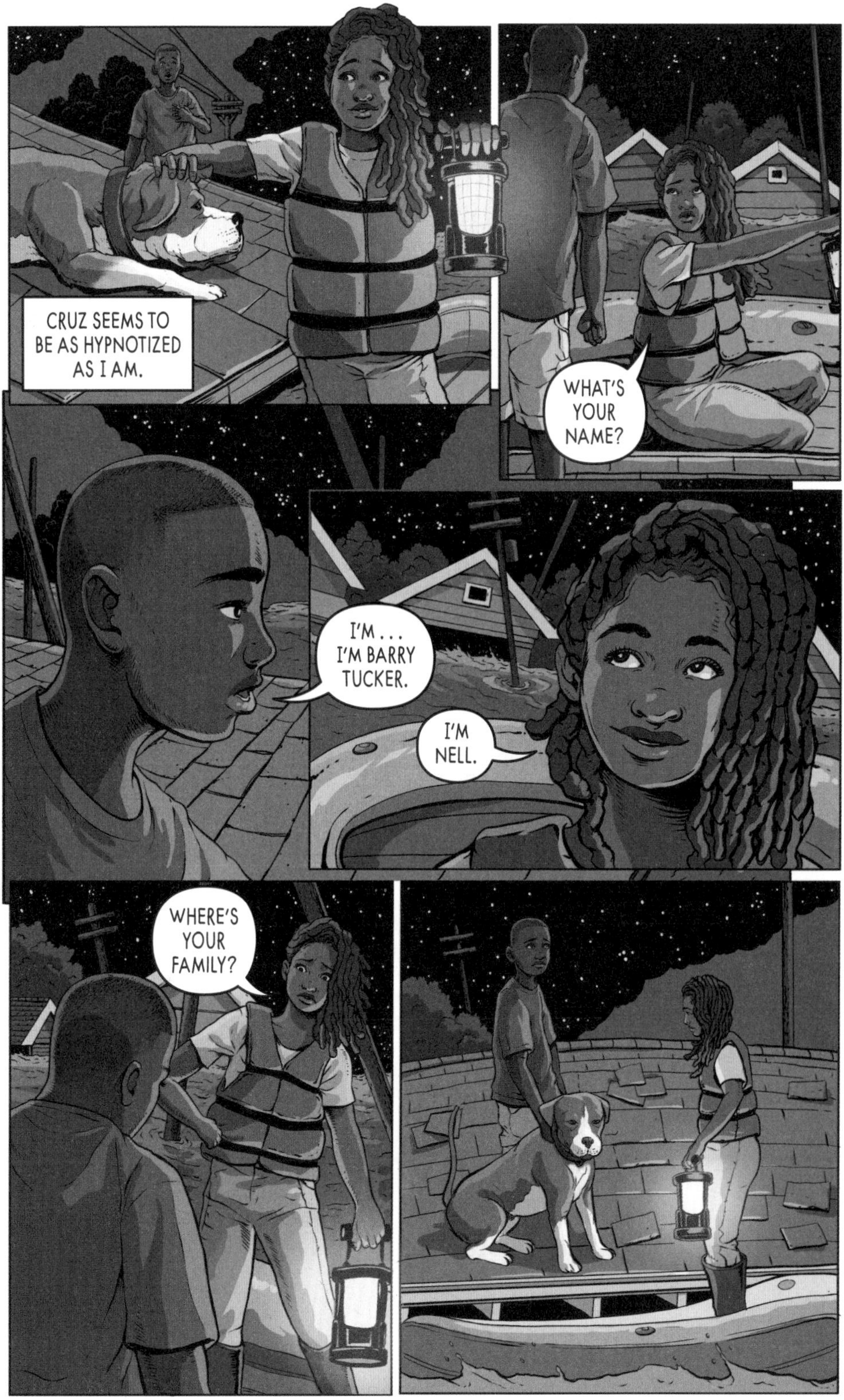
CRUZ SEEMS TO BE AS HYPNOTIZED AS I AM.
WHAT'S YOUR NAME?
I'M . . . I'M BARRY TUCKER.
I'M NELL.
WHERE'S YOUR FAMILY?

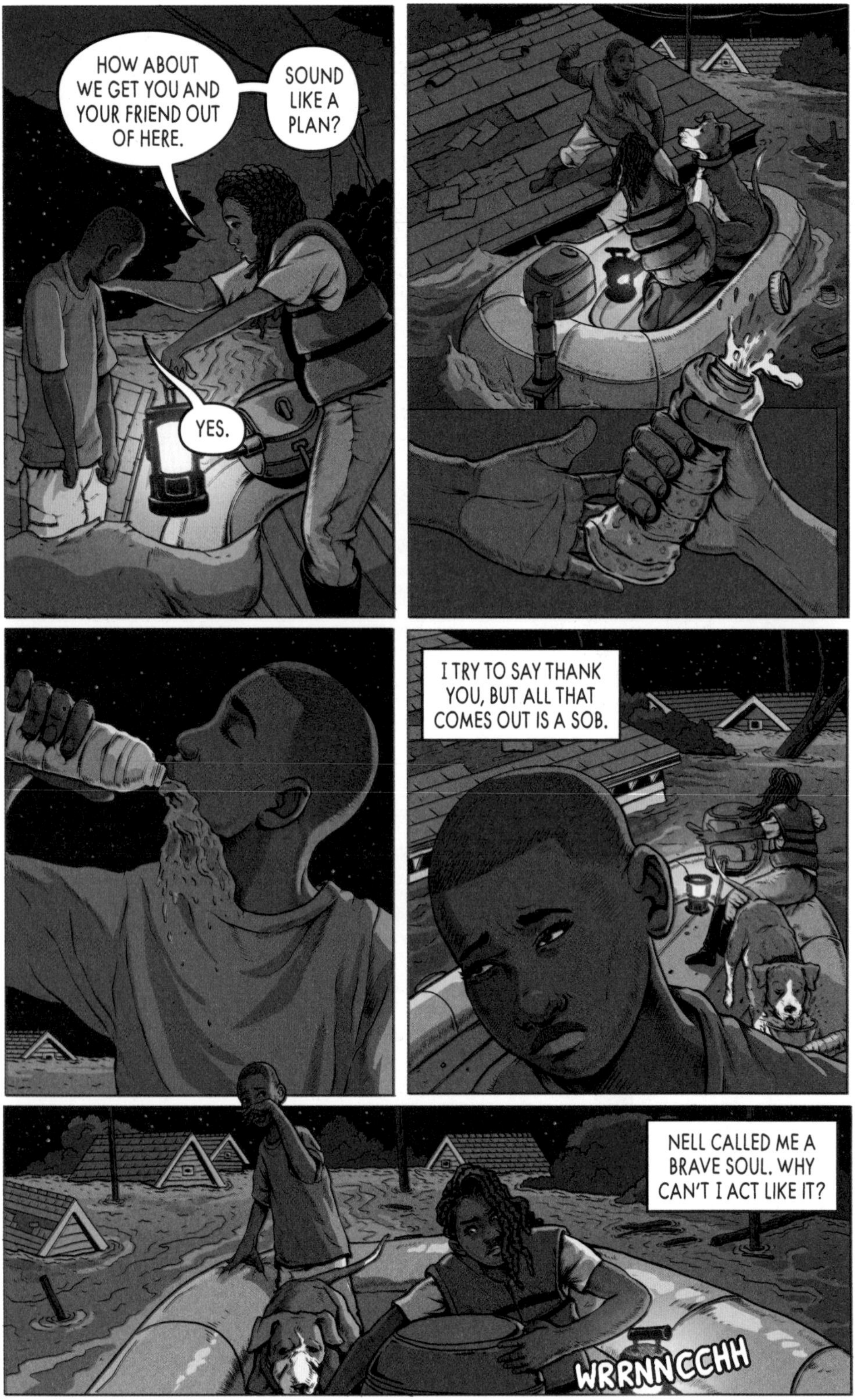
HOW ABOUT WE GET YOU AND YOUR FRIEND OUT OF HERE.
SOUND LIKE A PLAN?
YES.
I TRY TO SAY THANK YOU, BUT ALL THAT COMES OUT IS A SOB.
NELL CALLED ME A BRAVE SOUL. WHY CAN'T I ACT LIKE IT?
WRRNNCCHH

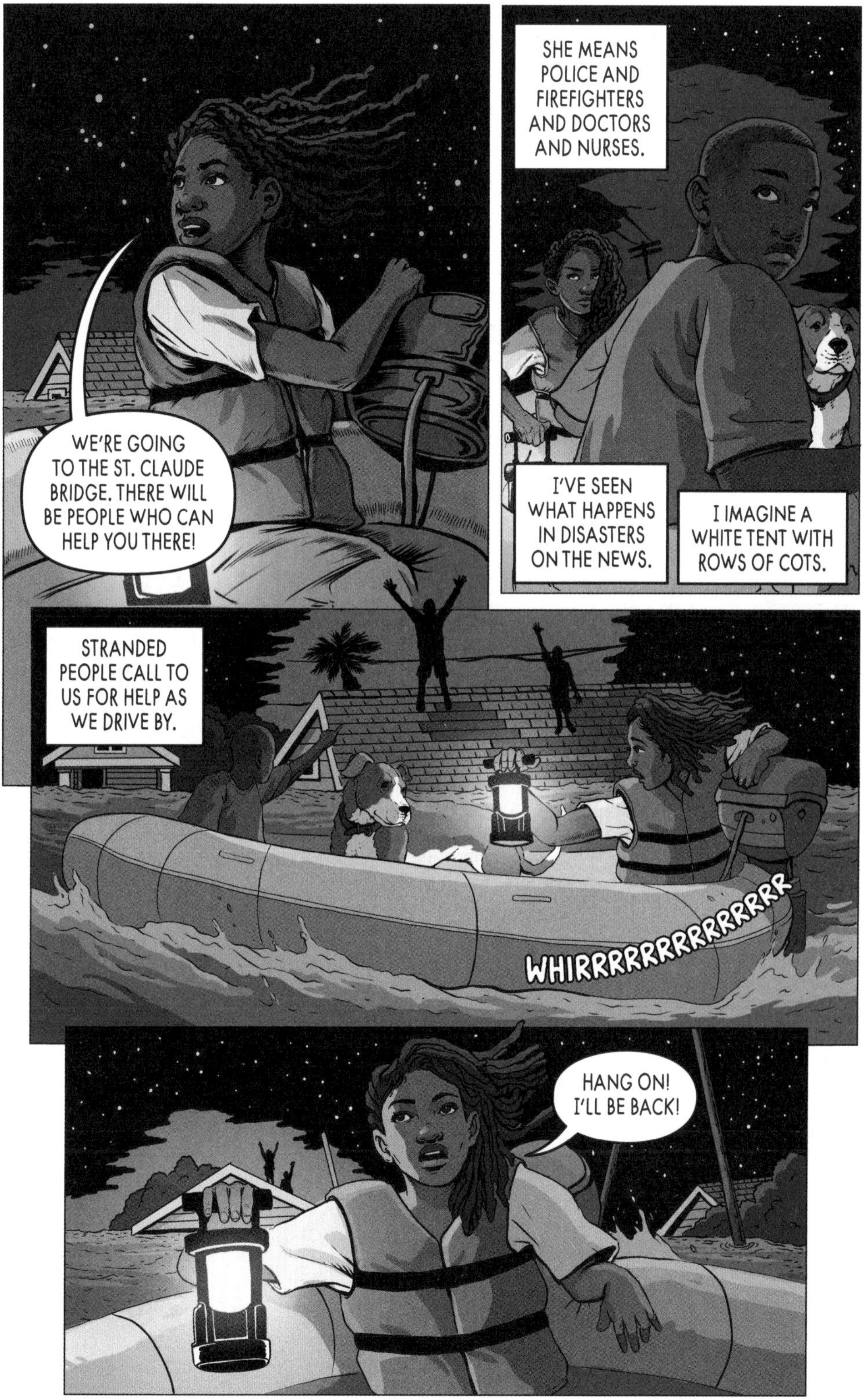
WE'RE GOING TO THE ST. CLAUDE BRIDGE. THERE WILL BE PEOPLE WHO CAN HELP YOU THERE!
SHE MEANS POLICE AND FIREFIGHTERS AND DOCTORS AND NURSES.
I'VE SEEN WHAT HAPPENS IN DISASTERS ON THE NEWS.
I IMAGINE A WHITE TENT WITH ROWS OF COTS.
STRANDED PEOPLE CALL TO US FOR HELP AS WE DRIVE BY.
WHIRRRRRRRRRRRRRR
HANG ON! I'LL BE BACK!

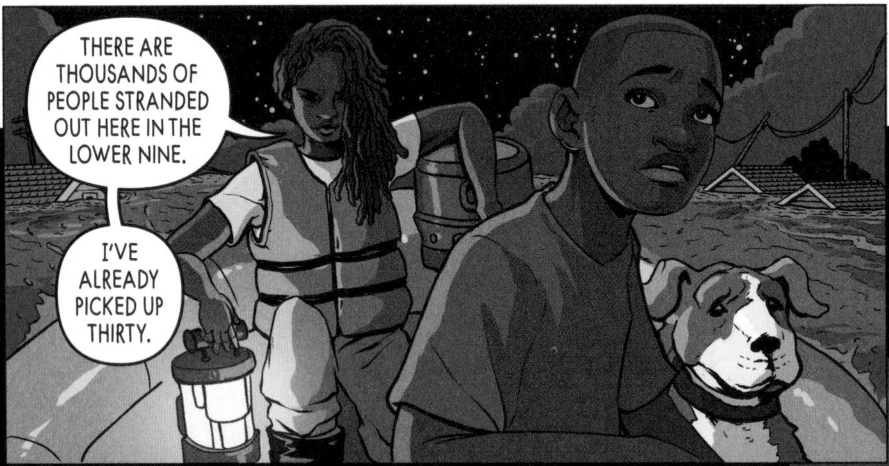
THERE ARE THOUSANDS OF PEOPLE STRANDED OUT HERE IN THE LOWER NINE.
I'VE ALREADY PICKED UP THIRTY.

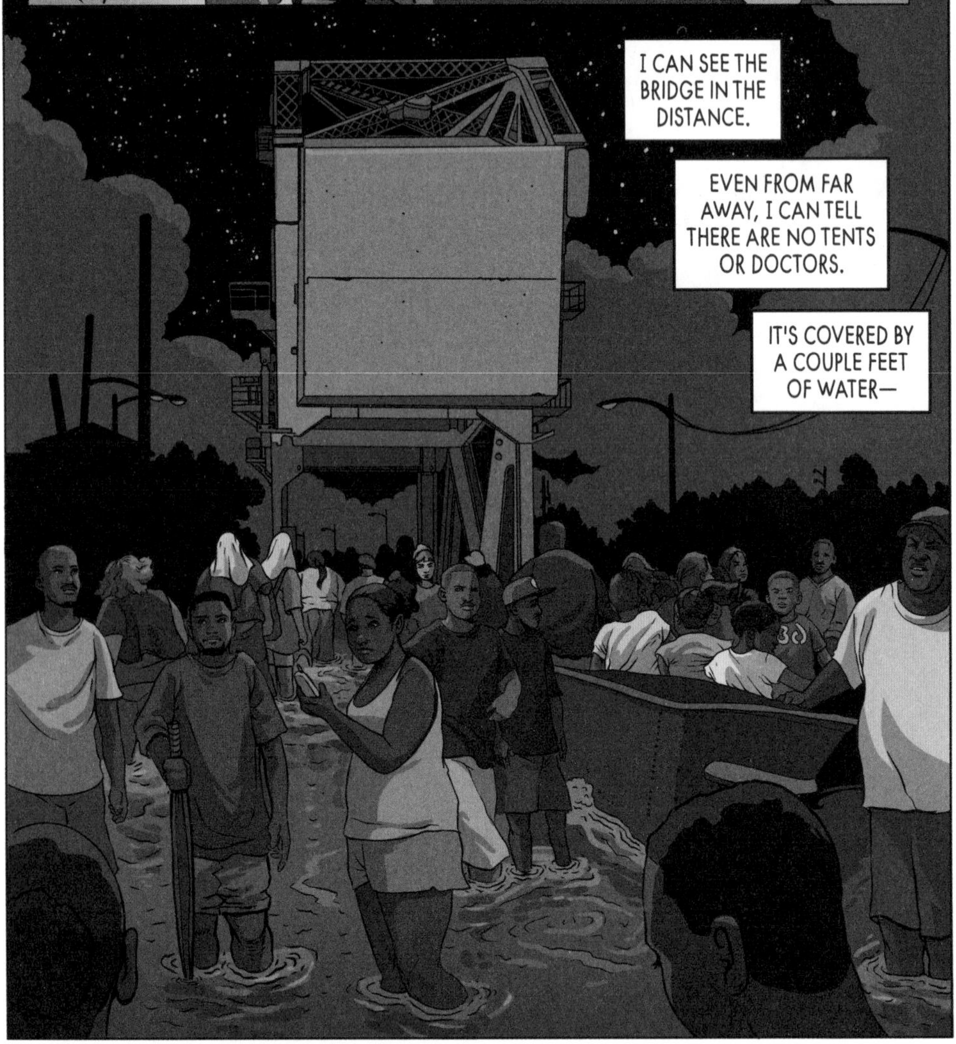
I CAN SEE THE BRIDGE IN THE DISTANCE.
EVEN FROM FAR AWAY, I CAN TELL THERE ARE NO TENTS OR DOCTORS.
IT'S COVERED BY A COUPLE FEET OF WATER—

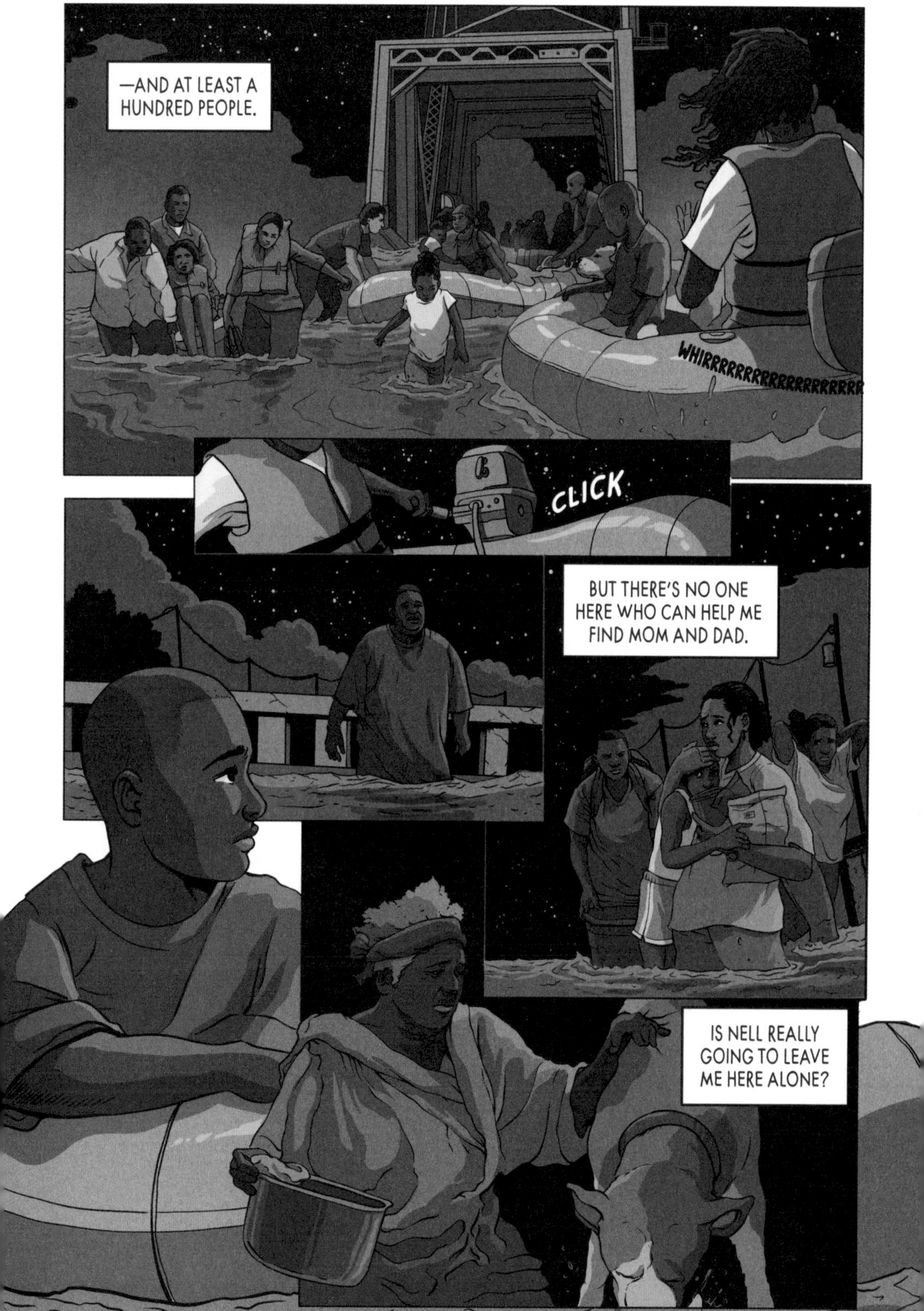
—AND AT LEAST A HUNDRED PEOPLE.
WHIRRRRRRRRRRRRRRRRRRRR
CLICK
BUT THERE'S NO ONE HERE WHO CAN HELP ME FIND MOM AND DAD.
IS NELL REALLY GOING TO LEAVE ME HERE ALONE?

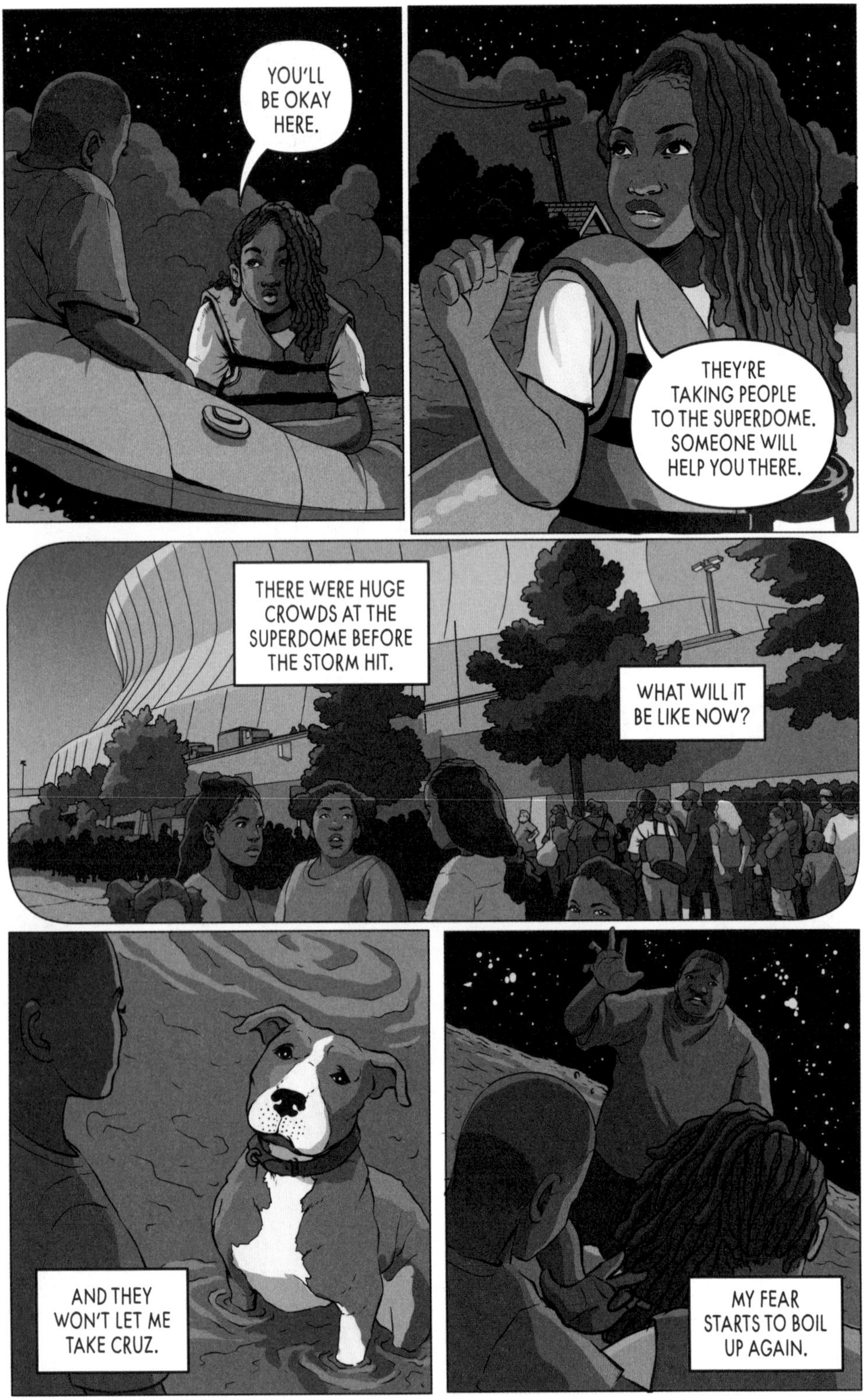
YOU'LL BE OKAY HERE.
THEY'RE TAKING PEOPLE TO THE SUPERDOME. SOMEONE WILL HELP YOU THERE.
THERE WERE HUGE CROWDS AT THE SUPERDOME BEFORE THE STORM HIT.
WHAT WILL IT BE LIKE NOW?
AND THEY WON'T LET ME TAKE CRUZ.
MY FEAR STARTS TO BOIL UP AGAIN.

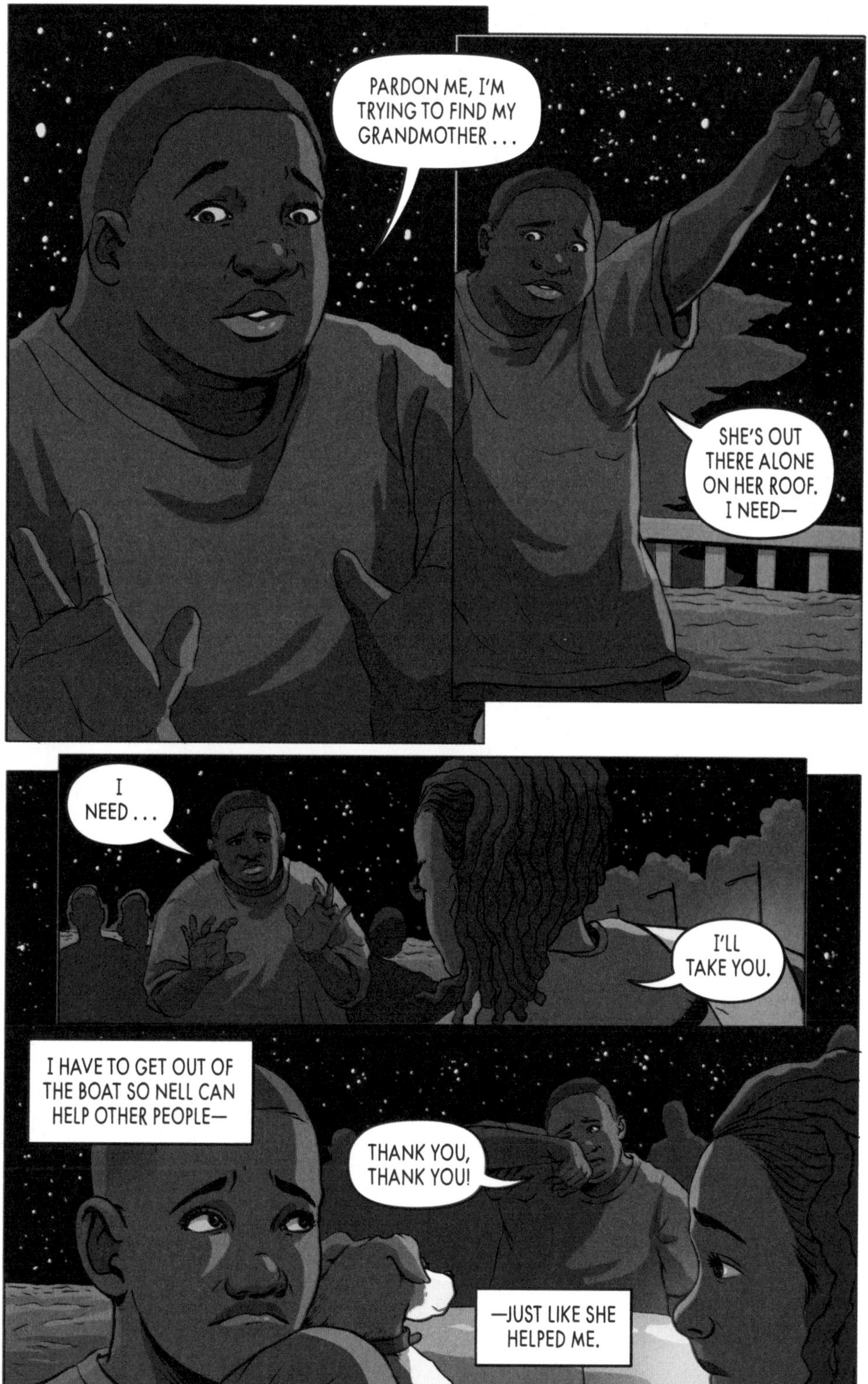
PARDON ME, I'M TRYING TO FIND MY GRANDMOTHER . . .
SHE'S OUT THERE ALONE ON HER ROOF. I NEED—
I NEED . . .
I'LL TAKE YOU.
I HAVE TO GET OUT OF THE BOAT SO NELL CAN HELP OTHER PEOPLE—
THANK YOU, THANK YOU!
—JUST LIKE SHE HELPED ME.

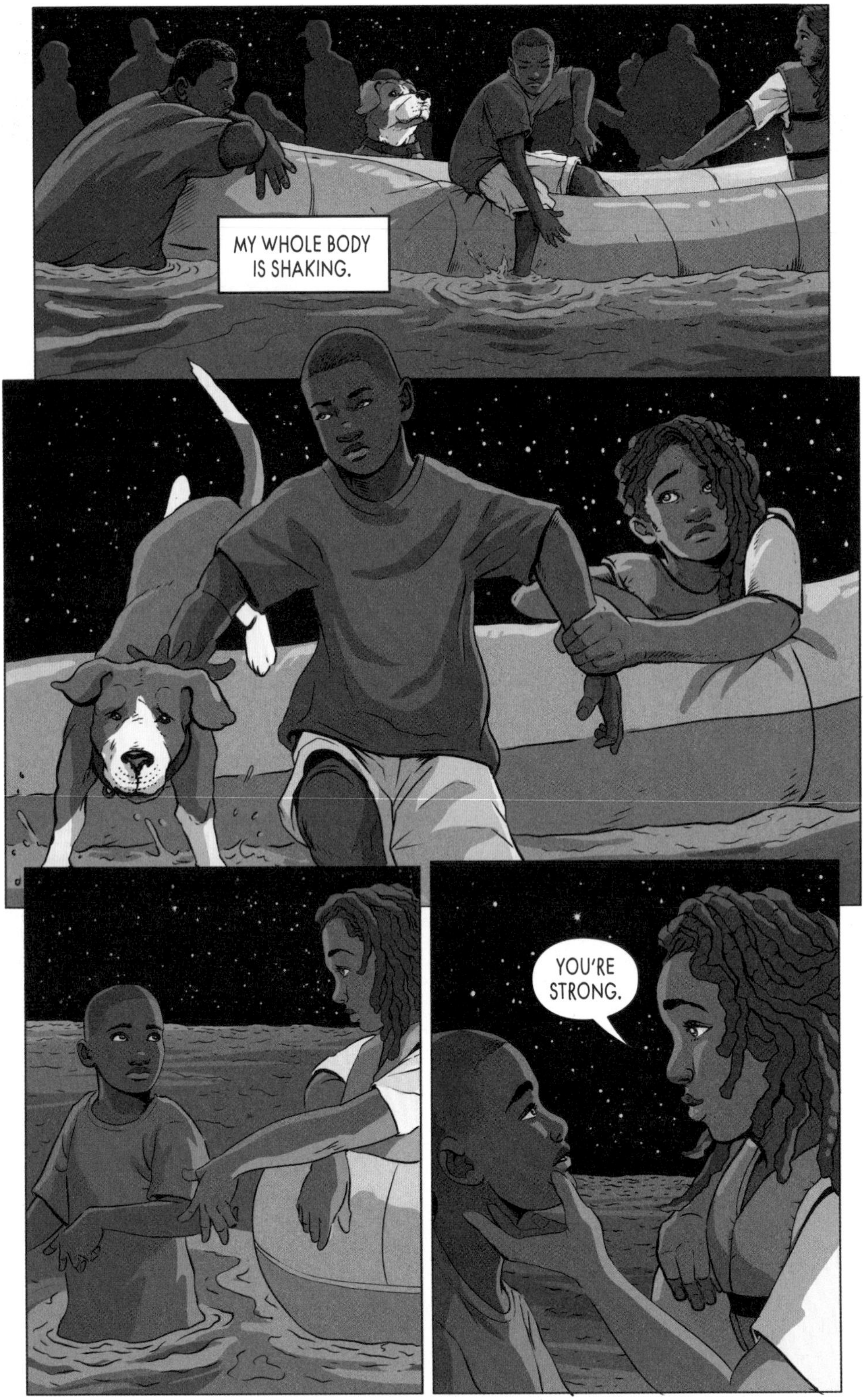
MY WHOLE BODY IS SHAKING.
YOU'RE STRONG.

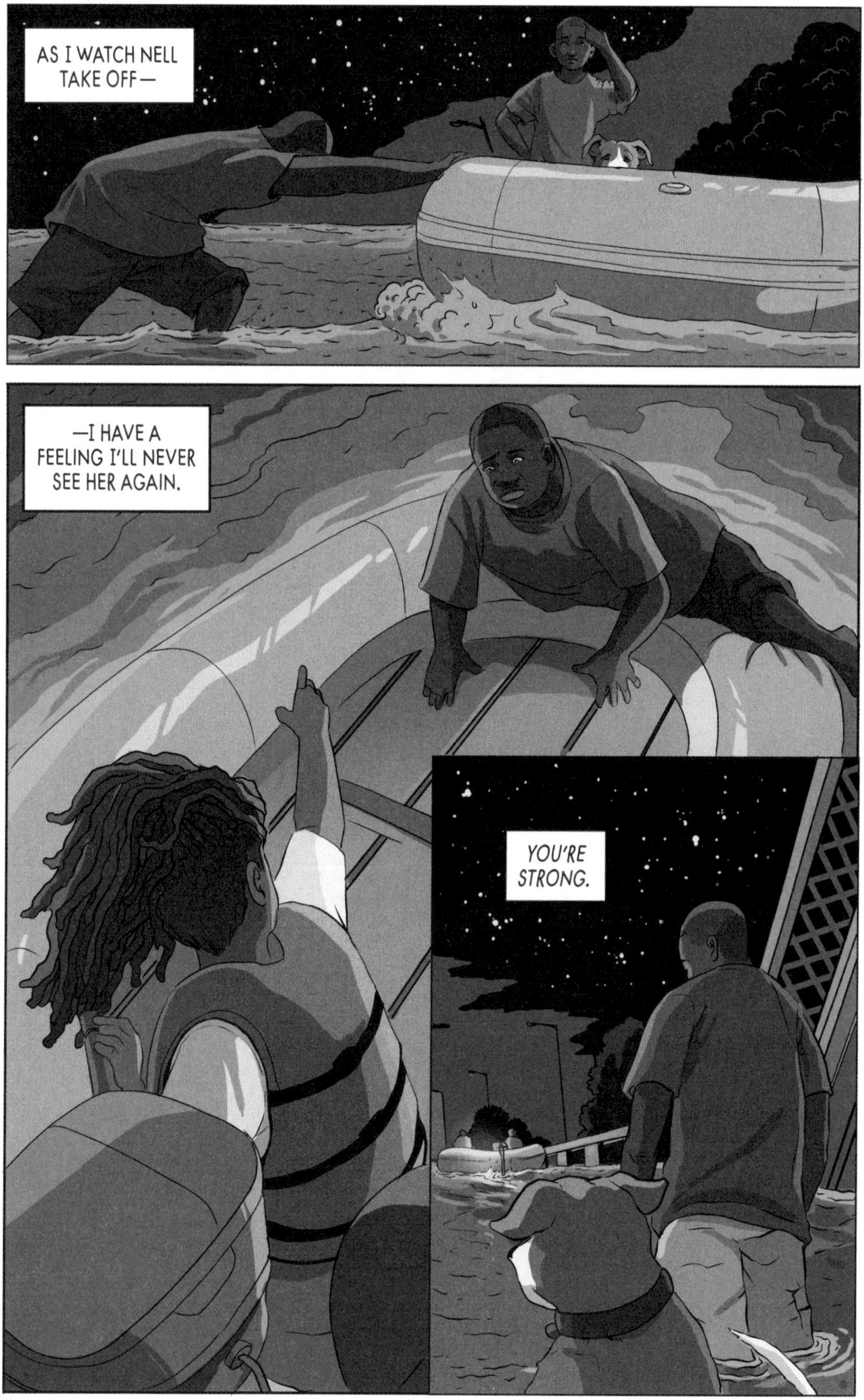
AS I WATCH NELL TAKE OFF—
—I HAVE A FEELING I'LL NEVER SEE HER AGAIN.
YOU'RE STRONG.

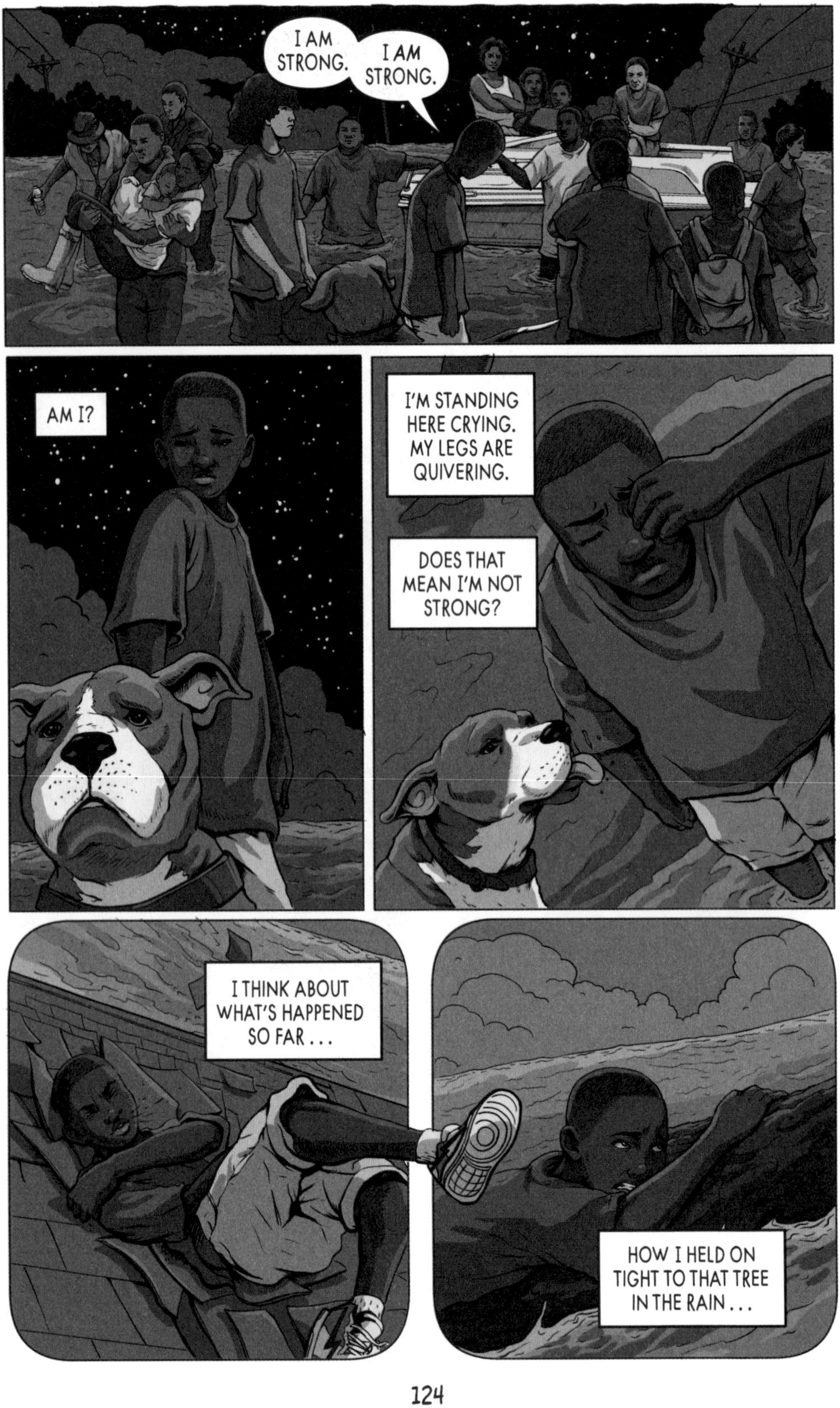
I AM STRONG.
I *AM* STRONG.
AM I?
I'M STANDING HERE CRYING. MY LEGS ARE QUIVERING.
DOES THAT MEAN I'M NOT STRONG?
I THINK ABOUT WHAT'S HAPPENED SO FAR . . .
HOW I HELD ON TIGHT TO THAT TREE IN THE RAIN . . .

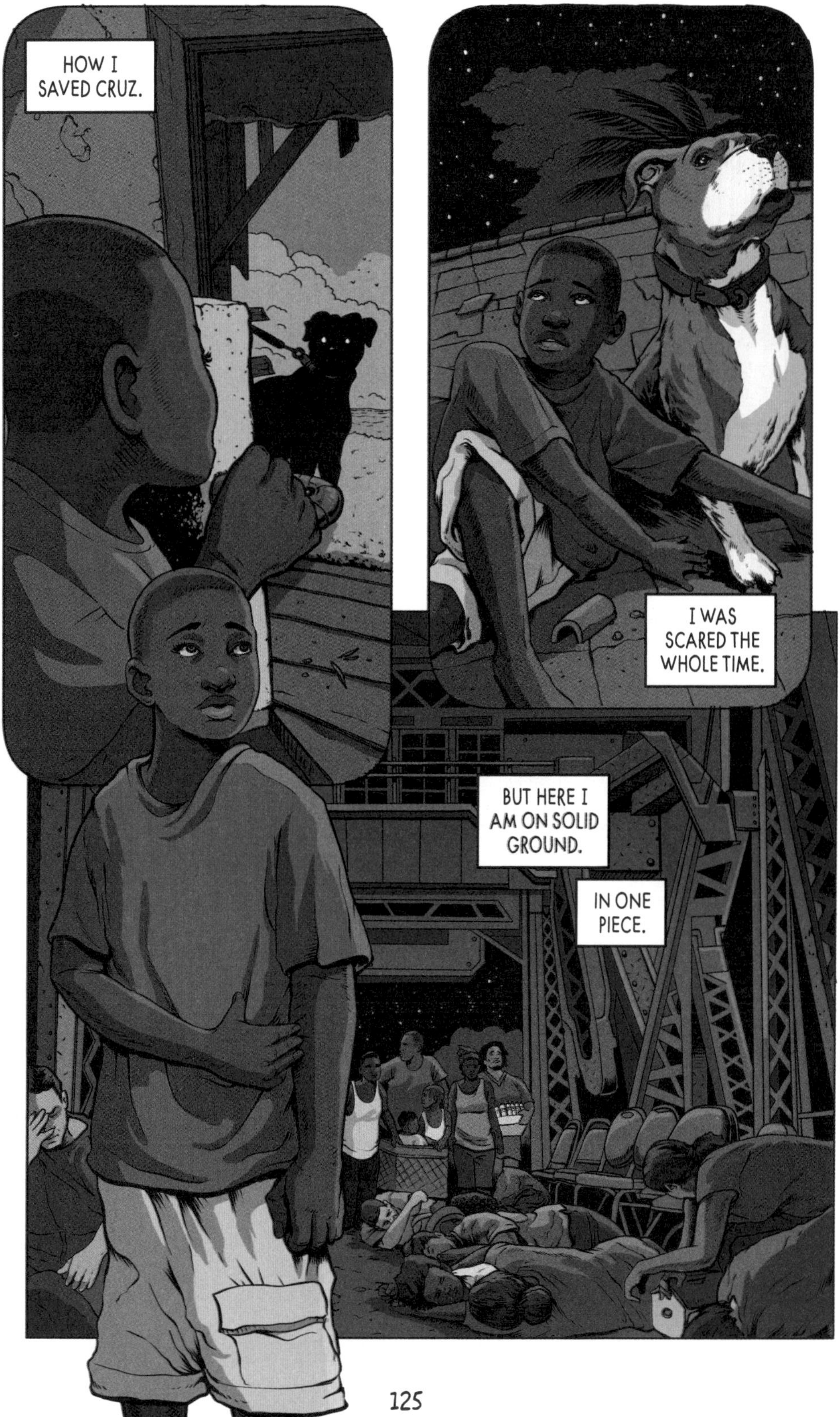
HOW I SAVED CRUZ.
I WAS SCARED THE WHOLE TIME.
BUT HERE I AM ON SOLID GROUND.
IN ONE PIECE.

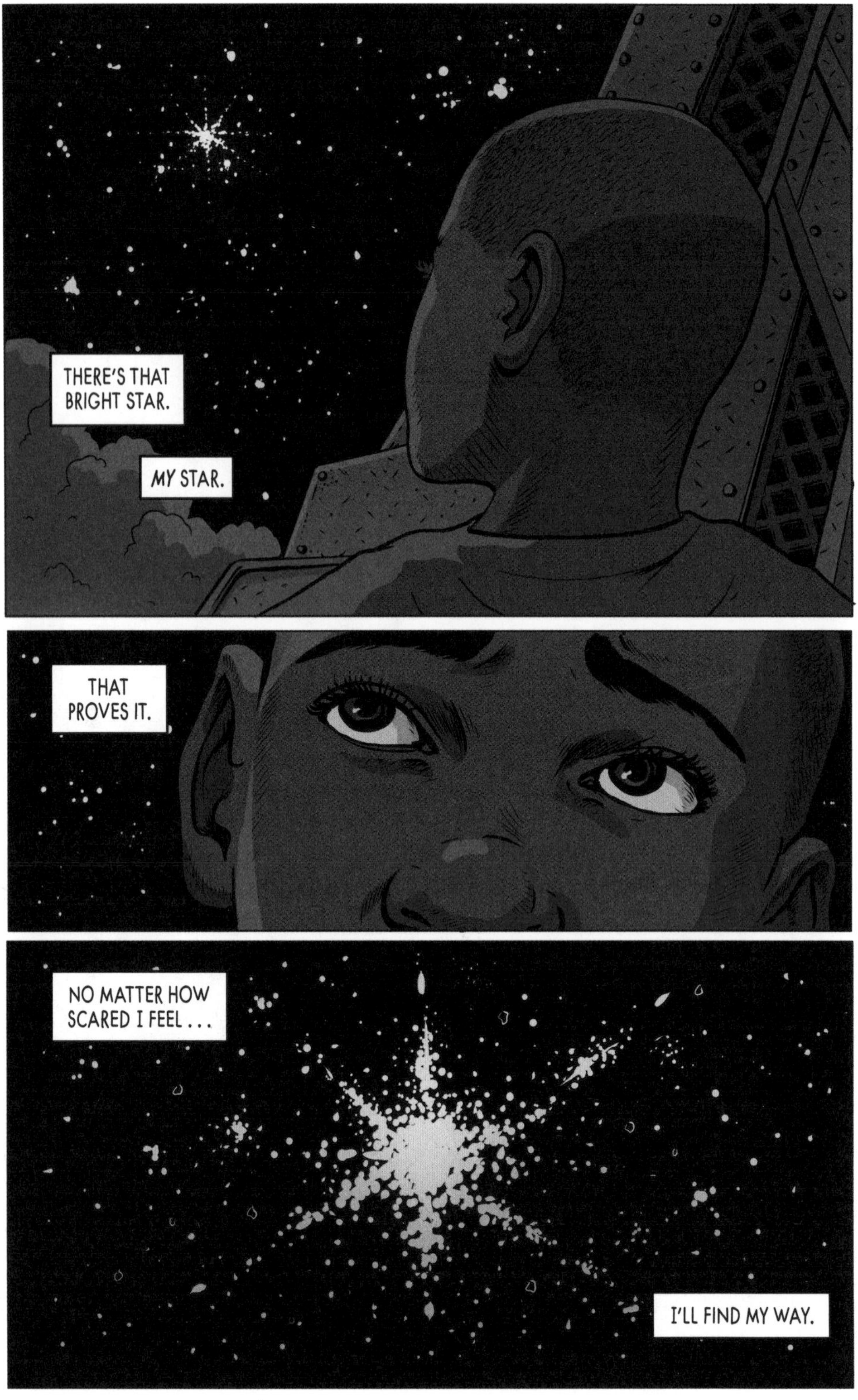
THERE'S THAT BRIGHT STAR.
MY STAR.
THAT PROVES IT.
NO MATTER HOW SCARED I FEEL . . .
I'LL FIND MY WAY.

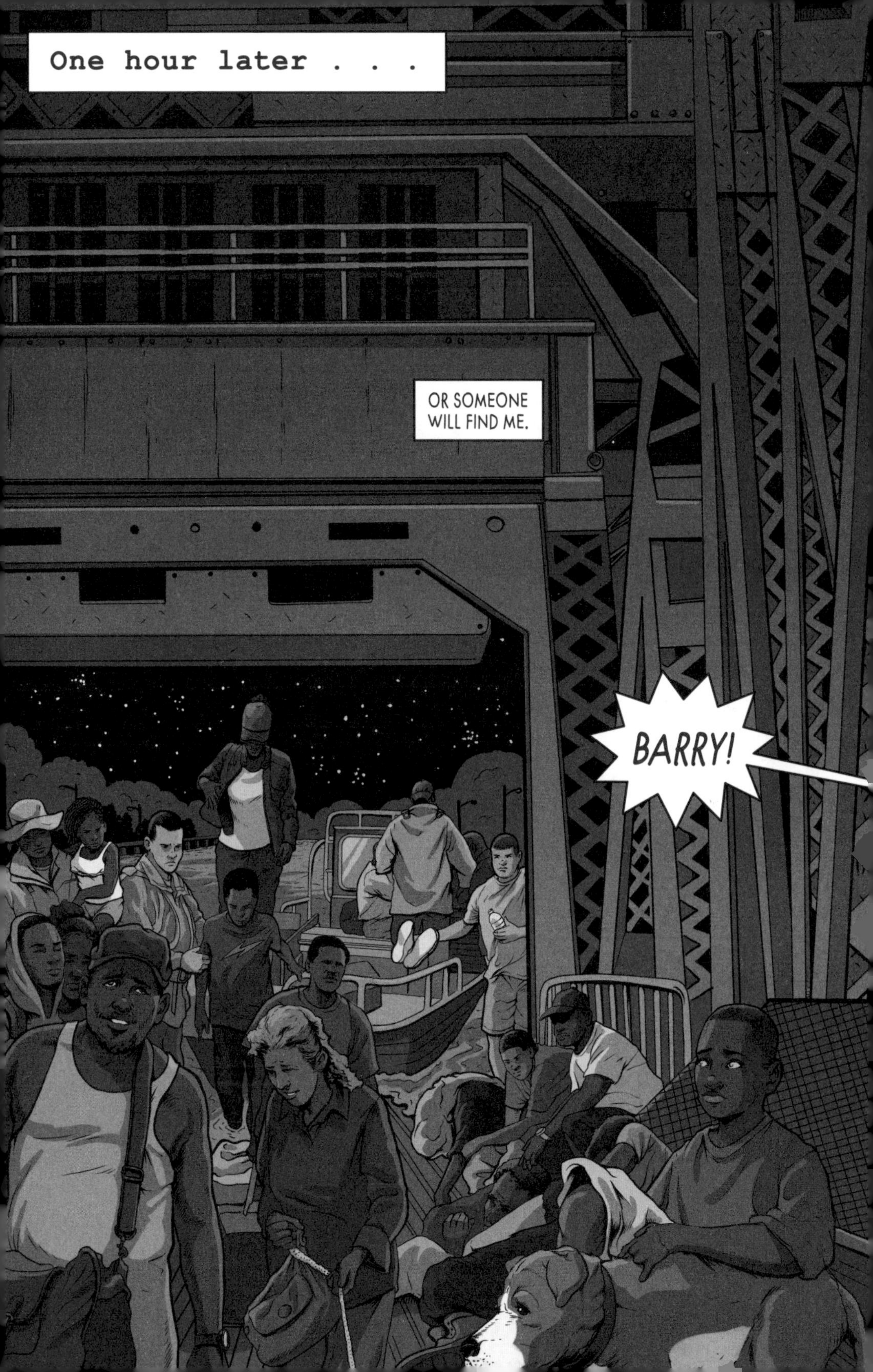

One hour later . . .
OR SOMEONE WILL FIND ME.
BARRY!

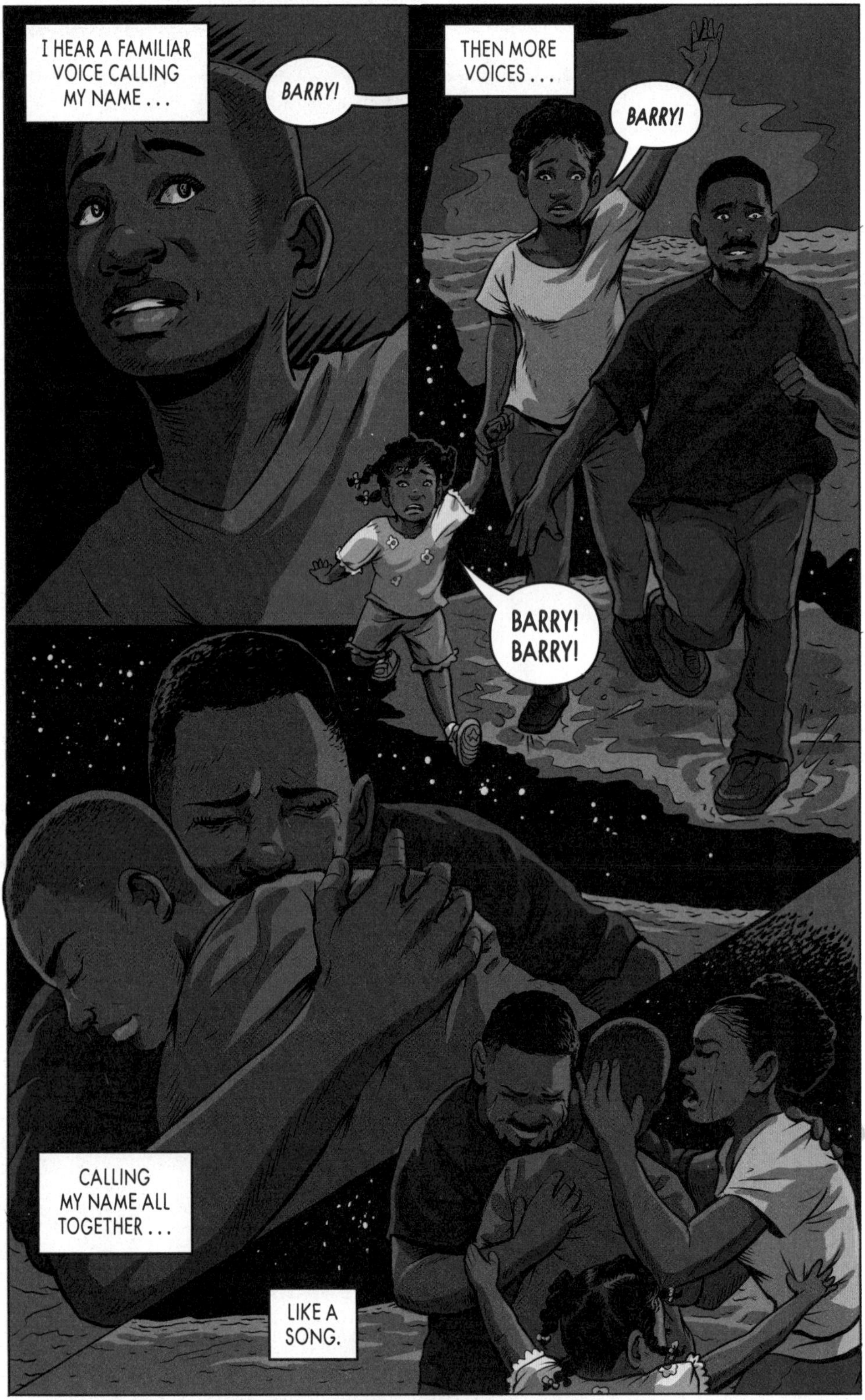
I HEAR A FAMILIAR VOICE CALLING MY NAME . . .
BARRY!
THEN MORE VOICES . . .
BARRY!
BARRY! BARRY!
CALLING MY NAME ALL TOGETHER . . .
LIKE A SONG.

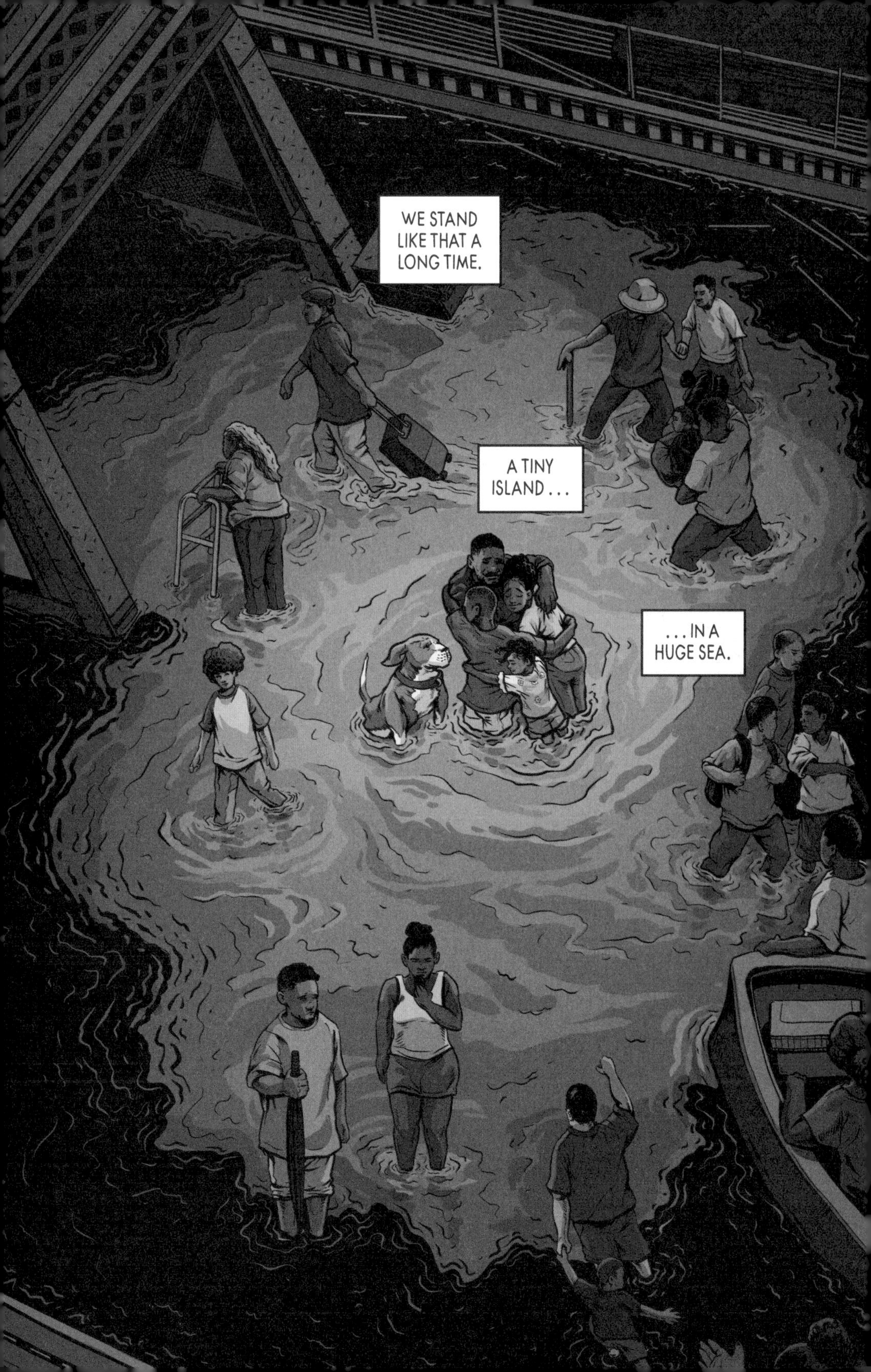
WE STAND LIKE THAT A LONG TIME.
A TINY ISLAND . . .
. . . IN A HUGE SEA.

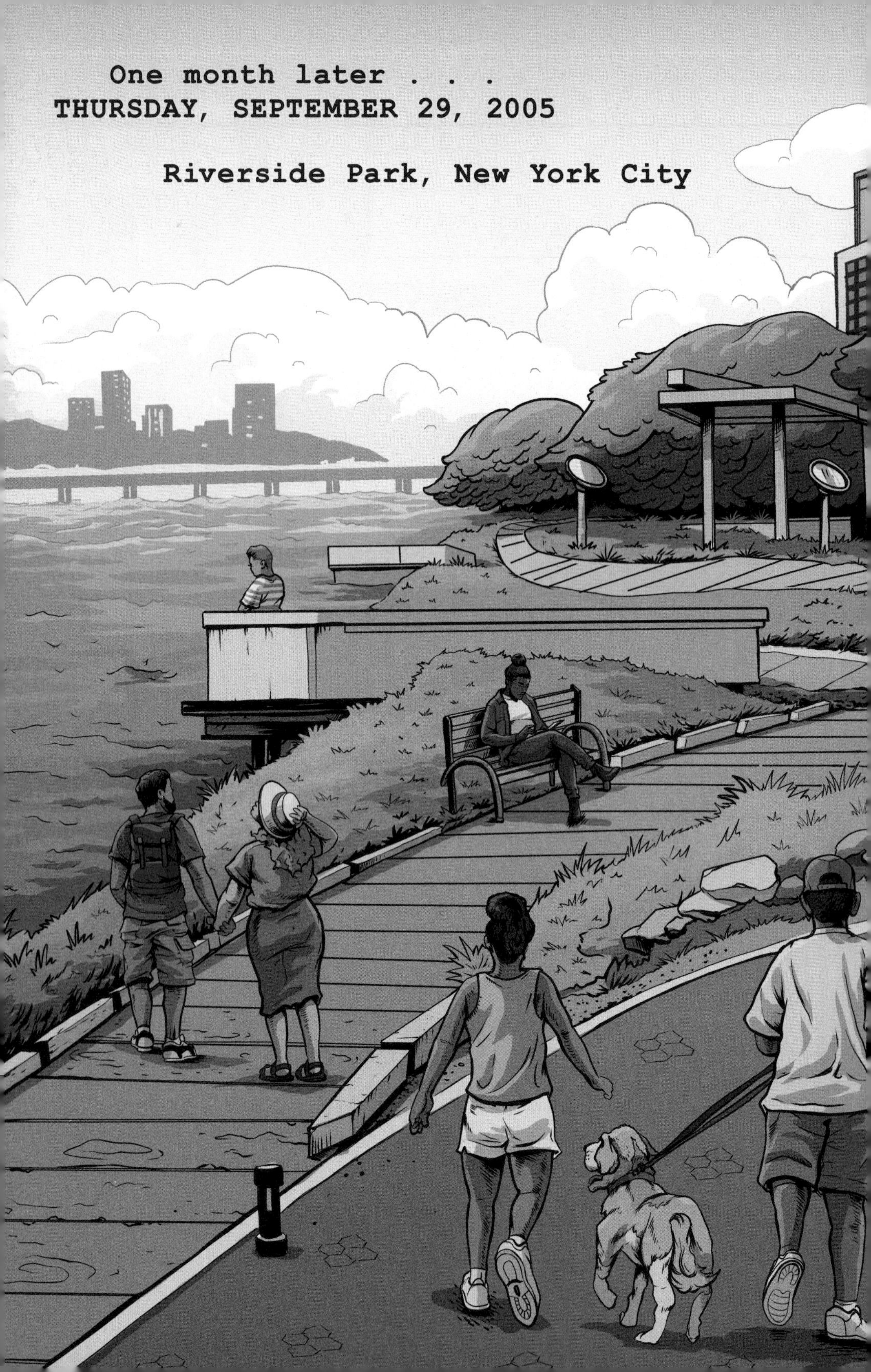
One month later . . .
THURSDAY, SEPTEMBER 29, 2005
Riverside Park, New York City

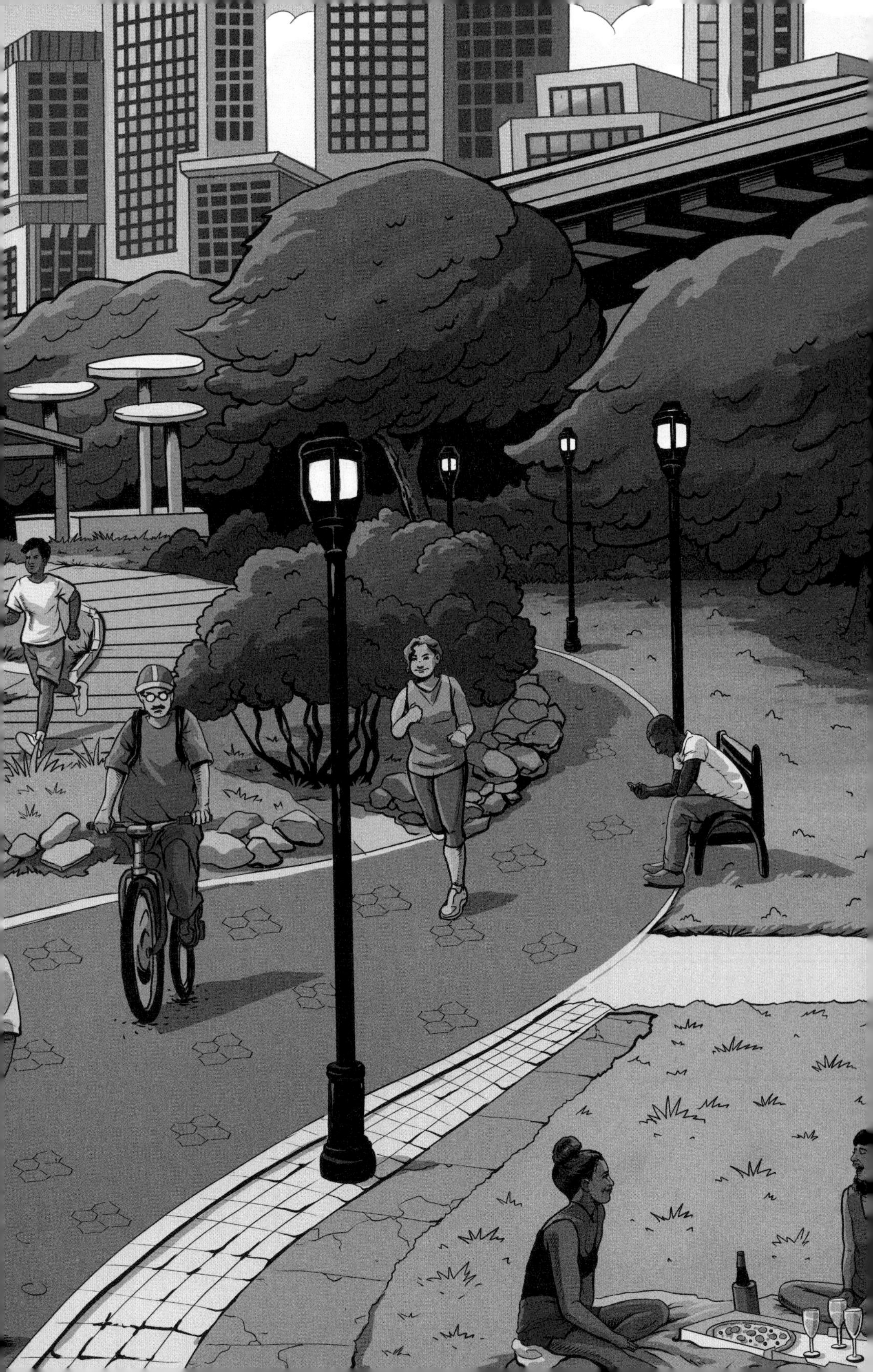

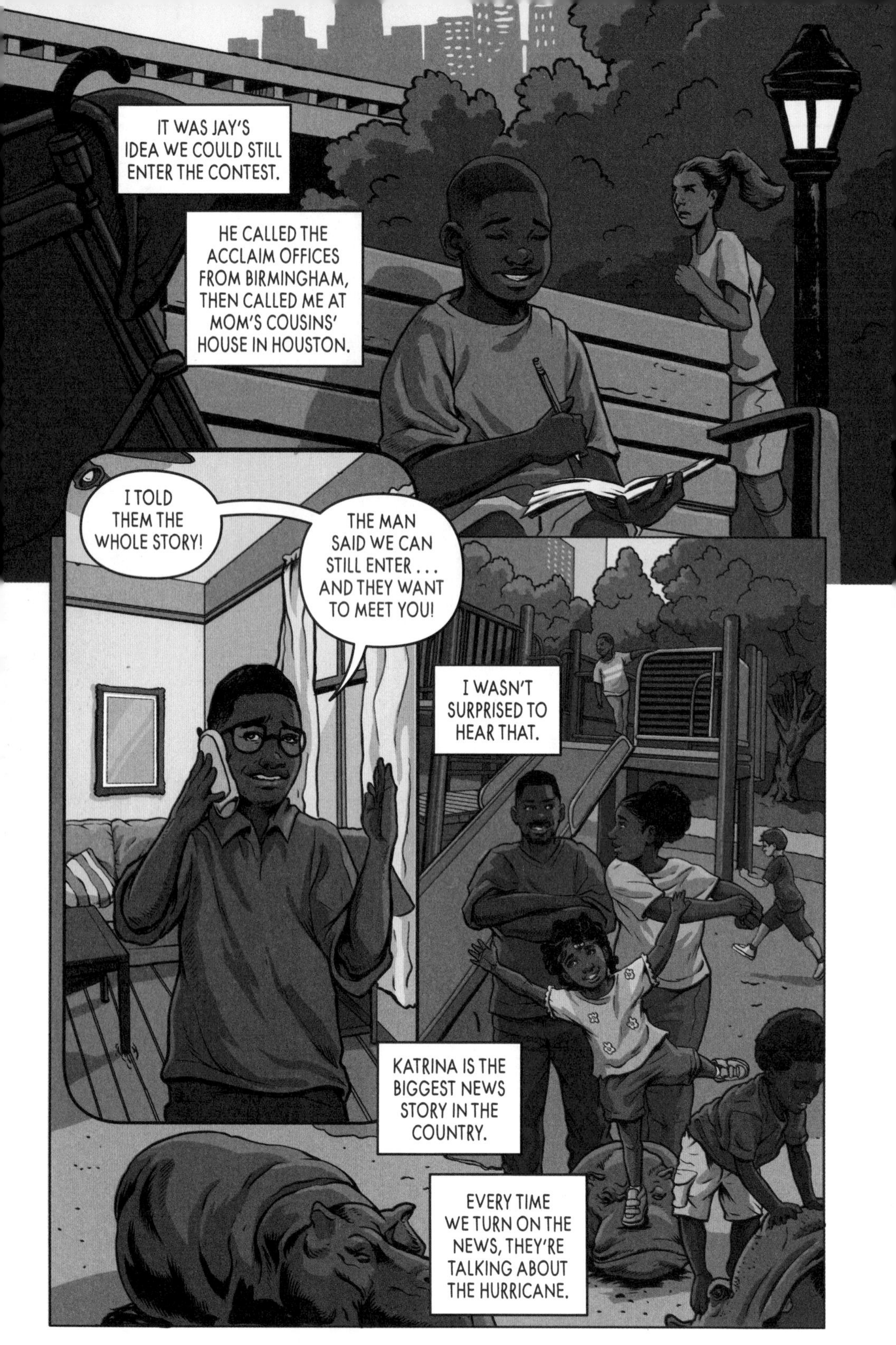
IT WAS JAY'S IDEA WE COULD STILL ENTER THE CONTEST.
HE CALLED THE ACCLAIM OFFICES FROM BIRMINGHAM, THEN CALLED ME AT MOM'S COUSINS' HOUSE IN HOUSTON.
I TOLD THEM THE WHOLE STORY!
THE MAN SAID WE CAN STILL ENTER . . . AND THEY WANT TO MEET YOU!
I WASN'T SURPRISED TO HEAR THAT.
KATRINA IS THE BIGGEST NEWS STORY IN THE COUNTRY.
EVERY TIME WE TURN ON THE NEWS, THEY'RE TALKING ABOUT THE HURRICANE.

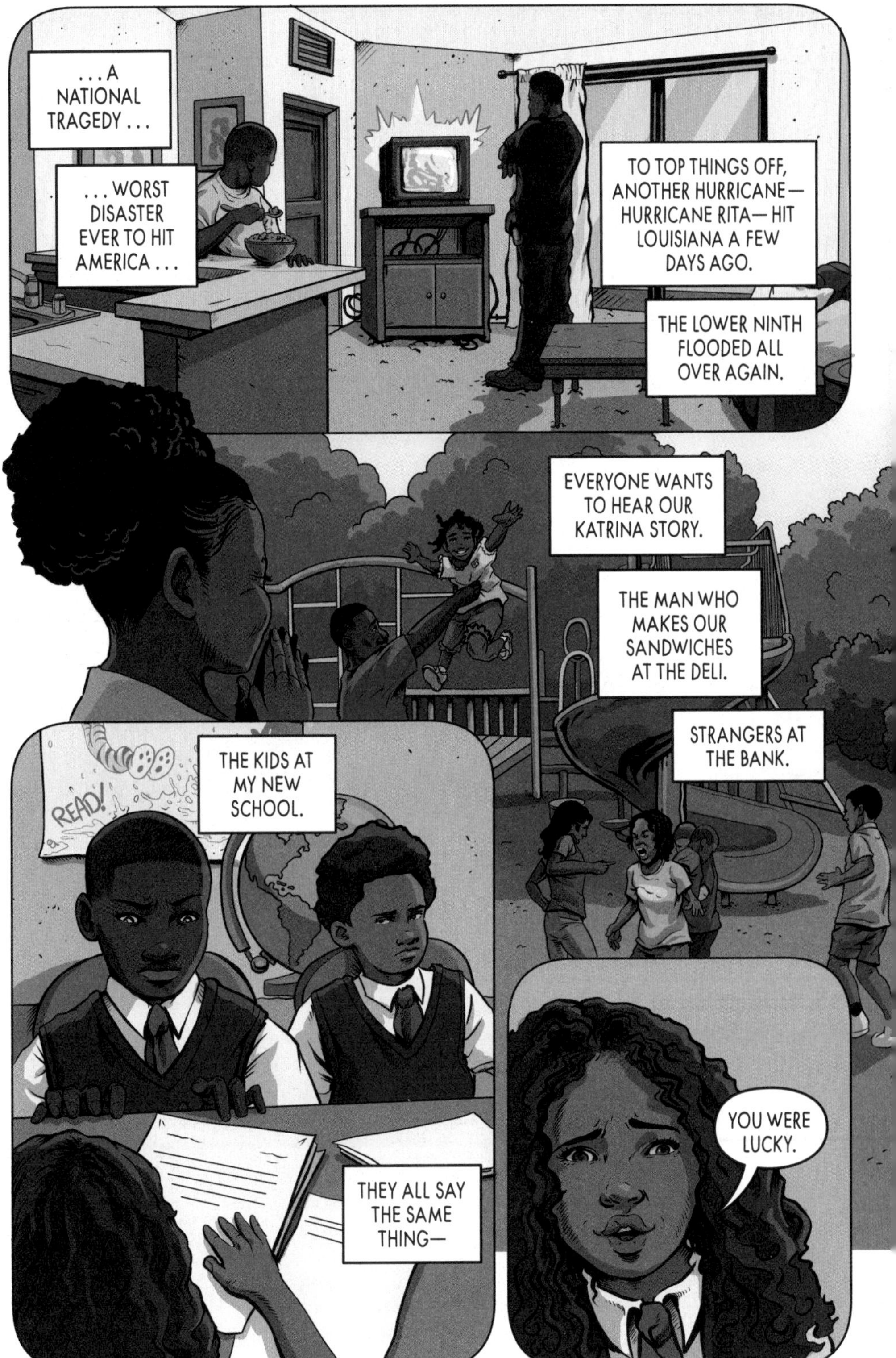
...A NATIONAL TRAGEDY...
...WORST DISASTER EVER TO HIT AMERICA...
TO TOP THINGS OFF, ANOTHER HURRICANE— HURRICANE RITA— HIT LOUISIANA A FEW DAYS AGO.
THE LOWER NINTH FLOODED ALL OVER AGAIN.
EVERYONE WANTS TO HEAR OUR KATRINA STORY.
THE MAN WHO MAKES OUR SANDWICHES AT THE DELI.
STRANGERS AT THE BANK.
READ!
THE KIDS AT MY NEW SCHOOL.
THEY ALL SAY THE SAME THING—
YOU WERE LUCKY.

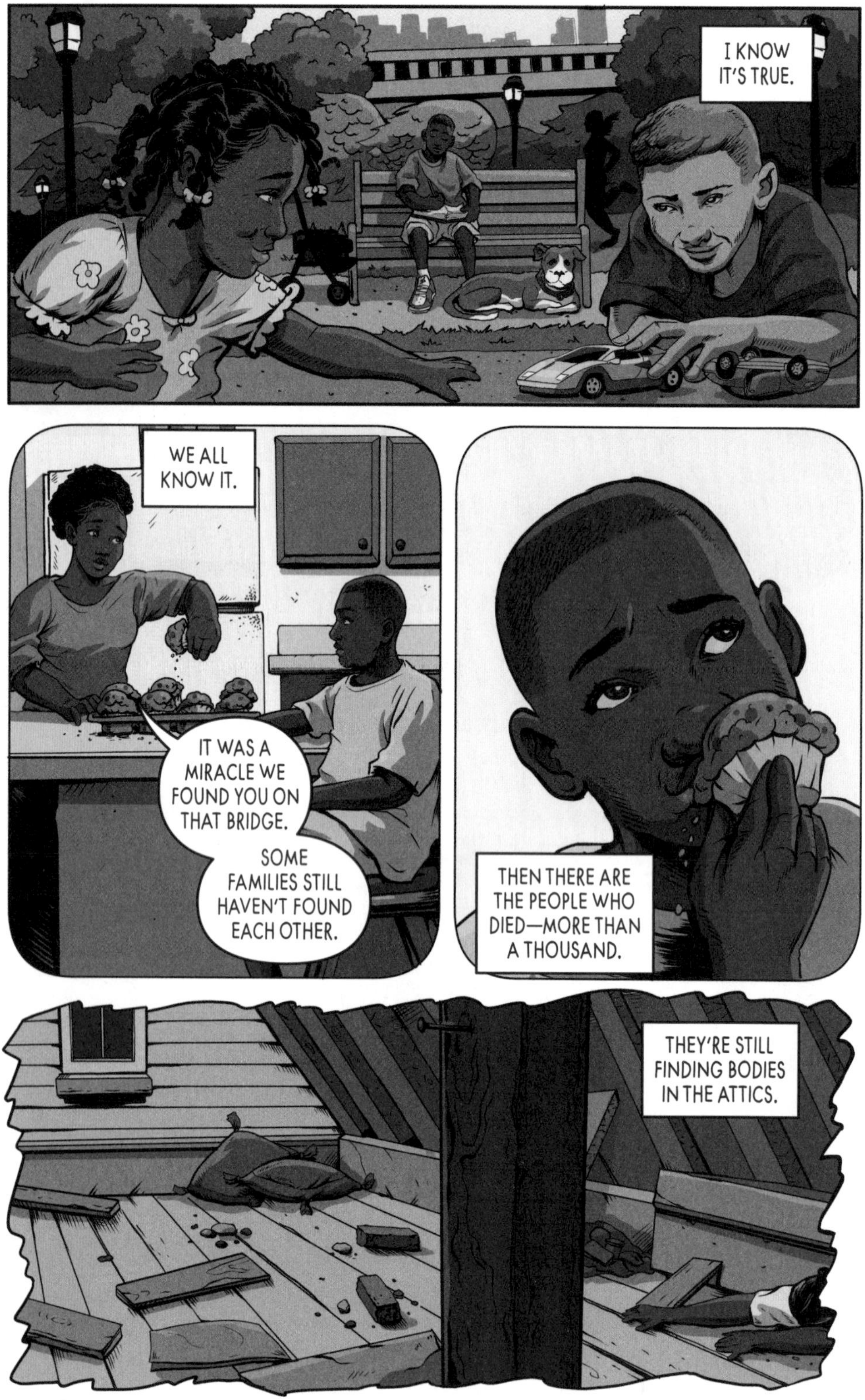
I KNOW IT'S TRUE.
WE ALL KNOW IT.
IT WAS A MIRACLE WE FOUND YOU ON THAT BRIDGE.
SOME FAMILIES STILL HAVEN'T FOUND EACH OTHER.
THEN THERE ARE THE PEOPLE WHO DIED—MORE THAN A THOUSAND.
THEY'RE STILL FINDING BODIES IN THE ATTICS.

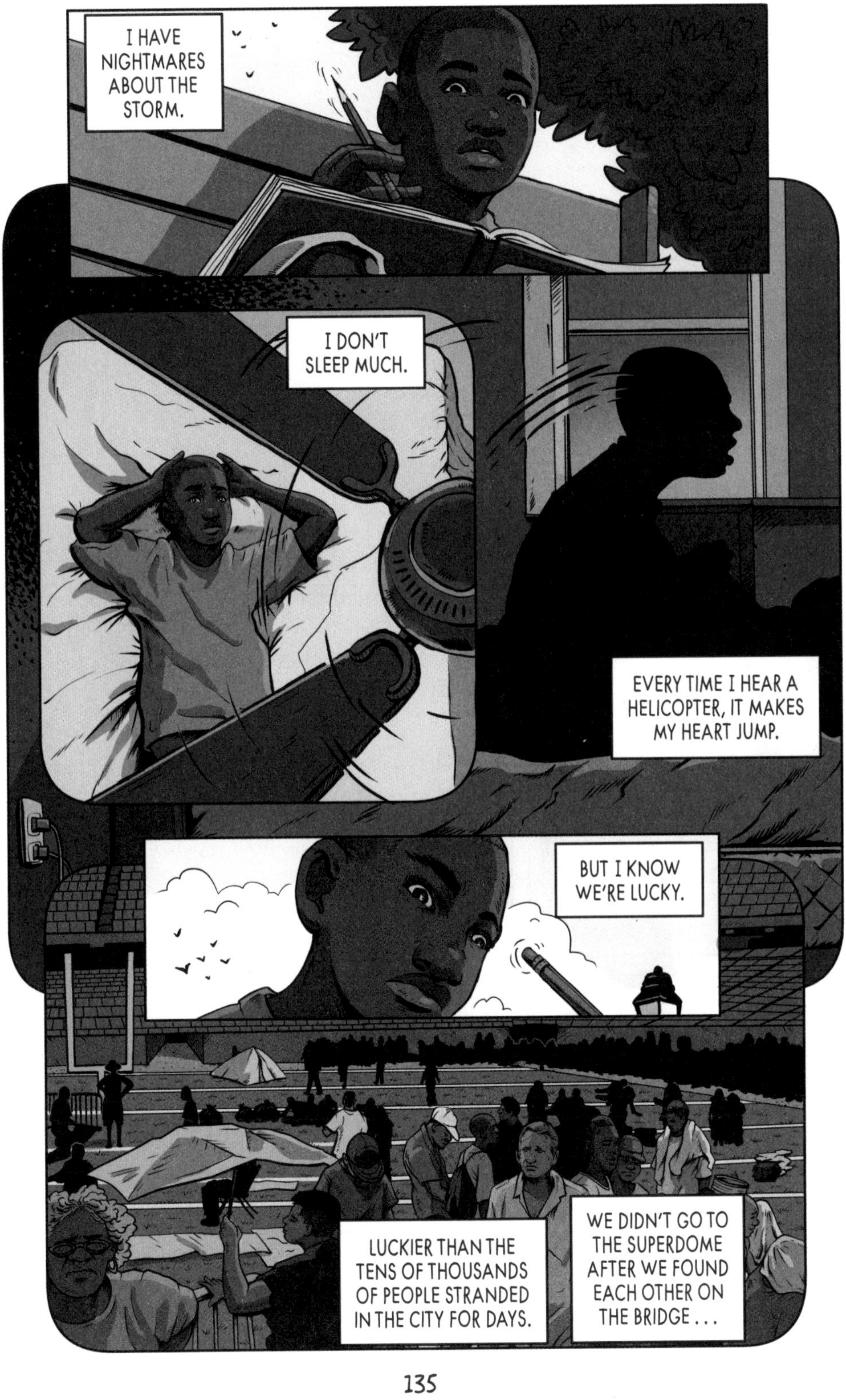
I HAVE NIGHTMARES ABOUT THE STORM.
I DON'T SLEEP MUCH.
EVERY TIME I HEAR A HELICOPTER, IT MAKES MY HEART JUMP.
BUT I KNOW WE'RE LUCKY.
LUCKIER THAN THE TENS OF THOUSANDS OF PEOPLE STRANDED IN THE CITY FOR DAYS.
WE DIDN'T GO TO THE SUPERDOME AFTER WE FOUND EACH OTHER ON THE BRIDGE . . .

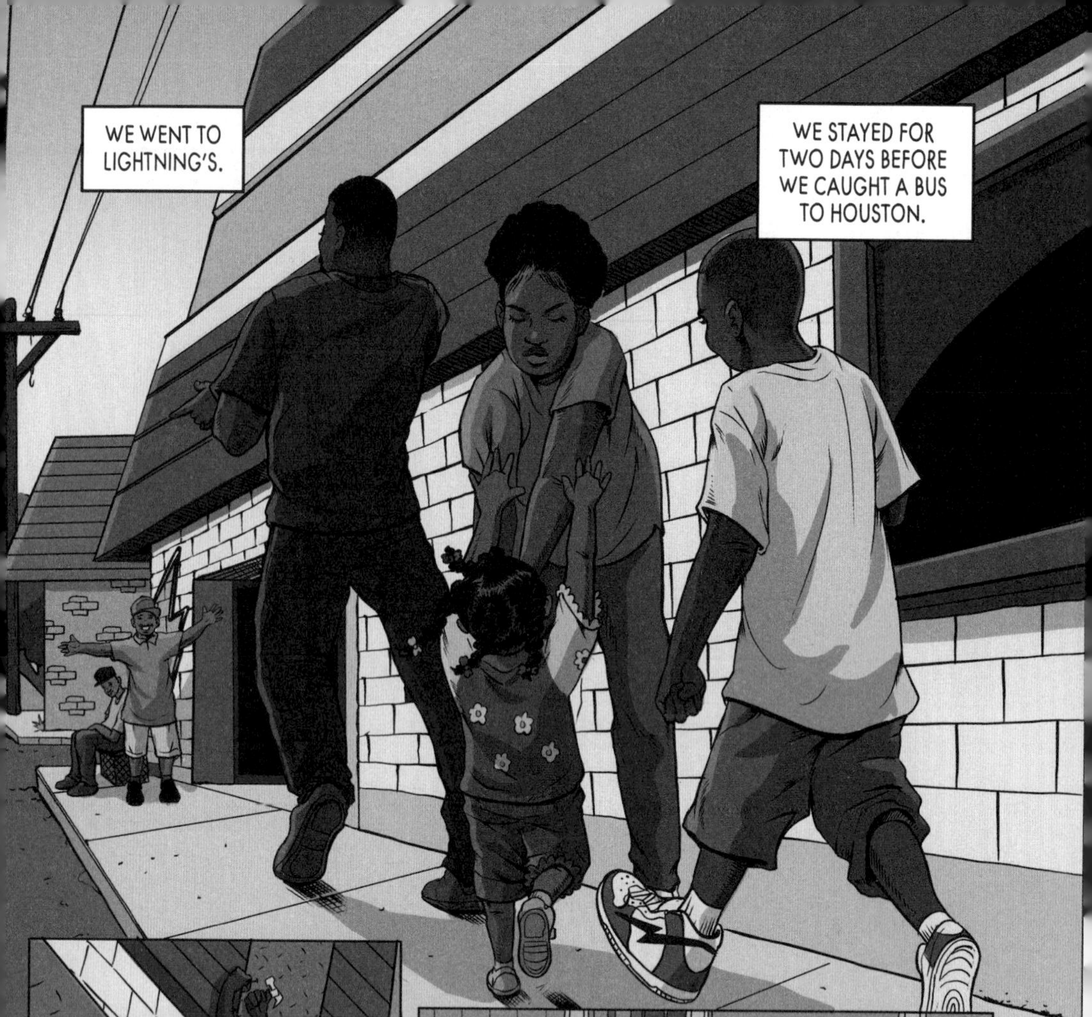
WE WENT TO LIGHTNING'S.
WE STAYED FOR TWO DAYS BEFORE WE CAUGHT A BUS TO HOUSTON.

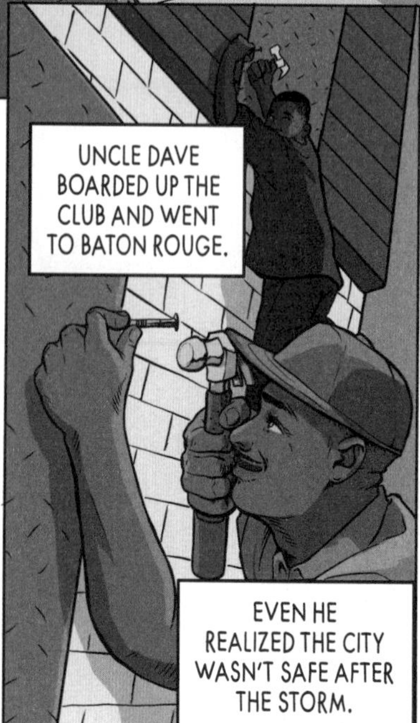
UNCLE DAVE BOARDED UP THE CLUB AND WENT TO BATON ROUGE.
EVEN HE REALIZED THE CITY WASN'T SAFE AFTER THE STORM.

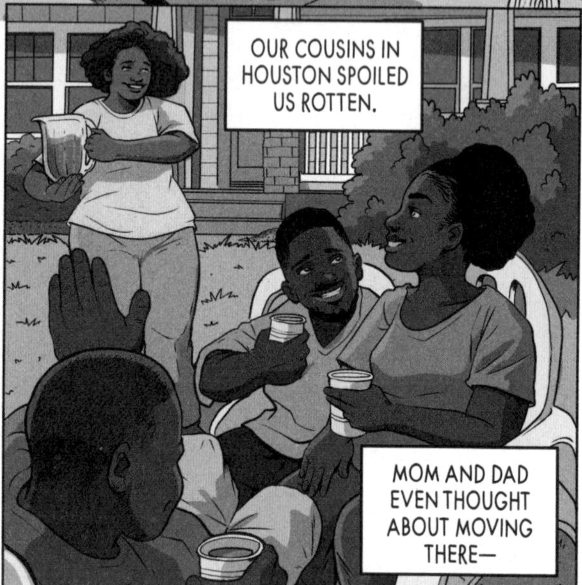
OUR COUSINS IN HOUSTON SPOILED US ROTTEN.
MOM AND DAD EVEN THOUGHT ABOUT MOVING THERE—

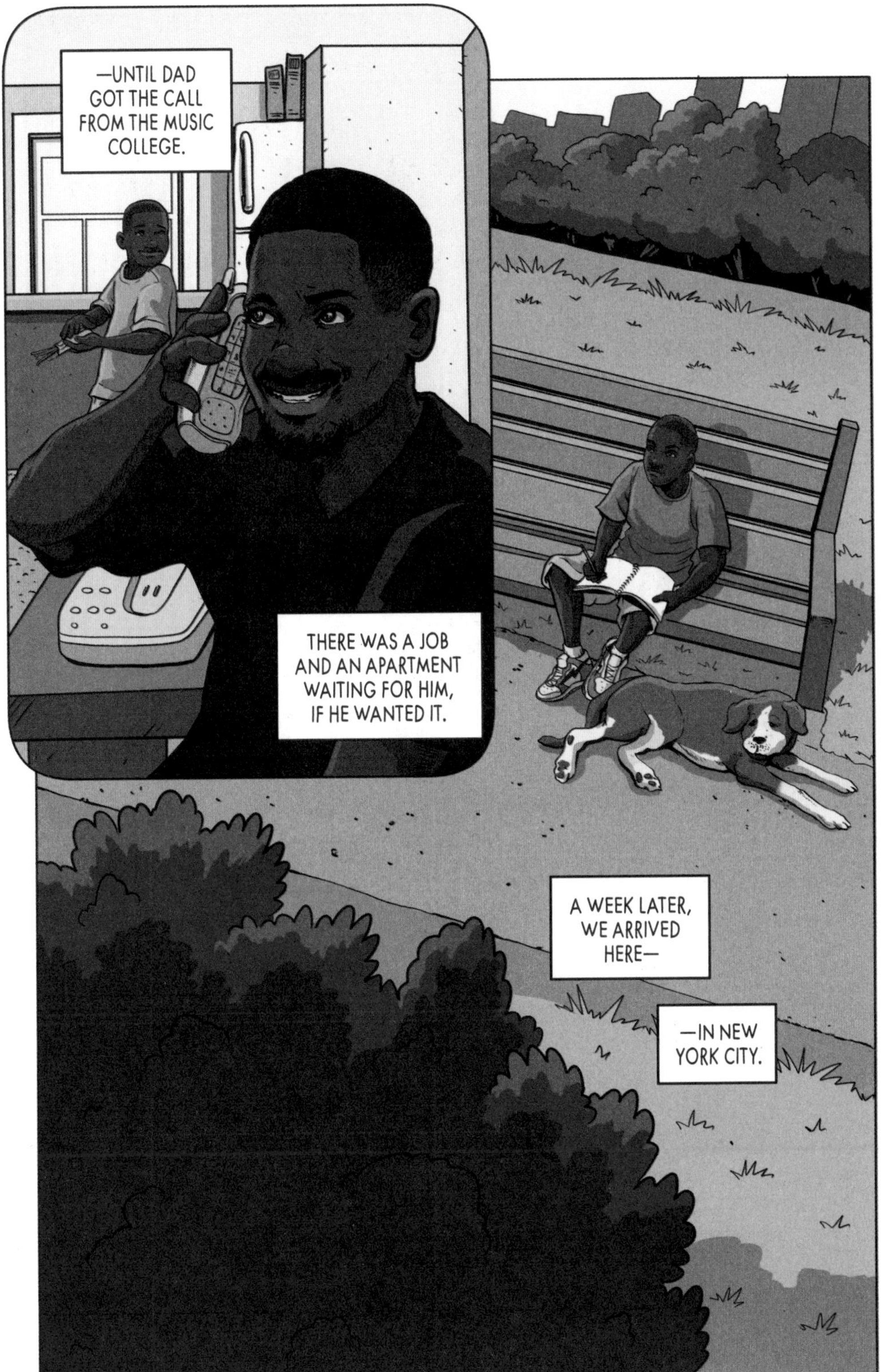
—UNTIL DAD GOT THE CALL FROM THE MUSIC COLLEGE.
THERE WAS A JOB AND AN APARTMENT WAITING FOR HIM, IF HE WANTED IT.
A WEEK LATER, WE ARRIVED HERE—
—IN NEW YORK CITY.

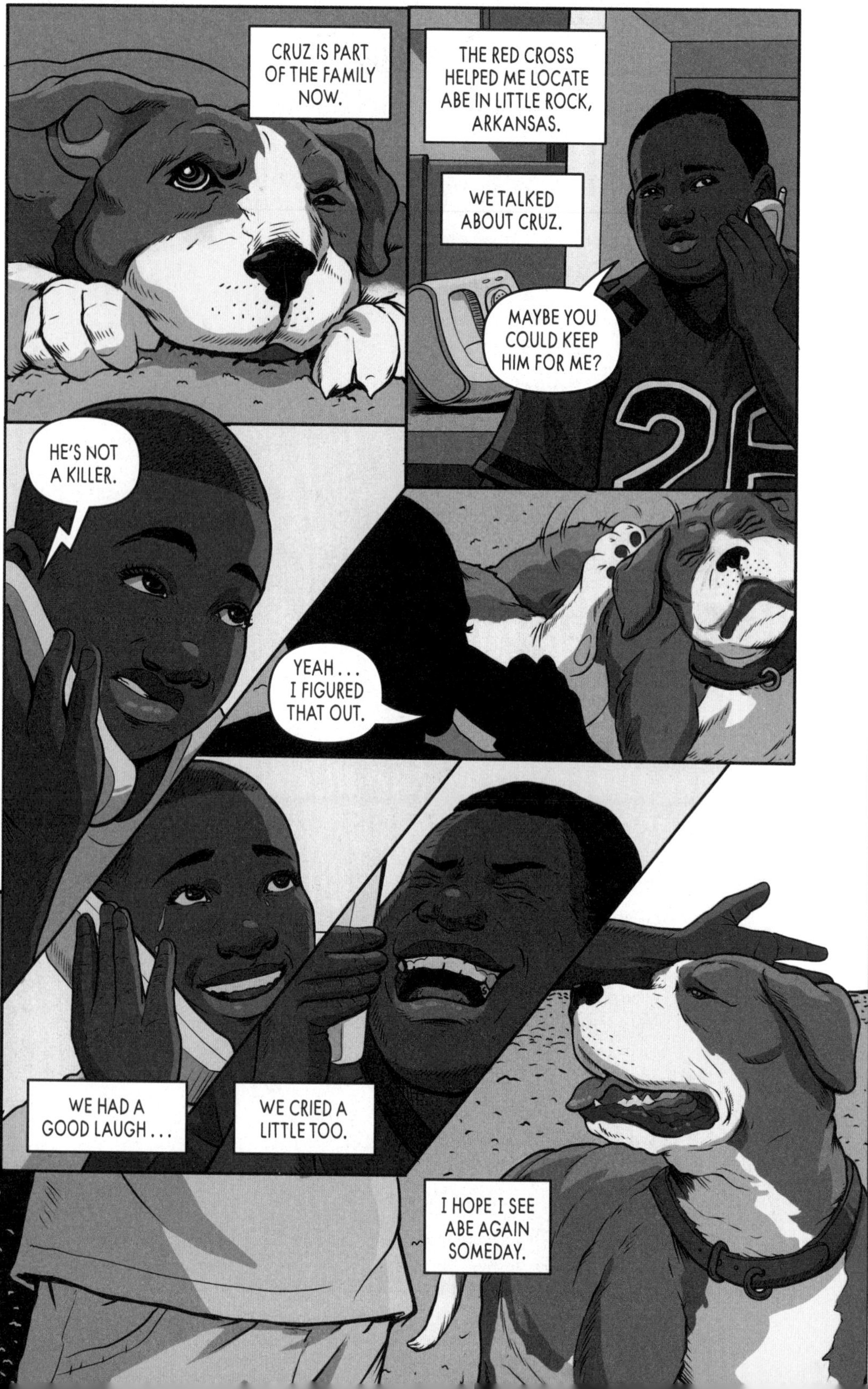
CRUZ IS PART OF THE FAMILY NOW.
THE RED CROSS HELPED ME LOCATE ABE IN LITTLE ROCK, ARKANSAS.
WE TALKED ABOUT CRUZ.
MAYBE YOU COULD KEEP HIM FOR ME?
HE'S NOT A KILLER.
YEAH . . . I FIGURED THAT OUT.
WE HAD A GOOD LAUGH . . .
WE CRIED A LITTLE TOO.
I HOPE I SEE ABE AGAIN SOMEDAY.

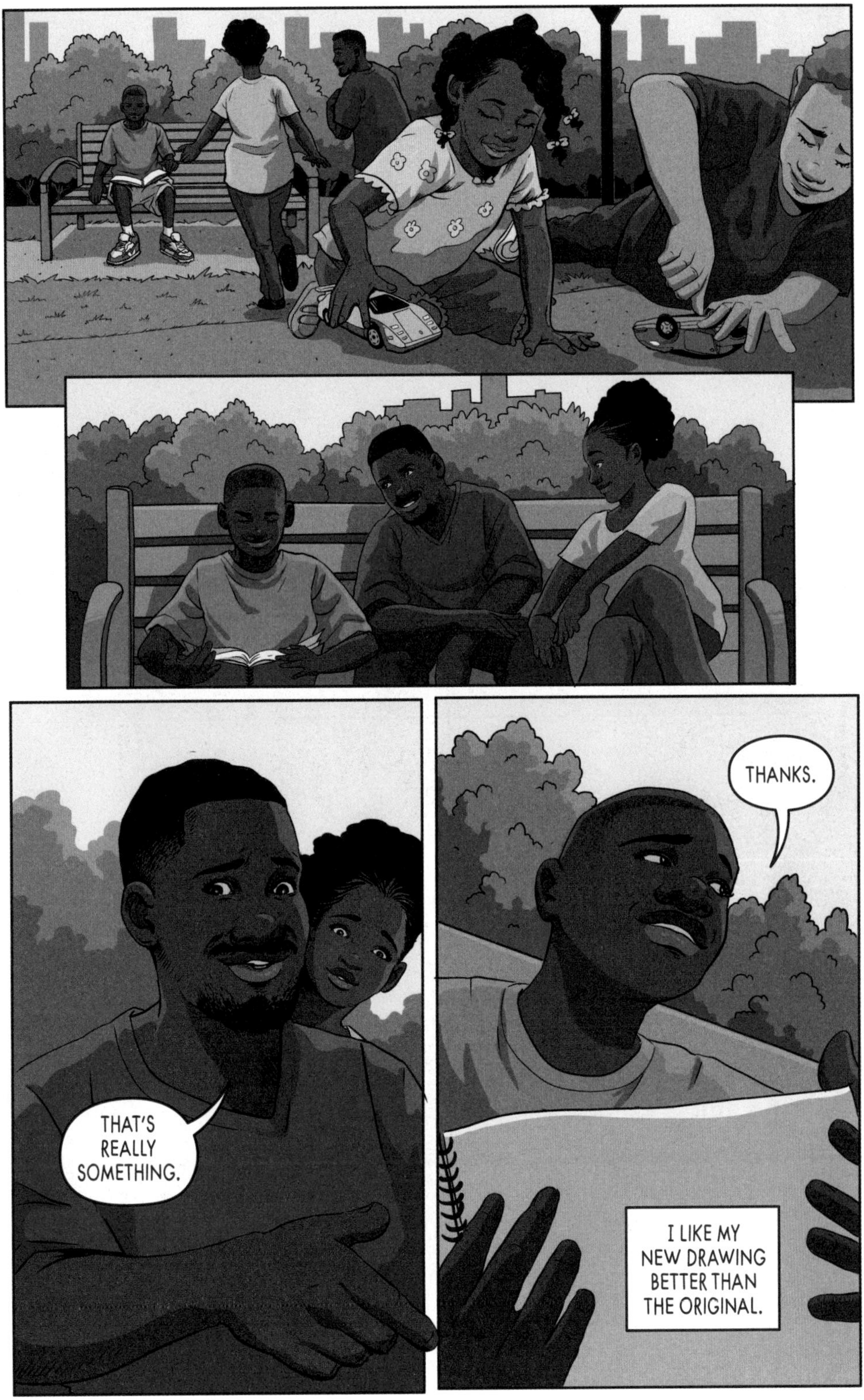
THAT'S REALLY SOMETHING.
THANKS.
I LIKE MY NEW DRAWING BETTER THAN THE ORIGINAL.

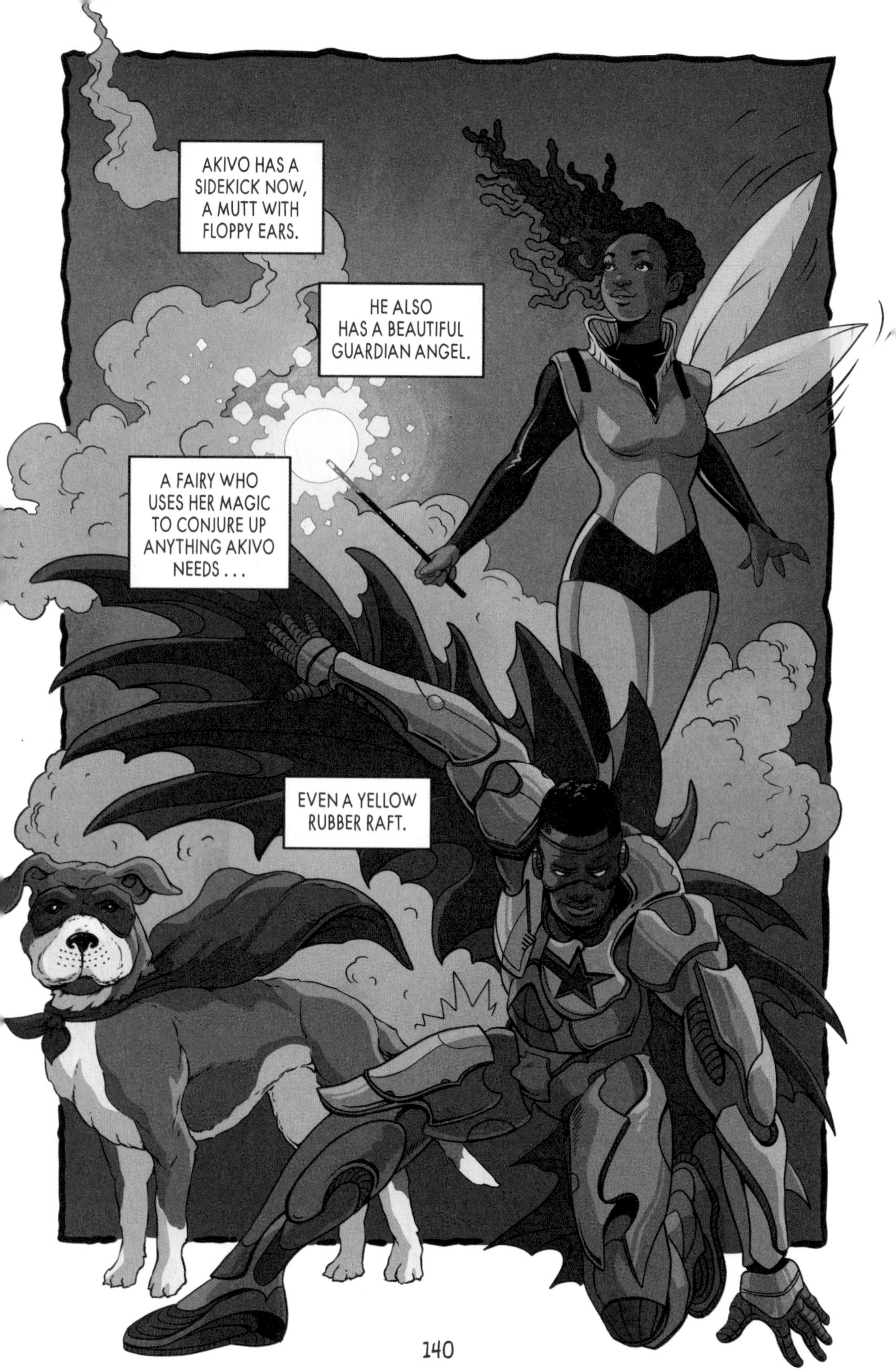
AKIVO HAS A SIDEKICK NOW, A MUTT WITH FLOPPY EARS.
HE ALSO HAS A BEAUTIFUL GUARDIAN ANGEL.
A FAIRY WHO USES HER MAGIC TO CONJURE UP ANYTHING AKIVO NEEDS . . .
EVEN A YELLOW RUBBER RAFT.

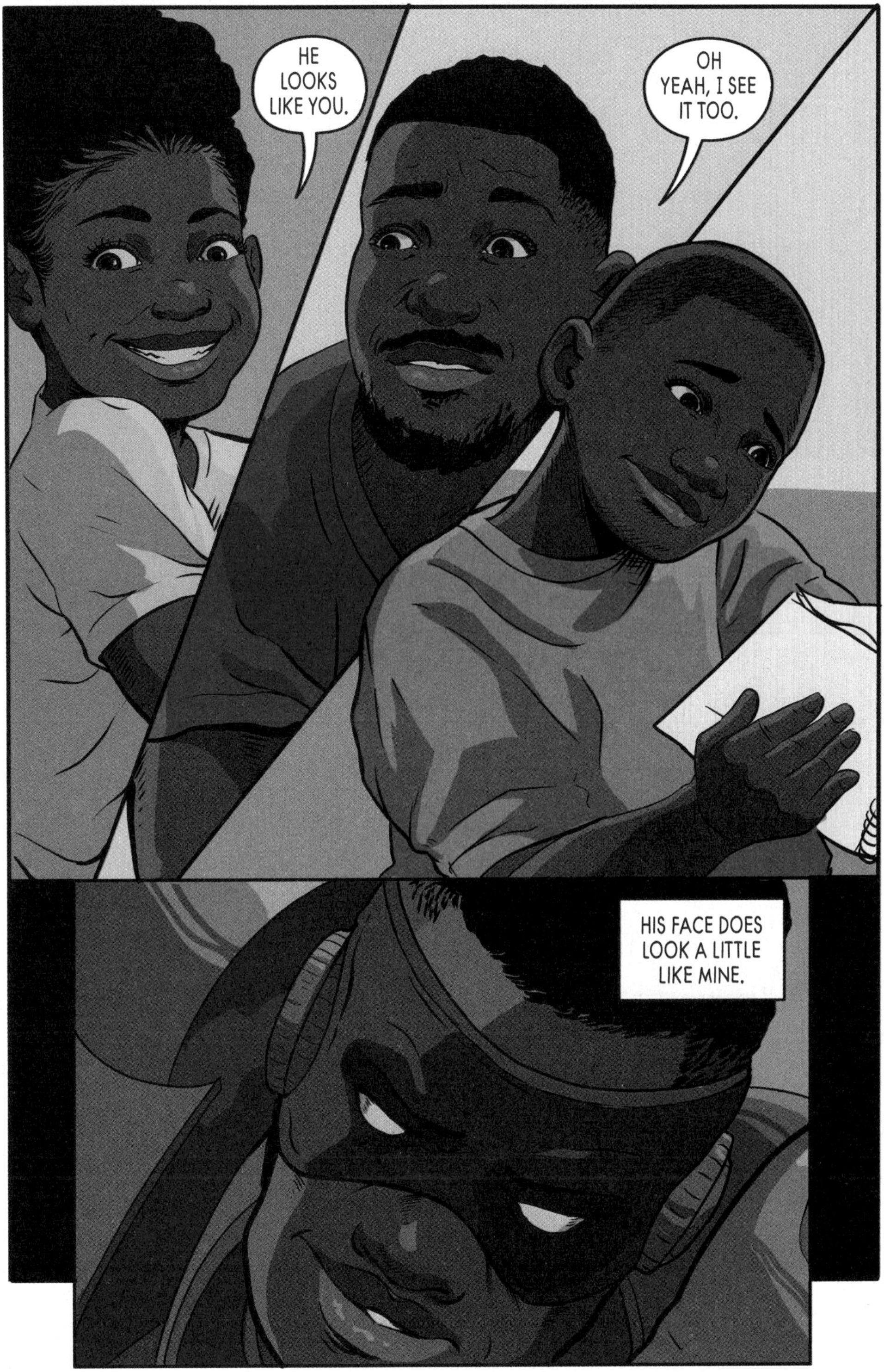
HE LOOKS LIKE YOU.
OH YEAH, I SEE IT TOO.
HIS FACE DOES LOOK A LITTLE LIKE MINE.

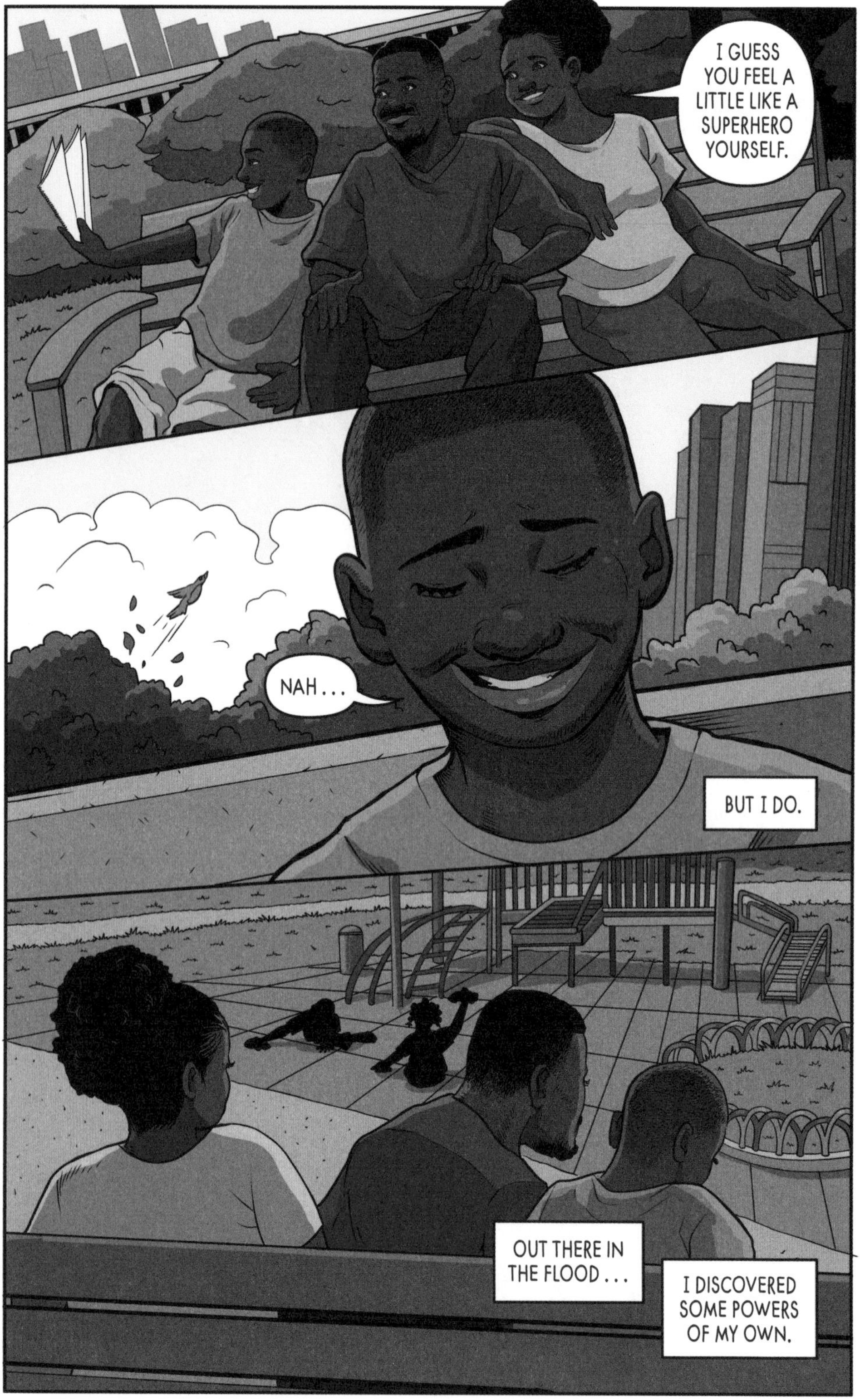
I GUESS YOU FEEL A LITTLE LIKE A SUPERHERO YOURSELF.
NAH . . .
BUT I DO.
OUT THERE IN THE FLOOD . . .
I DISCOVERED SOME POWERS OF MY OWN.

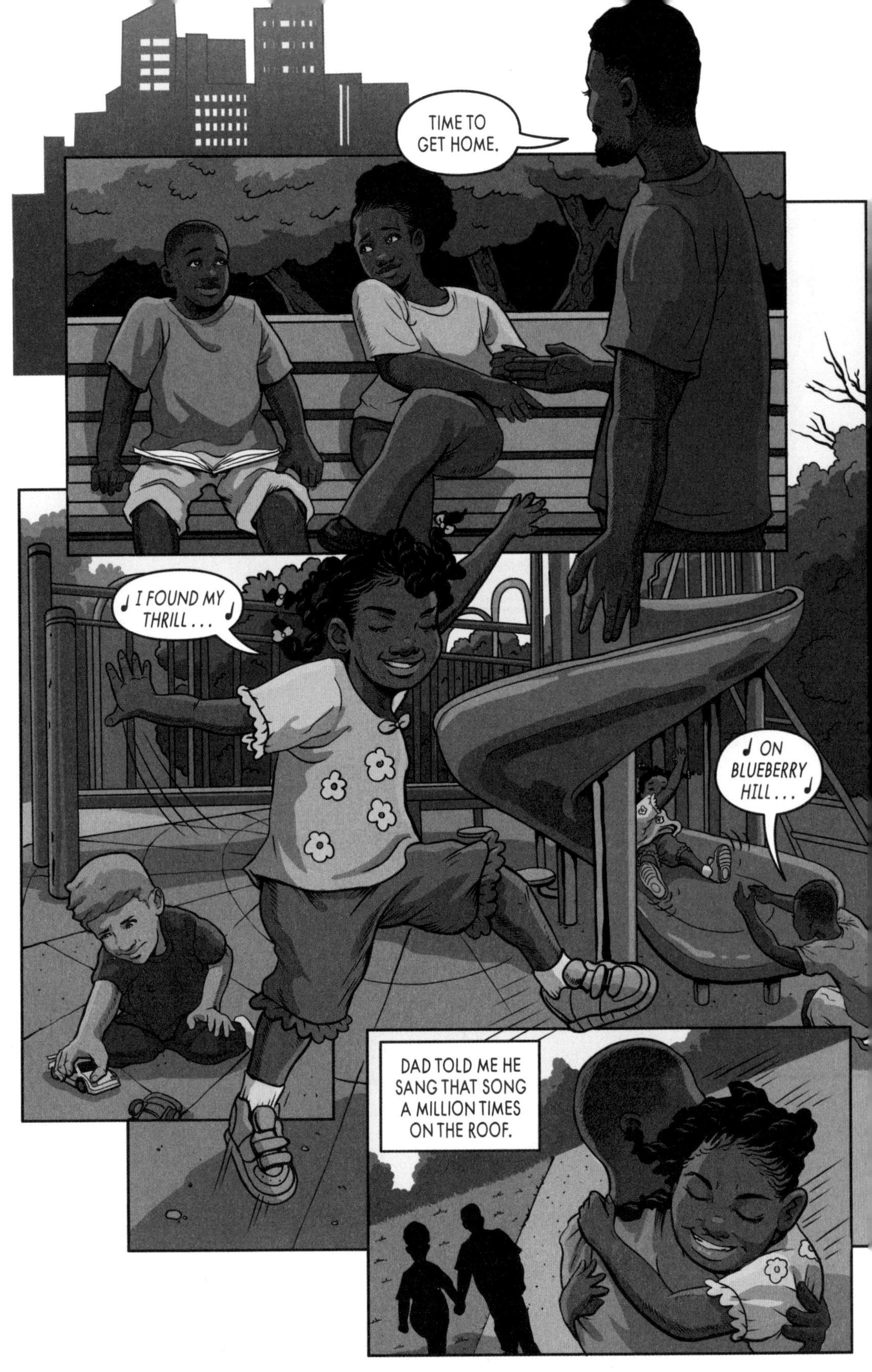

TIME TO GET HOME.
♩ I FOUND MY THRILL . . . ♩
♩ ON BLUEBERRY HILL . . . ♩
DAD TOLD ME HE SANG THAT SONG A MILLION TIMES ON THE ROOF.

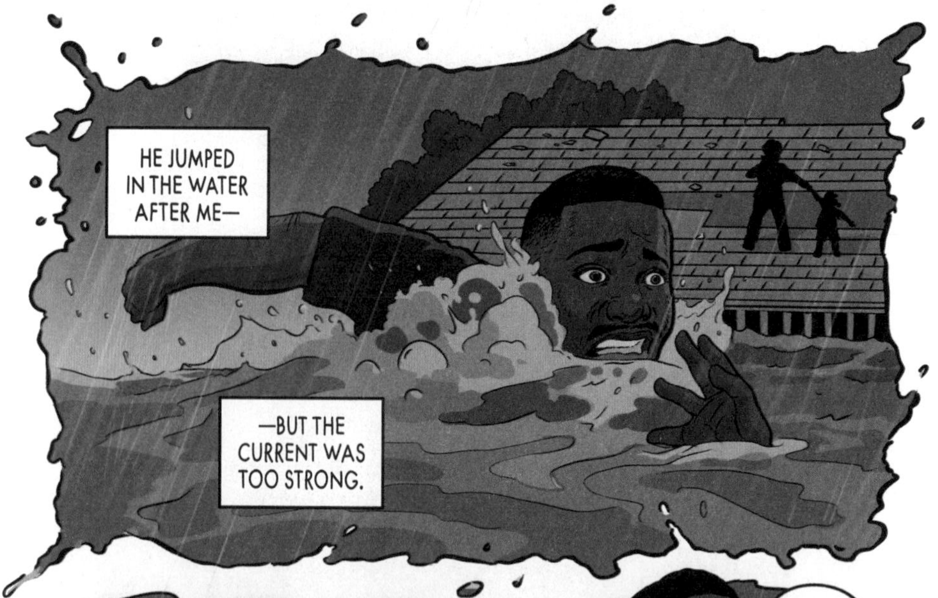
HE JUMPED IN THE WATER AFTER ME—
—BUT THE CURRENT WAS TOO STRONG.

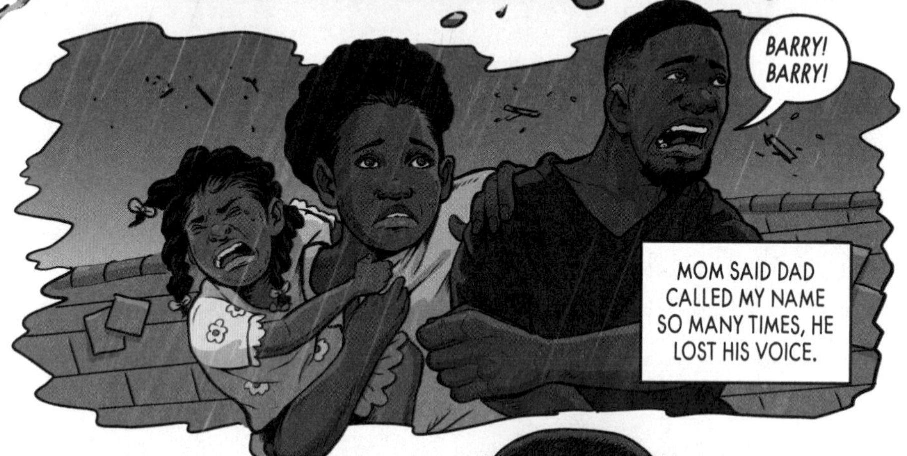
BARRY! BARRY!
MOM SAID DAD CALLED MY NAME SO MANY TIMES, HE LOST HIS VOICE.

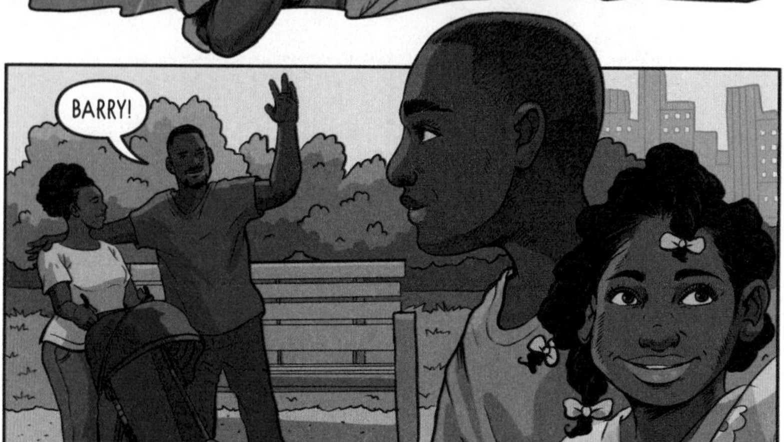
BARRY!

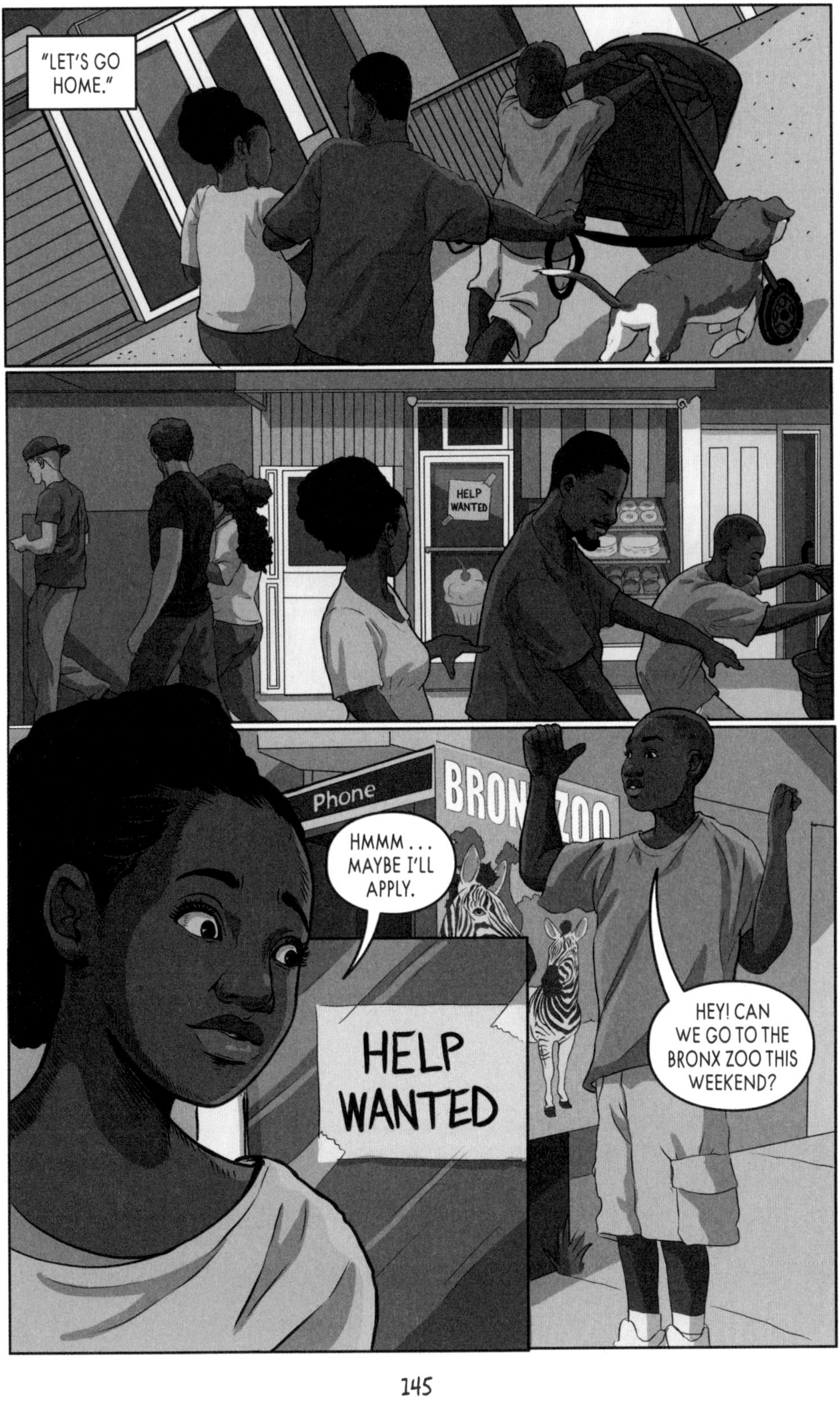
"LET'S GO HOME."
HELP WANTED
Phone
BRON ZOO
HMMM . . . MAYBE I'LL APPLY.
HELP WANTED
HEY! CAN WE GO TO THE BRONX ZOO THIS WEEKEND?

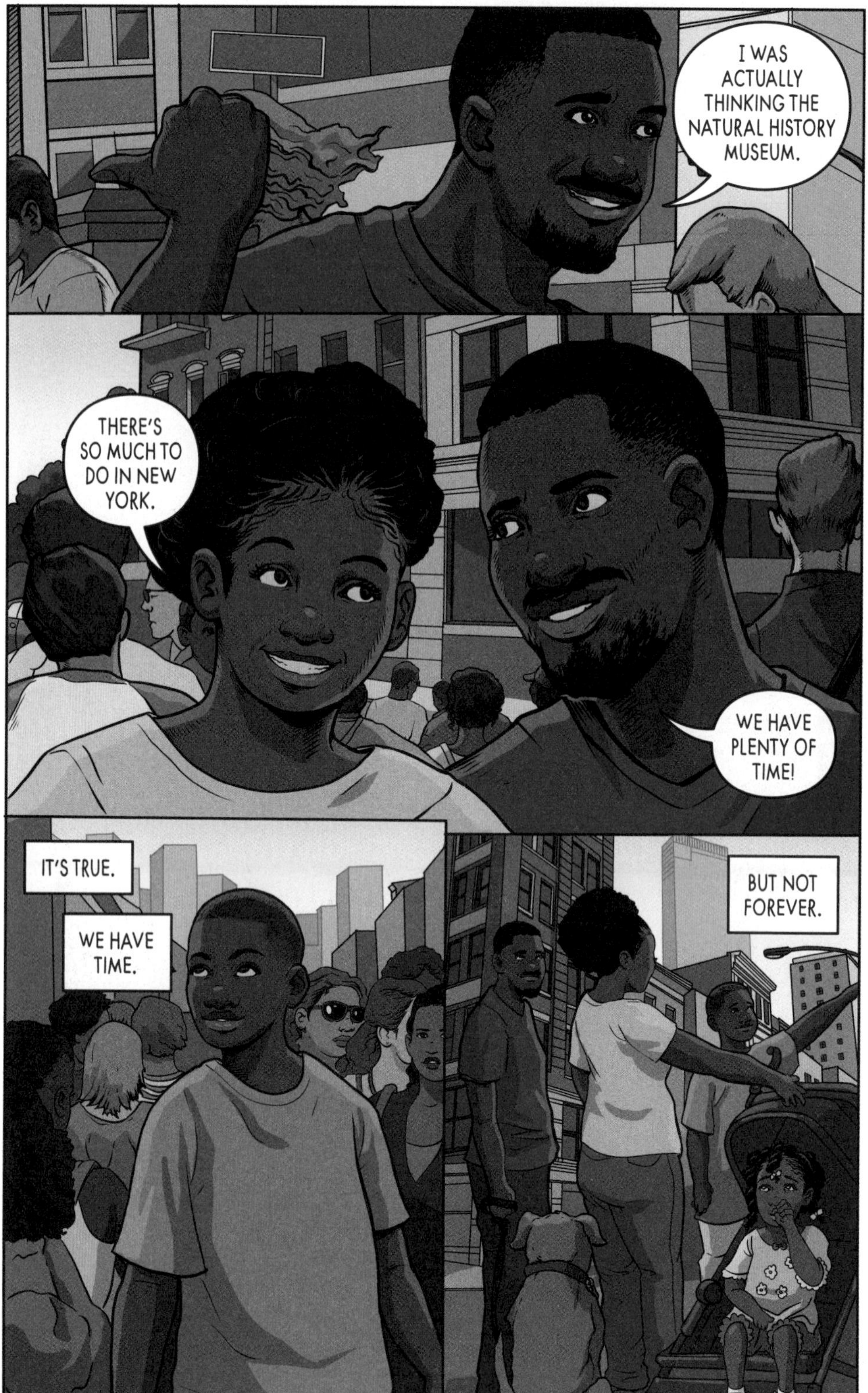
I WAS ACTUALLY THINKING THE NATURAL HISTORY MUSEUM.
THERE'S SO MUCH TO DO IN NEW YORK.
WE HAVE PLENTY OF TIME!
IT'S TRUE.
WE HAVE TIME.
BUT NOT FOREVER.

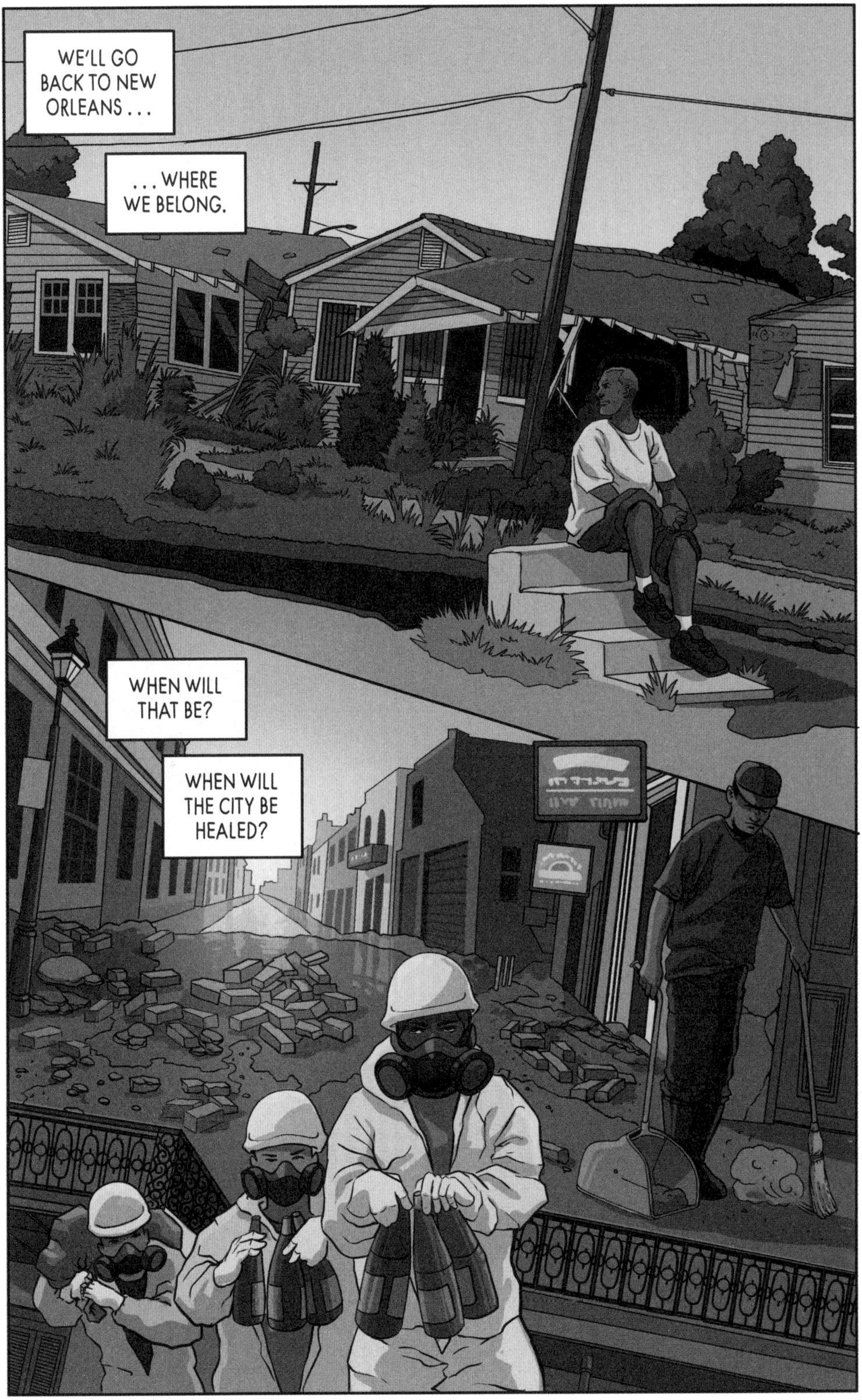
WE'LL GO BACK TO NEW ORLEANS . . .
. . . WHERE WE BELONG.
WHEN WILL THAT BE?
WHEN WILL THE CITY BE HEALED?

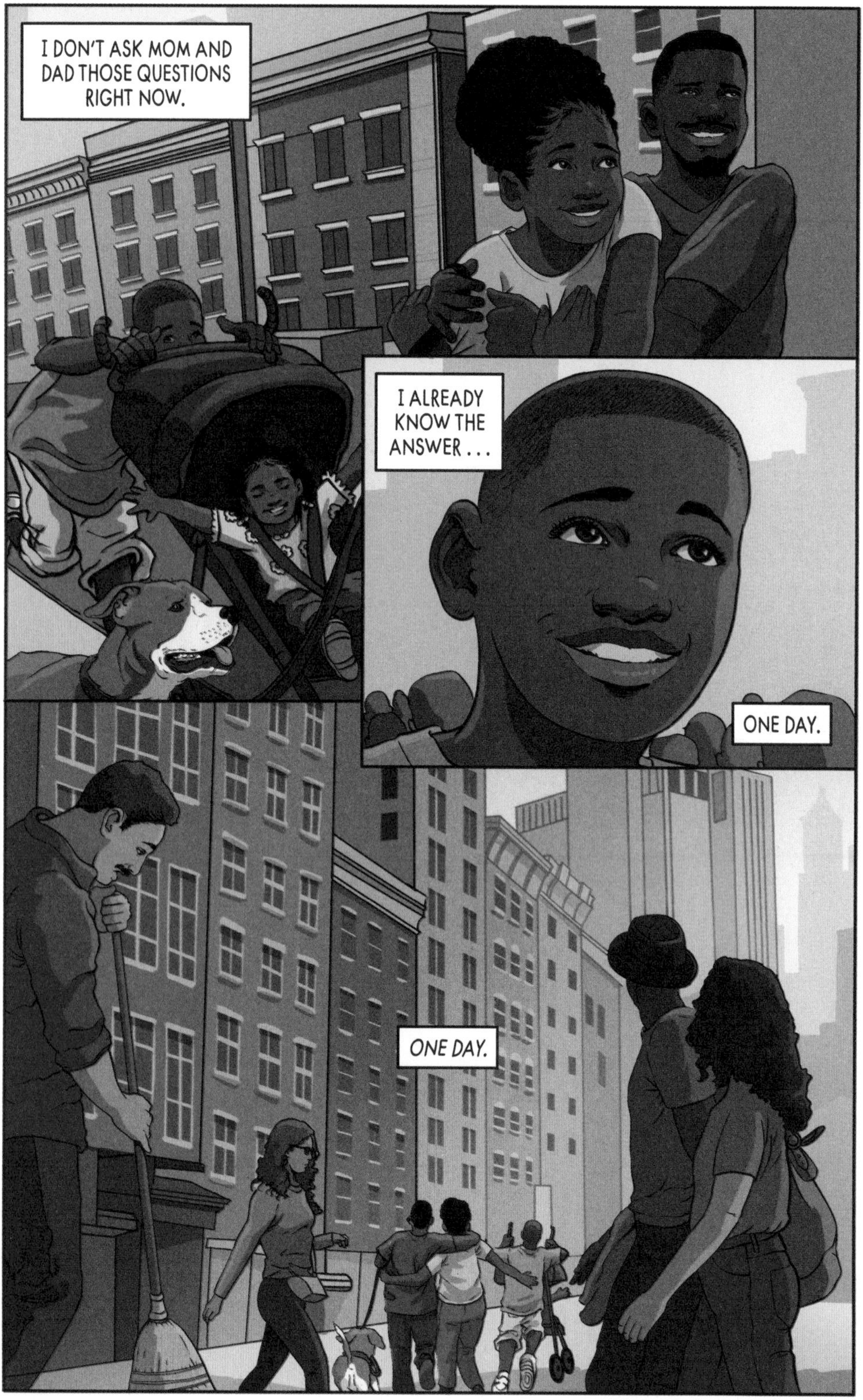
I DON'T ASK MOM AND DAD THOSE QUESTIONS RIGHT NOW.
I ALREADY KNOW THE ANSWER . . .
ONE DAY.
ONE DAY.

HEROIC RESCUES

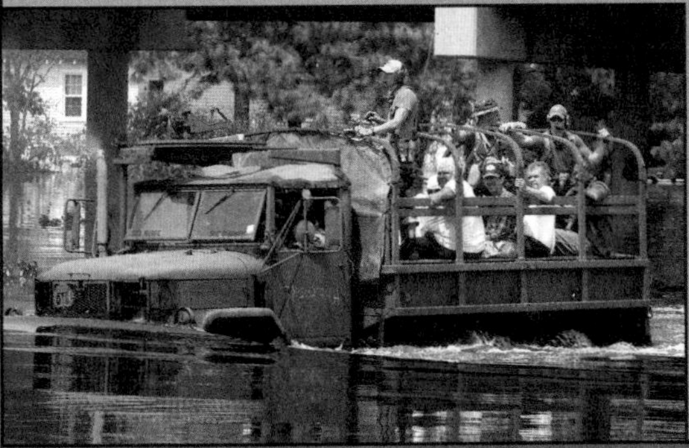

IN THE DAYS AND WEEKS FOLLOWING THE STORM, TENS OF THOUSANDS OF **U.S. TROOPS AND OTHER FIRST RESPONDERS** ARRIVED IN NEW ORLEANS WITH BOATS, HELICOPTERS, AND OTHER RESCUE VEHICLES. THEY RESCUED THOUSANDS OF PEOPLE FROM ROOFTOPS AND BRIDGES.

POLICE OFFICERS WORKED FOR DAYS WITHOUT REST. VOLUNTEERS HELPED FERRY PEOPLE TO SAFETY.

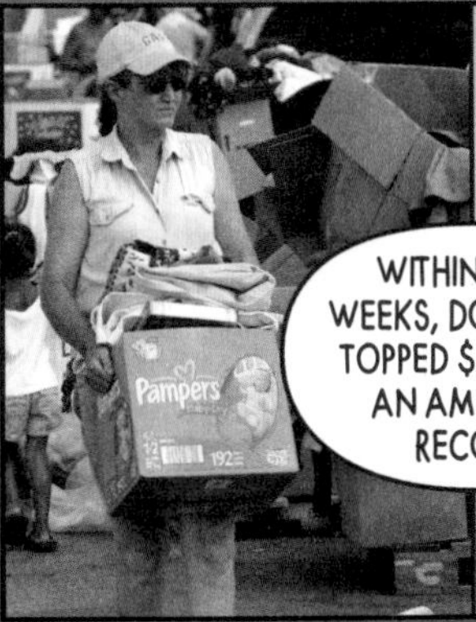
Pampers

DONATIONS OF SUPPLIES AND MONEY POURED IN FROM AROUND THE WORLD.

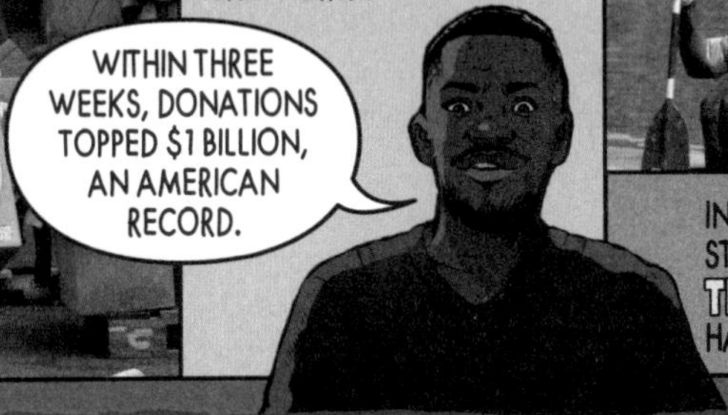
WITHIN THREE WEEKS, DONATIONS TOPPED $1 BILLION, AN AMERICAN RECORD.

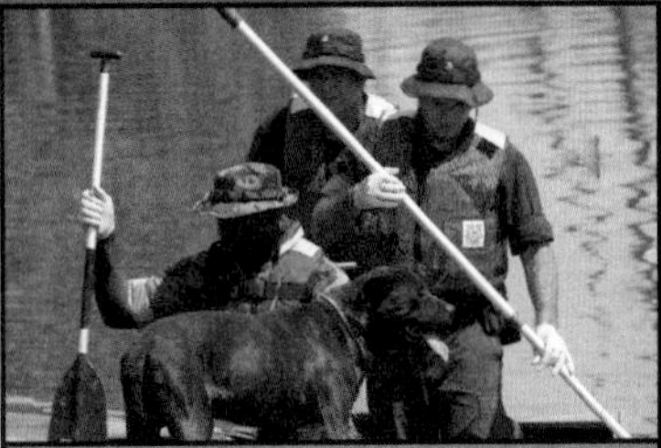

IN THE WEEKS AFTER THE STORM, VOLUNTEERS RESCUED **THOUSANDS OF PETS** THAT HAD BEEN LEFT BEHIND.

MAKING NEW ORLEANS SAFER

TODAY, A **STRENGTHENED SYSTEM OF LEVEES, GATES, BARRIERS, AND PUMPS** PROTECT NEW ORLEANS FROM HURRICANES.

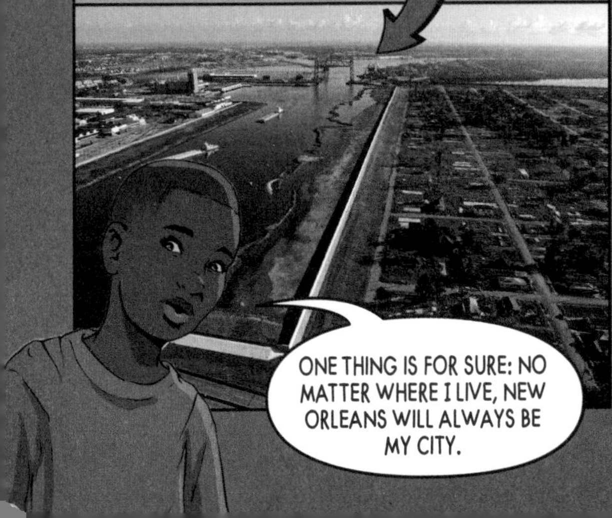
ONE THING IS FOR SURE: NO MATTER WHERE I LIVE, NEW ORLEANS WILL ALWAYS BE MY CITY.

IN AUGUST 2021, THAT SYSTEM WAS TESTED WHEN **HURRICANE IDA** STRUCK. THE NEW LEVEES AND PUMPS DID THEIR JOB. WHILE SOME AREAS OUTSIDE THE CITY FLOODED, THERE WAS NO SERIOUS WATER DAMAGE INSIDE THE PROTECTED AREA.

BUT WITH **CLIMATE CHANGE** THREATENING TO MAKE HURRICANES STRONGER AND MORE FREQUENT, MANY WORRY THAT NEW ORLEANS WILL FACE MORE RISKS IN THE FUTURE.

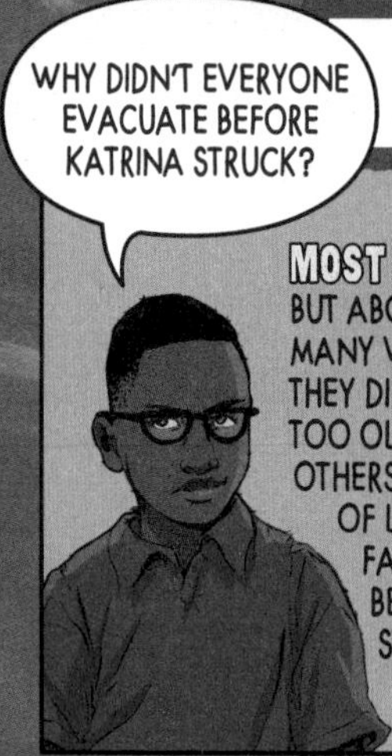
WHY DIDN'T EVERYONE EVACUATE BEFORE KATRINA STRUCK?

STAYING THROUGH THE STORM

MOST PEOPLE DID EVACUATE, BUT ABOUT **100,000 STAYED BEHIND.** MANY WERE UNABLE TO LEAVE BECAUSE THEY DID NOT HAVE CARS, OR WERE TOO OLD OR SICK TO MAKE THE TRIP. OTHERS COULDN'T AFFORD THE COST OF LEAVING—GAS, PLANE OR BUS FARE, HOTELS. SOME MISTAKENLY BELIEVED THEY COULD RIDE OUT THE STORM SAFELY IN THEIR HOMES, AS THEY HAD FOR PREVIOUS STORMS.

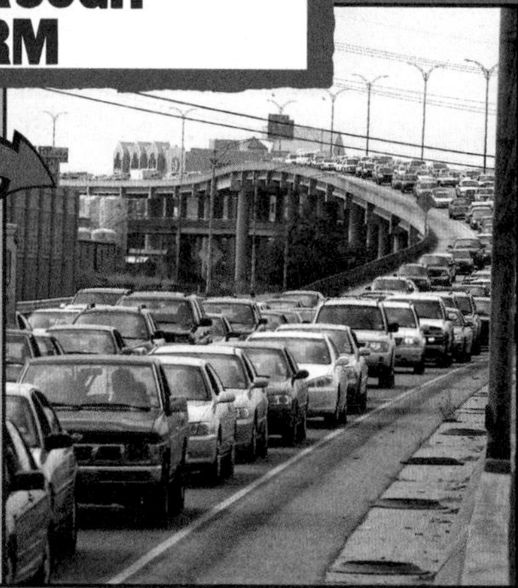

HUNDREDS WERE TRAPPED IN **ATTICS AND ON ROOFTOPS** IN SEARING HEAT AND HUMIDITY AND HAD TO BE RESCUED BY BOAT OR HELICOPTER.

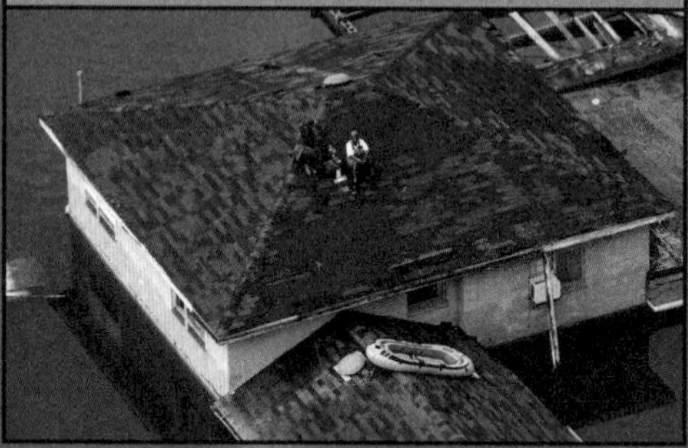

BEFORE THE STORM, THOSE WHO COULDN'T EVACUATE WERE TOLD TO GO TO THE **SUPERDOME**, THE STADIUM OF THE NEW ORLEANS SAINTS FOOTBALL TEAM.

CITY LEADERS WERE UNPREPARED FOR THE CROWDS SEEKING SAFETY AT THE STADIUM—AN ESTIMATED **10,000 PEOPLE**.

KATRINA'S WINDS DAMAGED ITS ROOF AND KNOCKED OUT POWER. THERE WAS NO ELECTRICITY. IT WAS ROASTING HOT. THERE WAS NOT ENOUGH FOOD OR WATER. TOILETS STOPPED WORKING.

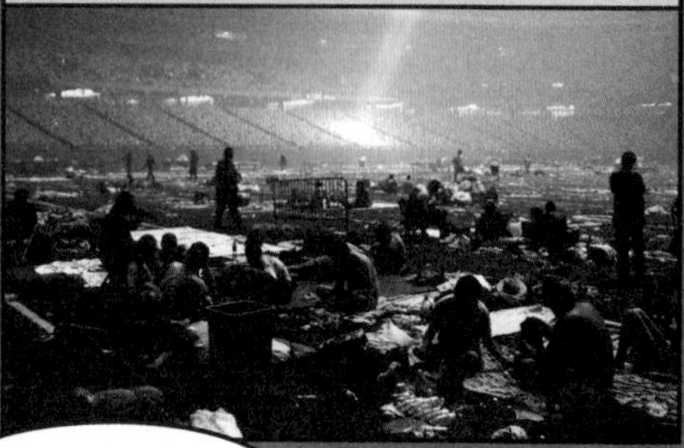

CONDITIONS WERE EVEN WORSE AT THE **ERNEST N. MORIAL CONVENTION CENTER**, WHERE FLOOD VICTIMS CHOSE TO GATHER.

ABOUT **25,000 PEOPLE** SHELTERED THERE AND ON THE SIDEWALK OUTSIDE, WAITING FOR HELP.

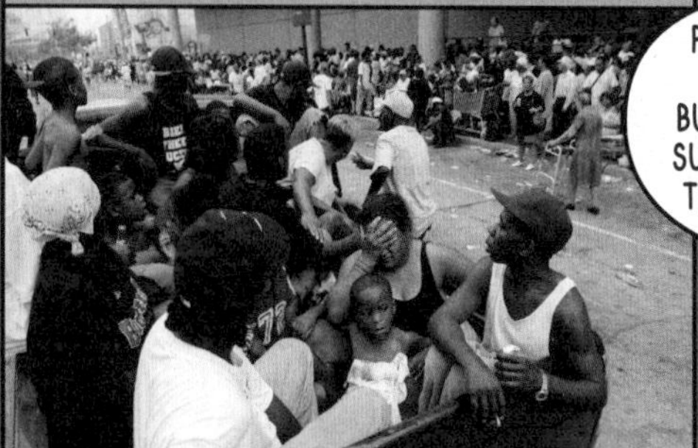

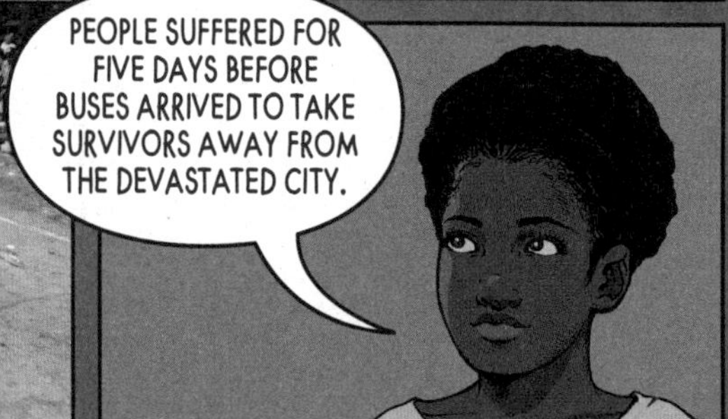
PEOPLE SUFFERED FOR FIVE DAYS BEFORE BUSES ARRIVED TO TAKE SURVIVORS AWAY FROM THE DEVASTATED CITY.

BATTLING THE FLOODWATERS

FOR AS LONG AS PEOPLE HAVE BEEN LIVING ON THE LOUISIANA COAST, THEY HAVE BEEN FACING STORMS AND FLOODS. THE FIRST PEOPLE WERE MEMBERS OF AT LEAST TWELVE DIFFERENT **NATIVE AMERICAN TRIBES**, INCLUDING THE ANNOCHY, CHITIMACHA, ACOLAPISSA, HOUMA, AND CHOCTAW, WHO HAD LIKELY BEEN LIVING IN SOUTHERN LOUISIANA FOR AT LEAST 1,300 YEARS.

THE FIRST RECORDED HURRICANE WAS IN **1722**, A FEW YEARS AFTER THE CITY OF NEW ORLEANS WAS FOUNDED BY FRENCH SETTLERS.

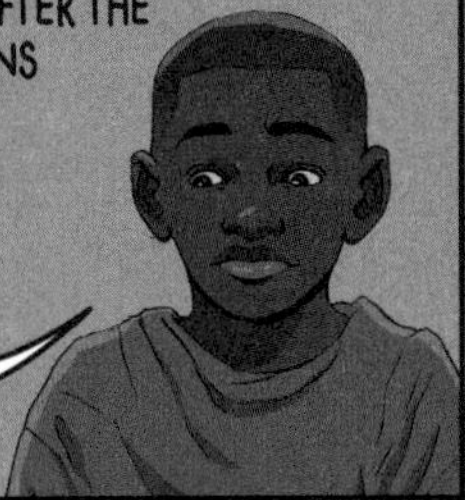
THE STORM DESTROYED EVERY SINGLE BUILDING.

AS THE CITY GREW, FLOODING FROM THE MISSISSIPPI RIVER WAS A CONSTANT PROBLEM. **THE FIRST LEVEES**—WALLS OF HAY, DIRT, OR WOOD TO BLOCK FLOODWATERS—WERE BUILT IN 1719, ONE YEAR AFTER THE FOUNDING OF NEW ORLEANS.

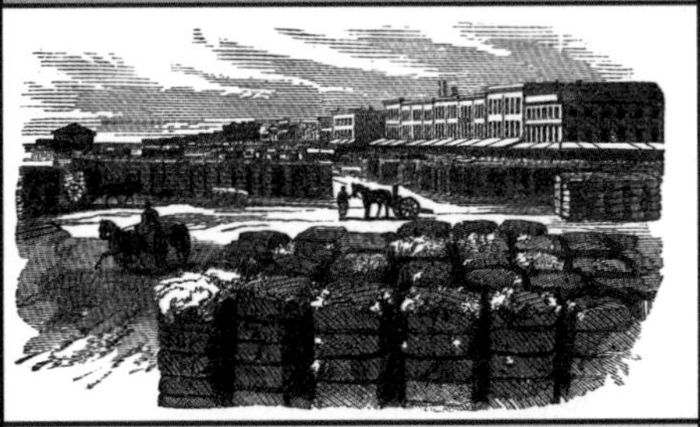

The Mississippi River riverfront in New Orleans in the 1700s

BY 2004, HUNDREDS OF **MILES OF LEVEES** MADE OF SOIL, AND SOMETIMES STEEL AND CONCRETE, ENCIRCLED NEW ORLEANS TO STOP THE RIVER AND LAKE FROM FLOODING THE CITY.

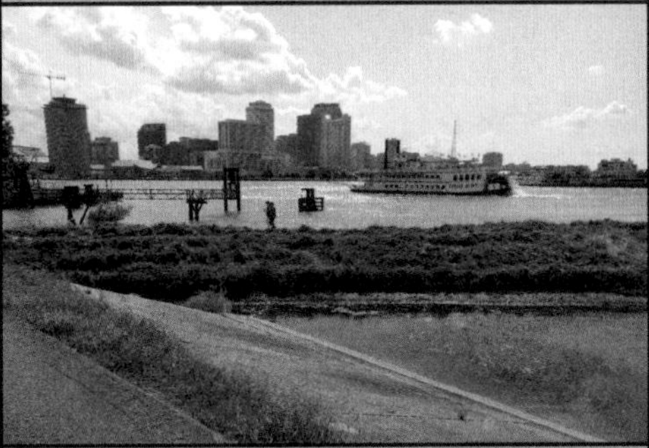

MEANWHILE, HUGE **ELECTRIC PUMPS** DRAINED STREETS AFTER HEAVY RAINS.

BUT SCIENTISTS WARNED THAT THE SYSTEM COULDN'T WITHSTAND A STRONG HURRICANE.

WITHIN HOURS OF HURRICANE KATRINA'S LANDFALL, **THE FIRST LEVEES HAD FAILED**. SOME CRUMBLED. OTHERS WEREN'T TALL ENOUGH TO BLOCK WALLS OF WATER.

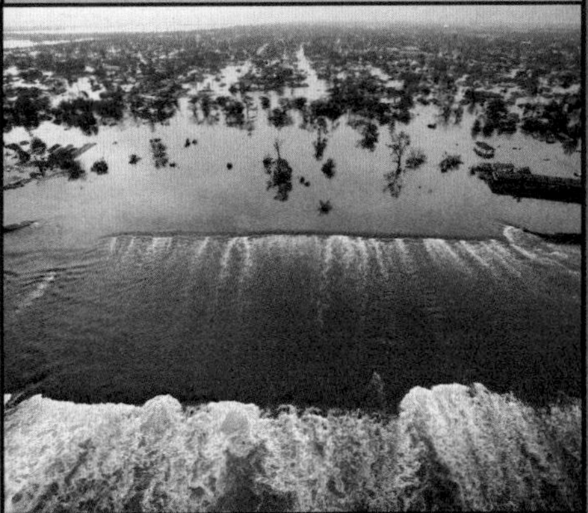

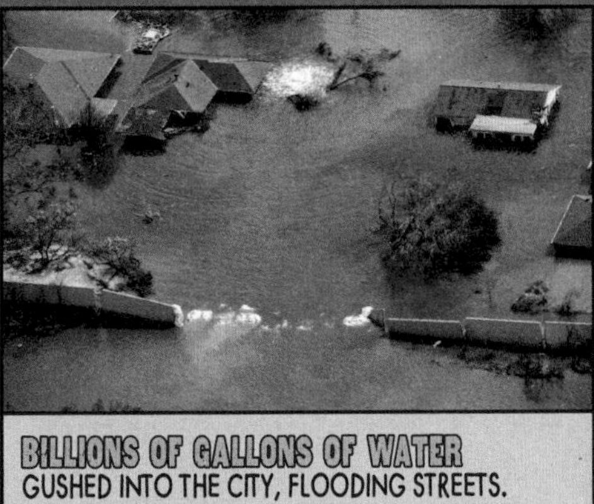

BILLIONS OF GALLONS OF WATER GUSHED INTO THE CITY, FLOODING STREETS. TENS OF THOUSANDS OF PEOPLE WERE TRAPPED IN THE FLOODWATERS.

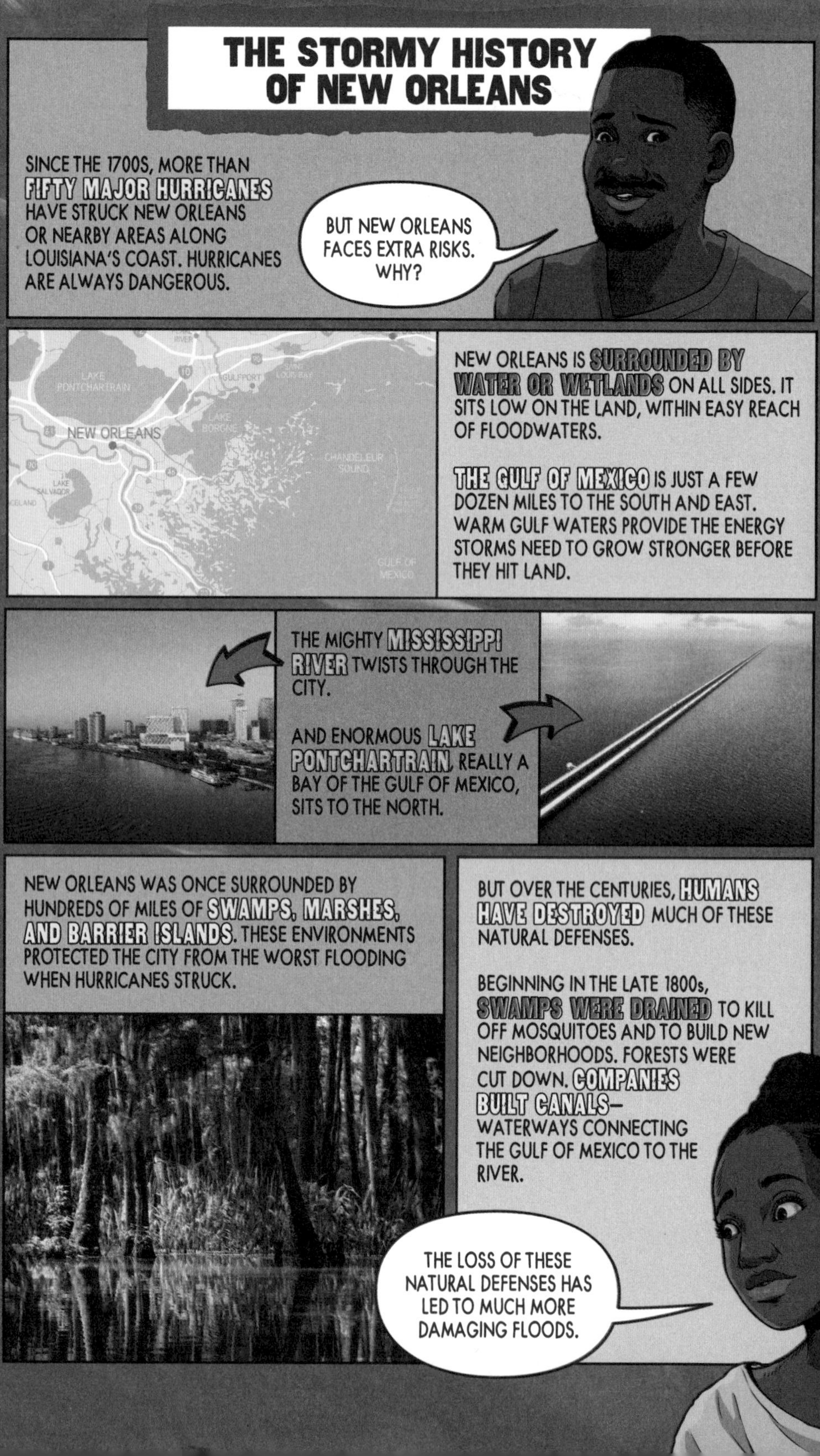
THE STORMY HISTORY OF NEW ORLEANS
SINCE THE 1700S, MORE THAN FIFTY MAJOR HURRICANES HAVE STRUCK NEW ORLEANS OR NEARBY AREAS ALONG LOUISIANA'S COAST. HURRICANES ARE ALWAYS DANGEROUS.
BUT NEW ORLEANS FACES EXTRA RISKS. WHY?
NEW ORLEANS
NEW ORLEANS IS SURROUNDED BY WATER OR WETLANDS ON ALL SIDES. IT SITS LOW ON THE LAND, WITHIN EASY REACH OF FLOODWATERS.
THE GULF OF MEXICO IS JUST A FEW DOZEN MILES TO THE SOUTH AND EAST. WARM GULF WATERS PROVIDE THE ENERGY STORMS NEED TO GROW STRONGER BEFORE THEY HIT LAND.
THE MIGHTY MISSISSIPPI RIVER TWISTS THROUGH THE CITY.
AND ENORMOUS LAKE PONTCHARTRAIN, REALLY A BAY OF THE GULF OF MEXICO, SITS TO THE NORTH.
NEW ORLEANS WAS ONCE SURROUNDED BY HUNDREDS OF MILES OF SWAMPS, MARSHES, AND BARRIER ISLANDS. THESE ENVIRONMENTS PROTECTED THE CITY FROM THE WORST FLOODING WHEN HURRICANES STRUCK.
BUT OVER THE CENTURIES, HUMANS HAVE DESTROYED MUCH OF THESE NATURAL DEFENSES.
BEGINNING IN THE LATE 1800s, SWAMPS WERE DRAINED TO KILL OFF MOSQUITOES AND TO BUILD NEW NEIGHBORHOODS. FORESTS WERE CUT DOWN. COMPANIES BUILT CANALS—WATERWAYS CONNECTING THE GULF OF MEXICO TO THE RIVER.
THE LOSS OF THESE NATURAL DEFENSES HAS LED TO MUCH MORE DAMAGING FLOODS.

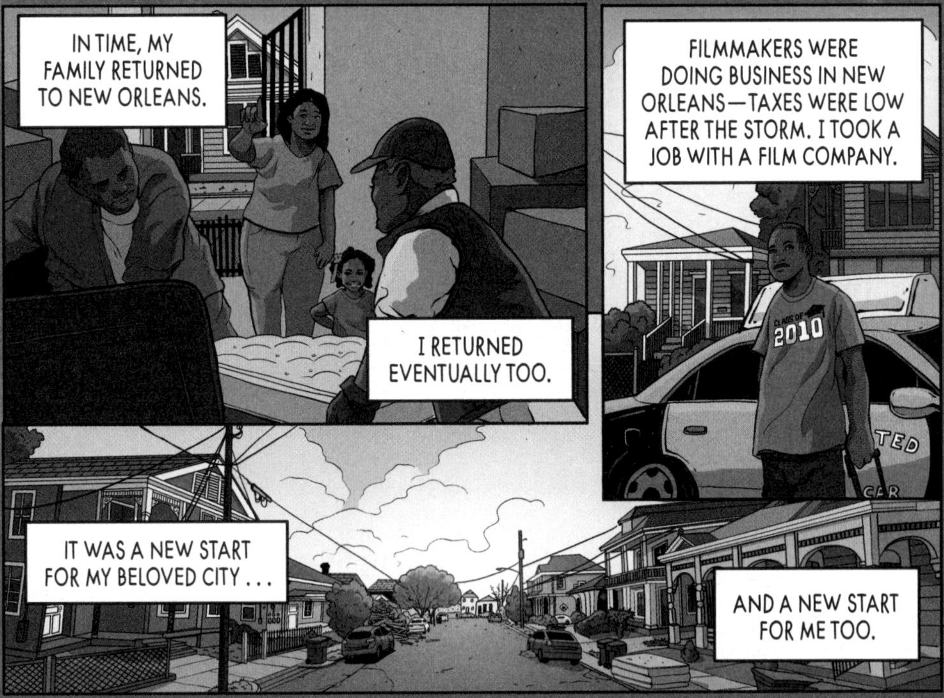
IN TIME, MY FAMILY RETURNED TO NEW ORLEANS.
I RETURNED EVENTUALLY TOO.
FILMMAKERS WERE DOING BUSINESS IN NEW ORLEANS—TAXES WERE LOW AFTER THE STORM. I TOOK A JOB WITH A FILM COMPANY.
2010
IT WAS A NEW START FOR MY BELOVED CITY . . .
AND A NEW START FOR ME TOO.

Alvin was among the lucky. His family had come through the storm. And he was able to return to the city he loved. But for so many others, Katrina was an endless nightmare.

Hundreds drowned that day, and over a thousand more died in the days and weeks ahead. Tens of thousands more were like the Tuckers—struggling to survive as water filled their homes. It took five full days for help to arrive, and another week before everyone was evacuated from the city.

In the weeks and months after Katrina, many wondered if New Orleans would ever recover. Entire neighborhoods were destroyed, as well as schools, hospitals, police stations, roads, and businesses. The city's residents—about 450,000 people—were scattered all around the country.

In the years after the storm, New Orleans has slowly recovered. If you visit it today, you'll be dazzled by unforgettable music and food, beautiful buildings and gardens, and streets that bustle with energy.

But some of the hardest-hit areas, including the Lower Ninth Ward, have not been fully rebuilt. Many people who left did not return.

And questions linger. Why didn't government leaders do a better job protecting New Orleans and its citizens? With so many warnings about flooding, why wasn't more done to make the levees stronger and higher? Why was help so slow to arrive? Have we learned lessons from Katrina that will keep New Orleans safe from future hurricanes?

Even now, all these years after Katrina, these questions remain unanswered.

Keep reading to learn more about the hurricane and its aftermath, with Barry, Jay, Dad, and Mom to guide you.

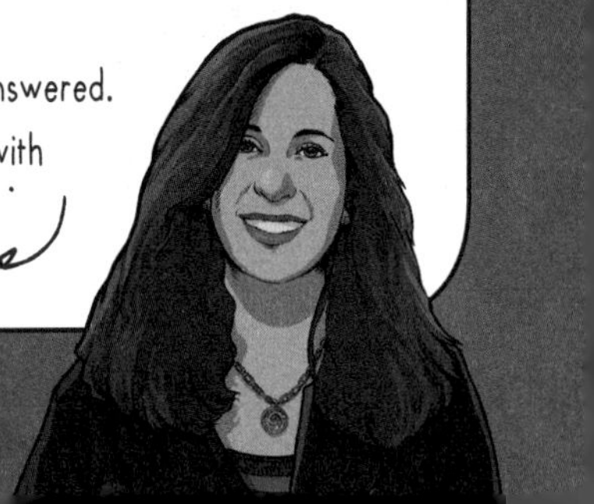

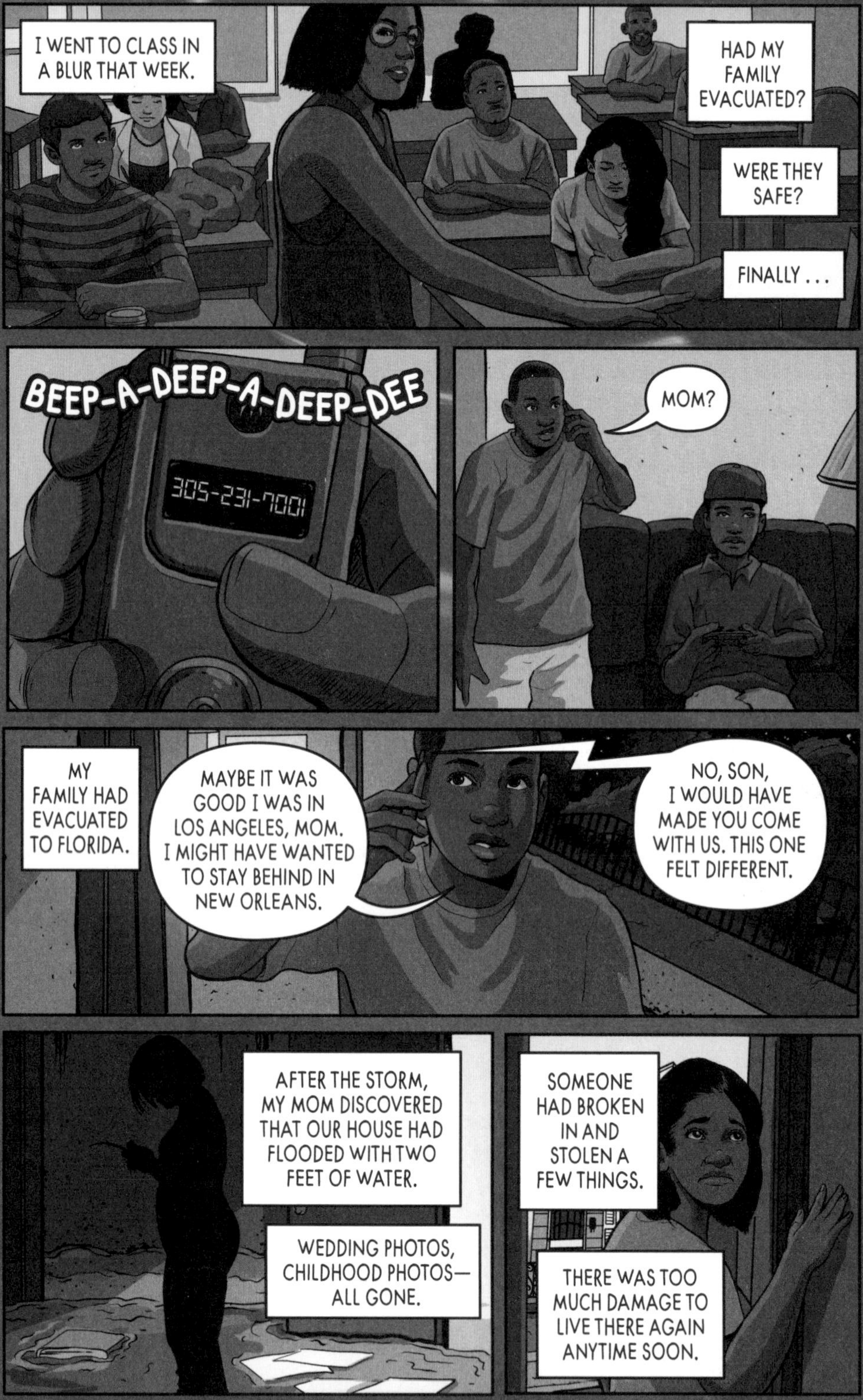
I WENT TO CLASS IN A BLUR THAT WEEK.
HAD MY FAMILY EVACUATED?
WERE THEY SAFE?
FINALLY . . .
BEEP-A-DEEP-A-DEEP-DEE
305-231-7001
MOM?
MY FAMILY HAD EVACUATED TO FLORIDA.
MAYBE IT WAS GOOD I WAS IN LOS ANGELES, MOM. I MIGHT HAVE WANTED TO STAY BEHIND IN NEW ORLEANS.
NO, SON, I WOULD HAVE MADE YOU COME WITH US. THIS ONE FELT DIFFERENT.
AFTER THE STORM, MY MOM DISCOVERED THAT OUR HOUSE HAD FLOODED WITH TWO FEET OF WATER.
WEDDING PHOTOS, CHILDHOOD PHOTOS—ALL GONE.
SOMEONE HAD BROKEN IN AND STOLEN A FEW THINGS.
THERE WAS TOO MUCH DAMAGE TO LIVE THERE AGAIN ANYTIME SOON.

SELECTED BIBLIOGRAPHY

Brinkley, Douglas. *The Great Deluge*. New York: William Morrow, 2006.

Eggers, Dave. *Zeitoun*. New York: Vintage Paperbacks, 2009.

Fink, Sheri. *Five Days at Memorial*. New York: Broadway Books, 2013.

Home, Jed. *Breach of Faith: Hurricane Katrina and the Near Death of a Great American City*. New York: Random House, 2006.

Piazza, Tom. *Why New Orleans Matters*. New York: HarperCollins, 2005.

The Times-Picayune, New Orleans, articles written about Katrina between August 29, 2005 and December 27, 2005.

FURTHER READING

You might enjoy these other I Survived books about extreme weather:

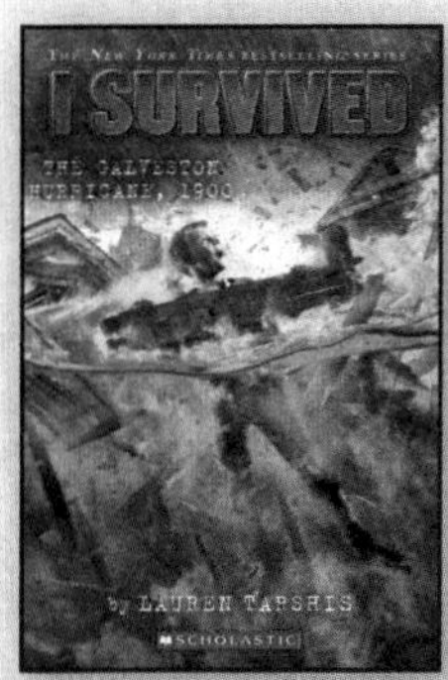
I SURVIVED
THE GALVESTON HURRICANE, 1900
by LAUREN TARSHIS
SCHOLASTIC

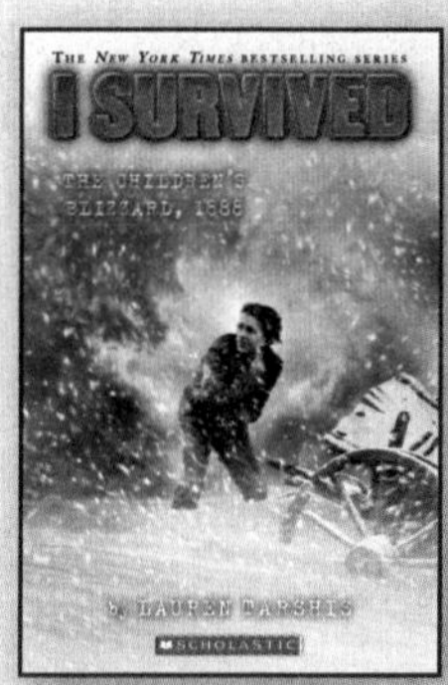
THE NEW YORK TIMES BESTSELLING SERIES
I SURVIVED
THE CHILDREN'S BLIZZARD, 1888
by LAUREN TARSHIS
SCHOLASTIC

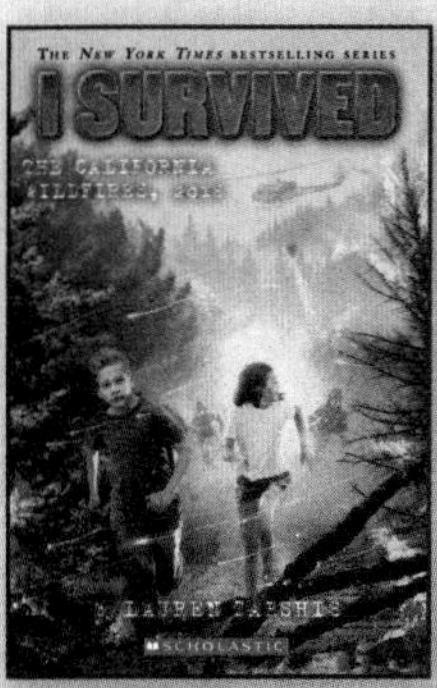
THE NEW YORK TIMES BESTSELLING SERIES
I SURVIVED
THE CALIFORNIA WILDFIRES, 2018
by LAUREN TARSHIS
SCHOLASTIC

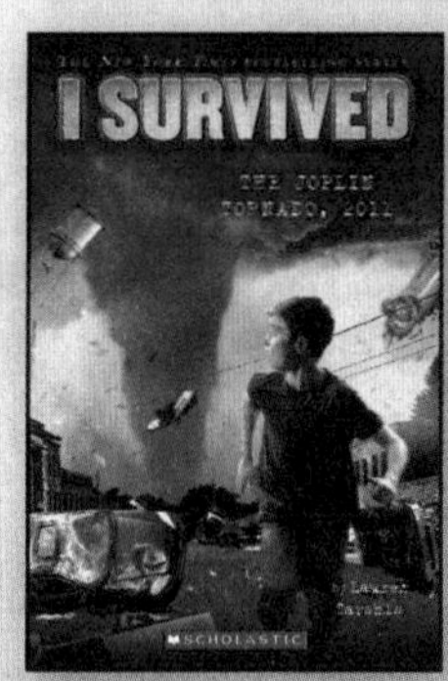
I SURVIVED
THE JOPLIN TORNADO, 2011
SCHOLASTIC

LAUREN TARSHIS'S

NEW YORK TIMES BESTSELLING I SURVIVED SERIES TELLS STORIES OF YOUNG PEOPLE AND THEIR RESILIENCE AND STRENGTH IN THE MIDST OF UNIMAGINABLE DISASTERS AND TIMES OF TURMOIL. LAUREN HAS BROUGHT HER SIGNATURE WARMTH, INTEGRITY, AND EXHAUSTIVE RESEARCH TO TOPICS SUCH AS THE BATTLE OF D-DAY, THE AMERICAN REVOLUTION, HURRICANE KATRINA, THE BOMBING OF PEARL HARBOR, AND OTHER WORLD EVENTS. LAUREN LIVES IN CONNECTICUT WITH HER FAMILY AND CAN BE FOUND ONLINE AT LAURENTARSHIS.COM.

GEORGIA BALL

HAS WRITTEN COMICS FOR MANY OF HER FAVORITE CHILDHOOD CHARACTERS, INCLUDING STRAWBERRY SHORTCAKE, TRANSFORMERS, LITTLEST PET SHOP, MY LITTLE PONY, AND THE DISNEY PRINCESSES. IN ADDITION TO ADAPTING LAUREN TARSHIS'S I SURVIVED SERIES TO GRAPHIC NOVELS, GEORGIA WRITES ABOUT HISTORICAL EVENTS SUCH AS THE WORLD WAR II BATTLES OF KURSK AND GUADALCANAL. GEORGIA LIVES WITH HER HUSBAND, DAUGHTER, AND RAMBUNCTIOUS PETS IN FLORIDA. VISIT HER ONLINE AT GEORGIABALLAUTHOR.COM.

ALVIN EPPS

IS AN ARTIST AND ILLUSTRATOR FROM NEW ORLEANS. HIS WORK OFTEN BLURS THE LINES BETWEEN FINE ARTS AND DIGITAL MEDIA AND HAS BEEN FEATURED IN COMIC BOOKS, ON ALBUM COVERS, AND IN MUSIC VIDEOS, FILM, AND TV. VISIT HIM ONLINE AT BYALVINEPPS.COM.

CHI NGO

IS A VIETNAMESE ILLUSTRATOR/ANIMATION ARTIST LOCATED IN LOS ANGELES. SHE HAS CONTRIBUTED TO BRANDS LIKE TRANSFORMERS AND CLIFFORD AND WORKED FOR CARTOON NETWORK, NETFLIX, HASBRO, AND BENTOBOX. YOU CAN SEE MORE OF HER WORK AT CHI-NGO.COM.

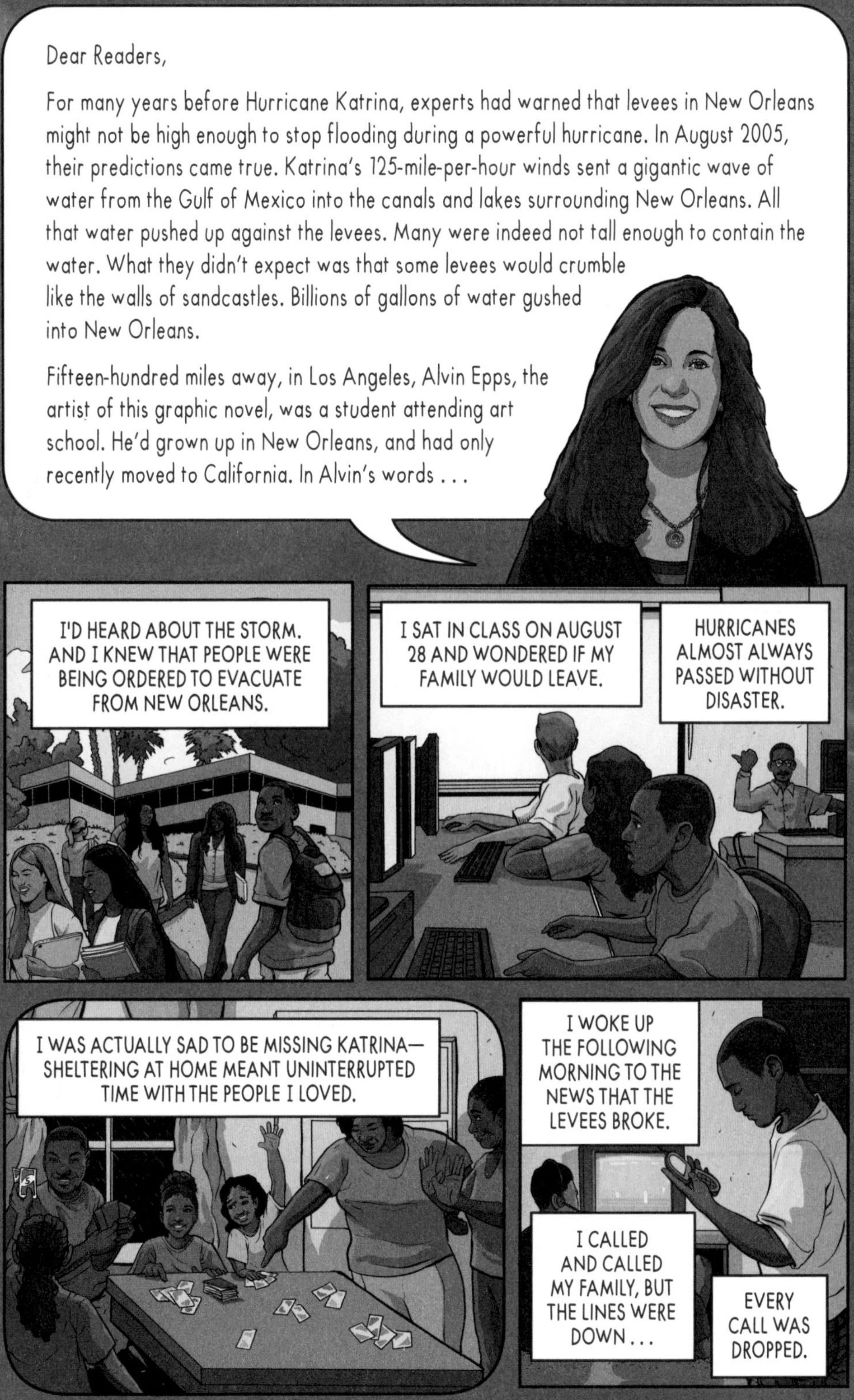
Dear Readers,
For many years before Hurricane Katrina, experts had warned that levees in New Orleans might not be high enough to stop flooding during a powerful hurricane. In August 2005, their predictions came true. Katrina's 125-mile-per-hour winds sent a gigantic wave of water from the Gulf of Mexico into the canals and lakes surrounding New Orleans. All that water pushed up against the levees. Many were indeed not tall enough to contain the water. What they didn't expect was that some levees would crumble like the walls of sandcastles. Billions of gallons of water gushed into New Orleans.
Fifteen-hundred miles away, in Los Angeles, Alvin Epps, the artist of this graphic novel, was a student attending art school. He'd grown up in New Orleans, and had only recently moved to California. In Alvin's words . . .
I'D HEARD ABOUT THE STORM. AND I KNEW THAT PEOPLE WERE BEING ORDERED TO EVACUATE FROM NEW ORLEANS.
I SAT IN CLASS ON AUGUST 28 AND WONDERED IF MY FAMILY WOULD LEAVE.
HURRICANES ALMOST ALWAYS PASSED WITHOUT DISASTER.
I WAS ACTUALLY SAD TO BE MISSING KATRINA—SHELTERING AT HOME MEANT UNINTERRUPTED TIME WITH THE PEOPLE I LOVED.
I WOKE UP THE FOLLOWING MORNING TO THE NEWS THAT THE LEVEES BROKE.
I CALLED AND CALLED MY FAMILY, BUT THE LINES WERE DOWN . . .
EVERY CALL WAS DROPPED.

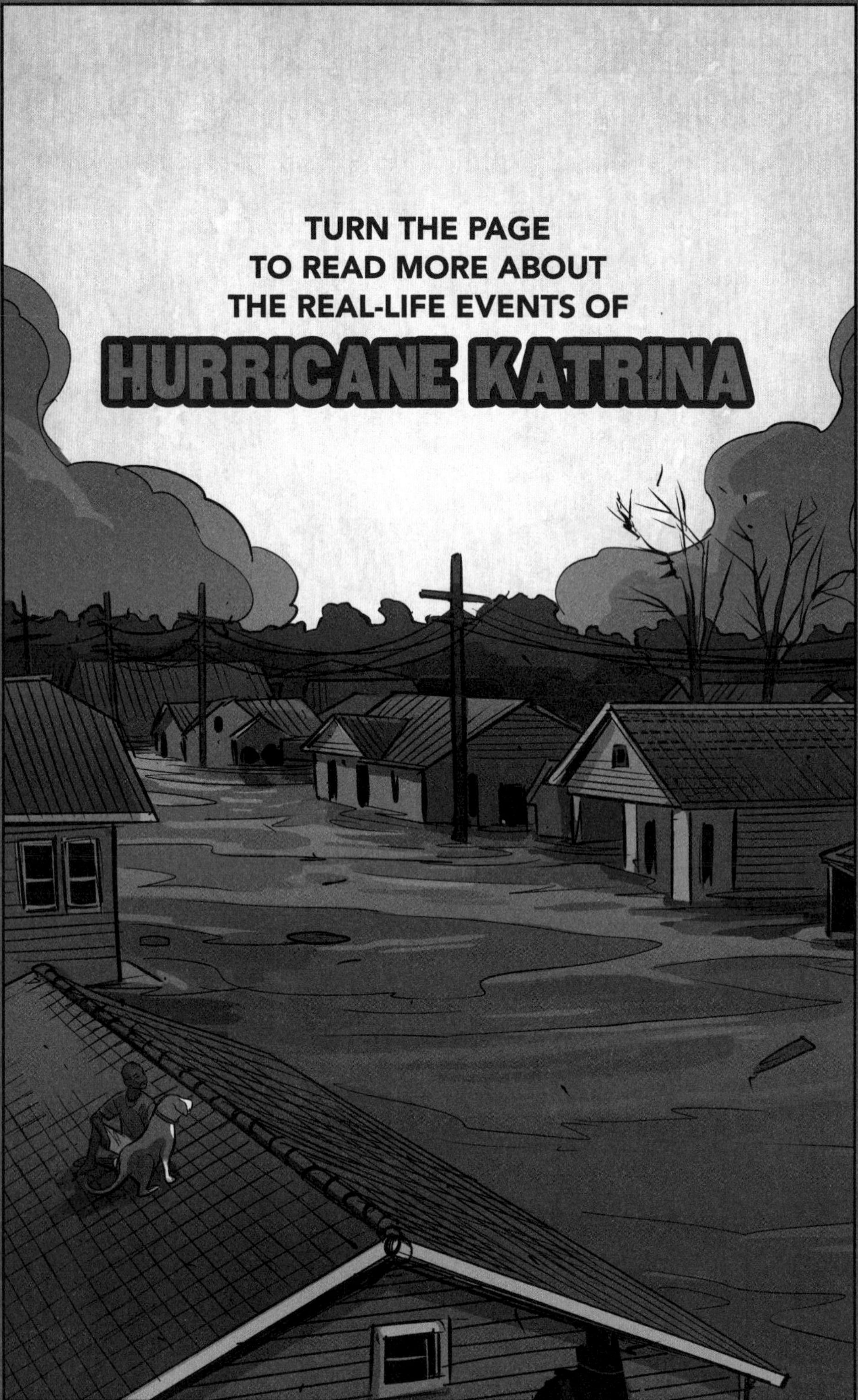
TURN THE PAGE
TO READ MORE ABOUT
THE REAL-LIFE EVENTS OF
HURRICANE KATRINA

I SURVIVED

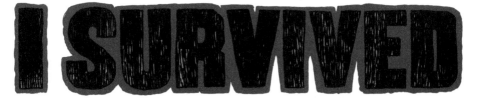

HURRICANE KATRINA, 2005

PHOTOS ©: 149–158 BACKGROUND: OLEG KOPYOV/SHUTTERSTOCK; 153 MAP: HEY DARLIN/GETTY IMAGES; 153
CENTER LEFT: PAWEL.GAUL/GETTY IMAGES; 153 CENTER RIGHT: ART WAGER/GETTY IMAGES; 153 BOTTOM LEFT:
PARKERDEEN/GETTY IMAGES; 153 ARROWS AND THROUGHOUT: JOHN GOLD/SHUTTERSTOCK; 154 CENTER LEFT:
MIKROMAN6/GETTY IMAGES; 154 CENTER RIGHT: AP PHOTO/GERALD HERBERT; 154 BOTTOM LEFT: POOL/AFP/
GETTY IMAGES; 154 BOTTOM RIGHT: JERRY GRAYSON/HELIFILMS AUSTRALIA PTY LTD/GETTY IMAGES; 155 TOP
RIGHT: REUTERS/ALAMY STOCK PHOTO; 155 CENTER LEFT: FEMA/ALAMY STOCK PHOTO; 155 CENTER RIGHT:
MICHAEL APPLETON/NY DAILY NEWS ARCHIVE/GETTY IMAGES; 155 BOTTOM LEFT: AP PHOTO/ERIC GAY,
GERALD HERBERT; 156 TOP: MARIO TAMA/GETTY IMAGES; 156 CENTER LEFT: AGENCJA FOTOGRAFICZNA
CARO/ALAMY STOCK PHOTO; 156 CENTER RIGHT: UPI/ALAMY STOCK PHOTO; 156 BOTTOM: DANIEL ACKER/
BLOOMBERG/GETTY IMAGES.

SPECIAL THANKS TO RICHARD CAMPANELLA AND TREMAINE KNIGHTEN-RILEY

LIBRARY OF CONGRESS CONTROL NUMBER: 2022938275
ISBN 978-1-338-76694-3

10 9 8 7 6 5 4 3 2 1   22 23 24 25 26

PRINTED IN THE U.S.A.   184
FIRST EDITION, OCTOBER 2022
EDITED BY KATIE WOEHR
LETTERING BY OLGA ANDREYEVA
INKS BY ALVIN EPPS & ÁLVARO SARRASECA
COLOR BY CHI NGO & LUKE GE
BOOK DESIGN BY BECKY JAMES, KATIE FITCH & SALENA MAHINA
CREATIVE DIRECTOR: YAFFA JASKOLL